They've Shot
the President's
Daughter!

Other books by Edward Stewart:

ROCK RUDE

HEADS

ORPHEUS ON TOP

They've Shot the President's Daughter!

Edward Stewart

Doubleday & Company, Inc.
Garden City, New York
1973

The author confesses that this book is from start to finish complete and utter fabrication. Any similarity between any person, institution, iniquity, or event in these pages and any actual person, institution, iniquity, or event, past, present, or forthcoming, is coincidental, unintentional, and hopefully inconceivable.

ISBN: 0-385-04236-1
Library of Congress Catalog Card Number 72–97275
Copyright © 1973 by Edward Stewart
All Rights Reserved
Printed in the United States of America
First Edition

This book is dedicated to the memory of
Frances deForest Stewart
and to some of the people she loved:
Dad and Shirley; Babbie, Morgan, Bill, Peggy,
Dorothy, Dick, Ethel, Nancie, and John;
with love and thanks to all of them

I: The Bullet

I've just discovered casseroles and the meat
grinder, which means that not much gets thrown
out in the way of food—there are so many
different ways of serving leftovers, things
that even Mom didn't discover!

> Darcie Sybert, letter to Fran Lawrence,
> intercepted by the Federal Security
> Agency and constituting Document 77 of
> File Z–145–6–239, code name "FLYPAPER."

Operatives must now cope with often submerged,
subtle and elusive ambiguities in the gathering
of intelligence and the pursuit of related
objectives.

> Dr. Erikka Lumi, inter-office memo to
> the Director of the Federal Security
> Agency

A well regulated Militia, being necessary
to the security of a free State, the right
of the people to keep and bear Arms, shall
not be infringed.

> THE CONSTITUTION OF THE UNITED STATES,
> *Second Amendment*

June 19: Monday

Certainly no one intended to walk into an assassination.

The idea was for the President and his wife and daughter to fly to his home town and lay a wreath on his parents' grave. Just whose idea it had been was not recorded. The President's advisers said it had been the President's idea, and he said that it had been his wife's. Everyone agreed, at the time, that it was an excellent idea.

The First Lady knew that she had had no such idea, for whenever anyone said "Whitefalls, South Dakota," her memory box flashed a picture postcard of a sepia town square in dustland, where the toilets had chains and the women's hair styles were ten years out of date. It was only to avoid discussion that she had canceled the Bolshoi Ballet and agreed to go. The First Lady, lately, had begun loathing discussion.

And so, at five-thirty in the morning on the day of the shooting, the First Family set out from 1600 Pennsylvania Avenue for Andrews Air Force Base.

It was still raining, and a lieutenant general stood by the limousine, frozen in salute. The President fell into conversation with him almost immediately. The First Lady preceded the men into the back seat. Lexie took the jump seat and stared out the window at buildings and monuments beginning to detach themselves from the night, and the First Lady stared for a moment at her daughter and tried to read the voiceless movements of her lips.

Through the wall of two-ply polarized glass that separated the front from the back seat, the First Lady recognized the carefully trimmed necks of the driver and the warrant officer. She had come to think of all the drivers and all the warrant officers in the singular: one held the keys without which she could go nowhere, not even shopping or out for a hamburger; the other held the daily changes of codes without which the President would be powerless to order a nuclear attack or retaliation. These codes were so important, those who knew told her, that the warrant officer and his little black attaché case were never more than ten yards from the President and his wife, whether they were in the bath or at the theater or driving to an airplane.

The First Lady, thinking that the warrant officer probably kept sandwiches in that case too, smiled secretly.

The uniformed guard at the gate waved them through, and the limousine turned fluidly onto the deserted avenue, and the First Lady looked back through the window at the White House, mantled in uncertain dawn and set against a seamless silken sky, its classic pillared profile as serene and changeless as the back of a twenty-dollar bill.

She had always viewed the White House—especially from this angle and in this light—with the residual awe of a twelve-year-old history student. Scooped out like a honeydew melon, the old insides thrown away and the shell buttressed with twentieth-century steel, it still seemed to her the tangible embodiment of a past that was a good deal nobler, if rather less detailed, than the age she inhabited.

The view of the pillars and rose garden, the lawn and fountains and the Jefferson Memorial, was as beautiful as any she had ever seen, and the west half of the second floor was hers to redecorate as she pleased, and yet it troubled her to live in the house where every President but Washington had lived. She kept feeling that a mistake had been made, she and her family had taken a wrong turn or turned a wrong key, the mistake would be discovered and they would be evicted. Other Presidents had made history, while her husband, it seemed to her, made only current events. She did not feel in the line of First Families who had made the White House the home of the nation's destiny shapers, and she despaired of ever possessing or even knowing it. The White House would never, could never, be her home.

She did not know whether this was her fault or its. But she

had entered with her husband and daughter as a family, and in all its space they had lost touch and now, even in the cramped leather hollow of a limousine, they could not find their way back to one another. A real home, she suspected, would not have done that to a real family.

The First Lady realized that people were talking beside her. The lieutenant general was saying something about the Senate Armed Services Committee. His was one of those red, Aztec-jawed faces that made all military men look alike to the First Lady. His single eyebrow ran temple-to-temple, like a misplaced mustache, and his ribbons lent him the slightly trinkety air of an ancient high priest. He sat absolutely erect, his back never touching the upholstery.

The President scratched his chin and nodded and said, "What kind of difficulty, Chuck?"

"Senator Evarts is trying awfully damned hard to blow the cover on air support for Arriagas."

"Guerrilla warfare's tricky. So's Evarts."

The First Lady took note of trees rising shadowy and two-dimensional along their route, casting slow nets of black filigree. She searched for satellites racing high above them, blinking and sputtering messages.

And as happened from time to time lately, when she sat in a closed space near her husband, she could neither slide away from him nor summon any thought of her own strong enough to ward off the even-edged blade of his voice. And it seemed to her, no disrespect intended, that these litanies of problems and crises and billions (of dollars, she supposed), these proposals and rejections that were whispered at her elbow, these schemes and tragedies and intrigues that fell from his lips in ever so slightly mocking a monotone were—though for the rest of mankind facts, real and hard and cutting enough—for him only mantras, aids in meditation, ways of getting his mind off petty aches and woes that would have submerged him if he had ever tried to cope. It seemed to her that he had his eye on the mountaintop only to avoid the puddles at his feet. It is easier, perhaps, to settle the affairs of a Latin American republic, especially if you don't have to live in Latin America, than to look your wife in the eye.

(*My God, he's talking so slowly! If I don't open this window I'll suffocate. What did I dream last night? Does he think that slowly, or is he just not awake? Could he have a cancer of the tongue?*)

The car eased through light early morning traffic, down the Memorial Parkway, turned east onto the bridge, brushed Virginia before taking the Beltway. The lieutenant general was fuming.

"You'd think after Vietnam the goddamned fool would have learned to keep his mouth shut!"

The President gave one of his half-smiles: the First Lady could see him measure it out. "The essence of a goddamned fool is that he never quite masters that art. Senator Evarts is feinting."

"Fainting, Mr. President?"

Even at five forty-five in the morning, the President could look very much the President. He had been born with the tall, naturally big frame of a Franklin Pierce, and thanks to daily scalp massages he had kept most of his hair, so he had the thick gray curls of a Zachary Taylor. His piercing blue stare was in fact the glimmer of German-made contact lenses, but so far as most observers were concerned he had the shrewd, lively eyes of a Chester Alan Arthur. From time to time he lightened the effect with a chortle straight out of William Henry Harrison.

"Fainting, Mr. President?"

"A boxing term, Chuck."

The President was handsome. The First Lady found him very handsome, and she supposed any woman in love with him—which she was not, not really, not so much as once—would find him insufferably handsome, for he had the sort of looks no woman could age well next to, the face that got craggier and bolder and deeper-tanned with the years; and for some time now he had moved and smiled, on and off camera, with the total assurance of a movie star under lifelong contract.

"Boxing, Mr. President?"

"I was using a term from the boxer's lexicon."

He wore clothes—any clothes—or no clothes at all—well; jackets could not but hang naturally on his still powerful swimmer's shoulders.

"Mr. President, we were discussing air reconnaissance."

"We're still discussing it, Chuck."

But the inside and the outside of him did not fit. The First Lady watched him charm senators and finagle businessmen, juggle the thousand and one chores of his office without a miss, and yet she sensed a discrepancy, a tiny crack. She was not certain how deep the fault ran. She knew he used an electric razor because he was terrified of cuts showing on TV, and she knew he had dropped over half a million tons of explosives on villages in Costa Rica. To him it was politics; to her it was a contradiction. Lately he had been screaming in his dreams.

Now the suburban ghetto oozed past the sealed, bulletproof windows, one endless garbage heap of broken concrete and shattered windows, snoring in the early light. Someone had scrawled a slogan on the side of a building and misspelled it.

(*We're forgetting everything. We can't even spell any more, and my husband couldn't take my hand even if I held it out to him.*)

"We'll have a chat with the *Post*—not for attribution," she heard her husband say. "Evarts may not change his tune, but he'll soften the orchestration."

"Six weeks—two months—and we'll clean up in there."

"I know, Chuck—and you'll get all the time you need." The President unhooked the intercom phone from the wall to tell the driver that the general would be getting off at the next red light.

For an instant the general looked as though this was news to him; and then he brightened and held out a strong, manicured hand. "Good-by, Mrs. Luckinbill—so long, Lexie. Good seeing you."

"Good-by, General," the First Lady said. She could not remember his name.

"And, Mr. President, thanks. If I can ever—"

The President's arm on his back hurried the general onto the curb. "No trouble, Chuck. Say hi to Betsy and the kids for me."

"You bet."

The general stood, one hand raised in salute, and diminished behind them into the dark. The mood seemed brighter without him.

It had been annoying getting up before the sun to jet halfway across the continent. Yet the First Lady found blessings in the rupture of routine. Today at breakfast she had not had to consult with the chief usher or the chief butler or the chief housekeeper; she had, for the first day in a hundred, eaten her pink grapefruit in tranquillity, cleared no appointments, selected no menus, seen to no household details. Her secretary had brought her no mail for decisions and brain-wracking personal answers; no suggestions for hair styles, no recipes, none of the thousand letters the White House mail staff sorted and passed on to her weekly. Today there would be no benefit luncheon, no national health or charity drive, no garden party for nine hundred war veterans, no afternoon tea for congressional wives. No Girl Scouts, no prime ministers, no state beauty queens today; at least she hoped there would be no state beauty queens at the graveside ceremony.

For the next several hours, speeding in a silver capsule from here to there, she need not worry whether she projected a personality too warm or too reserved, whether her handshake was too firm or too lax, whether Mary or Joan was the woman's name. These next hours of her life, in the negative sense of belonging to no one else, belonged to her; and she intended to savor them as selfishly as lemon drops dissolving on her tongue.

Her daughter spoke. "Mimi Moffett and I watched TV last night, Mom. We saw the rerun of the White House tour."

"Did you, Lexie? It must have been boring the second time around. I'm afraid I'll never make a TV personality."

"You were good," the girl said. "Really good."

The First Lady regarded her first and last and only child. The girl had full hazel eyes, sweeping lashes, arched nose with softly flaring nostrils, well-formed mouth and teeth of utter uncavitied evenness. Lately, since Lexie had become old enough to make up her own mind in such matters, she had worn her dark hair swept up, coiled in back in turn-of-the-century style. Her mother had at first disapproved, not because the style was too mature, but in shock that Lexie was old enough to carry it off. It was a giant step from pigtails to chignons, and Lexie seemed to have completed it in a hop. She was eighteen, going on nineteen.

"Only your dress was kind of icky," Lexie said, her eyes catching the flashes of highway arc lights. "You know the one I mean?"

"I remember it very well," said the First Lady. "The President of the Philippines gave me the lace."

"That pill!" Lexie cried, and the President, absorbed though he was in his thoughts, smiled slightly. "Well, it made you look dumpy. Honestly, it did. I hope you won't ever wear it on TV again."

"I can promise you that, darling. With your father's permission, I intend to stay off television for the rest of my life."

The First Lady smiled, careful to hide the warm pride she felt each time she looked at her daughter, a pride all the stronger for being frankly touched with envy. The girl had been born with something her mother had wrested from life only after thirty years' tutelage at the hands of hairdressers and cosmeticians and couturiers: beauty. And the shining eyes, so quick to narrow and flicker and change, hinted at an even more precious birthright. There was something secret and swift and cunning about the child, a sensibility and a sureness that it had taken the First Lady three decades to simulate and which even to this day sometimes failed her.

Whereas nothing ever seemed to fail Lexie.

"You could do a program on the rose garden," her daughter said, "or on the library or the paintings or a million things."

The First Lady smiled. "The *next* President's wife can do them."

"Or I could," Lexie said.

The First Lady gazed out the bulletproof window at the speedway, almost deserted at this hour, stretching like a fresh abdominal scar across the state. "I didn't know you were interested in television."

"I just think there could be so many great programs."

"I suppose." The First Lady heard her own voice, dead and muffled in the upholstered gloom of the compartment. *My God, I'm sounding like a prig! Let her do anything she wants—TV, astrology, Jesus—it's a free country.*

She kept her eye on the window and wondered how bulletproof, mobproof glass came to be so scratched. The green hills of Maryland were gray under the onslaught of rain, and the countryside shivered like a drenched dog's skin.

They were silent. Her husband still seemed to be thinking.

The presidential limousine maintained a speed of sixty-five miles per hour, fender flags snapping in the wet wind, slowing only at the turnoff marked Andrews Air Force Base.

The car took them straight to the air strip, and an army officer waited with a monster umbrella to escort them the ten steps to Air Force One, crouched like an outsized praying mantis ready to spring from its landing gear. Secret Service cars swung to a stop behind them.

"Good morning, Mrs. Luckinbill."

"Good morning." She did not recognize the smooth-shaven officer. Rain whipped her face and she drew up the collar of her raincoat.

"Awful weather, isn't it? Supposed to be clear in Whitefalls, though, with moderate temperatures and easterly winds."

"That will be nice," she smiled. Lexie huddled close to her as they moved toward the jet, and the President for some reason lingered behind, making a show of not needing the shelter of an umbrella.

And then she saw the little figure stumbling across the rain-slicked runway, and she recognized the limp of the President's assistant for national security affairs.

The officer moved the First Lady and her daughter to the ramp, wished them a good flight. The First Lady glanced back to watch her husband seize the little man's hand and pump it, and she saw they were both talking at once, standing in the rain, catching their deaths of cold. She shrugged, mounted the aluminum steps to the jetliner door. She felt the vibrations of Lexie's tread close behind her, almost in synchronization.

A figure materialized in the open doorway.

"Good morning all, welcome aboard the United States Air Force's Tequila Flight, our flying time to Acapulco will be exactly two hours, we should be so lucky!"

Mimi Moffett wore her hair blond and long and straight to her shoulder blades and had a way of letting it wisp across telephones and Xerox machines and door handles of Air Force jets. She also had a way of making stale jokes, and the First Lady tried to remember if she had ever stepped aboard a presidential flight when Mimi Moffett hadn't announced the flying time to Acapulco.

Of the President's three personal secretaries, Mimi Moffett was the only one to be young or female or to accompany him on long flights, and though her face had once had a way of cropping up in photos of protest marches, he seemed to rely on her to cope with most of the unclassified minutiae of his day-to-day existence. Observers speculated that she had some sort of understanding with her employer, and the speculations had reached the First Lady's ears, and lately she had begun to wonder.

The First Lady smiled at Mimi Moffett. They traded banalities, and the First Lady got a bigger banality than she gave and so, she supposed, came out ahead. She hesitated an instant before stepping into the plane. A hand seemed to grip her intestine—she felt a very definite contraction—and at the same moment the certainty came over her that the events of the morning, far from being random, were moving her and her family in an absolutely straight, purposeful line.

Mimi Moffett smiled at her, vapid and fake blond, and Lexie toyed with the fingers of her gloves, and through the open cockpit door the First Lady could see the pilot flicking switches and exchanging hand motions with a mechanic who was scooting about down on the runway. Everything was precisely as usual. And yet she had a sinking feeling that this morning's trivia were different, fodder for memoirs and magazine articles.

She felt that this could be the last morning of her life.

The First Lady stepped into the cabin and left Lexie and Mimi Moffett chatting over hair rinses.

Grounded, Air Force One sloped downward toward the tail, and with her high Italian heels tilting her even farther forward the First Lady had to grip the headrests of the passenger seats. She picked a comfortable chair—like all of them it was by a window—and slipped into her safety belt.

She stared up the sloping aisle and decided that Lexie was prettier, far prettier, than Mimi Moffett, and she wondered what her husband saw in such a calculated and grating kook. Her wonder gave way to gratitude that at least her rival—if Mimi was her rival—was a youngster: when Franklin Delano Roosevelt picked a mature mistress he had dealt Eleanor a bruise she had never managed to powder over. *At least I'm spared that*, the First Lady reflected.

And there was Lexie, hardly a woman and already discussing hair dyes and God only knew what else with that peculiar girl. Sex? Pot? No doubt Mimi Moffett was trying to enroll Lexie in one of her Ban-the-War barbecues.

What's happened to our children? the First Lady wondered, and her memory box flashed news photos of eighteen-year-olds pumping heroin into their veins and the shattered, pathetic body of a fourteen-year-old girl raped and thrown from a Greenwich Village rooftop and soldiers with deadened, doll-like eyes returning from never-ending wars on the other side of the earth. *What's happened to our children? One moment they're playing with toys and calling you to tuck them into bed, and the next they're grown up and gone and the house is empty and you don't know what's happening, you don't know if they're dead or alive or murdering other people's children. . . .*

The First Lady's thoughts had slipped into a familiar downward spiral. Ministers had cautioned her against it, and doctors had given her pills for it. She kneaded her purse and felt the familiar lump, hard as a warning in the breast. She snapped the catch open and took out the tiny, neatly labeled plastic bottle, rolled it in her fingers. *For headache as needed.*

It was as she swallowed the pill that she felt she was not alone in the cabin. The realization came to her gradually, like so much else that day, that someone was watching her, and watching her closely.

She turned in her chair.

"Good morning, Moni."

He was smiling at her, his small brown eyes peeping alertly from under thick eyebrows, his dark hair avalanching down over the wrinkled forehead. He had that high color which could signal apoplexy or stamina, or both, and even in that dark corner of the cabin, sprawled like a cowboy over two cushions of the sofa, he radiated a ruddy incandescence.

"Good morning, Dan."

Dan Bulfinch, Senate Majority Leader, stretched and half stifled a yawn and got to his feet, and she knew he must have been dozing there for some time; probably he had not even gone home to bed but, answering a presidential summons, had come direct from some all-night caucus; or some all-night bordello.

"Piss-poor weather," Senator Dan remarked.

The First Lady smiled at the mild and intentional indecency. Senator Dan always made a point of showing that he, alone of all mortals, did not regard the President's wife as a goddess—and she was grateful to him. Now, braced on his stocky legs, fists plunged into the depths of his overstuffed pockets, he extruded a tangible force and energy that almost seemed to threaten her.

"Good to see you, Moni. Looking so well."

"You'd be looking well yourself, Dan, if you could find a comb."

He ran his fingers through his hair, disarraying it further. "Last time I put a comb to this, I lost the damned comb."

"It's probably still up there," she smiled.

It was the First Lady's conviction that Senator Dan, like a child's room or a vegetable garden, needed looking after. His wife Cathy had looked after him with fanatical devotion during the twelve years of their marriage, and then like a Victorian curio she had died under a swift and senseless assault of tuberculosis. The loss had almost killed Dan, and drink had close to cost him re-election; but one night, when the First Lady had been no first lady at all, but mere Monica Luckinbill, senator's wife, a hiccupping, weeping, unshaved grizzly bear of a man had thrown himself through her kitchen screen door and she had fed him coffee and cradled his head and kept reporters at bay for twelve hours and listened to the whole pathetic outpouring: he had deceived Cathy, once, while she was dying; and Monica, thinking not of Cathy with her unbending kindness and her thin smiles, but thinking of her friend Dan, had said she was sure Cathy would have forgiven a single infidelity or even a bender or two, but she would have had no sympathy for a man's throwing his life into the bourbon vats.

Dan had—so far as the First Lady knew—never been drunk since. As for his women, she knew and wanted to know nothing about them. She loved him too much.

Senator Dan gave her a deep probe of a glance. "What's eating you, Moni?"

"Why, Senator," she laughed, "what makes you think anything would even be interested in eating me?"

"You're as easy to read as an IBM print-out." The senator's voice was pitched low. It was kindly and yet there was menace in it. He had the tone of a doctor about to examine a patient. There was affection but no comfort in his manner.

"If I'm such an open book," the First Lady smiled, "why bother to ask?"

"I'm a slow reader." His eyes held her in a stern focus that she could not evade.

"My husband has been lying to me." She said this softly, as though confessing a sin of her own.

"Oh?"

"Usually he's a good liar, a very good liar. That's part of his job, after all. Suddenly he's a bad liar."

"What sort of lies?"

"You know the sort. Yesterday he renounced chemical and biological weapons again. That doesn't count, it's a public lie. But lately there have been private lies too. Last Thursday he told me he had to meet with the budget director and some foreign advisers. He vanished at five in the afternoon and no one saw him till three o'clock the next morning. The budget director hadn't seen him, the advisers hadn't seen him. And never a word of explanation. Not to me, at least."

"Surely he does that sort of thing all the time."

"Last month he scheduled a meeting with Senator Dickens. They were going to spend the weekend at Camp David discussing Bolivia and the military expense. But he wasn't at Camp David. Lexie and the senator and I and forty security men had the place to ourselves. The wild berries were in bloom."

Senator Dan stared at her. "Come on, Moni. What's really the matter?" He patted her shoulder. It was an avuncular gesture and she could not help momentarily loathing him for it.

"What about this business today?" she flared. "For nineteen years he hasn't given a thought to that town and now he wants to fly fifteen hundred miles and put a wreath on his parents' grave. Now even you'll admit that type of sentiment is not like Bill."

Senator Dan's hands took her shoulders in two viselike grips, and she felt that with an ounce more pressure of the thumbs he could snap her collarbone. "Okay, Moni. Out with it."

She could barely make her voice audible. "He's been seeing another woman."

His jaw dropped. His hands dropped.

"What can a wife think when her husband's lies stop being plausible?"

"Moni, Moni. There could be a hundred explanations."

"There are too many little things he's said and done—and too many things he hasn't. For heaven's sake, Dan—a wife can sense it. She can count the nights since her husband last looked at her!"

"But another woman—a man in his position—" The senator made a puzzled face.

"I'd be the last to know, of course. The Secret Service would know because they've got to know his movements, and the press would know because they know everything, and you'd know, Dan. You'd know too." She did not spare him a direct, questioning gaze.

Senator Dan did not look away. "Moni, I swear. I haven't heard a word."

"He's under terrific pressure." She tried to sound cheerful. "And I know we've been married almost twenty years and there's a new morality nowadays. But I hate him, Dan, and I hate myself, and I hate her, whoever she is."

Senator Dan followed this, head nodding, eyes narrowing.

There was a thump at the front of the cabin, and Senator Dan and the First Lady separated, almost guiltily.

The President came down the aisle, pushing Nahum Bismarck ahead of him, perhaps out of respect for the man's seventy very odd years, more probably out of instinctive reluctance to let anyone but a Secret Service man walk behind him: "My back's too big a target," he had joked to his wife once, in the days when they had joked. Nahum Bismarck used a cane, arcing it in front of him like a radarscope, and with his slightly hobbled elfin gait he presented the appearance of a Prussian Ted Lewis.

This morning it disturbed the First Lady to realize that behind that Eisenhower geniality and that Truman brashness of her husband's there lurked an Adlai Stevenson's caution. She had not read the biographies of the other Presidents, and for all she knew every one of them had been crucified by clandestine doubt; but she did not think that men who had thrown off the British and held the Union together and dropped the Bomb could have leaned quite so heavily on such a creature as Nahum Bismarck.

He was a gnarled walking stick of a man, skinny and dark, with a shiny knob for a head, eyes the size of pennies and the brilliance of new silver dollars. She did not think he wore contacts: the thick horn-rims that had the glitter of bulletproof shields and always dangled by ten inches of fresh string around his neck were too much the apex and flower of his image. Caricaturists mocked them, Harvard professors imitated them, and

Nahum Bismarck himself from time to time raised them to his nose and sniffed, as though they had a magical power of magnifying or clarifying scent.

Now, shuffling through papers one-handed for an errant memorandum, he even looked through them, blinking as though they brought things a little too close.

Nahum Bismarck and the President nodded to the First Lady. Senator Dan went with them to the rear of the cabin. She heard civilities exchanged, coffee offered and ordered, and the soothing snip-snap of Mimi Moffett's hippie sandals scurrying to the galley.

"Mr. President, Senator," a voice insisted softly behind her, "we must be clear on one thing. This rider to the Administration's gun-control bill—it's no cause for panic, absolutely no cause."

Nahum Bismarck always spoke in a soft voice. The First Lady recognized the trick, and she distrusted it. The lowered tones were a means of gaining the ascendancy, of shaming the big, blustering generals and senators into shrinking their voices to the same level. Few men could plot matters of state in a whisper, any more than many track runners could win a race on tiptoe. But Nahum Bismarck was one of them, and if he could keep the talk to his level and the running to his rules, he could be sure nine tenths of the time of having his way.

"A die-hard in the House feels that by limiting guns the Administration is undercutting the Second Amendment. So to make his point, he attaches a rider repealing the entire Bill of Rights. You can't for one minute take the business seriously. The rider is a gesture, nothing more. Symbolic speech, as it were."

"Perhaps it began as symbolic speech, Nahum, but it could escalate into something a hell of a lot more dangerous than a symbol. Now I want you and Dan to tell me just how we're going to get rid of guns without jeopardizing the entire Constitution of the United States."

"What's the problem?" came the Oklahoma twang of Senator Dan. "Didn't the Supreme Court—"

"Exactly," Nahum Bismarck hissed. "The Court's on our side."

The First Lady tried to close her ears. Her eye roved the cabin for some distraction, and she wondered about having a painting on one of the walls. The Air Force technicians could probably rivet a Miro to the galley partition: it might look cheerful.

"The Supreme Court," said the President, "is still atoning for the Dred Scott decision. They must have been stoned when they handed down that opinion on New York's gun-control law, and we must have been stoned to try to hang a bill on it."

"It's a sound opinion," Nahum Bismarck said. "An ingenious opinion."

"I'll grant you," the President said in that tone that meant he was granting nothing, "New York was buckling under a plague of snipings and armed robberies and shoot-outs, and they had every reason to want to outlaw guns. But why the hell the Supreme Court had to pick that way of upholding them . . ."

"It was the only way of upholding them," Nahum Bismarck stated.

"The only way? To say that the U. S. Army bears the arms of the people?"

Watery premonitions of day filtered hazily through the two-foot veils of Dublin lace that covered the TV-shaped windows of the cabin. The First Lady had bought the lace on a stopover in Shannon, years ago, in the era of propeller planes. It had lain in the attic of the house in Virginia until, a little over ten months previously, she had had the idea of cutting it and hanging it to soften the razor edges of these windows. The delicate filigree blunted the light, broke it, and scattered it.

"Precisely. The right of the people to bear arms is vested in the Army, and since New York's law does not touch the Army it in no way infringes the right of the people."

"Nahum, I'm as much against guns as any thinking American, but once you buy the notion that the people's rights can be vested in proxies, you've just about abolished the people."

The cabin was long and large, comfortably dry thanks to air

control, though rain still splattered in huge, soggy droplets outside.

"I don't see the problem," Senator Dan said. "No one wants guns."

"The problem," said the President, "is that no one seems to want the Bill of Rights either. Look at the rider that congressman tacked onto our bill: he says since the guarantees of the Bill of Rights are vested in the Congress, they don't have to be vested anywhere else. Our gun-control bill frees the courts and the police to deal with guns, and that man's rider frees the courts and police to do anything they want to anyone provided they don't do it to a congressman. But what really alarms me is that the bill's coming up for a vote and there hasn't been nearly the type of outcry I'd expected."

"There've been objections," Senator Dan said.

"The country is tired," Nahum Bismarck said. "Apathetic. The apathy will pass. The bill will not."

"Now look, Nahum." The President's voice betrayed impatience. "The House is debating that bill today. By some fluke they may pass it. We've got to be sure, if it ever reaches the Senate, that we've got the strength to lick it. What do you think, Dan?"

The First Lady made a renewed effort to concentrate on her surroundings. To a surprising extent, the interior of the cabin mimicked an ordinary, earthbound room. The deep upholstered seats, moored like barber's chairs to the floor, were capable of turning at the touch of a lever to form different groupings as discussion might demand. There was even a spinet piano, bolted solidly to the wall, its case a deeply burnished mahogany, the gold letters that spelled STEINWAY gleaming from the underside of its lid. To the First Lady's surprise, it had a full seven-octave range, and except for a testy F-sharp in the bottom octave, it was perfectly in tune. She had learned that President Eisenhower, who liked to hear Mamie tinker with Chopin études, had put the piano in the old Air Force One; John Kennedy had taken the works out and moved the piano case to the new Air

Force One to house a bar; and Richard Nixon had reinstated the strings and the mechanism. The pilot had assured the First Lady that the spinet got a tuning up more often than his engine.

"I've taken an informal canvass." Papers rattled; Senator Dan hesitated. "The problem is, Mr. President, the minority leader is exploiting sentiment against our position on the supersonic jetports."

"Jesus," the President sighed, "build a jetport and suddenly the whole country wants to burn the Constitution."

Lexie emerged from the cockpit, pouting as though the pilot had refused to let her push buttons. She darted to the piano and bonged out the first measures of the C-sharp minor Prelude, standing. Her ferocity made the First Lady fear for the cloisonné vases that were moored to the spinet. She signaled Lexie to be a good girl.

The President and Senator Dan shot the First Lady quick glances of gratitude. Only Nahum Bismarck appeared saddened at the prospect of coffee without Rachmaninoff, but his drooping gaze quickly buoyed when he saw he had caught the First Lady's eye. He threw her a smile and she smiled back, wishing she could like the man and at the same time glad she did not.

Mimi Moffett, playing stewardess this morning, ambled down the aisle and plopped a newspaper, heavily folded, into the First Lady's lap.

"Good Lord," the First Lady exclaimed.

"Don't blame me," Mimi Moffett shrugged, "blame the Emerging Nations Supplement. They've got four sections, would you believe?"

The First Lady counted the sections and believed. Behind, the President was talking.

"I have a hunch the rider to the gun-control bill is only the tip of the iceberg, and in this case only one per cent of the ice is above water."

"What are you talking about?" Nahum Bismarck's voice rose above a whisper. "Iceberg!"

"Nahum, it took twenty years and a world war to restore the semblance of a democratic process in Germany. I don't think any of us is going to be around to take as relaxed a view as you apparently do, not the way the country is moving."

The Secret Service men entered the cabin and took their seats, and the safety-belt sign flashed on. It was a smooth take-off, and the complaint of suddenly jolted engines modulated seamlessly into a rising whine that always sounded to the First Lady like the sobbing of steel. She knew of course that steel could not sob, though peering through the lace at the rain-pelted wings she almost believed it could cry. The sob, even and long-keening, diminished upward into a hum that was either the faint abrasion of crystal spheres slightly off-center or the kibitzing of an attendant spirit.

The President's party was airborne.

The First Lady looked indifferently down out of her window. She was terrified of heights, but not of ridiculous heights.

A chunk of eastern seaboard, squeezed to the size of a schoolboy's map, its colors fogged over and out of phase, veered and tipped and spilled gradually behind them. Air Force One leveled out, and the men could be heard unstrapping their safety belts with loud clanks and gusto, as though loosening their breeches after a meal.

The First Lady stared across the empty aisle at her daughter turning the pages of *The New Yorker*. She hoped Lexie was looking at the ads, not reading one of those more and more frequent alarmist articles. But the whispers of the men, indistinct now that the motors were humming, were thick with alarms and disasters half-articulated. Alarm was the fashion, it was the lifestyle of a generation, and she knew there was no way even the First Child of the nation could be shielded against it.

The First Lady laid her head against the backrest and untethered her thoughts. She saw herself with her memory's eye, walking her dappled gelding across the hazy Virginia field. The dew was still heavy on the grass but she was wearing riding boots and jodhpurs. She had been a good-looking girl, her slim figure rounded where it mattered; no trouble with calories in those halcyon days. She had had a great curiosity about sex and by some round-about logic she had satisfied it riding and reading and painting and doing the things young ladies of that era did while waiting to lose their virginity or marry or both. Her mother had died while she was still unmarried and still relatively young and for a few years she had devoted herself to her father, who was very rich and did not need her devotion and, having just escaped one woman, was not about to tie himself to another.

Very tactfully he asked her to leave him alone.

She liked to ride before breakfast and she would refuse young men's invitations to dances and parties and movies because she liked to ride in the evening too. By nightfall she was usually tired enough of riding to fall asleep. Then she met young Bill Luckinbill, who was poor and persistent. She didn't ride nearly so much after that because Bill would simply not let her. He demanded her evenings, and somehow he got them; he demanded her afternoons and he got most of those too.

She painted less and her father smiled at her more.

Bill intrigued her because he was never tired. She secretly envied him. He was handsome in a way, not so handsome as he would become with age, but after her father's rejection she was flattered that any man should want her, especially a persistent, energetic, handsome man. Political life fascinated her because Bill, as a senator's aide, traveled to places and knew people she had only read about. She liked it when he said the nation needed a politics based on compassion; as a rich girl she had sometimes felt guilty about national poverty.

She did not know when exactly she had fallen in love with Bill, but she did know that when he went on long trips she was restless and frightened at having to be alone. Her father no longer seemed company at all and her gelding had died. When Bill proposed marriage she talked it over with her father, who said by all means, but why didn't Bill try for the United States Senate himself? Bill and her father had talked, and a year after the marriage her husband was elected to the United States Senate, where he served three consecutive terms.

Marriage and politics, in a hundred odd and surprising ways, had been totally different from anything she had imagined them to be. But she had never been able to imagine things ahead of time: not people, not places, not even her fortieth birthday. Everything in her life had been an unpredictable mixture of memory and disappointment and hope.

She smiled at that lonely girl who had once upon a time sneaked out of bed at five in the morning to steal a ride on her favorite horse, and who now sneaked out of bed to plop herself down on an airplane. She smiled that she had given up horses and given up her vague dream of going to Florence to study art and more or less given up all the vague ideas and vague dreams she had ever had.

In exchange, she had gotten a daughter. He had gotten the presidency.

It came to her that she was not especially happy. The problem was that she was not especially unhappy either. She could make do.

The men whispered and shifted papers and nodded their heads behind her, and Air Force One sped westward across the nation, in futile flight from the dawn.

*

At 12:12 P.M. a man in hunting boots and blue jeans and a checkered sports shirt entered the First Methodist Church of Whitefalls. He had the sort of windburned face that inspires trust and sells cigarettes. He was stopped inside the door by a Secret Service man who asked his business. He said he wanted to pray.

The Secret Service man apologized that the church was not open to the public till after the ceremonies in the graveyard. The bell tower, he explained, offered far too inviting a perch for snipers. The man smiled and said he understood. "The times we live in," were his words.

He turned as though to go, and the Secret Service man made the mistake of glancing away. Something struck him in the back of the neck and that was all he remembered before he crumpled.

The man in blue jeans, who had learned the blow in counterinsurgency school, withdrew a disposable, preloaded syringe from the breast pocket of his checkered sports shirt. He snapped off the protective plastic sheath and administered an intra-muscular injection, through the buttock of the Secret Service man's trousers, of 5 milligrams of ketamine. The dose, sufficient to produce fifty minutes' unconsciousness, had been found under certain conditions to produce an aftereffect similar to that of LSD.

But the man in blue jeans was not concerned with aftereffects. He went to the organ loft, where he had hidden his old-fashioned, German-made 7.65 bolt-action Mauser rifle. He took the weapon to the top of the bell tower. He checked the action and the telescopic sight and loaded the gun. He waited, and his fingers loosened the wrapper of a thick brown Havana that he had brought in the same pocket with the bullets.

He lit the cigar and savored the first rich intake of smoke and watched the flags that lined the route of the presidential motorcade.

*

The weather in the President's home town that day could not have been better for wreath laying. Temperatures for Whitefalls, South Dakota, and for the greater Wapsinicon River basin area were due to range from the mid-seventies to the mid-eighties. There was to be an easterly wind with a possibility of rain, but at noon skies were still clear with unlimited visibility.

The President's plane had arrived at 10:37 A.M., somewhat behind schedule, at Hobart, the nearest airport to Whitefalls. The mayor of Whitefalls himself was on hand to welcome the First Family and to join the motorcade back.

It was very much an *ad hoc* sort of motorcade. Local officials had encouraged pedestrians to join in, and every man, woman, child, and dog who had a mind to turned out to show his support of the Chief Executive. The composition of the parade varied bewilderingly from block to block, especially in the downtown area, where the movie house (dark these last twelve years) and the Pruninghook Arms Hotel (a proud nineteenth-century survival in the rutabaga Gothic mode) and the county court-

house all fronted on Whitefalls' historic town square, in which
William Jennings Bryan had once campaigned.

Local police estimated that virtually all of Whitefalls' 4,000
citizens, as well as some 3,000 well-wishers and sightseers
from the surrounding metropolises and farmland of the greater
Wapsinicon River basin area, had turned out that day, box
lunches and noisemakers in hand, to pack the sidewalks, litter,
wave flags, shoot off flashbulbs, and shout their damnedest.

It was a regular Fourth of July.

At Wetstone Avenue several dozen more pedestrians joined in
the motorcade. In defiance of all security regulations in effect
since November 1963, many shook the President's hand, and
in fact the Chief Executive seemed none too shy of offering it.
A lot of the women tried to kiss the First Lady and her daughter
Lexie, and one unidentified, heavy-set woman almost pulled the
girl from the back seat of the open black convertible.

By the time the motorcade and the stragglers reached the
intersection with Missouri Avenue, things had slowed to a decided march, and Mrs. Abbie Loudeen, housewife and amateur
movie buff, was able to secure a position on foot some twenty
yards behind the presidential car, which she maintained almost
up to the Walnut Avenue stoplight. Mrs. Loudeen was able to
get some almost-in-focus candid shots of the President and his
family with her Japanese-made movie camera.

Authorities speculated, afterward, that if Mrs. Loudeen had
not run out of film one block short of the entrance to the
Whitefalls Cemetery, the government might indeed have had
an invaluable record of the prelude to that day's tragic events.

State troopers at the cemetery gates redirected unofficial
members and vehicles of the motorcade to the Seventh Street
and Eighth Street sidewalks, both of which commanded excellent views of the burial ground. At the request of security
agents, attendance at the wreath-laying ceremony was restricted
to the presidential party, the press, local government, and members of the Whitefalls Junior High School Marching Band.

The presidential car and motorcycle guard came to a stop just
inside the gates, and the President and his family continued on

foot, escorted only by three armed Secret Service men, the mayor of Whitefalls, and the president of the Whitefalls Chamber of Commerce, who carried the memorial wreath which the Chief Executive was to lay upon the grave of his mother and father.

The Whitefalls Cemetery occupies three choice acres in the northwestern quadrant of town. Its average elevation is twenty-three feet above that of Whitefalls itself. The grave of Eustace and Wilma Luckinbill (they were moved to a joint resting place in 1962) is situated on the southern face of the upper extremity of the cemetery knoll and is, at thirty-two feet, one of the highest places in the entire Whitefalls town limits. Only portions of Wapsinicon Drive, some two miles distant, can top it.

A memorial statue representing the Spirit of Vigilance marks the Luckinbill grave. This alabaster representation of a female person rises to a height, including pedestal, of eight feet seven inches. Its wing span of five foot three precludes anything approaching a clear sighting of the grave from the north or northwest. Visibility from all other directions is, however, virtually unobstructed, except that a modest, three-tiered grandstand had been set up ten yards southeast of the grave to accommodate representatives of the three wire services, of radio and television, and of the national and international press.

The grandstand was completely full by 12:38 P.M. on the day of the shooting.

At approximately 12:40 P.M.—accounts vary by a matter of several seconds—the Chief Executive, his wife and his daughter, and the mayor of Whitefalls and the president of the Whitefalls Chamber of Commerce reached graveside and stood at attention, gazes fixed on the Spirit of Vigilance.

The United Press International wire service recorded that the Chief Executive wore a three-piece, conservatively pinstriped dark suit; the First Lady wore a white ensemble, the skirt of which came to five inches below her knees; and eighteen-year-old Alexandra ("Lexie") Luckinbill wore a simple, attractive, and utterly appropriate white cotton dress, knee-length.

The mayor made a brief speech welcoming the Chief Executive home to his birthplace; hoping that the First Lady and her daughter would enjoy their stay and perhaps have the opportunity to visit the Whitefalls Agricultural Museum, recently established under a much appreciated federal grant; and recalling to those there gathered the sacrifices of the gallant men and women, many from small towns every bit as humble as Whitefalls, South Dakota, who had given of their life and limb in two world wars, three United Nations peace-keeping actions, and seven American interventions, that democracy, liberty, and the pursuit of happiness might not vanish from this earth.

His words were carried locally by station KICK, and some of them could be heard echoing back from the many transistor receivers in the vicinity. Three radio networks carried the ceremony nationally, and the occasion in its entirety was filmed by the cameramen of CBS-TV, which had promised to share its footage with all comers.

A spattering of applause as the speech finished was quashed by a claque of shush-ing and sss-ing. The President of the United States thanked the mayor for his kind words, thanked the men and women of Whitefalls for their gallant and unforgettable reception of his family and himself, and thanked those who could not be here—the men and women who had given their lives in the many and tragic conflicts of this century—for their part in preserving our mixed free enterprise heritage.

The President expressed confidence that the nation would resolve its many dilemmas in democratic fashion, and then he accepted the wreath from the president of the Chamber of Commerce. Holding it aloft in his right hand, he approached the grave of Eustace and Wilma Luckinbill.

The wreath was a four-foot, eight-pound, aluminum-reinforced horseshoe of intertwined ivy, myrtle, and American beauty roses; designed and executed by Fleet Florists of nearby Hobart, South Dakota, it bore a pink silk ribbon with satin letters spelling LUX AETERNA.

As the President knelt on one knee at the grave, the bandmaster raised both batons in the air to prepare the kids for the

downbeat of "Hail to the Chief." The Whitefalls Junior High
School Marching Band had been especially augmented with
extra piccolo and euphonium, and the kids had been practicing
Tuesday evenings for over a month. The plan was for the music
to commence as soon as the Chief Executive finished laying the
wreath and got back to his feet.

The President laid the wreath. A premature piccolo twittered,
solo and naked.

Something cracked in the air overhead.

It cracked sharp and swift and vicious, staccato as lightning.
It triggered a ghastly silence, and the silence was engulfed in a
rising tidal wave of shouts and screams of terror and recognition
as understanding swept the marching band and the reporters
and the Secret Service men and the police and the crowds who
had pressed against the gates and fences for a better look; and
the First Lady threw herself across the victim's body, screaming
"Oh my God! My God! Lexie!" and the President, without
even rising from where he knelt, dove across the grave in the
attempt to shield his wife and child; and the ashen-faced band-
leader lowered one baton but forgot the other, and three Secret
Service men, guns drawn, rushed to the grave and fell over one
another in burbling, sobbing determination that no bullets
would cut down yet another President of the United States;
and the crowd, buckling under the fear of more gunfire, volatil-
ized into a panicked, trapped swarm, and with a second crack,
this time of a huge tree toppling, the three-tiered grandstand
gave way, and reporters spilled like dice across cables and one
of them tripped the newsreel camera, and eight hours later TV
viewers sitting at home the nation over and wondering what
was going on out there in Whitefalls saw a single flash of a
young reporter's uncomprehending face hurtling toward them
before the screen went black, and, a moment later, a commercial for dogfood came on.

*

Because sightseers blocked the roads it took thirty-two minutes for the ambulance to reach the graveyard and another forty-

eight for it to get Lexie to the hospital. The President and
the First Lady and the warrant officer rode with the body, and
even if they had wanted to talk the science-fiction screech of
the siren would have prevented their hearing one another.

A flotilla of police followed. The motorcycles were strung out
as far as the First Lady could see, stretching further than the
asphalt horizon.

Halfway to the hospital Lexie's hand stopped twitching in
her mother's.

The hospital was a square, prisonlike building set down at
the edge of a wheat field. A great many reporters had gathered.

Orderlies came for the stretcher, and the President and his
wife and the warrant officer followed like mourners at a burial.
Four men with submachine guns walked with the procession as
far as the waiting room, where a nurse brought coffee with
powdered cream substitute. She asked the First Lady for an
autograph, and the First Lady signed a napkin.

The President sat oddly still, his thumb probing the dimple
of his chin as though to dislodge a piece of lint. Several times
he told the First Lady, "This is my fault."

"No," she said, "don't say that." But in her heart she agreed.

She went to the bathroom, and a policewoman went with
her and watched her splash cold water at her eyes.

"Need any help?" the policewoman asked.

"I've been pregnant three times in my life," the First Lady
said; and she went from towel dispenser to towel dispenser and
found them all empty, and stood with ice water running down
her cheeks. "I lost the first and the third. Lexie's the second."

"That's too bad. Here, use some toilet paper."

The toilet paper made sharp edges and stung the First Lady's
face. "Lexie took twenty-eight hours, just getting born. My
father was with me all the time. He read to me. My husband
was campaigning."

"You be brave now."

"I don't suppose she'll take nearly as long dying, do you?"

"No one's going to die."

But the First Lady saw a priest in the corridor, expressionless and patient as a vulture, and she felt rage grow in her heart till she wanted to cry out.

The young doctor returned, smiling. "Mr. President, Mrs. Luckinbill," he said, "your daughter suffered a mild concussion when she fell. The bullet grazed her shoulder, but she's in pretty good shape, considering."

"She's alive?" the First Lady asked, not believing it.

"Very much so," the young doctor said. "You can see her."

The President, his wife, the warrant officer, the policewoman, and the four armed guards followed the young doctor Indian file down the corridor and around three right-angled turns. The parade came to a halt outside a room guarded by two Secret Service men who rose from their chairs. Nurses stood scattered along the hallway, watching, and two orderlies rushing a patient to the operating theater stopped to stare.

The President and his wife went in without their guards and without the President's codes.

They couldn't see much of Lexie: her forehead was bandaged where she had bruised it falling; thick, broad strips of adhesive plaster hid an entire cheek and half her chin. The sheet lay touching her throat, and except for an arm with needle taped to it, there was no more of her to see.

The young doctor reached down a thumb and forefinger and opened the patient's left eye—a dull, glazed marble that stared at the First Lady with frightening lifelessness.

Without thinking to ask permission, the First Lady reached out a hand to feel the exposed skin of Lexie's face. It was flushed and hot, throbbing like the membrane of a tambourine.

The First Lady leaned toward her daughter. "Lexie. It's Mom. Can you hear me?"

"She won't be hearing anything for a few hours," the young doctor smiled, and the First Lady realized that he had caught her and the President in the Jesus Christ sweep of his out-stretched arms and was moving them back toward the corridor. They rounded a right angle, and Nahum Bismarck was coming toward them, one hand clenching the head of his cane, the other a Coca-Cola bottle.

"Mrs. Luckinbill," he said softly, "I'm very sorry at the turn of events." And he turned to the President. "The House Rules Committee is sending the bill to the floor. With the rider."

"Good Lord," said the President. And he went with Nahum Bismarck, and the warrant officer and two of the guards trailed after them.

The First Lady stood wondering where to go and dreading the thought of another six hours in that waiting room. And then, because she felt ridiculous keeping a policewoman and two armed men dawdling, she began to walk.

She must have walked for fifteen minutes. She found herself staring into the huge inverted bottle of a water cooler, watching her reflection squeeze in and out of focus, thinking that the events of her life had never been fair, or even logical, but merely painful: thinking that this child, whom it had almost killed her to bring into the world, whom doctors had told her to abort rather than risk carrying, this child who would have been her posterity, her justification, the redress for the years and the marriage of utter emptiness, this child was even now being taken away from her.

Why couldn't the bullet have hit me instead? she wondered.

"Ma'am?" came a voice at her elbow: the policewoman's.

The First Lady shook her head, poured herself a cup of ice water and downed it in a numbing gulp.

When she returned to the waiting room Senator Dan Bulfinch was there.

"Moni." He took her hands.

"Comb your hair." She offered him the comb from her purse. He ignored it. "Are you all right, Moni? You weren't hurt?"

"I'm not hurt."

"Lexie?"

"Why did they have to shoot her? They don't like the War or Welfare or arms for Israel? Why shoot Lexie?"

She collapsed onto the straight-backed sofa. Senator Dan sat beside her, and she found it incongruous that his hand should be smoothing her hair.

"Why should a child have to suffer like that? It isn't fair!"

"I'm sure she's not suffering, Moni."

She took the senator's hand and held tight.

"Mrs. Luckinbill?" She looked up to see a white-haired man with a kindly smile standing with one foot on the doorsill. It was an odd time for smiles, even kindly ones. She recognized the mayor of Whitefalls. "You and the President must be tired."

She had no time to agree or disagree. He was holding out a doorkey tied to a huge wooden tag.

"You can borrow my house. It's not much, but it's near, and it's a home, and I think you need one."

*

"All right, Woodie," said the President, "what do we know?"

Waiting for a reply, he offered the sherry around again; there was nothing else in the house to drink. It was an old house: things creaked and there was too much lace on the windows and lampshades and chairs. Some surprised-looking heads of animals stared down from the walls, suspended between crossed sabers and rifles, ornamental fishing rods and sealed gas jets.

"Somewhere between a little and a lot," came the reply. "We've interviewed the witnesses, we've done a rush on the ballistics, and we've combed the TV footage."

The President nodded. "Good."

The mayor had been kind to lend them his house, and it was not his fault, really, if there was nothing stronger in the cupboard than sherry; it was merely his preference. The First Lady speculated that the mayor was a reformed alcoholic. She re-crossed her legs and refused sherry. The head of the Federal Security Agency uncrossed his and accepted a third glass. He considered his fingers as though they were sticky and he would have liked to lick them.

"The statements of observers as to the direction the shot came from," he continued, and the President stood with a half-smile that meant I am listening, not I am amused, "are just about as contradictory as you can get. For that matter so are the statements as to which way the victim was facing when the shot was fired. Since there is no photographic record of the victim's position, and since even the next-of-kin contradict one another on the matter—" The man paused to sip his sherry, and his eyes flicked up accusingly, over the rim of the glass, at the President and then, less hurriedly, at the First Lady.

Woodrow Judd was the only human she had ever met who managed to speak slower than her husband. Of all the things that day that had made her want to scream, this fat man was the one that made her want to scream loudest. Her lungs shrieked for air, her ears shrieked for silence, and he droned on and on, spitting words out one or two at a time, like rejected sourballs.

"—the angle of entry of the bullet is conclusive evidence of nothing except that the assassin shot the victim from the rear."

"Mr. Judd," the First Lady interrupted, "could I ask you not to use the word *victim?* Her name is Lexie."

The President intervened, a frown worrying the smile. "Woodie is reading from a report, hon. *Victim* is a standard locution."

"My daughter is not a standard locution and she's not dead yet."

"Glad to," Woodrow Judd said, and he continued in the same halting, dead monotone. "Now the assassin—let's call him a sniper, since he hasn't actually killed anyone yet—he probably hid in the bell tower of the First Methodist Church. We had a guard there and he was jumped this morning."

Woodrow Judd wore his hair almost crew-cut. It was a little blacker than seemed natural, and the First Lady had the impression that the same zeal and tactic had been brought to the battle against gray as to the battle against subversives.

"Moreover, our men have found a single ejected cartridge, still sulfurous incidentally, under the bell of the church tower. Apparently it rolled there and the sniper either didn't notice or didn't care. So it looks like the church tower, at least for the moment."

Woodrow Judd's face was shapeless in the way of an Irish potato, and his eyes recalled a potato's in color and in the suggestion of sightlessness. His skin was freckled, but the freckles could have been a plague of liver spots, and they were glossed over by a tan that had come from a bottle or a sun lamp. At first glance, or from the photos, the First Lady would have believed the official statement that he was sixty-five; but sitting six feet from him, she was more inclined to think him seventy.

"The type of rifle can be hazarded from this empty cartridge case—probably an old-fashioned German-made Mauser 7.65. This is pretty much corroborated, as far as such things ever are, by the bullet that struck the shoulder of the—Miss Luckinbill's shoulder. The bullet is fairly well mangled, almost beyond recognition."

The First Lady wanted to scream, *What about my daughter, isn't she mangled?*

"The time of the shooting is a matter of public record, so we can pretty well assume the sniper went up into the tower just after twelve o'clock, when the guard was jumped, and came down a little after twelve-forty."

Something in the man aspired to the dandy: the white silk handkerchief testified as much.

"The sniper might not have taken the gun with him—could have planted it there ahead of time—but he sure as hell took it down with him, because it's not there now. So we're asking people if they saw anyone of that description with a gun."

What description, the First Lady wondered: *you have half a telephone book there and you keep leafing through it, but you haven't given us a description.* He had been sitting in the chair when she and the President had turned on the light in the room, and he had not gotten up. He had said he'd flown straight from Washington when the teletype flashed word, as though that explained his being too tired and too busy and altogether too important to rise.

There was silence in the room; abruptly the President seemed to realize the fact.

"I know you're doing your best, Woodie, and it sounds as though you've gotten off to a damned good start."

"There's a question, Mr. President."

"A good many questions." The First Lady could not help sounding angry.

"Yes, ma'am." Woodrow Judd's eyes stayed with her. "We don't know whether he was shooting at the President and happened to miss, or whether he was shooting at the girl, at Miss Luckinbill, and found his mark."

The First Lady exploded. "Isn't it perfectly obvious that this lunatic was shooting at my husband? How can you even think someone would purposely aim a gun at my daughter? She's never hurt a soul in her life; she's not even involved in politics!"

"Except by blood, ma'am."

"By that kind of logic the man could have been trying to shoot *me!*"

"Yes, ma'am."

Aside from her husband, there were two others in the room, and they had both gotten up when she'd come in. One of them was the man with great cistern eyes who sat on the piano bench staring at the animal heads, and to whom no one had offered sherry. Woodrow Judd had called the man his stenographer, and if there had been a name she did not remember it, and she would have put his age five years south of Judd's. He seemed to be trained to say very little and to nod a great deal, and he carried a small tape recorder.

The other had been a miniature poodle jumping to the name Mon Ami Pierrot. The animal had attacked the First Lady's skirt, tried to rip her belt loose in its teeth, and had vanished under a cloud of cluck-clucks and shames to the hollow beneath some overstuffed chair where it could still be heard breathing hotly. Woodrow Judd had laid ownership to the poodle as well as to the man, saying that the First Lady had to forgive the little mutt: he'd never seen a celebrity before. For an astonished moment the First Lady had not realized which of the two he meant.

And now, while the poodle chewed noisily on a corner of the mayor's rug, they were talking of death. The First Lady made her voice absolutely firm.

"Mr. Judd, the sniper intended to kill my husband. He did not. Your men could have taken security precautions. They did not. Why in God's name wasn't the bell tower better guarded? If you'd had two men there instead of one my daughter wouldn't be in a hospital, dying, now!"

"Now, hon," the President interposed, "she's not dying, we don't know that."

"If Lexie dies," the First Lady cried, and did not finish.

"Now, darling." The President put his well-exercised arm around her. "Woodie, you've got to forgive Monica."

"No, Mr. President, I'm the one who should be asking both your forgivenesses. I'm responsible for this, same as I'm responsible for anything the Agency undertakes. And Mrs. Luckinbill, Mr. President, I want you to know, if your daughter dies, I'll hand in my resignation."

Several things about Woodrow Judd did not cause the First Lady to believe or trust him; that remark confirmed her doubt.

She had heard him referred to as a Fascist, and though she would have been hard put to define the word, other than to say it was someone who used his power to oppress poor people and symphony orchestras, she saw nothing in his appearance or behavior to contradict the accusation. She felt disoriented in his presence, like a compass that had been banged with a magnet. She could not focus on her grief but kept drifting into resentment.

"Your resignation," she said, "won't bring Lexie back."

"Hon." The President tightened the grip of his arm, gave a little pack-up-your-troubles smile that was engagingly pathetic and, the First Lady realized with some surprise, probably sincere. "She's not gone yet."

The First Lady moved free of the arm. "Every minute of our lives we're followed and spied on and told where we can go and who we can see, and we live like prisoners, all in the name of some pious fiction called security, and the one time that there's a threat, that these men could actually fulfill some purpose, where's the security? Off in some bar tanking up on beer? Puffing marijuana it took ten men to confiscate from some student? I'm sorry, I've lived with security almost three ycars, I loathed it when it started and I loathe it now, and seeing this man face-to-face, I just wonder where and what is all that law and order he prattles about, what the hell are we paying for, beefsteak for that ridiculous poodle?"

And the First Lady saw that her husband's hand was trembling and his brow was damp and his eyes were pleading with her; and the realization came obliquely, glancingly, that there was a power in the land higher than the President, and it was the men who were custodians of all Presidents and all secrets. It had taken fifteen administrations and fifty years and an act of God to dump J. Edgar Hoover and dismantle his Bureau, but conceivably the power he had amassed survived undiminished in the hands of his former colleagues and in the sister organization, and perhaps, like Rockefeller money, the power was so large it just kept growing, and no matter that the man who wielded it was rude and not much taller than Toulouse-Lautrec.

"Hon, Mr. Judd has come all the way out here to help, and I think you may be doing him an injustice, and maybe we'd better continue this discussion aftcr you've had a chance to rest." The arm had caught her again and was moving her in no uncertain terms toward the door.

"I'm sorry," the First Lady apologized. Since Inauguration, she had gotten almost accomplished at lying.

"If anything happens to your girl," Woodrow Judd said, "I will personally find the man that pulled that trigger and when I do, your husband will have my resignation. You have my solemn oath."

She forced her lips into a wan smile.

"Why don't you go upstairs and take one of those pills?" the President suggested.

It was the first she had realized he knew about the pills. "I'll be all right. Please forgive me, Mr. Judd."

"My pleasure," the fat man said. The poodle came running to him, offering in its mouth a swatch of saliva-drenched carpet, and he made a great show of being interested in the gift. The First Lady disliked the way Woodrow Judd deferred to his pet and treated his stenographer like a dog; and so she went to the stenographer and offered her hand.

"Good night," she said. "Please forgive me."

The stenographer, startled, stumbled to his feet. She felt sorry for him. Something in the eyes suggested a glimmer of artistic ability.

"Good night," he said in a sickbed voice.

In the hallway the First Lady passed a man who had not been there when she had come in, and whom she did not bother to look at now. He rose, perhaps as a sign of respect, or perhaps only in surprise. And when she did not notice him, he slid back down onto the bench where he had been sitting and stared at his fingernails as though one set did not match the other.

She had not closed the living-room door; the men were audible.

"You've got to excuse Monica. She's upset. But the hospital says Lexie's in fair shape and getting better all the time. She may just pull through."

A stopper rattled in a sherry decanter.

"I hope so, sir. I sincerely pray she does."

Outside the house, the night wind screamed through a sieve of electric and telephone wires.

"Monica has been under a lot of strain, don't ask me why. Maybe Washington hasn't turned out to be quite the banquet she expected. And she reads a lot of Agatha Christie, so please forgive her when she starts doing your work for you."

"Nothing to forgive. Matter of fact, she's probably dead right."

Silence.

"Mr. President, the assassin was shooting at you. We know that for a fact."

The living-room door creaked further open, and Woodrow Judd's head appeared for a cuckoo-clock instant in the hallway. "Agent Hiram Quinn, come in here a minute."

The man from the hallway came into the room.

He betrayed signs of wear, but not specifically of age. He could have been a dilapidated thirty-five or a youthful fifty. His hair could have been silver-blond or totally grayed; the light in the room was ambiguous. His brow and jaw formed a square, and his nose and ears were so eroded that they in no way modified the geometry of it. His eyes were no more than indentations above the flat cheeks, and he kept them narrowed.

There were no introductions.

"Mr. President," Woodrow Judd explained, "a little over two months ago a letter was sent from Whitefalls to the White House. It was unsigned, and it threatened your life. I believe its wording was, *Stop killing or we will kill you.*"

"It was worded," the agent corrected neutrally, "*Stop killing or you will be dead you.*"

"*You will be dead you?*" the President mused. "I was never told of this."

"It's the Agency's job to take care of that kind of mail," Woodrow Judd said. "You've got more important things to look after."

"At this point I'm not certain I do."

Woodrow Judd moistened his lips with sherry. "Mr. President, ninety-nine and forty-four one hundredths per cent of these letters threatening your life—and you get five hundred a month if you get one a year—most of it is the work of cranks and kids and frustrated cab drivers. Naturally we look into each and every one of them, because there's always that point fifty-six per cent that's for real, and it's our job to find out who they are and to stop them."

The agent listened with the concentration of a musician evaluating a taped playback. His eyes had retreated into twin slices.

"Unfortunately the law provides a maximum five-year penalty for using the mails to threaten the life of the Chief Executive, and, as you know, the courts have taken to reading a freedom of speech issue into some of this."

"I know, Woodie: you've got your work cut out for you, and I appreciate the fact. All the same, if there's a potential assassin sitting in Whitefalls, and he announced the fact, I'm curious you'd let me come out here."

The agent's fingers could be seen working the frayed edges of his shirt cuffs, searching out threads.

"I can only say by way of mitigation, Mr. President, and I know it's not much, that if we had known who wrote the threatening note, we would certainly have passed that information on to the Secret Service."

Woodrow Judd faced the agent and spoke even slower.

"Now Hiram Quinn here has been in charge of the investigation since April 17. He is one of our best and most tireless investigators, he has an excellent record in this type of trace, and it was on the basis of his recommendations and findings that we were in the process of downgrading the Whitefalls investigation, which is to say, phasing it out."

The President still faced Woodrow Judd, as though refusing to place responsibility with any other person. The silence stretched to breaking. The poodle stopped chewing carpet. Woodrow Judd made no move. It was the agent who finally spoke.

"Mr. President, we've taken a long and close look at the mail flow in this town, and we're satisfied that the person who wrote that note doesn't live here."

"If he doesn't live here," said the President, "he certainly commutes."

The agent blinked as though he had been slapped.

"That will be all, Agent Quinn," said Woodrow Judd.

The agent left the room. The security guard at the front door let him pass without a glance.

*

Hiram Quinn, veteran of twenty-three years with the Federal Security Agency, kicked gravel under a sputtering sky and aimed his steps at the only bar in Whitefalls, South Dakota. Cutting through the town square he took jabs at the stone dignitary and bruised his knuckles on the pedestal. He spat into the drinking fountain, but violence did little to curb the lion in his heart.

You run away from home at twelve, he itemized in his head with a curse for his drunk mom and the pop that beat shit out of her; you enlist in the Army at fourteen, go to State U. at seventeen, you join the FSA training academy at twenty-one, you graduate eleventh in a class of three hundred forty-two; in twenty-three years you take a minimum of bribes, if even that, you keep the cleanest hands of any agent in mail reconnaissance, and don't think you couldn't have laid your mitts on a few money orders and negotiable securities and some of the cash that passed under your nose, and what the hell did you do it for, to end up framed and lynched and holding the bag in White-falls, South Dakota?

The north side of the square was deserted at that hour, and no one saw Hiram Quinn turn down Third Street and duck into the door beneath the blinking light.

"What'll it be, Hi?" the bartender asked.

"Blended," said Hiram Quinn. "Give me the bottle."

And with his first gulp, Agent Hiram Quinn, nice guy no longer, signed finis in blood to a quarter century of I-pledge-allegiance. In between gulps of straight blended he eyed the occupants of the bar, old men on stools fumbling for their one conversation of the day, kids dancing to the traffic accident that was pouring from the jukebox.

A face and body detached themselves from the convulsing mob and moved with a familiar step toward him. "Something the matter, Hiram?"

She was a good kid and a loving one, and he couldn't help thinking she deserved a little better than him.

"First they send me into this latrine and then they empty the goddamned pail over my head," he spat. "I'm supposed to sit still for that? What do they think I am, some kind of congenital schnook?"

"Hiram, what's a schnook?"

He looked at her and saw innocence and felt reproached. "A schnook is a patsy, and you got your nose two inches away from one, so take a deep sniff, you are smelling the last of Hiram Quinn, boy agent *par excellence* and straight arrow *ad infinitum*, he just got busted in two back there."

"Hiram, look at me." She put a finger beneath his chin, tilted his bleary gaze up toward hers. "Now if something's wrong, tell me. Something I did?"

"Screw off," Hiram Quinn said, wondering why it was he always ended up being mean to her. He slid off the stool and stumbled out the door.

She came after him. "Hiram!" she called.

Loping like an escaped circus bear, Hiram Quinn cut across the town square and up the steps of the Pruninghook Arms Hotel. She pursued the lumbering shadow uncertainly and hesitated at the hotel door. She saw that the desk clerk was barricaded behind a Hobart *News and Gazette*, evening edition (ASSASSINATION ATTEMPT! screeched the headline), and she tiptoed across the open-weave straw rugs.

Hiram Quinn took the stairs two, three steps at a leap, and he went up like ricocheting birdshot, one hand skimming the banister and the other fending off walls. She followed as best she could, but the gap between her and Hiram Quinn widened to a floor and a half.

When she reached room 47, Hiram Quinn, his lips grimly determined, was trying to cram a three-piece double-vent gabardine wash-and-wear into a suitcase half the size of her purse. She wondered about his clothes.

"Hiram, don't those stores ever make alterations?" She went to the closet and creaked it open. "Are you taking your bathrobe?"

"No, I'm not taking the bathrobe." His voice was vinegar. "Throw me some underwear and a change of socks."

She went to the bathroom and leaned in. "What about your razor? And you've still got some shaving cream in that can."

"I can buy that crap on the road."

She turned to see Hiram Quinn go to the chair, flip the cushion over, and pull a tiny cardboard pillbox from a hole. He tried to stuff the box into the suitcase, then frowned.

"Take care of this, will you, sweetie?" He threw the box to her.

"How should I take care of it?"

"Just take care of it."

"Hiram, what kind of trouble are you in?"

He slammed the suitcase lid down, disregarded a coattail trailing out the side, and jimmied the lock shut. "The worst, and let's save the discussion. Got any money? I spent my last three in that bar."

She counted out bills and change and a postage stamp from her purse. "Five seventy-three enough?"

He looked at her, and his expression suddenly went soft, and she felt her knees slacken. "Keep it, sweetie, I've been an A-1 *goniff*; some day I'll make it all up to you."

He snapped open the suitcase and pried up a revolver from beneath the shirts. He tucked the gun into his belt, almost popping the leather, and shut the suitcase again. He threw her a kiss and spun out the door.

"Hiram!" she shouted after the departing shadow, but it didn't bother to answer.

*

Midnight observers of the Wapsinicon River Drive would first have heard the coyote howl of a solitary motor speeding down from Whitefalls. Ninety seconds later they would have seen a west-roving finger of light brush trees and roadside warning signs, and in another ninety seconds they would have seen that this finger reached out from the one extant headlight of a renegade, runaway black '63 Chevy, its body a half-completed crossword puzzle of dents and gashes. Swerving with a cockroach's instinct from highway lights, this indomitable near-ruin of a car scuttled toward the Route 3 turnoff and held to the dark side of the road with the tenacity of a damned soul. It was going close to ninety miles per hour.

As the Chevy was banking for a broad left onto Route 3, it was caught by an easterly fist of light, the converging headlight beams of a car that swung out onto the highway from the dirt siding.

The light must have surprised or blinded the driver of the '63 Chevy, for instead of turning onto Route 3 the car turned into a rain ditch and rolled to a stop with two of its wheels spinning in air. The driver of the other car doused his lights. The flames of the '63 Chevy gave more than enough light to make out the first few rows of a cornfield.

A little under thirty seconds later the passenger door of the '63 Chevy opened upward, like a ship's hatch, and a man hoisted himself and a little black bag through. He jumped clear of the flames, patted out the sparks on his cuffs and lapels, and squinted at the outline of the new-model station wagon that had moved dead center into the crossing.

"Jesus P. Christ!" the man muttered, and he ran the other way, into the corn.

The cornfield at the juncture of Wapsinicon River Drive and Route 3 is a large one, a hundred acres, and a fertile one, average yearly yield over a thousand bushels. By mid-June the corn is tall enough for a man to run through head bent and be as good as invisible.

The field is a diamond twisted askew, bounded on two facets by the intersecting roads and, on the far facets, by a forest that the county is planning to cut down and by the river that gives Wapsinicon River Drive its name.

He followed the lanes of corn, running full-throttle now. His bag and his outstretched hand jostled the shoulder-high stalks, and the ears of corn took hard retaliatory swings at his chest, clobbering him sometimes like baseball bats and knocking the breath out of him so that his voice made the endless entreating sound of a low-pitched siren.

He tripped over stalks that had fallen of the weight of their own corn, and he collided with a wheelbarrow and almost lost his kneecap to its blade-sharp edge, and something cold turned over in his stomach. His run became thick and his feet became inaccurate and he slowed and wobbled down an unexpected slope. He grabbed a cornstalk to hold him back but pulled the plant with him and heard it splash at the same time he did into the crotch-high Wapsinicon.

He stopped and listened, but his breath had risen to the velocity of a gale, and it blanketed every sound except his heartbeat.

He took a sighting on the opposite bank and moved toward it, and with one hand tried to hold his suitcase clear of the current. There were enormous potholes in the riverbed, and a single step could skid him off rock and put him in mud three feet deeper than he had stood the second before. He ventured out a gingerly toe to taste the depths before each step, and with caution he managed to fall only three times.

When he pulled himself by a fallen tree up the other side, his clothes clung to him like cold compresses, and his calf muscles began going into cramp. He slowed and bent to pound them with his fist and with his suitcase, then hopped and hobbled a little farther and stopped to pound again.

His progress was no faster than a mother's pulling a stubborn child.

This side of the river was called County Park, and the idea had been to develop it with lawns and flowerbeds and statues, but the best the county had been able to do thus far had been to prune twice yearly, though funds—they said—were finally coming through.

Beyond the park ran the outer tail of Watson Lane, and it was toward the road through pincing thickets that he stumbled, and it was at the road's ungroomed edge that he set down his suitcase and waited till he heard, through his own subsiding breath, the unhurried approach of a car.

He put out his thumb, but seeing how small and unreliable the thumb looked in the unsteady dawn of headlights, he waved one arm and then both, and shadows of trees striped across him.

The car began slowing at the bend, stopped several yards from him, and sat with motor purring. With the headlights full in his face he could discern neither make nor driver.

He picked up his suitcase and limped toward the passenger door, took the handle, and—smile prepared—swung it open.

"Thanks," he said, and he made the syllable laughing, as though he were Huck Finn fresh from a dip in the creek. "You're saving my life."

The driver wore blue jeans and a checkered shirt. "My pleasure," he said. The voice seemed familiar but the face was in shadow.

Hiram Quinn put a foot into the station wagon and was about to slide the rest of him in, when the driver placed something against his heart which it took him a moment to recognize as the barrel of a rifle.

At the instant of recognition he heard a noise, swifter and sterner than thunder, and was thrown backward to earth again. He fell faster than Lucifer, bag and all.

June 20: Tuesday

The room is hot. The First Lady was thinking this so as to avoid thinking, *My daughter is dying.* Beside her she heard a man saying, "The only thing we have to hate . . . is hate itself. . . ."

The guards had brought extra benches and chairs into the county courthouse, and reporters were allowed to sit on the floor as well. The room was packed with three times the people it could comfortably hold. They listened silently, with something approaching respect. There was almost no coughing.

"Let's not speak of darker days. Let's speak, rather, of sterner days. . . ."

There was an almost distracted regularity to the way the President kept stopping in mid-sentence, mid-phrase, mid-word. The air conditioning in the shuttered windows became audible, skipping beats with the insistence of a far-distant train. Whoever had put the speech together had rifled an entire thesaurus of homily: John Donne and Sir Winston Churchill and staff writer fell from the President's lips in tight, grief-choked quanta.

"I do not hate even now. . . . My wife does not hate. . . . Nor must we, as a nation, hate. . . . Hate is the heroin of the people. . . ." He read the speech, his longest since the inaugural, in a high, garroted voice, and the First Lady held his hand out of sight, behind the lectern where he had placed the neatly typed, pencil-revised sheets.

They had told her she had to come to the press conference.

"All too often . . . in our pursuit of power . . . both as a nation and as individuals . . . we tend to forget. . . ."

Today the TV cameras kept a considerate distance. It was for their sake that the windows were shuttered: they could not cope with daylight and artificial at the same time. Daylight threw the color off.

The reporters' expressions ranged from a sort of skeptical, grudging sympathy to the outright distress of children watching the sad parts of a Lassie movie.

"Our Federal Security Agency . . . is pressing forward on all fronts. . . . The Director informs me . . . that this is not the work of a conspiracy . . . but of some poor, lonely, pathetic brute. . . ."

A guard by one of the doors caressed his hip holster with a roving fingertip. In the front row of seated reporters, a stocky woman with bobbed, graying hair closed her note pad with an audible slap that made the First Lady glance her way.

". . . and, according to the latest hospital reports . . . our daughter stands an excellent chance . . . of recovery. . . . Other than the unity of our nation, my wife and I could ask . . . nothing more."

Silence, as after a funeral oration. And then, because no one had yet died, applause. The First Lady smiled palely at her husband. He smiled back, and the smile was an apology for subjecting her to all this.

"Mr. President," a reporter wanted to know, "is the First Lady available for comment?"

"We have made our comment," the President said.

"Mrs. Luckinbill," the reporter persisted, "how do you feel about all this?"

"Mrs. Luckinbill," said the President, "feels as I do."

The gray-bobbed woman spoke up. "Mrs. Luckinbill, after the birth of your daughter Alexandra were you not told that you could have no more children?"

"My wife's discussions with her doctor are her own affair. Any other questions?" The President appealed to a reporter who had not even raised his hand: an ally. "New York *Times*."

The *Times* man rose. "Mr. President, there has been some speculation that the shooting ties in with the renewed wave of student unrest. Do you have any opinion on this?"

"I think that the shooting is symptomatic of the confusions

and anxieties of the transition period in which our nation finds itself. I think it is up to each and every one of us to search his own conscience. The roots of violence are widespread."

The gray-bobbed woman kept right on charging. "In view of the fact, Mrs. Luckinbill, that it cost you two miscarriages to bring one child into this world—"

"Will that woman shut up?" the President shouted.

"Why did you, as a mother," her voice rose, "permit her to ride in an exposed car on an obvious vote-catching junket?"

The First Lady could only wonder why this woman was going at her with a relish, a hatred almost personal.

"Is it true," the *Times* man asked, "that the White House has received threats to the President's life from the Whitefalls area?"

"The Secret Service and the Federal Security Agency inform me," the President stated, "that such threats from various areas are not uncommon."

The Chief Executive placed a steadying arm around the shoulders of his wife, and—stepping her gently, as though she were a rare and breakable thing, down from the little raised platform— he guided her with swift grace through the clustered advisers and the rapidly gaining implosion of reporters.

The gray-bobbed woman was waving her pad like an up-stretched picket. "Do you consider your behavior as setting a good example of parental—"

"Thank you, ladies and gentlemen," the President said. His glance held them off, and the First Lady's silenced them, for they saw that they had made her cry.

He hurried her into the next room, and a guard closed the door, and there was tea. She did not recognize the hand offering it. She took a long, scalding swallow, and it made her feel better, a punishment endured.

There were faces around her, mostly official, several familiar. They all bore an identically stamped grief which she realized with shock was as close as they could come to copying hers.

"Moni," they said, "Moni . . ." and it was like keening.

Her gaze poked among those masks and she saw the strain

of tears forced, the swift sideways dodge of eyes avoiding con-
frontation. She went among them curiously, not knowing what
to make of these people or the grief they professed, wanting to
tell them they needn't bother, not for her sake.

"Thank you," she said, "thank you," as though something
had died and these were the mourners.

"God bless you, Moni, you handled that bitch like a trouper!"

The woman who cried this, and who blocked the First Lady's
way, wore a gray suit, but that was the only subdued thing
about her. She had the voice of an upstaged mother and the
delivery of an umpire, and she lodged a kiss with dead-on ac-
curacy on the First Lady's surprised cheek.

"Our hearts go out to you, Moni," said the man beside her,
ashen and stone-faced in a dark, dark suit. "We're really broken
up, just shattered."

The woman grabbed the First Lady's upper arm, as though
feeling for muscle. "Don't you worry, honey, that kid's a
champion, it's going to take more than a bullet to stop her."

"Thank you." The First Lady's feet made backtracks. "You're
very kind."

"Kind, my ass, we're telling it like we sees it," the woman
cried. "Right, Howie?"

Howie, in the dark suit, was the Vice-President of the United
States; the woman in gray was his wife.

"Of course," Howie said.

The President, sensing a disagreeable situation, came rapidly
through the crowd. "Moni's a little tired." He put an arm
around his wife.

"Damned right she's tired." The Vice-President's wife slipped
her own arm around the shoulder already occupied by the President's, and by a skillful upward maneuver she eased his loose
and remained in complete and sole possession of the First
Lady's sobbing person.

"You just come over here and sit down, honey," the Vice-
President's wife coaxed, "and put your head on old Maggie's
shoulder."

That Maggie Tyson had a secret weapon that day had been

perfectly apparent from the moment she rat-a-tatted into the room, for she held what appeared to be a tightly rolled map under one arm and let it stick out with all the subtlety of a blunted sword.

"I'm not that tired, really," the First Lady said, but she could neither duck nor pull loose from the protection of that arm.

"Just you relax a minute, honey, and let's have us a brief little heart-to-heart. There's something I think you ought to know."

Maggie Tyson walked the First Lady to the edge of the room. Two empty chairs awaited. They sat. Maggie took her paper bazooka in hand and, with a single flap as sharp as Old Glory snapping in a breeze and as attention-getting as the report of an assassin's bullet, she threw it open to the First Lady's eyes.

"Someone's printed up a few hundred thousand of these," Maggie explained. "They're swamping the campuses."

The First Lady looked and winced as though someone had baptized her in carbolic acid.

The poster that Maggie Tyson had unfurled was last year's official photo of Lexie Luckinbill, a Karsh of Ottawa job that had caught an elusive note of pouting and yet somehow endearing virginity. A rifle target had been superimposed, and a caption ran beneath: NEXT TIME AIM BETTER!

"I just thought you had a right to know," Maggie Tyson said, "what those damned college kids are up to."

The First Lady, hankie to mouth, could only whimper. "Who could hate Lexie? What's she done?"

"That's okay. You just cry your heart out. Maggie will take care of it."

"For chrissakes, Maggie." The Vice-President stood before them, looking vaguely astonished. "Did you show it to her?"

Maggie rolled up her poster. "She has a right to know."

The Vice-President patted the shoulder of the First Lady, whose lips were quivering soundlessly on the edge of her fist. "It's okay, Moni, just a bunch of college kids—they don't mean anything."

"Don't mean anything," his wife cried despite his significant stare, "they shot Lexie, didn't they?"

An arm intervened. It was the President's, trying a second time. "Moni's a little tired. You've got to excuse her."

Maggie Tyson made no attempt to pry the arm off. "Damned right, she's tired—and I'll tell you who else is tired—sick and tired. Yours truly. Are those reporters still out there?"

Maggie took three giant, swift steps into the corridor. She lingered a moment in the doorway of the press room, letting the voices fall silent and waiting for a quorum of heads to turn her way. Then she moved, bestowing glances and smiles like the King's alms. She took up her position at what her instincts told her was the center of gravity of the crowd.

"Hiya, fellas," Maggie let loose, "howzit goin'?" Then she smiled at the woman with the gray bob, who was syndicated in 234 papers. "Say, Lydia, you've been using a lot of pepper in that column lately."

The laughter was chummy and warm, and she knew she had the suckers.

"I've just spoken to Mrs. Luckinbill," she said. "Now the poor kid's in a terrible state. No need to bulldoze her with a lot of twaddle about pregnancies. Moni has asked me to tell all of you this:—"

Pads flipped open and pencils poised at the ready. Maggie took a good deep breath and dove.

"The First Lady is appalled and stunned and revolted and hurt—yes, personally hurt—that in this great, free nation, the freest nation on God's earth—freedom of the press should be perverted into pornographic and irresponsible incitement to murder."

She let this sink in, took inventory of the sneers and arched eyebrows and my-aching-elbow moans.

"I am referring to, the First Lady is referring to, the doctored photograph that appeared this morning in certain so-called underground publications. The First Lady says we have reached the point where, if we are to survive physically and morally, we must distinguish between freedom and filth."

The reporters were bored; pencils had slowed to a sit-down.

"Sounds like the same old war cry, does it, fellas?" Maggie gave them one of the softening-up smiles. "Well, maybe some of you haven't had a chance to see what the First Lady is talking about."

Maggie Tyson happened to have well over a hundred 8½ by 11-inch photo offsets of the picture in her purse, and she began passing them out. They went faster than cake in a breadline.

"The same hands that gave us heroin, homemade bombs, and anarchy," Maggie Tyson cried, "are grinding out this filth! This is the work of people who advocate the death of our children!"

"Says who," the gray-bobbed woman challenged in a whiskey baritone: "you or the First Lady?"

"Okay," Maggie confessed, "I'm saying it for her, because that poor gal's so heartbroken she can't even open her mouth! This is your freedom of the press, fellas!"

Maggie said *freedom of the press* in the same tone of voice that someone else might have said *open sewage*. If there was one thing that could cop headlines nationwide, it was an attack on freedom of the press; and if there was one way of getting your message to Mr. and Mrs. John Q. America, it was nationwide headlines. Maggie waved a poster and flashbulbs popped and she wondered whether the New York *Times* would run the shot.

"Freedom of the press? You wanted it and you've got it and *this country has had it!*"

*

Senator Dan had to walk faster to keep up with him. "But why, Evan? You must have a reason."

Evan Beaupré, the very smiling and very suntanned junior senator from Alabama, stopped and gazed at the huge chandelier with its twenty electric bulbs that hung over the circular stairwell of the Senate. He gestured in a noncommittal way, and his hand brushed one of the thirteen pillars commemorating the thirteen original states. "Let's just say I had a talk with my conscience and my conscience and I agreed to disagree with Bill Luckinbill."

"Believe me, Bill's as upset as anyone in this country over the shooting, but that's no reason to change your vote."

"I'm not changing anyone's vote. Before I said *maybe*. Now I've made my mind up. That's all. No change. I'm being honest with you, aren't I? Wouldn't you rather I told you now?"

"I'm disappointed."

The junior senator from Alabama smiled the most heart-breaking of smiles. "I'm disappointed that I've got to disappoint you, but I don't see that I have a choice."

"There's always a choice."

"Not this time."

"Then I'm sorry for you."

They had reached the bottom of the stairs, and Evan Beaupré held out his hand as though in farewell. It was a young, steady hand. Senator Dan shook it and then stood and watched his colleague vanish among the sightseers mobbing the corridor that had every flower and tree and animal of North America painted on its walls.

Dan Bulfinch felt cheated: not because Evan Beaupré had gone back on as implicit a commitment as a man could make—that was politics; but because of the way he had done it—yet that was politics, too. Your average senator, Dan Bulfinch reflected, was rarely overtly dishonest, hardly ever unpleasant. He had assistants to lie and make promises and make threats for him, if necessary to backstab for him, while he himself was free to be charming and smiling. Your average senator was smooth and worldly and well-traveled, for wherever he went—across an ocean or even on the private underground railway connecting his office with the Senate floor—he traveled at public expense. Your average senator was suntanned, for despite his workload he had leisure to play golf, for his secretaries, his researchers, his speech writers and his ghost writers, his masseurs and his drinking companions and his automobile repairmen and even his marital infidelities were paid from the public purse. Your average senator received the best public housing in the nation, for the govern-

ment provided him with office space and even paid to re-
upholster his armchairs.

Senator Dan disliked thinking of himself as the average senator, and in at least one respect he was not: every other senator
had a suite of four or at most five rooms, but Senator Dan,
majority leader, had six; and it was to his sixth room that he
strode. Linda Parsons, a handsome, soft-eyed divorcée from
Missouri and his personal assistant of twelve years, was trying
to make his percolator work, and she greeted him with a smile
and offered a cup of coffee.

"Robert Harrison's been trying to reach you. Emergency.
Ditto Herb Cranley. You're invited to the National Symphony
tonight. It's Bruckner."

"You go, Linda. I'm bushed."

"I'm afraid the invitation is non-transferable." Linda Parsons
arched her left eyebrow in a way that meant Anita Sands,
widow of the late Secretary of the Treasury.

"Tell her I've got flu."

"It could be bubonic plague and she'd still want you. Fight
your own battles, Lochinvar." Mrs. Parsons extracted the plastic
spool from the Dictaphone and, grinning, headed toward the
door.

"Say, Linda, what do you hear about the President's love
life?"

She turned and cocked her head as though the senator looked
a little bit less nuts seen on a bias. "Love life? I thought it
was strictly straight and narrow since he moved into the White
House."

"So did I. But wasn't there a woman—some kind of blonde—
while he was still a senator?"

"Marion Holmes? That's prehistory."

"No one since?"

"Not that I've heard of. Sorry about that."

Mrs. Parsons was gone, and the senator loosened his necktie
and fell into an armchair. He looked over the list of phone
calls, penned in Linda's beautiful hand that belonged on parchment, not memoranda.

Harrison would be a deal, and a not very delectable one, and because certain ends dictated certain means, Senator Dan intended to accept. He would have to stall Cranley till he had sounded out Lucky Bill in a bit more depth, but he decided to hold off on that until the First Lady and her daughter had returned to Washington. He saw that Evan Beaupré had phoned four times, and he understood the apparently chance meeting on the stairway.

He wondered if the junior senator's defection was a fluke or the first pebble heralding a rockslide, and he couldn't help thinking that the Administration, despite his every effort, was going to get buried under the rocks. In politics as in economics, Senator Dan was a pessimist: the most he could hope to accomplish as senator was to keep the weak from becoming too hopeless or the strong too vicious, and if the process proved to be irreversible, at the very least he wanted to slow it.

His politics had been formed late in life, long after his election. The death of his wife had taught him the futility of a life from which compassion has been banished, and the Nixon years—he had seen farmers break down in tears at being paid no more for their hogs than it had cost to truck them to market —had taught him that it takes the poverty of ten men to make the wealth of one, and he applied the same ratio to nations. Though he was called an innovator and a progressive and some even thought him radical, he saw himself as no more than a brake slowing his nation and his government in their ceaseless striving for an ever more perfect and suicidal injustice.

But brakes could burn out, he reminded himself. They could burn out very quickly indeed.

The phone on his desk went off and he lifted a wary hand toward it.

*

Belinda gave her signal: ten rings, then nine, then eight, then seven. Then six, five, four . . .

At three he opened the door, and she could tell from the way he said "Hi," in the tone of voice he would have used speaking to a chair, that she was in for trouble. His shirt was buttoned wrong, his tie was looped around his neck and shoulder like a misapplied noose, and his belt was hanging out of its loops like a tail sprouted from his right hip.

He had been home sick for several days, and his hair was mussed, which was nothing new, and his eyes had that red, rabbity look they got when he rubbed them too much or when he started reading those tiny-print political pamphlets.

This time it was the pamphlets.

She took three steps into the studio apartment and saw a whole shower of fine print littering the unmade day bed.

"I picked up something for you," she coaxed.

She whisked aside the curtain that hid the walk-in kitchenette, waved "Skat!" at cockroaches that had taken up positions on the dishes in the sink, and started putting away the groceries she had brought him: candy bars, gourmet soup, sour cream. He was always thin, never ate enough.

"You didn't have to bring all that stuff," he said.

She turned, a sixty-eight-cent grapefruit balanced in one hand, and saw him scowling at her. "Someone's gotta feed you," she chirped. "But look what I got you."

She aimed a toe toward the flat, two-by-four-foot plain-wrapped package that she had set by the baseboard.

"It'll look real campy over the bed. Go on, open it."

She pretended to be making room in the fridge for the celery, but with one ear she was keeping an eye on him. She heard him grunting as he tried to loosen the strings with his fists.

"Hey."

She wiped the grapefruit knife on the dish towel (that towel needed changing: some of those gravy spots looked three weeks old) and held it out to him, handle first. He mumbled thanks, and she heard the strings sing out and snap under the sawing of the blade, and then the crackle of brown paper hitting the rug (Jesus, that rug needed vacuuming) and then the quick intake of breath.

"Where did you get this?"

He was holding it out arm's length on a crooked diagonal,

his head cocked to rectify the horizontal, and his face had that characteristic expression, somehow made even more so by the leftward forty-degree tilt. His frown, a furious wrinkling of wild Irish eyebrows, a clenching of lips that had barely outgrown the fullness of a baby's, had no more authority than a little boy's swagger; and when he gave his head that irritable cocker spaniel jerk, a strand of hair fell forward and brushed the tip of his nose, and he tried to deflect it by the sheer air pressure of a snort.

He never looked so much the kid as when he was angry. For a moment she was lost in contemplation of him.

"You don't like it?" she hazarded.

"It's obscene."

"Come on, obscene is contrary to community standards. This isn't contrary to a goddamned thing."

She took the portrait from him, scrambled onto the bed, crunching pamphlets underfoot, and took a shoe off and held it hammerlike.

"How's that?" She positioned the gift.

He grumbled something.

She pulled down the calendar, which was two years old anyway, and using its nail and her own medium-high heel she thwacked the poster into place. Several of her swings missed and the wall looked as though someone had been grinding out cigarettes on it.

The plaster answered with four *fortissimo* broom-handle thumps.

She backed across the room, her eye evaluating the straightness of the poster. "It's a rifle target," she explained, "and that's the President's daughter. Isn't that wild?"

"Wild," he said sullenly, and she heard him go into the kitchenette and turn faucets and gas jets.

"Make me a cup too!" she sang out, and she gave the poster a little leveling touch.

She crept into the kitchenette behind him, sneaked her arms up around him as he stood measuring out instant decaffeinated into two unmatching cups. She noted that he had lit the burner under an empty pot. She switched the pot and the water kettle around.

"I thought you'd like the poster," she said. "It's political after all."

"So that's what politics has come to."

Her eyes scanned the pamphlets that her foot had sown all over the floor: mimeographed, humbly stapled things with names like *Western Destiny* and *Cultural Imperative*. Her offering seemed almost frivolous by comparison.

"It's sort of pop politics," she said lamely. "First they shoot Jack Kennedy, then they shoot Bobby Kennedy, and then they shoot Lexie Luckinbill. It's sort of a progression. If you can call that progress."

His hand stopped in mid-air. "Who did they shoot?"

Now it was her turn to look at him aslant. "Jack Kennedy, remember? And then Bobby—"

His frown was as mean as a dissenting Supreme Court Justice's and she wondered what she had said wrong.

"And who else?" he asked.

"Who do you think?" She shrugged cheerfully and tipped the whistling kettle at the two cups, but mostly she poured a steaming rapids between them.

He grabbed her elbow and whirled her around. A tail of burning water lashed the wall. A potholder hanging by a hook made a singeing sound.

"Ouch!" She rubbed the red spots on her arm.

"Will you stop playing your goddamned games?" His eyes had narrowed to nasty little razor edges. "Who else did they shoot?"

It came to her suddenly that he didn't know. He collected pamphlets the way some people did stamps; he had economics and political philosophy in cardboard cartons up to his ceiling; but he hadn't seen yesterday's headlines or turned on his TV.

"Lexie Luckinbill was shot. You know, Lucky Bill's daughter?"

"Where?" His face was white except for some very red, prominent veins shooting down his forehead.

"In the shoulder."

What came next was a thoroughly unprovoked shout, as

though he were trying to make a deaf man hear him. "What *town*, for God's sake?"

"Some town out West. Lucky Bill's home town. If you'd look at television once in a while, you'd know."

"Were they laying a wreath on his parents' grave?"

"Something like that."

She moved out of first-strike range. Not that under ordinary circumstances he would hit her, but the static electricity in the room suddenly did not seem ordinary. She gave the TV knob a yank and a twist and the set pinged and panged. With a mortar-shell burst of chicken-soup commercial the picture came on. She recognized the friendly face of the man who did the early evening news roundup. He was talking about Costa Rica.

"It was my idea." The cold, flat knife-edge of the statement caught her.

"What was your idea?" she asked.

He was sitting with Napoleonic gloom in the overstuffed chair that she had found on West Fifty-fifth Street, that she had phoned him about the minute she spotted it before anyone else could grab it, that they had carried together through thirteen blocks of midday midtown traffic, one year ago to the day. His legs were thrust out and his little Cupid's fanny had almost skidded off the cushion and his posture was a terrible slump. His head lolled on a forearm.

The telecaster talked of higher prices and riots in Belgrade and the strange shooting in Manhattan of an entire methadone rehabilitation clinic.

She went to him, cozied down on an arm of the chair, and rubbed his head. He had thick, tangled hair, and his pout was ferocious. She was afraid that if he kept grinding his teeth he might snap the lowers off.

"What was your idea?" she coaxed.

He was leaning forward now, beyond caress, his hair evading her fingers, and his eyes glared at the ping-panging black and white screen. She followed his gaze.

It was the same day-old footage, fractured from reruns, of the First Family's motorcade, the gates of the cemetery, the President moving toward the grave with the outsized wreath in his right hand.

And then the camera lost balance and rocked back, swung blurrily to one side, to an ill-focused something that lay white and huddled on the ground. There was a jump-cut to a sharper focus, and the First Lady was throwing herself on top of her daughter and the President was falling on top of his wife and suddenly complete nonentities were jumping into the picture and flinging themselves onto the bodies as though this were all a game of king of the mountain.

Then the camera showed a roadside sign: WHITEFALLS, SOUTH DAKOTA, POPULATION 4000 CHEERFUL PEOPLE, PLUS A FEW GROUCHES.

The telecaster's face came back on, still friendly. He was shuffling typescript just on the edge of camera range. "Alexandra Luckinbill is still reported to be in serious condition. At his press conference today, the President stated that the shooting is symptomatic of the confusions and anxieties—"

"Bullshit."

Belinda was as shocked at the intrusion as if someone had shouted an obscenity during a church service. She shushed him.

"A source close to the First Lady," the TV continued imperturbably, "states that she is, quote, stunned, revolted, and personally hurt that in this great, free nation, freedom of the press should be perverted into pornography and incitement to—"

He sprang from the chair. His fists were tight and colorless and she instinctively ducked. He stomped to the television set and for a moment seemed to be considering the pros and cons of smashing the screen. Instead he smashed the OFF button, and the picture wobbled and faded while the voice wound up in an aborted hiccup.

"Jordie," she pleaded. "What are you angry about?"

He moved to the window and stared down into the street. She tried to read his expression, but it was hieroglyphic.

"Something I did?"

He flung the curtain shut, went to the table and played with the lamp.

"You're wasting the bulb," she cautioned.

His scowl darkened into an eclipse.

"You're not upset over Lexie Luckinbill!" Of course, anyone who could take the American Civil War and the Nuremberg Trials personally could find reason for grief in the Tokyo weather report. But he still, sometimes, amazed her.

"Why shouldn't I be upset over Lexie Luckinbill?" He was peeling Scotch tape off the shade.

"Because she's a dumb, spoiled, obnoxious nobody, and if anyone deserves a bullet in the lung, it's that brat. Where does she get off, telling us to bomb Costa Rica? You should hear the *other* things she says!"

"I know the other things she says." The patch came loose and he began detaching another.

"Well? Don't you think she's an idiot?"

"A useful idiot."

"She's about as useful as the garbage under your sink, but at least the garbage feeds cockroaches! If you want my opinion she got what was coming to her and I'm glad someone in this country had the guts to pull the trigger!"

He gave her a long, iced-over glare. She had a feeling it signaled a turning-point in their relationship.

"You're a real credit to the culture-bearing stratum."

She had never in the year and a week she'd known him been certain just what the culture-bearing stratum was, but she knew sarcasm when she heard it, and it never failed to cut her. Sometimes, with no more than a word, he could cause her to wilt in one second flat. She fought just this once to keep her bloom up.

"What did you mean when you said it was your idea? *What* was your idea?"

"Nothing was my idea."

"Something was your idea and you're not telling me!" A year of snide put-downs and gnarled eyebrows sped past her mind in rapid reverse play.

He made a face.

A genius Belinda was not. In her own book she was a moron and, despite the pretty face and nice figure, a loser. Believing herself a moron and a loser, she longed for, she craved, she would have given her pretty face and nice figure *and* her right eye for one gram or Roentgen of intelligence; and so she prayed and schemed it might rub off on her by touching this boy, as the chalk of some impossibly complex differential equation might stick to her shoulder if she leaned against the blackboard. And here she stood worshiping and begging, and genius was making a face, and the face said she was stupid.

"How are we ever going to make it," she burst out, raining tears in a 360-degree arc, "if you won't share things with me?"

He shrugged.

She looked at him, could not bear the verdict in those eyes which so exactly matched the verdict of her own mirror. She grabbed her purse and didn't even bother to slam the door behind her. She heard him close it, quietly, as she stood jabbing the elevator bell.

She cried all the way down to the unguarded lobby.

II: The Scenario

In such dangerous things as war, the
errors which proceed from a spirit of
benevolence are the worst.

CARL VON CLAUSEWITZ, *On War*

Some wars might easily result in the
creation of large areas that one would
not wish to live in.

HERMAN KAHN, *On Thermonuclear
War*

June 21: Wednesday

"We're relettering the layout," the supervisor told him. "That'll mean an inch less of blurb."

"Okay." Jordie placed a fresh sheet of paper in the center of his desk. The fresh sheet always got the point across that he attacked fresh problems in a fresh way, and in three years it had gotten him close to two thousand dollars in raises.

"Can you bring it to my office around eleven?" the supervisor asked.

Jordie glanced at his watch and said he might be able to manage.

As soon as the supervisor had thanked him and moved on, he crumpled the blank sheet of paper and turned his back on the corridor so as to shield his desk from passing eyes. Once again he opened the manila folder of clippings on the Luckinbill shooting.

The more Jordie reread, the more he was convinced of one thing: he had been robbed.

The trip to the parents' grave. The wreath. The wife and daughter. The whole cornball production went beyond coincidence.

Down to the last detail, it was his scenario.

Jordie's life had been a tapestry woven of two threads: disappointment and injustice. His mother had been taken from him by a stupid twist of a steering wheel; his father had disowned him; two colleges had suspended his scholarships because he had spoken his political opinions; a sweetheart had lasted only three days, and those three days, the happiest of his life, now hung like a curse over the rest of it; and a bitterness he had once harbored only for his father now extended up the entire management ladder to God himself.

Jordie had managed to keep going only by regarding disappointment and injustice as Sisyphus must have regarded his rock, or Prometheus his vulture: as tangible, irrefutable recognition.

But today he felt he deserved more than mere recognition.

At eleven o'clock he took the revised copy to his supervisor, and at eleven-fifteen he slipped out of the office into the automatic elevator.

Nobody noticed.

Jordie stepped off the elevator at the twenty-second floor. The receptionist did not look up from her paperback mystery. He went through the door not so quickly as to arouse suspicion, but like a man who had business on the other side.

He caught his breath and reconnoitered. The far corner office, with windows north and east and gilt on the door, would be the director's. He considered the best method of getting across the room full of typewriters and secretaries without anyone's noticing.

The name on the door was GILLESPIE. A woman sat at a typewriter in the nearest cubicle working her nails over with an emery stick. At that instant the office door opened and a tall man in a dark suit stepped out.

The man walked at a near jog. Jordie intercepted him three steps from the elevator.

"Mr. Gillespie, I'm sorry to bother you, but—"

The man turned a look of carefully tailored, aquiline surprise on him. "Yes?"

"I'm Jordie Watts, from the copy department, and . . ."

The doors opened on an empty elevator. Mr. Gillespie got in and Jordie followed. Mr. Gillespie pushed the button for the ground story. "Yes?"

Jordie spoke quickly. "Do you remember last April 7, you sent out a memo to the employees?"

"I send memos to the employees every Friday."

Above the door, the floor indicator flashed diminishing arabic numerals.

"You asked every employee to describe what events or sequence of events would make him or her feel the least or most sympathy for the President of the United States. Do you remember that questionnaire?"

"I remember several questionnaires along that line." Mr. Gillespie spoke with the unflawed diction of a classical disc jockey. "From time to time we've handled political clients."

"Do you remember my answer to that questionnaire? My name is Jordan Watts. People call me Jordie. I wrote nine single-spaced pages."

The manicured smile stiffened. "Anyone who remembered every reply to every questionnaire would have to have the retention of a computer and the brain of a trash basket."

"I said shoot the President's daughter."

Mr. Gillespie's finger contacted the STOP button with the practiced authority of a generalissimo's pinkie. "No, Mr. Watts. I do not remember that reply. Was it a joke?"

"No sir. I gave the matter a good deal of thought. And I was wondering if—"

Mr. Gillespie was one of those old men whom magazines call youthful and whose youth, being a matter not of years but of will, is sturdier than any young man's. He stood straighter than Jordie and spoke stronger and had eyes far brighter: and he now focused a fierce energy through them. "What were you wondering, Mr. Watts?"

"If maybe—"

"What did you say, Mr. Watts?"

Jordie glanced down and saw that Mr. Gillespie's shoes were far more expensive and far shinier than his own.

Mr. Gillespie released the STOP button, but his eyes did not release Jordie. "Are you feeling all right?"

"A little pain," Jordie mumbled. "In my stomach."

"You'd better take the day off and see a doctor."

Jordie nodded. He would have liked to think it was a deceptively meek nod, but he was afraid it lacked deception. His legs were trembling and, worst of all, an external oblique abdominal muscle was going into spasm.

Sisyphus had a rock; Prometheus a vulture; and Jordie Watts

an ulcer. It had come upon him in his eighteenth year and had thrived through six years of cottage cheese, teetotalism, and medical tests. He had no intention of blowing yet another fifteen dollars on yet another doctor: from a bottle in his desk labeled PUSHPINS he took a pill to inhibit the spasmodic muscle. From his middle drawer he took several sheets and envelopes of office letterhead.

With his supervisor's permission he left work to go, he said, to the hospital. He hailed a taxi and went home.

*

Jordie sat planning his letter.

Woodrow Judd, Esq., Director, Federal Security Agency, he roughed. Not knowing the address but certain that the post office would, he added *Washington, D.C.* For a message he had gotten no further and no better than: *Dear Mr. Judd, May I have five minutes of your time to discuss an urgent matter?*

A fly circled his typewriter twice, then landed on the margin release. He wondered at the animal's stupid courage, but was too preoccupied to squash it.

The message, he saw quite clearly, was insufficient.

He scratched his head and was annoyed when his scalp, which had behaved itself for several weeks now, began itching. He stared at his fingernails. He *x*'ed out the message and began again, keys hitting paper like bullets.

Dear Mr. Judd, May I have five minutes of your time at your earliest convenience to discuss a pressing matter?

Pressing matter somehow failed to sound pressing.

He attacked the typewriter with new ferocity.

Dear Mr. Judd, I must have five (5) minutes of your time to discuss a matter of supreme importance to the Republic. I can be in Washington upon four (4) hours' notice. . . .

June 22: Thursday

"I sometimes wonder," the First Lady said, "if it's a place to bring up a child."

The President looked puzzled. "If what's a place?"

"The White House."

"Come on, hon, Lexie's not a child any more."

Slowly, hand-in-hand, they moved along the bank of the Wapsinicon River, where the President had swum in the buff as a boy.

"I suppose you'll be going back there," the First Lady said. "To the White House."

"I should have been back yesterday."

"I suppose I'll be going back too."

"I think you ought to stay here with Lexie."

"And when she's well we'll both go back."

"Is there somewhere else you'd rather take her?"

The sky was restless, blue, freighted with oak scent. The trees rose on either side of the footpath, enclosing the President and his wife. The forest was alive with wild things and triggers and invisible security guards, and somewhere not too far behind them a warrant officer in a dark suit carried an attaché case of codes just in case the unthinkable ever actually started happening. There had been talk that the Chinese and, in some way, the Romanians might be behind recent events.

"Somewhere else?" the First Lady wondered. "Somewhere safe. That's impossible, though."

"Hon, they were shooting at me. Not at her."

"Then they'll shoot again."

"There are risks you take in any job. Getting shot at happens to be an occupational hazard of the presidency."

"But Lexie's just a child. Why should children get shot? This isn't Vietnam or Costa Rica."

"Lexie's not going to get hurt. Cheer up. The doctors say she'll pull through without a scratch."

The First Lady felt something pressing down on her, numbing her. It could have been fear or it could have been her husband's hand or it could have been the soft choking mass of his concern, filling her like an antiseptic foam. She tried to analyze the weight she felt, and it seemed to be made of all the days she would have to go on living in uncertainty.

"I just don't know if she ought to go back to the White House."

"Hon, she'll be guarded."

"She was guarded in the cemetery."

"No one's after Lexie. Get that through your head. They're after me."

A helicopter buzzed. She watched the sky. According to the radio the air pressure was falling and there would be a storm. She saw no sign of it. She went with her husband, down paths of his choosing.

"Sometimes I wish you weren't President. Sometimes I wish you were just a senator again. Or a farmer. We could be happy on a farm."

He bent down to pick up a rock and skip it across the water. "The way this country's moving, we may be on a farm in two years."

"It wouldn't bother me if you weren't re-elected."

He grinned. "Thanks for the loyal support."

"That's not what I meant."

"I know, hon. We're both tired and we both need a rest and no one's going to get shot, so let's just stop worrying." The voice, even and insistent as a blade, cut neatly into the soft gray cotton of her brain. She looked at a tree, and it seemed to her an odd and enviable thing that trees could live without ever asking questions.

His arm was around her again, his step faster. "Come on, I'll show you the oak where I had my first tree house."

"There's probably a bronze plaque on it."

He gazed at her and chuckled. "You're a great gal, you know that?"

June 23: Friday

Dear Mr. Judd, he read and pondered: *I must have five* (5) *minutes of your time to discuss a matter of supreme importance to the Republic. I can be in Washington upon four* (4) *hours' notice. . . .*

For almost an hour and forty-five minutes Woodrow Judd had been sitting in the old swivel chair, with its squeaky axle and frayed leather cushion, that he had carted with him from office to office since the founding of the Agency. He had shifted pieces of paper from this folder to that with such practiced economy of movement that it seemed to the assistants who drifted in and out of the room that he had not moved at all, but had simply sat there asleep with his eyes open a crack; or, what was more likely for a man of his years, that he had quietly died.

. . . supreme importance to the Republic . . .

That he was not dead could be seen from the tiny movements, as remote as quakes on the moon, that disturbed both corners of the mouth; from the quick, almost contemptuous scanning motion of the eyes, which dropped entire lengths of pages in a single swoop as though watching the fall of meteors; and from a probably unconscious gesture of the left hand, which repeatedly checked the alignment of his yellow polka-dot bow tie.

. . . four (4) *hours' notice. . . .*

Word fragments kept igniting in Woodrow Judd's head like firecrackers hidden there by some prankster. He tried very hard, with the patience of the aged, to piece the fragments together. He tried very hard to think.

Under Woodrow Judd the Federal Security Agency had maintained a friendly and co-operative relationship with the other government intelligence organizations. It was a testament to

Judd's skill as a diplomat that the FSA had prospered and grown through years of Cold War and Insurrection and Anarchy and ultimately attained a supra-legal potency, untinged by the jealous rivalry that had undermined J. Edgar Hoover's Bureau.

Woodrow Judd knew he had built a good agency: the toughest and probably the most result-producing in the field. He also knew that he was going to die, and he was determined that, when he let go the helm, he would leave an agency so shipshape, so formed in his own image and competence, that it could function for administrations and administrations and need no touch of another leader's hand. The Agency was to be his epitaph, writ deep enough to last the centuries.

He had enough dirt on the Congress, enough dirt on the nation's last six Presidents and enough dirt on its next five, to ensure that no legislature or executive could ever boot him out. Now that the dirt was computerized, Congress had taken to passing bills every five years or so giving him life tenure and, lately, extending that period "so long as Mr. Judd shall deem himself capable." He was, as they said in the trade, secure.

And then, two months, two weeks, and three days ago, Woodrow Judd, who had dedicated his life to crushing the enemies of his nation, who could sniff a traitor at ten miles, had been himself betrayed. Early on the afternoon of April 6 as he sat at his desk fingering a report of campus drug use, sniffing a goblet of Pouilly Fuissé, contemplating a wedge of ripe Camembert on a slice of diet-rye melba toast, his heart had stopped beating. Simply, unconditionally gone on strike. The room had turned green and tipped like a sick gyroscope. A band of hot steel had gripped his stomach and pinched, and he had begun vomiting his life onto the blotter he had always kept so neat and spotless. He had barely managed to push a button.

His men had rushed him, helpless as a carcass of beef, to the hospital. Doctors jabbed adrenalin into him; tattooed his heart with metal valves and printed plastic circuits; hauled him back bodily from the valley of the shadow and told him to take a vacation for the rest of his life, which if he was a good boy might be as long as a year or two.

"Are you calling me an old wreck?" Woodrow Judd demanded.

"How old *are* you?" a pup of a doctor asked.

"How old are *you?*" Woodrow Judd replied in thunder. And from his bed he instructed his men to get the dirt on those doctors and to get the dirt on that hospital. And he got the dirt. And he told the doctors and he told the hospital that Woodrow Judd had never, but never, experienced heart failure at all, that it had been a simple question of one or two hemorrhoids. And the hospital told the press that Woodrow Judd had never been gamer, spryer, or stronger. And Congress passed a message of get-well-soon, sore-ass.

He returned to work after a three-week absence; took up where his second-in-command had left off; and from time to time wondered about mortality. Having personally shaken Death's hand, he was inclined to view the Reaper in the manner of a foreign head of state; less an enemy than an equal.

He threw himself especially into the trivia, for trivia was the stuff of life. He forced himself to take an interest again. When the President's daughter was shot he jetted to the scene, though a fat lot of good it did. When an oddball letter came in, he read it himself; he even read the accompanying report, trying very hard to focus on its exact meaning. Lately his mind had been drifting off into all-is-one generalities, and he found he had to fight to keep a grip on specifics.

He fought now.

Intelligence spot report, they had written.

USAFSABIC SR NO. 56–J–578–986
1. HQ, NYC 107TH MI SP
2. 109–6077–146
3. JORDAN ("JORDIE") WATTS
4. NONE
5. EST 1440 22 JUNE, 1560 MADISON AVE GILLESPIE OGILVIE THORPE PUBLIC REL AND 341 EAST 68TH STREET APT 14D
6. NONE

7. JORDAN ("JORDIE") WATTS AGE 24 CAUCASIAN MALE COPY CLERK FOR GILLESPIE OGILVIE THORPE PUBLIC REL AGENCY ON JUNE 21 MAILED THE ATTACHED LETTER TO DIRECTOR OF AGENCY REQUESTING FIVE (5) MINUTES OF DIRECTOR'S TIME.

A) JORDAN ("JORDIE") WATTS IS A SUBSCRIBER TO THE JOHN BIRCH SOCIETY PUBLICATION "AMERICAN OPINION."

B) RIGHT AND LEFT THUMBPRINTS, RIGHT INDEX FINGERPRINT ON LETTER DO NOT MATCH ANY PRINTS ON FILE IN PRINT BANK.

C) CRYPTANALYSIS NEGATIVE. NO LATENT CODE OR CIPHER.

8. GILLESPIE OGILVIE THORPE HANDLED PUBLIC REL FOR LUCKINBILL ELECTORAL CAMPAIGN. JORDAN ("JORDIE") WATTS MAY HAVE HAD HAND IN COPY WRITTEN FOR THIS CAMPAIGN.

9. DRAFT STATUS OF JORDAN ("JORDIE") WATTS 1-Y EXEMPT EXCEPT IN TIME OF NATIONAL EMERGENCY. EXAMINING MD NOTES EMOTIONAL INSTABILITY EXTREME RIGHTIST POLITICAL TENDENCIES.

10. DISCONTINUE INVESTIGATION.

11. NYC FSA

12. PROBABLE CRANK.

13. NO ADDITIONAL INFORMATION CONCERNING THIS MATTER WILL BE SOUGHT. JORDAN ("JORDIE") WATTS' THUMB AND FINGERPRINTS HAVE BEEN ADDED TO THE NATIONAL BANK.

14. USAFSABIC SR NO. 56–J–578–986 CLOSED.

Woodrow Judd tried to push Death from his mind, tried to give all this its due weight. Failing, he raised an eye toward the door. Upon this signal an assistant ushered in the visitor who had been waiting the better part of a quarter hour: Woodrow Judd's second-in-command.

"Hello, Erikka." Woodrow Judd did not rise; they had been friends too long for that kind of nonsense.

Erikka Lumi slipped smoothly into a chair.

"One of our agents," Woodrow Judd said, "one of our agents in Whitefalls, Hiram Quinn, has been murdered."

The assistant, so quiet as to be faceless, left the room and closed the door behind him. The air in the doorway was suddenly compressed. This single, short compression passed as a disturbance across the room, over the heads of the two occupants, and gave a sudden push to the curtains hanging in the window.

"Ballistics analysis came in." Woodrow Judd indicated one of the folders on his desk top. "Seems that the bullet that blew Hiram Quinn's insides out left a fragment—microscopic fragment, they say, but they're always saying that—and this fragment is 'not dissimilar' to the bits of bullet that the doctors found in Miss Luckinbill."

"Same rifle?"

Woodrow Judd shrugged a shrug that wasted no effort of shoulder or neck. "Same or similar. Looks like whoever shot Miss Luckinbill killed our mail investigator." His eyes peeped up watchfully.

"Possibly the mail investigator posed some kind of threat to the assassin."

Woodrow Judd was aware that the twin inertias of time and bureaucracy would, after his death, heave this woman up into the directorship; and Erikka Lumi was aware of the fact; and so they spoke as equals of a sort. At times he felt a sort of affection for the woman and her competence; he liked to think the feeling was reciprocated, but she was coquette enough for him never to be sure. He smacked his gums.

"I met Hiram Quinn out there, and I've been reading over the file on the Whitefalls mail surveillance, and I've been reading over Quinn's reports, and if he was any kind of threat to anyone, well—the threat's pretty elusive."

Erikka Lumi seemed to sit taller in the chair, and yet no one part of her had shifted.

"These intercepts have got to be the biggest load of crap since the President's inaugural." Woodrow Judd tapped the folder with a finger whose ring lent the tap added weight. "Love letters, ads, bills . . . I'd be tempted to say Quinn was goofing off. What would you say?"

Erikka Lumi always wore a dark dress which somehow never lost its press no matter how long or grueling the work day. Woodrow Judd had rarely seen so much as a strand of her black hair out of place.

"The investigation was going slowly," she said. "We'd turned up no satisfactory leads as to the identity of the sender of the threatening letter; and we were within a week of terminating Operation Flypaper."

Woodrow Judd made a face. "How well did you know Quinn?"

"He was a good agent."

"Was he mixed up in anything besides mail?"

"I doubt it."

"Did you have him under surveillance?"

"The budget for Operation Flypaper did not permit us to keep tabs on our own men," Erikka Lumi said. "Quinn had been with the bureau for twenty-three years. I believe he was absolutely trustworthy. He didn't drink, he rarely touched tobacco, he avoided personal entanglements."

Woodrow Judd began stacking folders like playing cards. "To shoot a mail surveillance agent, to shoot anyone, takes a motive."

Erikka Lumi glanced up from under thick dark eyebrows, aiming a long and shrewd glance as though reluctant to express an opinion before hearing her superior's. But Woodrow Judd was silent.

"The surveillance so far," Erikka Lumi said, "had turned up nothing. So it would be my opinion that the assassin was worried what the surveillance was about to turn up."

Woodrow Judd nodded. "I want another agent sent to continue mail surveillance. I want you to detail a thorough, patient man to the job. An older man. Somewhere near retirement. Show him the back file, fill him in a little. Not too much. That won't be necessary. Just a little."

"Are you planning to sacrifice an agent?" Erikka Lumi inquired.

"Why do you ask?"

"Because such a consideration would affect the choice of operative."

Woodrow Judd's left hand adjusted a bow tie that needed no adjustment. "Let's just say that I want that assassin's head, and I want it on a twenty-foot pole, and I want that pole up on the Capitol dome."

June 25: Sunday

He confronted himself in the mirror, smiled with perfunctory optimism. He ran the water, turning his hand under the flow. When in eight and a half minutes it became lukewarm he plugged the drain and moistened his cheeks, his jaw, and his throat with quick, stinging slaps.

He did not know why his superiors had sent for him. They had pulled him off an investigation of stolen money orders in Abelard, Kansas. They must have had their reasons. He had learned, in his years with the Agency, to ask as few questions as possible, and as a result he had trained himself to wonder about very little.

They had put him in a hotel room in Washington, D.C., and they had ordered him to read certain documents: background, they had said. He had read the documents. They were mail intercepts, and they puzzled him.

He watched himself carefully as he shaved. He was in the habit of thinking he had a face wholesome as good bread and fresh milk: no longer young—though even in childhood snapshots he had never had a juvenile face—but certainly not yet irreparably aged. That would come. The hair was going gray, but the bristle cut helped disguise the fact; the jaw did not yet sag and the lip had held its stiffness. The gray-to-colorless eyes were ageless as salt water, and the ginger eyebrows grew trimmed and aligned of their own accord and crossed the line of his nose straight and blunt as the top of a T-square. It was a face that had learned a weary, wary kindness but somehow avoided softness.

They had said they would phone, but in twenty hours the phone had not so much as murmured.

He squinted at the mirror-image of his cheekbone, a trouble spot he sometimes missed. Soap-stained water ran from the razor down his forearm, raining off his elbow onto the tile. With a last clean flourish he finished off the night's growth of shadow.

He returned, drying his face, to the bedroom. He supposed he had time to review the documents.

REF. "FLYPAPER" (Z–145–6–239) DOCUMENT 38 AT-TACHED. OLIVETTI LETTERA 44 PORTABLE TYPE-WRITER, 1961 MODEL. "E" UNALIGNED. TOP SE-CRET.

Whitefalls, Thursday April 20

Dear Fran,

Thank you for your wonderful letter. It was such a comfort. Excuse me for taking so long to answer, but I hope you understand. Funeral yesterday, church next door (First Methodist). Mom would have liked it, I think. Reverend Jannings read from Ephesians, her favorite, and at the end we sang "Lead Kindly Light," do you remember she taught us that when we were little? I cried all the way through it and wasn't able to pay much attention but everyone says Mom would have loved the service.

I tried to get lilies and white roses for the altar, but they were so expensive I decided against. We asked for no flowers to be sent, but for people to send checks to the Road Safety Foundation instead, so there wouldn't have been any flowers, but Reverend Jannings donated daffodils out of his own pocket. He is a kind man and has been wonderful these last few days. The burial was in Whitefalls Cemetery up on the hill, do you remember where we used to play hide and seek? Mom has a nice plot overlooking town, and Reverend Jannings has arranged time payments on the plot which makes things a lot easier.

It has been hard adjusting. It seems to cost me more to buy food than it cost Mom, and when I cook everything turns out dry and hard to chew, even though I'm using the recipes she kept in that little notebook. Bobby and Dad have been very patient and not complained, and Bobby helps with the dishes. It takes me hours to cook a lambchop and stringbeans. I don't know how Mom did everything so quickly. I suppose I'll learn.

Poor little Bobby came into my room last night and crawled into the bed and cried for three hours. I tried to say something, but if I'd opened my mouth I would have been crying as bad as him, and I just can't let them see how broken up I am. They depend on me and they think I'm managing, if they weren't counting on me I suppose I'd go to pieces.

Dad has moved his wheelchair onto the sleeping porch and he just sits there all day with his old magazines, but I know he's not reading them, because he hasn't asked for any new ones this week. He doesn't like us to see him crying, but I heard him yesterday morning when I was sweeping the downstairs porch.

I guess none of us can really believe she's really gone for good. Every time there's a sound at the front door I think it's her. They say it takes months, sometimes a year to get over it. They say there's nothing to do but keep going and try not to think too hard. Besides, what with exams and housekeeping, I have a lot to keep me busy, which is not a bad thing. I'm answering the letters in Mom's desk.

Mr. Morrow, the man Mom worked for, came by yesterday and returned the things she left at work. Two paperweights. He seemed nice but quiet. Mom never spoke much about him and I never met him. I gave him a cup of coffee and there was no cream, so I used condensed milk, but he didn't say anything.

Bobby is very worried about having a tooth pulled. I told him novocaine is a real "trip" and he feels better about it.

I have to put on the leg of lamb. Wish me luck!

Thanks again for the letter. It made all the difference.

Love, Darcie

At his request, the hotel had given him a window on the air-shaft rather than the street. The room was costing the Agency seventeen dollars a day, plus tax. He went to the blinds and with one finger tilted a slat up half an inch. It was perpetual night in the shaft. Scraps of paper spiraled like moths in the warm currents. A few horizontal scars in the darkness indicated lights behind other blinds.

He let the slat fall with a plastic snap.

The hotel had given him—besides the two beds—a standing lamp, a television, a chair, and a mirror. The chest of drawers was flush with the wall, but he had nothing to unpack.

He refilled his glass.

REF. "FLYPAPER" (Z–145–6–239) DOCUMENT 38 AT-TACHED. UNDERWOOD PORTABLE ELECTRIC TYPEWRITER, 1971 MODEL.   TOP SECRET.

Excelsior Springs, Saturday, April 29

Dearest Darcie,

Thanks for taking the time to write. I must say, you seem to be managing wonderfully by yourself and in no time I bet you'll have the house running smooth as clockwork. Probably you'll be tossing off cordon bleu dinners with a flick of your wrist! I really do envy your ability to adapt. It seems to run in your family.

I don't think I've ever met the Reverend Mr. Jannings. But he sounds like a wonderful man.

Guess what— I was looking through some old letters from your mother. I had completely forgotten that she lent me a hundred dollars seven years ago, when I graduated and needed money for the dress. This seems as good a time as any to return it. I am enclosing a cashier's check so that you'll be able to credit it to your account immediately.

Must run to get this in the next mail. I'm writing from work, on school time! My love to Bobby and to your father. I'm send-ing him a batch of old magazines I found in the attic—I hope he enjoys them.

Love and kisses,
Fran

He had seen this type of material before. Often intercepted letters meant no more than what they said. That was the hell of trying to make sense of them.

REF. "FLYPAPER" (Z–145–6–239) DOCUMENT 39 AT-TACHED. OLIVETTI LETTERA 44 PORTABLE TYPE-WRITER, 1961 MODEL. "E" UNALIGNED. TOP SE-CRET.

Whitefalls, Tuesday, May 2

Dear Fran,

You're a grand old pal but you'll never make even a middling-good fibber. You're wonderful to think of sending a hundred dollars and I can't tell you how much I appreciate the thought, but we really can't accept it. I've done some detective work through Mom's checkstubs and bank statements, so I know that you invented the whole thing to try to help us.

You're an angel, Fran, but things aren't quite so bad, fi-nancially, as I made them sound in the last letter. Dad's govern-ment pension comes the first of every month, and the money the army gave us for Willard is not much, but it helps. I'm going to get a job after graduation, and maybe Bobby will find some part-time work. Also, Mom left an insurance policy, five thousand smackeroos. So we're not in any straits at all and I'm returning the check with all our love and gratitude.

The magazines came this morning. Shame on you, Fran, twenty of them, all new, and you sent them first class. Dad is in seventh heaven. They couldn't have come at a better time and they've taken his mind off everything. Fran, you always do the wonderful thing at the wonderful moment. I don't know how in the world to thank you!

But thanks. Only promise never to do it again! Old maga-zines in the attic my eye! We all love you, Fran. Any time you want I hope you'll come up and stay with us—this summer per-haps. Dad would love to see you again.

Love,
Darcie

The packet of photographed letters had to have some meaning, and he had an aching hunch that if he could only lay them out in the right order a pattern would leap to his eyes. Someone had jumbled the letters—no agent would send documents back in such confusion—but still he could almost deal them out in suits, like a deck of playing cards.

He hiccupped and swallowed from his glass.

There were letters from Mrs. Roosevelt, Sheyenne Avenue; a note from Chuck Gormley, Eighth Street; he glanced at these and saw that they were one or at best two of a kind; no replies, no follow-ups; dead ends. One suit far outranked the others: the girl Darcie.

REF. "FLYPAPER" (Z–145–6–239) DOCUMENT 43 ATTACHED. HANDWRITTEN BALLPOINT. TOP SECRET.

Whitefalls, S.D. Thursday May 4

My very dear Fran,

How sweet of you to send the old magazines you found in your attic. I am reading them now, three a day, and will soon have finished the lot.

Life for me has not been the same since Natalie went. It is not that I saw so much of her, but I was able to when I wanted and that made a difference.

I shall be delighted to unburden you of any other old magazines that might be taking up space in your attic. There is not much to read in the house, and Darcie rarely thinks of bringing magazines home for me.

I have carnations in the window box on the sleeping porch and am eating strawberries. If ever you come back to Whitefalls you are welcome to stay with us as long as you like. It would be pleasant having you in the house and hearing your voice.

Since I began this letter I have read two more magazines and now have none left. Fran, please write to me, but quicker than I have been in replying. I have no excuse. I want to write and thank you, yet have not done so. Why?

Well my dear I shall close. All my love,

Harry (Sybert)

The glass was suddenly empty. He took ice from the paper bag that sat leaking on the window sill and mixed another vodka and root beer.

REF. "FLYPAPER" (Z–145–6–239) DOCUMENT 46 AT-TACHED. OLIVETTI LETTERA 44 PORTABLE TYPE-WRITER, 1961 MODEL. "E" UNALIGNED. TOP SE-CRET.

Whitefalls, Friday, May 5

Dear Fran,

I ought to have my head examined for writing you while I have four exams to study for—but I doubt that I'd be able to get much studying done around this house anyway, with all the dishes that are piled up in the sink, Bobby lying in bed scream-ing with a new toothache, his cheek swollen as large as a grape-fruit, Dad yelling at me every five minutes, wanting a fresh glass of juice or wanting his chair moved into the sun or out of the sun.

Bobby keeps turning on because he thinks it helps the pain, but all pot does frankly is make him more paranoid, and I do get nervous when he smokes that stuff all the time—there have been some arrests in Hobart on dope charges and that is all we need!

I almost lost my temper when Dad called me a "selfish little gadabout." I suppose it's hard having to sit in a wheelchair fifteen years with nothing to do but stare at flowers growing in a window box and reading magazines. But it made me angry, for a minute I was about to say something horrible. After all the only places I've been gadding about to are the grocery store and school and that damned (excuse me) kitchen, fixing meals for Dad. He hardly touches them and of course he never thanks me either.

But then he never thanked Mom. She used to say that beneath all that bad temper he had the lovingest heart in the world. I guess she must have known, after all she married him.

This morning five magazines came in the mail for Dad, new ones. I didn't see the return address because Bobby brought them in. But Fran, if you sent them, please don't send any more. Dad and I are both grateful to you of course for everything you've done, but I'm trying to ration the magazines and get him to read one a day straight through instead of the best parts of five or six. He goes through them in a minute if I let him get hold of a bunch at a time. So I'm telling him that each magazine is the last in the house, and that way he takes longer.

I took four away from him this morning and he's furious at me, but it's the only way I can stretch them out, and till the insurance comes we can't spend as much money as we used to when Mom was working and alive, and I don't want him to get in the habit of more than one magazine a day.

Then again, maybe you didn't send the magazines and maybe I'm pestering you for nothing. Bobby is howling again, I'd better close for now. Wouldn't you know it, there isn't a grain of codeine or a single Darvon in the house. I think Dad eats it like candy. So I'm giving Bobby brandy to wash his gums with. Do you suppose that works?

Sorry to be so frantic. Lots of love,

Darcie

P.S. Please don't forget about the magazines.

I'm here for a reason, he told himself; *they don't call you twelve hundred miles without a reason, do they?*

REF. "FLYPAPER" (Z–145–6–239) DOCUMENT 49 AT-
TACHED. HANDWRITTEN BALLPOINT. TOP SECRET.

Whitefalls, S.D. Saturday May 6

My very dearest Fran,

   Thank you so much for the magazines. Darcie has taken them
all away from me. She is out at choir practice now, so if I write
quickly this letter may reach the mailbox before she gets back.

   I think that she is jealous we are friends. She cannot understand that you would have the thoughtfulness to send a lonely
old invalid a few magazines that were cluttering up your attic.
Basically, Darcie is a far from generous person, and she cannot
forgive in others behavior which she herself cannot comprehend.
You see, dearest Fran, Darcie is incapable of kindness.

   She has hidden the magazines and refuses to let me have
them. In fact she is pretending that they never came. The
minute they arrived she seized them, and I have seen neither
hide or hair of them since. I have been sitting for two days,
watching my carnations. I think they are dying.

   I wish Natalie were with us. Darcie hasn't the slightest idea
how to run a house. Meals are late and in general poorly cooked.
Last night the pork was underdone, the mashed potatoes were
watery, the string beans soggy. She is a slovenly housekeeper.
There are rings in the bathtub. She complains that my wheels
squeak and when I beg her to buy me some oil she asks why I
can't just sit still.

   She opened that brandy that I had intended for Natalie's and
my twenty-fifth wedding anniversary and has been washing out
Bobby's mouth with it. She does not bother to make beds any
more. The linen needs changing but she hasn't had time to do
the laundry. Yet she can spend two hours on the telephone
gossiping with some feather-brained classmate. She has no power
to discipline Bobby, who now spends all his time watching
television instead of studying. I think he has become a "junkie."

   I wish you were here, Fran, to see the state in which we live.
Perhaps you would be able to influence Darcie.

   I suppose it would be useless to send any more magazines. She would only take them away. You see, I cannot even protect my own property. I wonder if she sells them again.

Well my dearest I shall close. All my love,

Harry

He mixed another vodka and root beer, easy on the root beer. Wistfully he wondered if there was a good Western on TV.

REF. "FLYPAPER" (Z–145–6–239) DOCUMENT 54 AT-TACHED. OLIVETTI LETTERA 44 PORTABLE TYPE-WRITER, 1961 MODEL. "E" UNALIGNED. TOP SE-CRET.

Whitefalls, Monday May 8

Dear Fran,

If only you or Mom or someone was here who could help. I've locked myself into my room because I don't want them to see me like this but I have to pour it out to someone, so I guess you're the lucky winner.

Dad's been criticizing me for over a week, and it's starting to get to me. He won't let me phone friends to discuss home-work and he says I'm trying to give him food poisoning and that I'm stealing from him. He's turned Bobby completely against me. When I was coming through the vacant lot after choir practice yesterday I saw Bobby dropping a letter in the corner mailbox, and later Dad told me he had written "someone" about me. Bobby wouldn't tell me who the letter was addressed to. I felt so angry and helpless, I wanted to cry.

I didn't know how hard it would be without Mom. If it's go-ing to be like this last week, I don't want to stay with them. Isn't that an awful thing to say. I can't go out any more, can't have my own life or friends. They act as though I'm selfish to spend time studying, when in the long run it will be far better for all of us if I get good marks and can get a halfway decent job. As it is now, I may not even pass my exams—four years wasted! Some-times I think Dad enjoys seeing me cry.

The worst thing Fran is being alone. There's no one I can

talk to any more, except you, and you're wonderful, but before Mom was right here and she always seemed to have an answer for everything. I guess we all have to find our own answers, but I can't understand people the way Mom did. I can't even understand my own family. Bobby called me a "bitch" and Dad didn't even scold him.

I'm so afraid of failing, Fran. Failing school and failing everything and everyone around me. Help me.

Darcie

What do they see in this, he wondered; but, shift pages as he might, no answer appeared: only hints—submerged, subtle, elusive. Nothing on TV but Shirley Temple.

REF. "FLYPAPER" (Z–145–6–239) DOCUMENT 57 ATTACHED. UNDERWOOD PORTABLE ELECTRIC TYPEWRITER, 1971 MODEL. TOP SECRET.

1231 Kansas City Avenue, Excelsior Springs, Mo.
Wednesday, May 10
The Reverend Mr. Jannings, First Methodist Church, Whitefalls S.D.

Dear Mr. Jannings,

Darcie Sybert has mentioned you often to me. I believe I am doing the right thing in sending you these letters. The only reason Darcie has not taken her problems to you herself is that she has a natural fear of being a burden to others. Might you have time to talk to the Syberts?

Darcie may not have told you about her father. He has been an invalid for many years and was totally dependent on his wife. In recent years I believe he has developed into an eccentric and will not leave the house—not even, apparently, for his wife's funeral. Natalie Sybert's death has been a terrible loss for the family, following so closely upon the loss of their elder son, Willard. Mr. Sybert and I hardly know one another, and his letters came out of the blue. The whole incident of the magazines seems to camouflage something far more serious, don't you agree?

I hope you'll have time to glance over these letters and to look into the problem. I know the Syberts would be grateful for any help you could spare. From so far away, there is little I can do except send moral support through the mail, and in this situation that is totally inadequate.

In a way, I'm an ex-parishioner of yours. The Syberts and my family were neighbors for almost ten years. Darcie and I went to the same school (I was seven years ahead of her, though I am only five years older.) We moved from Whitefalls the month before you came, but we are Methodists and went regularly to the First Methodist Church.

I know how deeply Darcie appreciated the help you gave her last month, and how much it would mean to her if somehow you were able to help her now.

With so very many thanks,
Fran Lawrence

AGENT'S NOTE: XEROX COPIES OF DOCUMENTS 43, 46, 49, 54 ACCOMPANIED DOCUMENT 57.

He was a man who had come home one day after monitoring intercepts on a drug case to find his wife cleaning marijuana with the kitchen flour sifter. His cases had taken him out of the city and sometimes into other states; and once, in Chicago, when he didn't have change for the pay phone, he had neglected to call home. After that his wife and he had begun to say less and less to one another.

He had begun noticing small things, dust building up on the window ledges, smudges on the panes that seemed to indicate a face had been pressed against them. He had once found a half-finished letter in the typewriter, left there perhaps for him to find; and because it was part of his work and training to read other people's mail he read it, even though his sense of self-preservation told him not to; and the letter said, *I spend most of my time moping, but at least I have a decent stereo.*

Perhaps another page had preceded. It worried him that she wrote *I* when in fact the stereo belonged to both of them; he had bought it with his third raise. He was bothered not because she was denying him his property, but because something in the letter seemed to deny his existence.

REF. "FLYPAPER" (Z–145–6–239) DOCUMENT 62 ATTACHED. IBM DESK ELECTRIC TYPEWRITER, 1968 MODEL. CARRIAGE RETURN UNEVEN. TOP SECRET.

First Methodist Church, 4702 Sheyenne Avenue, Whitefalls S.D. Saturday, May 13

Dear Miss Lawrence,

Thank you for your letter of May 10th. I shall most certainly call on Mr. Sybert tomorrow.

You are quite right that Darcie has never mentioned any of these problems to me and quite right, I believe, in advising me of them. I understand and admire your concern for the Syberts.

I have the highest regard for Darcie and every confidence in her character and personal abilities. I am sure that we shall be able to master this crisis and that soon you will have good news from your friend.

Most sincerely,
Oscar Jannings✝

He had married at twenty.

Corinna was a difficult choice to explain; at least, in retrospect, difficult to explain to himself. He had chosen her because he went one bored night to a church dance where the air conditioning wasn't working; because the p.a. system kept lulling him with the same Elvis Presley ballad and because his wash-and-wear shirt had caught static electricity and was sticking to his ribs and to hers; because she wore tiny fake pearl earrings and because there were little fair hairs curling at the lobes of her ears; and because something was happening in his premanent-press khakis that had never happened before in church. Chiefly it had

been because of that first touch of her skin, a memory that—
even years later—never ceased to crucify him.

His mother had liked her, too.

"You need someone to take care of you. I'm too old to wash
your socks and iron your shirts. Corinna's a nice girl. Stronger
than she looks."

REF. "FLYPAPER" (Z–145–6–239) DOCUMENT 71 AT-
TACHED. OLIVETTI LETTERA 44 TYPEWRITER,
1961 MODEL. "E" UNALIGNED. TOP SECRET.

Whitefalls, Monday May 15

Dear Fran,

Do you believe in miracles? I sure didn't until yesterday afternoon. I was coming back from school (biology), really feeling
sorry for myself. As I was coming in the side door of the house I
noticed that the television wasn't turned on. You couldn't hear
those gunshots and screams and quiz shows that Bobby switches
on every afternoon. Guess what—he was lying on the floor studying math! And he wasn't smoking pot either!

I couldn't believe my eyes. The pillows on the sofa had been
fluffed up, the rug was vacuumed, and when I went into the
kitchen, all the dishes were done. I ran back into the living
room and I said, "What's got into you, Bobby, did you clean up
the house?" He looked sort of shy and said, "I felt like getting
some exercise," and then he said he couldn't talk to me any more
because he had to solve some algebra problems.

He had put himself through a night college on Long Island
to earn the degree his father wanted him to have.

"A college degree takes a few hours a day, costs you two, three
thousand dollars, and it's worth eighty thousand dollars in
earning power, now how can you beat an investment like that?"

"But, Pop," he had said, "that eighty thousand's spread out
over a lifetime."

"I wish to hell it was spread out over mine! When you're an
old man like me, you don't want to be running a candy store."

"But you and Mom have a good store," he had said, and his old man had made a face like a dirty word and gestured with a Moxie bottle, and for the first time ever in his twenty years he had realized that his father did not like the little shop on the corner of Highland and Jamaica.

"Good, you call this good?" His father had jabbed a fist at the rack where *World-Telegrams* and *Journal-Americans* shrieked the latest: "This is to line your garbage pail with. And this?" He had thumped the cooler where the pop bottles were stored, a bright red tub big as a washing machine, ice-cooled and not electric. "Drink three of these a day and you burn out your stomach!"

The stomach had always been a big point with his pop; there had been three operations, and it had become his most valued investment.

"Listen to your old man. Go to college, you'll be a million-aire."

Marriage and night college had overlapped, and he had taken a job with the New York City Transit Authority as a transit cop, riding shotgun on the Queens-Coney Island express every day from 8 A.M. to 4:30 P.M., with a half hour off for lunch at one of the underground hot dog and sauerkraut stands. Every week he brought home sixty-seven dollars and a few pennies, in those days good pay for a twenty-year-old with a wife and a sixth-floor walk-up to support and no college degree.

Corinna, a Slovenian Catholic with hereditary superstitions about banks and cookie jars, would give him ten of his dollars back, slip ten in the sugar bowl, and divide the rest between a savings and a checking account. Sometimes toward the end of a week there would be two or three suppers of hot dogs and cabbage but Mondays he could always count on pork chops or ground chuck beef.

Occasionally in those first months of marriage, in their own renovated rent-controlled walk-up, he sat with a can of beer listening to Corinna clank pots in the kitchen, and he said to himself, *So this is it.* He recognized that he had come up in the world from the leftover stews that had been the days-at-a-stretch specialty of his parents' table; and, true, he had a pretty girl in bed, a bright girl, inventive with cheap cuts of meat.

But somehow he had expected something a little more, and from time to time, when she thumped a pot in the kitchen, he got the feeling she had too.

They hid their disappointment well, if it was disappointment; never discussed it. And of course when his parents asked how Corinna was, he always said, "Fine, fine," and changed the subject. Even after marriage he still went to have dinner with his folks once a week. Sometimes Corinna came, but she never really seemed to enjoy it, so mostly she stayed home with some excuse like a cold or cleaning up.

Well was I ever confused! As I was going upstairs I heard voices from the sleeping porch. I thought, this is it—Dad's talking to himself—he's gone bats. But guess what! Dad and Reverend Jannings were sitting there drinking coffee and laughing! Dad said they'd formed a widowers' club. I've never seen him look so darned happy in all my life. He had a great stack of old (but really old) magazines. Reverend Jannings said there were millions more in the parish house and Dad could have all he wanted.

Then Dad got serious and asked about Mom's funeral and Reverend Jannings described it to him—but beautifully, Fran, I could have cried all over again. I made fresh coffee and we all had a laugh about condensed milk. Reverend Jannings said that when he was an army chaplain in Laos they had powdered milk, and it always tasted bitter because they had to use chlorinated swamp water to mix it! So I guess we've got a lot to be thankful for!

Well I'm sure grateful for one thing—that Reverend Jannings came over (just on an impulse, he says—kind of makes you believe in ESP!) Dad adores him and you can't imagine the difference it's made in the house. Like the windows were open and all the air was changed. I mean I can breathe again, I don't feel like crying every fifteen minutes, and nobody shouts at anybody.

He's a wonderful man, Fran. And that's my miracle. What do you think of it?

Love and kisses,
Darcie

It was two years after his marriage that an armed, heroin-starved bandit held up his parents' store and put a bullet through his pop's head, a clean shot entering the left temple and exiting the right. His mother, who rushed to the old man's defense with some lunatic notion of stopping the bullets with her own body, died three days later in the hospital, not so much from the wounds, her son suspected, as from a refusal to bother with more living.

She spent those last hours mumbling in a language that was not English and she did not seem much to understand or care when her son promised that he would find the bandit and bring him to justice.

REF. "FLYPAPER" (Z–145–6–239) DOCUMENT 77 AT-TACHED. OLIVETTI LETTERA 44 PORTABLE TYPE-WRITER, 1961 MODEL. "E" UNALIGNED. TOP SE-CRET.

Whitefalls, Thursday May 18

Dear Fran,

Just a quick note. Guess what—I passed biology! Bobby passed algebra, which was the great worry.

Dad is really eating up his magazines and not worrying about a thing, so the house is more or less peaceful. However, Reverend Jannings told me it may take some time to collect on Mom's insurance policy, which means I'd better start looking for a job as soon as I get through my other exams and graduate, etc. I might skip the graduation ceremony, the dress being rather expensive and all, and rehearsals taking up so much time.

I've just discovered casseroles and the meat grinder, which means that not much gets thrown out in the way of food—there are so many different ways of serving leftovers, things that even

Mom didn't discover! Sometimes in the kitchen I feel like Christopher Columbus—I guess Dad and Bobby do too when I bring out the dinner. Last night we had "supreme de supreme" (my own name for it), sort of a cauliflower and pork hash thing in jellied chicken soup. Bobby said he liked it. Dad finished most of his but left a little on the side, a hint I think that he didn't care too much for it.

Why don't you and I collaborate on a cookbook? You'd be the sensible one, and me the nut!

Love and Kisses,
Darcie

An orphan, a husband, and a college graduate in the same year, he had gone direct from the Transit Authority to a full-time job with the Agency.

He tried to explain his reasons to Corinna when she asked why he didn't get a better job, something in insurance, something with money.

"It wouldn't be right," he said. "Not the way I feel now."

"You're never going to find that punk," she told him.

At the beginning he had done well: the Agency had started him at a base pay of fifty-eight hundred, up thirteen hundred from his Transit Authority salary. He'd been able to take Corinna out one or two nights a month, and there were steaks on the table, and they had been able to buy a television—used, but it worked.

He got two promotions and raises totaling six hundred dollars. Corinna was sending his shirts to the laundry instead of doing them herself, and the bathroom no longer looked like a Laundromat; there was meat four, five times a week, and they even had bottles of wine, and from time to time friends dropped by for dinner and television.

He felt prosperous, successful: they'd even talked about having a baby; there was almost enough money for a third mouth. They laughed a lot, mostly at TV shows, but they were laughing together.

Then something went wrong. He had never known exactly

what, but some time during his third year with the Agency, everything—his job, his marriage, his life—began to unravel at the edges.

REF. "FLYPAPER" (Z–145–6–239) DOCUMENT 81 ATTACHED. UNDERWOOD PORTABLE ELECTRIC TYPEWRITER, 1970 MODEL.   TOP SECRET.

Excelsior Springs, Sunday May 21

Dearest Darcie,

I'm sending you my graduation dress via United Parcel. I hope it fits. I haven't used it for years, so do please keep it and make any alterations necessary. Do attend your graduation. It's a once in a lifetime event, a real summing-up and turning-point, and even if you feel it's a lot of pain and trouble, you'll look back on it and be glad you took part. And I know it would mean so much to your father to see your photograph in the paper.

Congratulations on the exams.

I know what you mean by things' being frantic—flu has felled half the faculty, and I have two hundred and eight final essays to correct and grade!

Good luck finding a job—I know you'll land a dilly!

love and kisses,
Fran

A job came up involving a Soviet trade attaché. The incentive pay was fifteen hundred, way above the usual, and it was hinted that the Director of the Agency would promote the men who could plant the mikes. He volunteered along with a first year guy called Harvey Johnson. Harvey was a blond-haired, bright-eyed boy who sweated a lot and talked about a wife and two kids.

The target was a brownstone in the West Nineties of Manhattan. The Agency had said it would be deserted between three-thirty and five in the afternoon, and he and Harvey arrived at three thirty-five in a Telephone Company truck, dressed as repairmen. They broke and entered through the kitchen door and took forty minutes planting mikes in the baseboards of seven of the eight rooms.

The Agency's instructions had been to put microphones in all seven rooms, and he and Harvey disagreed as to whether this meant a total of seven mikes, or a mike in every room, which would have been a total of eight. There were spares in the truck, and—believing that the Agency wanted a bug in every room—he told Harvey to wait while he went back for an eighth.

The truck was parked across the street from the brownstone, and while he was getting the extra mike and batteries, he saw a yellow taxi pull up in front of the house. A woman got out, paid the cabby, and went to the front door. The cab pulled away and she stood looking through her purse for a key.

He watched her.

At first he felt only a curious detachment: his eyes merely took note. The face and hands filled out a blank, and now he knew what a Soviet trade attaché's cook looked like. He could almost tell what her food would taste like: his mother's.

She was a heavy woman, Slavic in features, squat. She wore a clean uniform and wore it badly, and one hand kept going to her hip in attempts to pull the cloth down.

She dropped her key on the step and bent down to snatch at it.

Something in the way her hand chased that key sent a memory banging up against the top of his skull. The shape of old breasts pinned down beneath starched white, ankle and heel exposed and red as the foot slipped out of its shoe, these forms and colors seemed to have happened before, and for some unidentifiable reason he felt sorry for her.

She straightened up and as she opened the door and stepped into the house she turned. He could not tell whether she saw him or not, but he half expected her to recognize him and felt obscurely hurt when she did not. The door closed and she was gone.

Eight minutes later Harvey slipped out the same door and hurried to the truck.

"Any trouble with the cook?" he asked Harvey. He started the motor.

"No trouble," Harvey said, asking if they could go to a bar someplace.

Agents were not supposed to drink on duty, but he felt sorry for Harvey, who was new and had just had a close brush. He said okay.

They went to a bar and he had a root beer and Harvey had three double ryes, taking them in quick, breathless succession and knocking over the salt shaker with his elbow. Finally he said why didn't Harvey go home, he'd turn in the report himself.

In the afternoon papers the next day was a story about a Soviet trade attaché's cook who had been beaten to death in her kitchen. He almost vomited when he read it.

He said to Harvey, "I've got to know, and I swear it will never get past me: did you hit that woman?"

"I didn't touch her," Harvey swore.

They both had long, separate talks with their supervisor, and he told everything he knew and said he didn't think Harvey had touched the woman. Naturally there was no incentive pay for the job. He followed the story for the week that the papers ran it. Police never came up with anything except a statement that the cook must have surprised a burglar.

Within a matter of months he started getting assignments to out-of-town jobs. More and more of these jobs involved reading mail and monitoring taps. What they came down to, in a year, was sitting in government rooms across the nation studying documents; he had been virtually retired from the field. Within two years he had to start wearing glasses to read small print, and he began getting headaches, and when aspirin stopped helping he took to pouring vodka into his root beer.

"Don't you see what happened?" Corinna asked him. "That other guy put the blame on you, he got the promotion and you got the boot, and we're in a sixth-floor walk-up!"

He said he was sorry, but she was wrong. She said she was leaving him. He said she had to try to understand.

"What don't I understand?"

"You don't understand that kind of thing doesn't happen in the Agency." He was almost crying. "The Agency's straight. It's the last straight thing in this goddamned country."

And then inflation; and then they were back to hot dogs.

REF. "FLYPAPER" (Z–145–6–239) DOCUMENT 91 AT-TACHED. OLIVETTI LETTERA 44 PORTABLE TYPE-WRITER, 1961 MODEL. "E" UNALIGNED. TOP SE-CRET.

Whitefalls, Wednesday May 24

Dear Fran,

It's over—as of twelve-thirty yesterday, when Mrs. Galston called my name and I went up on the platform to take my diploma and shake her hand—first time I've ever done *that!*

Your dress fitted perfectly. I didn't need to change a thing, not even the hem. I hate to boast, but I thought I looked ten times prettier than any other girl there. But we'll wait for the photos to come out. I'll send you one and see if you don't agree. I mean I was really a knock-out! Boys were staring etc. All the credit goes to your dress of course. Do you really mean I can keep it?

I'd love to, not that I'll be doing any dancing or partying for a long while yet, but it's always good to have something in reserve, and the dress couldn't be more perfect. With a sash it would look a little more contemporary and maybe I could raise the hem and let the neck down a little. That is, if you're really letting me keep it. Anyway, thanks a million!

And one day, after monitoring the intercepts on a drug case, he came home and found his wife sitting at the living-room table with the flour sifter, grinding marijuana into a Pyrex mixing bowl, and he shouted at her, "Why do you use that stuff?"

"I like it," she said, and these were her first audible words in some time. He took the bowl. He was going to empty it down the toilet, but it looked like forty dollars' worth and instead he just pushed it away from her, and then he sat, one forefinger tapping his temple.

That night, after dinner, he had three root beers and vodka instead of two, and he was dozing through the flicker of a late late Western. He had long since given up wondering whether she would come to bed or sleep out on the sofa: she claimed that sometimes she was so tired she just fell asleep wherever she happened to be, and more and more often it happened to be some place where he wasn't. But that night she got into bed with him, naked, and she slipped his shorts down off his legs and his undershirt up over his shoulders, and it surprised him how much she knew about undressing a man.

That bothered him, and though they made love for the first time in six months and she brought him to a brass-band climax, it was the reason, the next day, that he asked for longer assignments away from home.

After the ceremony I went to the cemetery and left my bouquet (yes, we carried flowers—Mrs. Galston's idea) on Mom's grave. The grave is in wonderful shape. The grass has grown nicely over the mound, and the tombstone is simple but lovely. And guess what else! It is almost next door to the grave of the mother and father of President Luckinbill! Some luck, hey?

It really is because of Mom that I didn't need to go to work four years ago, and was able to get an education, and I wanted to thank her for the graduation. You were four-hundred percent right, Fran, it would have been a mistake to miss the ceremony, if only because Dad (and Mom too, I know) had been looking forward to that day for so long, and it meant so much to them both.

Bobby came to the ceremony and said I was the prettiest girl there and the only one that stood straight when I went to get my diploma. Thanks to Mom again, remember how she used to nag about posture? I guess I owe Mom a heck of a lot, don't I! And I'm really feeling it these days too, I don't know why. Graduation seems to be the end of something, and now I'm beginning something else—I don't mean just the job (yes, I got one!!) but life—but skip it before I get too corny. I cried at Mom's grave. A family was photographing the Luckinbill grave and I had to pretend to be sneezing when they saw me!

She wrote him letters for a while: *Hi, they're raising the rent 15%; we've got new neighbors.* But he sensed spaces between the words and lines; and he wondered where she had learned to do things like that in bed; and he wondered if she was in love with someone else, maybe a man who smoked pot and liked the things she did.

He answered with postcards: a photo of the Drake Hotel in Des Moines with a window circled in ball-point: *Hi, this is my room;* the tabernacle at Salt Lake City, *Hi;* a sunset in Sioux City, Iowa. After a while she stopped writing—the last he ever heard from her was that the Laundromat had raised the price of an eight-pound wash and spin-dry to thirty-five cents. A letter he wrote her on Holiday Inn stationery came back to the Agency in eight days, *addressee unknown.*

They never divorced, and he continued to wear the wedding band. It was something to twist on his finger in those moments when a man needed to fidget, and in the Agency a man had to be married if he expected to advance above a certain level. Nevertheless, despite the wedding band, he did not advance.

After twenty years he was still reading other people's mail.

About the job—you'll never guess! My good angel (the other one—you're the main one) told me just after the ceremony that he had arranged a job for me at Whitefalls' one and only Bank! I train for a week and then I take over for the summer when the regular goes on vacation. If I like it, and they like me, I stay on. There's a chance for advancement and the pay is fairly good considering that I'm not experienced—ninety-five dollars a week, minus withholding tax, etc., which comes to seventy-some take-home pay. Hours are just great, with forty-five minutes off for lunch.

Bobby is still having a little tooth trouble, but that hasn't stopped him from starting up his own lawn-mowing business for the summer. So far he's lined up five people, not bad for a start. Ten hours a week, he's charging a dollar seventy-five an hour. I'd better watch it or he'll be earning more than me!

Dad is being a lamb, I just don't recognize him. Reverend Jannings brings him a pile of magazines every other day (I think he collects them from the congregation, and some of them are so old you never even heard of them!) so that keeps the old man out of trouble and out of my hair!

Well Fran, wish me luck with the job, I'll need it, and thanks again for the dress. It made all the difference.

Love and kisses,
Darcie

He went to the window, poked a finger through two slats of blind and peered into the eternal, premature night. Something dropped on the asphalt floor of the airshaft, seventeen stories below, with the bright joyless ring of an empty beer can.

*

Lexie and the First Lady returned to the White House in the early evening. A heavy Secret Service guard shielded them from the furious scrutiny of public and press. The First Lady had wired the head housekeeper to track down some of Lexie's old toys, and her daughter's room had been made ready for the arrival of an invalid.

The stuffed animals stared at the First Lady, bears of mismatched button eyes, giraffes with necks droopier and sadder than any forlorn peacock's tail. From the pile the First Lady chose Lexie's favorite, a creature of unclassifiable genus and species, gingerbread brown, with sad, wide eyes that hungered for affection.

The doll had two legs—or three, depending what you called the tail-like thing. Its arms and neck were blistered with the kisses and sucks and bites of a love that had lasted a good deal longer than many marriages. Lexie had given it the name Ichabod and had maintained that it was not a she or an it, but a he.

Once Lexie had said, "Ichabod will never hurt me. . . ."

The First Lady always felt odd returning to the White House, and she felt a little queer holding Ichabod again after all the years that he had lain in the attic chest of dead memorabilia. "We almost burned you," she confessed, and at that the creature looked at her so pitiably she had to kiss it. "But if you help Lexie get well, you can stay in her room always."

And she placed the animal in a position of honor on Lexie's pillow.

It looked sad there, and weak, and for some reason it reminded the First Lady of those napalmed orphans that one had seen too much of in the wars of these last twenty years. But it had, after all, survived: that took a certain strength.

The White House itself, she reflected, had seen the full gamut of human strength and oddity and weakness: Abe Lincoln and Teddy Roosevelt had romped here with their sons, and Teddy had almost lost an eye playing with his boy Quentin in the dark attic; and Andrew Jackson had served a 1,400-pound cheese in the Entrance Hall, and Abigail Adams had hung her laundry in the East Room, and the corridors had echoed to the groaning wheelchairs of Wilson and Franklin Delano Roosevelt; Presidents had died in the house and their children had been born and died in it; yet once there had been greatness too, and it was the greatness that the First Lady missed. She kept feeling it had left the room just before she came in or stopped speaking just as she started listening. The house had doctor's and dentist's offices, a barbershop and a movie theater, radio and TV studios and a subterranean swimming pool, 150 rooms in all. It had crystal and china and silver to feed and serve hundreds and linen to sleep dozens and it buzzed with the activities of 156 assistants and aides and secretaries who themselves had assistants and aides and secretaries; and it had air conditioning; and it had armed security; and once—in history books—it had had greatness.

And so when the First Lady returned to the White House that evening her awe had a question mark. The house had become part of her life; in it her daughter had passed from girlhood to young womanhood and in it she and her husband had become almost total strangers. In it she was empress of a staff of maids, plumbers, gardeners, engineers, laundresses, painters, housemen, electricians, cooks, carpenters, doormen, waiters, butlers, eighty-two servants who rotated around the clock and who somehow consumed over sixty-three pounds of floor wax a month. Here she had her own florist and her own hair stylist. Here she had entertained and shaken the hands of and to an extent gotten to know cabinet members, congressmen, judges, civil servants, diplomats, military men, reporters, and newscasters. Here she had charted and navigated state dinners for a hundred and formal receptions for two thousand and fed tournedos Rossini to crowned heads and, once, watercress soup to a party of Coptic Christians. Here, strangely, she and her husband and daughter had lived longer than in any other home, and there was a wonder, an oddity about it that should have faded with familiarity but instead grew greater each day and now threatened to drown her.

Lexie was carried to her room in her own special bed, on long legs and silent wheels. The First Lady tried to put Ichabod into the bed with her, but the nurse took the doll and said that the risk of contagion was too great. "You should burn this old thing," she added.

The First Lady felt an obscure hurt, as though someone had reproached her taste in dress.

"Lexie loves it so. I thought it might be good. Psychologically."

The nurse dropped Ichabod with a quick movement, like garbage, onto a safely distant chair.

The First Lady would have liked to be alone with the child, but she sensed that the nurse was going to permit no such liberty; and she had to content herself with staring down into the steel bed. Fleeting muscular movements beneath the skin, as of shadows shifting, suggested her daughter might be dreaming. The bandages were gone, and there were no more tubes or needles, and the girl's complexion had achieved the icy, flawless perfection of marble.

The First Lady realized with a peculiar pride, quickly shunted aside, that the girl would be beautiful even in death.

"Mom?" came a voice from a shadow on the steel bed.

"I'm here, Lexie."

"Where am I?" The voice was pitiable, frail, like the piping of a broken penny whistle.

"You're home, darling."

"Are we at the farm?"

The question startled the First Lady; she had never realized Lexie cared for the farm in Virginia, let alone considered it home. "No, darling. We're at the White House. You're in a special bed near the window. If you listen you can hear the traffic outside."

The girl breathed heavily as though there were a weight on her chest. "I hear waves. Are we in Grandpa's cottage by the sea?"

"No, darling. We're in the White House. But you can go to the farm if you'd like, or to the sea. As soon as you're well."

The girl absorbed the meaning of this. "Am I sick?"

"You were hurt. But you're much better now. The doctors say you've made a splendid recovery. They say you're a brave young woman."

Yet, looking at the child, the First Lady thought she saw wounds deeper than any doctors' diagnosis.

"How was I hurt? What happened?"

"Never mind that. It's over."

"We were standing in the graveyard and Dad went to lay the wreath and then something hit me in the shoulder. . . ."

"Don't remember. You're safe and that's all that counts."

Lexie's hand gripped a flap of plastic tent. "The gunshot!"

The First Lady flung her arms around the girl with a ferocity that almost uprooted her from the bed. "No one will hurt you, not ever. You're safe. Mother's here. Go to sleep."

She heard a noise at the doorway. Turning, she saw the familiar black-jacketed shape of the warrant officer, codes dangling from the right arm. She could make out whispers just around the bend of the corridor, and a moment later the President was beside her, staring down at the girl.

"Hi, Lexie."

The girl smiled. "Hi, Dad."

He took his daughter's hand and squeezed it. "Do you feel up to that dinner, hon?" he asked his wife.

It was a dinner for campaign contributors. She knew they would be disappointed if she wasn't there in a new dress right beside her husband.

"You'd rather be with Lexie," he said. "So would I."

"No, Bill. We owe it to them. Lexie's got a nurse."

He kissed her. "I'll try to keep the speeches short."

The First Lady kissed her daughter and went to her dressing room. It seemed there was never any time. She felt a headache beginning and took two of her pills.

*

"Suddenly my mail—everybody's mail—is running three to one in favor of that bill and that goddamned rider."

"Mmm-hmm."

"Something's happening to the country. Something just happened in the House, and something's about to happen in the Senate."

Two men sat in the largest bathroom at 1600 Pennsylvania Avenue: the Senate Majority Leader on the closed, needle-point-covered lid of the toilet seat; the President in the bathtub with the eagle etched on the side. It was Senator Dan who was talking.

"Half my own men won't even look me in the eye. They're scared."

"Wonder what of," the President said, soaping.

"Scared of me, of you, of the nation, I don't know. But I do know this: the longer it takes to get to a vote in the Senate, the less of a lead we're going to have to defeat that bill. Mr. President, if your own senators won't do it for you, you may have to veto your own gun-control bill."

"I'm aware of that fact, Dan."

The President flexed and floated, scrubbed and scratched, made wave after wave and sent them to nibble the clean porcelain shore. Cowboy-lanky, lean as a good pot roast, with only a sprinkling of salt at his temples and a few crow's-feet at his eyes to attest that his years exceeded two-and-a-quarter-score, the President of the United States stretched full-length in the six-foot-six bathtub and wiggled his toes under the hot-spouting tap.

"I may be overreacting, Mr. President, but I think we've got the biggest mess on our hands since the South seceded. The nation's seceding, the whole goddamned Union, from Alaska to Texas. It's going to be tough to fight that kind of confederacy."

To hear Dan Bulfinch tell it, in a mere six days the nation and the Congress had taken a U-turn for the absolute, unmitigated worst. It was the fault of the economy; it was the fault of the war; it was the fault of the shooting—and how by the way was Lexie doing?

"As well as could be expected."

The damnable thing, and the Senate Majority Leader emphasized this, was that there was no way of knowing for dead sure where the nation stood until the actual vote—and that would probably be too late. One had only to look at the facts: the Administration had told its forces to vote against the amended bill, but it had passed the House by an astonishing and unprecedented 315-vote margin, and the telegrams of approval had outnumbered the protests 18 to 1. The Administration clearly had far fewer friends—inside and outside of the government—than it had supposed.

"Sure," Senator Dan said, "we've got the newspapers on our side, some of them at least, and some of the TV networks see things our way. But we haven't got the people on our side. It buffaloes me, Mr. President—we're on the people's side, but the people aren't!"

The President stroked himself with a Japanese sponge which the importer claimed would flake off dead skin cells. He nodded.

"What happens if the people don't want liberty, Mr. President? What happens if the people rip up their own freedom and burn it?"

The President wrung his sponge dry.

"We could be a full-fledged police state in under a year," Senator Dan said. "South Africa and Spain and the Soviet Union in one big jelly roll. We could be everything our enemies call us."

"More," the President said. "Much more. Our enemies underestimate us." He gave his head a puppy-dog shake. The Senate Majority Leader recoiled clear of the soapy droplets.

"Do you think Napoleon had one like this?" the President asked.

Senator Dan was surprised and obscurely hurt to see that a part of the President's anatomy was peeking through a ring of soapsuds and that the Chief Executive was giving it and not the senator his attention. "At least you could cover that damned thing up. You're worse than a twelve-year-old boy."

The President gave the senator an uncharacteristically playful wink. He rose from the tub, a priapic Neptune, clothed only in soap bubbles. The senator threw him a towel.

"Wrap that around you, will you please?"

"Do my best," the President smiled. He fixed the green cloth with a thick granny knot around his thirty-two-inch waist: and the senator wondered enviously how the hell the man managed to run the nation and still keep fit. In his years in politics, Dan Bulfinch had seen Chief Executives turn gray, go bald, put on pots the size of garbage cans, develop angina and ulcers and barbiturate habits. But not Bill Luckinbill: if anything, he had slimmed down; his step had become springier; and that damned boyish smile had smeared itself to his lips like some permanent Tootsie Roll stain.

A mountain of suds belched drainward, and the President stood dripping on the bathmat and began splashing himself in talcum powder. "How many votes can we count on?"

"I'm not promising," Senator Dan said. "But I think we've still got a five-vote lead."

"Five!" The President unspooled a yard-long stretch of dental floss and began running it through his teeth. "Sunday we had six. You said six for sure."

"Evan Beaupré defected."

"I'll have his scalp." The President brushed his hair: fifty strokes with the pig-bristle brush. "I'll have his balls and nail them over that door!"

Senator Dan could not help glancing with a shudder at the class photo that hung framed over the bathroom door.

"What about the others?" The President held the senator's eye in the mirror. "Standing firm?"

The senator spoke softly. "I pray to God they're standing firm."

"Prayers to God are not enough!" With an abruptness that was almost schizophrenic, the President was shouting. "I've seen a twenty-vote lead dwindle down to five in less than a week. What the hell is going on? What kind of a majority leader are you? And where in damnation is that majority?"

"Mr. President." The senator was shaken into an almost apologetic tone. "It wouldn't help if we controlled ninety per cent of the Senate. The bill is not a partisan issue."

"I'm making it one. Who else is wavering?"

"I get vibrations from two or three."

"Get on that phone." The President's ring finger flashed out at the red telephone nestled in a cranny above the toilet paper. "Talk to them now and pin them down."

"Mr. President, it's one thirty-five A.M."

"It's going to be one thirty-six A.M. if we don't get off our asses."

In two steps the President crossed the bathroom, grabbed the receiver from its cradle, and thrust it into the senator's astonished hand, where it lay humming a dial tone.

The senator consulted his pocket directory, a leatherbound gold-initialed gift from his assistant, Linda Parsons. He found the home number of the junior senator from Nebraska and began his phone canvass. Twelve minutes later he wearily replaced the receiver.

"Bailey and Smith and Hendricks have defected." He glanced up at the President and found that the Chief Executive's eyes were awaiting his, cold and unsurprised, and for the umpteenth time since he had known the man, Senator Dan wondered if he was a clairvoyant.

The Senate Majority Leader wiped sweat from his eyebrow. "Jesus, we're in trouble."

"If that bill passes," said the President, "it will be by the greatest acclamation since Hitler took Austria. We've got to stop it, Dan. I don't care how. But it's got to be stopped, or this government and this country are finished."

*

Mark Hendricks, senior senator from New Jersey, allowed the receiver to drop back into the cradle.

"Luckinbill?" his visitor asked.

"Bulfinch." Senator Hendricks' voice was drained and his eyes stared as though they needed pennies to keep the lids down.

"Same difference," his visitor said. "You look like you could use a brandy. Matter of fact, I wouldn't turn one down myself."

"And I wouldn't offer you one."

Senator Hendricks' visitor got up from the chair. "Well, well. Miles to go before I sleep, so *hasta luego*, chum. Oh, you can keep that." A blunt-fingered hand gestured toward the two yards of furled print-out that Senator Hendricks held in a bloodless white grip.

"You had no business putting that filth into a computer," Senator Hendricks said.

"And you, Senator, had no business committing that filth." His visitor held out a hand. "Welcome to the team. And stay well until the vote. And do shout your *yea* loud and clear."

Senator Hendricks ignored the hand. "You know the way out."

"Yes indeed."

*

It was close to four in the morning when the First Lady for the third time surfaced from sleep to consciousness and found herself still alone in the king-sized double bed. The whisperings in the presidential bathroom, two doors distant, had ended; and she had dreamed or heard footsteps and muted good-bys in the dressing room.

Now, as she craned her ear toward the door, there seemed to be total silence, broken only by the occasional scratch of a match striking.

The First Lady realized that, after almost two years on the wagon, her husband was smoking again. More than that, he was pacing barefoot, risking a head cold in the air conditioning; at the very least sniffles. She toyed with the idea of going to him, and her feet crept from under the sheets and searched the floor for her slippers. But then some instinct told her to hold off: to let him come to her when he wanted, if he wanted.

For the First Lady, the events in Whitefalls had had a happy ending: her daughter was safe and home and almost good as new, the doctors said. Yet she sensed that, for the man on the other side of that door, there was no happy ending in sight.

And, for an instant, before sleep again pulled her down, she was surprised to feel an emotion she had not known since the earliest days of her courtship and marriage.

She was sorry for her husband.

June 26: Monday

"This," the woman said, "was received several months ago. Does anything about it strike you?"

The hand offering Borodin the sheet of paper showed signs of recent manicure. The paper was a Xerox copy of a bad-tempered little postcard. Using both the message and address space, the author had compiled letters and words from different newspapers and magazines, with an eye toward variety of typeface that was almost dizzying. Fine lines in the Xerox suggested that he or she had used transparent gummed tape to hold the bits into place.

Stop killing or you will be dead you, the message ran. The author, in keeping with the conventions of the genre, had not signed his name.

"The letters," the woman explained, "were for the most part clipped out of a back issue of *Look* magazine. *Look* stopped printing some time ago. They were Scotch-taped to a postcard of the Luckinbill statue in the Whitefalls town square. The card is on sale throughout the Dakotas. Some latent fingerprints have shown up; they don't match anything in the print bank. Anything about it strike you?"

"The way the letters are taped on," Borodin said. "Imitating a nut."

"Imitating?" The woman's hair was onyx-black, her skin white and unlined as Antarctic snowdrifts. Her eyes had the slightly too intense glow of signal buttons on a computer. Borodin suspected her of practicing the small cosmetic deceits of all lovely women.

"Nuts paste the letters on in nice neat lines," he said. "They don't zigzag around like this. And they know their grammar and punctuation. They don't mix upper-case and lower-case letters. Small *s*, small *t*, capital *o*, capital *p*—no nut would spell *stop* like that. It's a put-on. This is the kind of note someone who doesn't know anything about nuts thinks a nut would send."

"You've had experience with nuts?" The woman recrossed her legs, as though to draw attention to their slenderness.

"I've seen nuts send notes to bank presidents saying *You are doomed*, I've seen an old schizo shaking with palsy get out scissors and a newspaper and clip out a *d* and an *m* and two *o*'s and suffer, really suffer, getting the letters straight on the page. Nuts take pride in their work."

"Don't we all?" The woman had said her name was Dr. Erikka Lumi. She kept looking at Borodin as though he bore out a favorite hypothesis.

"Not the way nuts do," Borodin disagreed. "We can't afford to. Only one kind of person would send this kind of note, and that's a joker with plenty of spare time."

"The joke's punishable by a five-year jail term."

"If you catch the joker."

"Don't you worry; we'll catch him." She handed him a second Xerox, this of a stamped, postmarked envelope addressed by typewriter to the President of the United States. It had been mailed in Whitefalls, South Dakota, on April 12.

Borodin muttered, "Jesus."

"Is 'Jesus' all you have to say?"

"No, ma'am, not quite. I've been an investigator for the Agency for longer than I like to think, and it's my humble hunch that this note has nothing to do with that shooting."

"Then why the postmark?"

"Because it's a gas, a murder note to the White House from the old folks at home. I've run into some jokers would drive two thousand miles for a laugh like that."

"The fact remains that this postcard was mailed from Whitefalls, and someone did subsequently shoot at the President in Whitefalls."

"Or at the kid."

"We're investigating that possibility."

They sat in a windowless, gray-walled concrete cube, perhaps ten feet on a side. Three rectangular holes like slots in a projection booth punctuated one of the walls, but for the moment no sound or light came through them. Two fluorescent tubes x'ed the ceiling, and electrical currents whined softly in them.

The table and the chairs they sat in dropped heavy steel shadows onto the floor. These shadows leaped silently between two slightly different positions as the lights overhead shifted intensities. There was no other furniture.

Borodin made a face.

Dr. Lumi smiled neutrally. "I think you have a comment."

"No. No comment."

"Any comment you have could be of use in the investigation. You've seen some of the intercepts. Enough to get the flavor. What's your reaction?"

Borodin's lungs ached vaguely in the artificially dried cold.

"All right, I'll tell you. When the President got this letter, it was just a routine threat, a one in ten thousand chance that it meant anything. So you sent a man out to Whitefalls, right? He looked around to see if any old friends of the President were still living there. He talked to the people at the post office. He thought maybe they don't sell that many Walt Disney commemoratives. Maybe they remember some movie nut came in and bought three sheets. Only no one remembered. So he asked the police if there were any nuts in town. And he checked whether anyone in Whitefalls ever wrote a note to the White House, ever signed a petition to the President, anything like that. Say there were one or two. He watched them. And he watched the ministers. And the teachers. And the potheads. And the troublemakers. He read the mail that came in to these people and went out from these people. He looked for fingerprints. Scotch tape. Typewriter face. Something. Anything. He ended up watching the whole town, more or less."

"And what happened?" Dr. Lumi, smiling in an interested way, began tapping a plastic pen on the steel-topped table, ever so softly.

"You're asking me? He watched till the money ran out. He

watched till your budget was screaming and you couldn't afford
to keep him in that town nosing around and nothing turning up
but letters from schoolgirls like Darcie What's-it. He told you
someone in a convertible must have driven through town one
Saturday and dropped this thing in a mailbox. And you would
have believed him—except there was that shooting."

The pencil came to a standstill. "Why do you say someone in
a convertible mailed this postcard?" Dr. Lumi cocked a glance of
amiable curiosity at Borodin's thumbs.

"Figure of speech." Borodin tried to think why he felt the beginning tremors of antagonism toward her: because he didn't
think women should be running government agencies? Because
he suspected all doctors? Because she had Corinna's eyes?

"You seem to have a definite conception of the sender of this
card. Just glancing at some Xerox copies, some snippets of news-
print, a few pieces of tape." Something in the doctor's smile
alerted Borodin to cunning. She wore her face with the accomplished falsity of a mask.

"You bet I have a definite conception. A college kid in a convertible. And I'll tell you something else: odds are, you'll never
catch him."

"Never?" Her smile suggested this was hard to believe.

"You may catch the joker that pulled that trigger. But the
joker that mailed this note? Nope. Not on the kind of budget
you have for tracing letters. It takes money and time and men to
monitor a town, and unless you're willing to invest enough to
finish the job, it's not worth starting. And if you do invest
enough to finish the job, it's still not worth finishing, because
you spend close to half a million dollars and all you catch is a
joker—and not even the right joker. I'm telling you: an assassin
with talent shoots. It's the stay-at-homes that write in. And the
joker that wrote this did not pull that trigger."

"I'm not as sure of that as you." Dr. Lumi drew herself up; her
voice took on an explanatory tone. "Notice that the words are
made up of groups of letters scissored *en bloc*, not letters in-
dividually clipped out. Notice, too, the wording: *stop killing or
you will be dead you.* It's repetitious, clumsy. Does it suggest that

the sender planned his message, counted the required letters, and went to the trouble of finding them? No, he used quite a different approach. The note plainly indicates that he seized on an impulse and a back-issue magazine and slapped together the first semi-coherent string of words that approximated his meaning. The sender is not neat. He cannot plan. He cannot postpone satisfaction. And that is the classic description of a dangerous psychopath."

Borodin shrugged. "Lots of people don't make plans or postpone satisfactions. But I don't see the dangerous. And I don't buy the psychopath. And I don't see that it's got to be a he."

"The sender is a man."

"That's certainly a possibility."

Dr. Lumi's eyes glinted like mica-flecked rock. "Women do not send threatening notes to the President. That type of hostility, that way of expressing it, these things are not in their psychological make-up. I have never seen a single case of a woman sending this type of note."

"You say no women are writing these fan letters because you haven't caught any? I say women are smart, man, smart."

A silence passed on tiptoe.

"Do you by any chance hate women?" she asked.

"Some. And it's not by chance."

"I see."

"No you don't."

Her wand waved. "A computer has checked the intercepts for latent code or cipher."

"You think there's code or cipher in that crap?"

Lumi angled a glance of aquiline understatement at Borodin's necktie. "Not beyond the realm of possibility. Note the references to old magazines. This girl Darcie and her brother and her father all had access to them."

"Who the hell doesn't have access to old magazines? I could get at an old copy of Look if I wanted. So could you."

"The girl's older brother was killed in a United States police action in Costa Rica. This might conceivably have given rise to anti-government sentiment in the family."

"Now wait. If she was using code, why would she tip you off about the magazines? If she was covering her tracks, wouldn't she cover all of them?"

"Some criminals have a high self-hatred component. They give themselves away intentionally."

"But you just got through telling me the threat was not sent by a woman."

"And you just got through telling me I was wrong."

"Look, either you're kidding, or we're not quite connecting."

"You'll take the evening flight to Whitefalls."

"Jesus Christ, you must have a platoon out there already."

Lumi neither acknowledged nor denied. "Your job will be to continue mail surveillance. You needn't worry about any platoon."

Borodin was aware that by some sleight of tongue and rank, she had gotten him onto the wrong side of an abyss. She was looking at him pleasantly, but all he could wonder was, *Why the promotion? Why me?*

"The last thing I was in complete and sole charge of," he said, "was an investigation of stolen money orders in Abelard, Kansas."

"We liked your work on that case."

"So you're giving me a step up?"

"We're giving you this job because we think you're the man best suited to it."

"What happened to the guy before me?"

"He was shot."

Little bits of electrical circuit began clicking together, and Borodin saw the glimmer of a light bulb. "So I'm the stakeout."

"We liked your work on the Abelard case," Dr. Lumi repeated with the mild, kindly emphasis of a schoolteacher.

"That case is still pending. Lose me, and you'll have to break in a new guy."

"We have no intention of losing anyone."

"Well, do I have a choice?"

Dr. Lumi smiled benignly. "No."

*

INTER-OFFICE MEMO. LUMI TO JUDD. COMMENTS ON CONVERSATION, JUNE 26, WITH AGENT FRANK BORODIN. TOP SECRET.

Like many men recruited during the early Cold War/McCarthyite period, Borodin embodies in his attitudes, assumptions, and methods some considerable residue of the Wild West/rugged individualism/John Wayne mythos which experience of recent years has indicated not to be the happiest trait in agents. Operatives must now cope with often submerged, subtle and elusive ambiguities in the gathering of intelligence and the pursuit of related objectives. Mental flexibility is therefore at a premium.

For this reason Borodin has in recent years been relegated to relatively unimportant and low-risk tasks in low-population areas, where chances of conflict between his rigid norms and values and the evolving norms and values of the local populations are minimized.

Like many of our older agents, Borodin has demonstrated little growth beyond the crusader-like mentality of the 1950's and 60's with their sharply delineated lines of conflict (or, to put it in a less exact fashion, their clear though arbitrary distinctions between *right* and *wrong*). He is, in today's terms, a policeman, not an agent, and he belongs on the beat, not in intelligence. However, for obvious reasons, we cannot put him out to pasture. He knows a great deal.

In general we do not assign such men to responsible positions in on-going investigations. In the present instance I believe an exception is well warranted. In the first place, Borodin will be at all times under surveillance by our own men. Secondly, the tracking down of an anonymous letter-writer is a slow, boring, and unrewarding task. Though Borodin has expressed doubt as to the efficacy of such an effort, he has expressed none as to its *moral value*, and there can be no question but that he will be highly motivated to pursue and uncover a violator of his own most closely held authoritarian values. There is little possibility of his being slowed in the job by tedium, questioning of relevance, or intellectual restlessness.

In conclusion: The origins of Frank Borodin's truly monstrous hostility are apparent but, in this instance, irrelevant. Though he is a relic of now-superseded employment criteria, a man with his capacity to hate is always a tireless and dedicated investigator. In this instance we may disregard the agent's protective façade of cynical indifference verging on defeatism: since failure in this case would be tantamount to an admission of impotence (his deepest dread), he will produce results willy-nilly, or, as it were, "die in the attempt."

At the same time, should worse come to worst, he is a man whom it would not be difficult to replace.

I see many advantages in using Frank Borodin, far outweighing possible objections.

LUMI

*

At 6:38 P.M. Dr. Erikka Lumi signed her black Volkswagen out from the subterranean 1,300-car garage of the Agency Building. One hour and twelve minutes later, with brown paper bags of groceries and liquor piled on her back seat, she skidded the car down a single-lane dirt road in the Maryland woods and pulled to a stop before an isolated one-story cottage that was built of far too much glass ever to have been a farmhouse.

Balancing packages, she let herself in the front door.

A whisp of cigar smoke, like the exhaust of a hovercraft, swayed in the air above an armchair. Humus-caked hunting boots rested crisscrossed on a wooden stool; blunt fingers tapped an idle rhythm on blue-jeaned thigh, and a windburned face turned a half profile toward her. Logs spat flames in the fireplace. "Hello, darling," Erikka called.

A familiar grunt answered her. She set down her packages in the hallway and checked her hair in the little antique mirror. She came down the pine steps into the sunken living room, patting a strand of raven's black back into place.

"How did it go with Judd?" came the grunt.

Erikka saw that her visitor had a half-finished drink in hand; brandy and soda, to judge by the bottles left out on the sideboard.

"Judd is convinced that Hiram Quinn and Lexie Luckinbill were shot by the same person. He wants to replace Quinn and see if the assassin moves against the replacement."

"He must be senile to try a stakeout like that."

Though it was not her favorite drink by any stretch, Erikka fixed herself a mild brandy and soda for sociability's sake. She sat on the straw mat and cuddled against the booted legs. Blunt fingers played in her hair, and Havana ash dropped onto her shoulder. She let it stay there.

"I suppose he is senile," Erikka nodded. "And desperate."

"Who are you sending?"

"His name is Borodin. He's a mediocrity and a paranoid." Live sparks blitzing the straw rug made it difficult to concentrate on conversation. Erikka moved the copper mesh screen nearer the fire.

"Paranoids have a way of meddling."

A pine knot popped like a gunshot. Erikka caught her breath.

"His record indicates very low initiative. Fascist-passive-anal personality profile. Authoritarian receptive." Erikka glanced up. "You haven't kissed me."

They kissed. Long after their lips had separated, Erikka's remained puckered in recall.

The house they sat in had been built of the rawest, most unadorned materials; huge cinderblocks, plate glass, unbleached pine. Whatever human comfort there was in the look of the place came from the walls of bookshelves and the leather sofa and chairs. Sliding doors hid a completely automated kitchen. Another door hid shelves of appliances for cleaning and mending and maintaining. A third door, Erikka noticed, had been left ajar.

"Who's been here?"

The cigar hesitated in mid-arc, shed a Havana ash, glowed a renewed pink. "No one's been here. I went out to bring in some more logs. You were running low."

Erikka got to her knees and, with a little more effort, to her feet. "That door should be kept locked."

"It makes a nice draft."

"I don't care. It should be kept locked."

The visitor chuckled, reached out a hand in a gesture that combined affection, condescension, and masculine arrogance. Erikka refused, for the moment, to be coaxed or wheedled. She evaded the caress, went quickly to the offending door. She peeked down the unlit hallway, looked, and listened.

The doors to the bedroom, guest room, and bathroom were all shut. The back door was not. Erikka darted to the end of the corridor and stood at the screen, sniffing the forest as though for human scent, peering into the towering evergreen darkness. She closed the back door and slid the bolt, shutting out the army of trees. At the guest room she paused, ear to the wood. Hearing nothing, she was satisfied.

She came back into the living room, twisting the key behind her. "We must be more careful," she warned.

"Who's going to see us? Chipmunks?"

"Hikers sometimes come this way. And lost tourists. And you never know when Woodrow Judd's got a security check on you." Erikka came back to her place by the fire, by the boots.

"How much additional time will this Borodin permit us?"

Erikka pondered. "The Agency won't expect results for at least a week or so. He'll need to settle into the job."

The visitor calculated on blunt fingertips. "A week could be just long enough."

"We're so close to winning; and so close to losing everything." Erikka sighed and gripped the boots. "I wish it were over."

The visitor gave her a long, drawling smile. "Why don't you draw the curtains so the chipmunks can't see?"

Rising on swift high heels, Erikka Lumi obeyed.

*

REF. "FLYPAPER" (Z–145–6–239) DOCUMENT 103 ATTACHED. OLIVETTI LETTERA 44 PORTABLE TYPEWRITER, 1961 MODEL. "E" UNALIGNED. TOP SECRET.

Whitefalls, Sunday May 28

Dear Fran,

This has been one of the most wonderful Sundays of my life! We went to the farmer's fair (in a beautiful new Buick, robin's

egg blue, stereo radio, convertible pushbutton canvas top, red
leather upholstery) and we spent eight hours just roaming the
fairway. We won five kewpie dolls! Made ourselves sick on hot-
dogs and French fries and spun sugar candy, rode on the roller
coaster, just a tiny one and still I was screaming my head off,
both entered the pie eating contest, they tied our hands behind
our backs and we had to see who could eat a huge blueberry
pie fastest (it was delicious). That fat little Jones girl won first
prize. You should have seen her with that great blue grin!

I figured it was better (out of respect for Mom) not to be seen
galavanting around in the evening, so I said I had to go home
after the pig judging contest. They gave the ribbon to the ugliest
sow you ever did see, dung colored and bristles and stinking like
a privy. The cutest little pig, the one we were rooting for, was
disqualified on a technicality. I wanted to adopt it, it looked so
sad. Anyway I explained about Mom passing away and all and
so instead of staying out in public we went to a movie in Hobart
—a musical, not very good.

I got home around eleven-thirty (an hour ago.) It turned
out Bobby spent the evening out too with some of the local
hippie-types and Dad hadn't had any dinner, so I warmed up a
can of ravioli for him and told him about my day (leaving out
most of the details!!) Then I took a long hot bath and here I
am, ready for bed, sitting at the dressing table (typing on my
knees—scuse me if it jiggles) and when I look in the mirror I
just don't recognize the three me's (it's Mom's old bureau with
the three-panel mirror, the one I always wanted. I've moved it
into my room). I mean I look so idiotically happy, and to think
how terrible everything was a couple of weeks ago and me going around afraid the world was coming to an end!

Dad is screaming for his malted milk nightcap, excuse me, I'll
be right back.

A shrill discharge of static shot through the airplane. Borodin's
startled neighbor, a jacketless man across the aisle, dropped his
plastic tumbler of gin and tonic. Forty thousand feet below,
earth slipped by at five hundred miles an hour. From overhead,

amid recessed reading lights and air valves and hidden oxygen masks, a voice rattled with the ubiquity of God himself.

"This is Captain INCOMPREHENSIBLE reminding you that while you are seated aboard our Astro-Jet Flight 734 to Hobart, South Dakota, we recommend that you STATIC."

I ought to have my head examined, here I am raving on and on and you don't even know who I'm talking about. First question: is he anyone you know? No, you've never met him. Second: would you like him? You'd love him!

Guess where I met him—in that morgue, of all places, at work! Yes, he came in to cash a check! Is he a doll? Fran, let me describe him—only you'll probably hop the next jet and grab him yourself. He's tall, has brown hair, cut medium-short but wavy, and hazel eyes and long lashes, aristocratic nose and strong chin. He stands very veddy straight, and he has a wonderful speaking voice. In fact it gives me shivers!!

The sky outside Borodin's window had gone dark and blank, and airplane and air seemed motionless. Across the aisle the windows were pink with the last radiations of a setting sun, and wisps of cumulus trailed past, hurrying in the opposite direction.

"We should be landing in Hobart in about SILENCE. You should be able to see the lights of Butte, Montana, those of you seated on the right side of the plane. It'll be night by the time we're over the Wapsinicon, but I'll point it out to you, those of you who are interested in geography."

Fran, I could have died when I saw this guy amble into the bank. I mean my eyes were really popping out of my head, and he has a really cute walk, hard to describe, but distinctive. So he asked how he could cash a check. He was leaning over the desk. I could smell his after-shave lotion!

Of course I didn't hear a word he was saying, his voice was so damned sexy. It still gives me shivers! I just looked straight at him and nodded. He has the whitest, straightest teeth I've ever seen in a human mouth!

Lights blinked like squadrons of fireflies in the port window. Borodin suspected they were the street lights of some minor American metropolis, but because their square geometry filled the windows entirely he had a queasy impression that the plane's horizon had tilted at right angles to the earth's.

Incidentally, I was wearing your white dress, this being a special day, with the sash I mentioned to you, and some of Mom's perfume (the stuff her brother sent her from Europe, the one who's in the Army.) He said I smelled like Christmas, which I thought was cute of him. He took me to lunch, the drugstore, and we sat in a booth. He ordered a really excellent spiced knackwurst on rye—and I ate two of them!

He read my palm, told me there had been tragic losses in my life in the last year, that my father did no traveling and there was a younger person about whom I felt serious concerns. I was amazed! He said some nice things about the future and a few other things I won't tell you about (take a guess!!) I just couldn't keep my eyes off him, Fran, and I still can't believe he's interested in ditsy little me! But is he ever—oh boy! I practically had to pry him loose with a crowbar after the third "goodnight"! Anyway, wish me luck!

Much love and kisses,
Darcie

Borodin watched an old woman two seats forward nibble a candy bar and turn the pages of a plastic-encased magazine, untroubled by questions of gravity or direction. Peanut crumbs speckled her lace collar.

In the starboard window, Ursa Majoris hung steady.

Later, Borodin felt rumblings beneath, wheels banging into position.

The plane sliced down through layers of wind, cloud and rain, and jolted against a water-slicked runway. Jets reversed and the plane skipped forward, walls quaking, like a stone across a pond. Blankets, briefcases, umbrellas rained from the overhead rack. A woman screamed. Lights within the cabin flashed pleas, NO SMOKING; FASTEN SEAT BELT.

Outside, weather-drenched workers waved flag code; lights at the edge of the runway blinked cipher. A mechanic ducked, head tucked beneath forearm, and ran. The air terminal, a squat spider of glass and prestressed concrete, moved toward them.

At the front of the cabin, a stewardess in red plastic, shining as though she had showered in it, enunciated into a microphone, drowning the upper partials of the jet. "Welcome to Hobart. Temperatures are in the mid-eighties. We look forward to having you with us again soon."

Borodin smiled at her as he passed. Her dress crackled as her thighs shifted. "G'by now," she said. Her knees were tan, and Borodin could see she had been taking advantage of the airline's underbooked Caribbean flights. He reflected that he had not been in the sun for twelve years.

He hurried down the portable stairway and across the no man's land of wind-harried rain into the terminal. He surveyed the half-dozen raincoated men and women who stood dripping at the gate. As planned, there was no one to meet him.

He bore left past vending machines and toilets, through slow-moving flows of nuns and soldiers. Near him, a silent man stripped a candy bar naked and devoured it in quick chews; a studious woman centered her reflection in the coinbox of a telephone and checked make-up and hair spray.

"Flight six thirty-seven," an electronic voice called sadly, urgently.

He noted that there were almost no neckties; few jackets; aside from wedding rings and wrist watches, little jewelry. There were no smiles. Faces betrayed anxious concentration. Feet hurried; a few ran.

A recorded bell bonged the hour and rained harmonics down on the voyagers.

A skycap helped him get his bags aboard the bus. The driver asked for two dollars. The eight travelers already seated had settled into frowns and boredom, and they watched with indifference as Borodin moved down the aisle to the very last seat. He sat in the corner, where no one could read over his shoulder.

REF. "FLYPAPER" (Z–145–6–239) DOCUMENT 107 AT-
TACHED. UNDERWOOD PORTABLE ELECTRIC
TYPEWRITER, 1971 MODEL. TOP SECRET.

Excelsior Springs, Wednesday May 31

Dear Darcie,

It's wonderful to hear that you're fitting in so well at your new
job and that you enjoy your work there. I hope you'll keep doing a good job, as I'm sure you are.

I don't mean to sound disgustingly maternal, but a few things
in your last letter bothered me.

The bus eased out from the curb and into the congestion of
cars fleeing the airport. Rain spattered the windows and roof
with staccato nonchalance. Borodin peered between drops and
could make out the three-foot blue neon letters girdling the
terminal. HOBART AIRPORT. Men and women clustered beneath
the letters, as though their light were protection from wind and
wet.

If you feel a mad crush coming on, don't plunge right into it.
Hold back a little. I'd try to let the friendship aspect of things
develop a little before taking any drastic steps. And forgetting to
come home and fix your Dad's dinner is a drastic step, I think
you'll agree—under the circumstances.

I'm sorry if I sound like an old maid schoolmarm, and I hope
I don't, too much. Of course you can keep the dress. Alter it
any way you'd like to—make a bikini out of it if you want!
Hotcha!

Love to your father and brother.

Love and kisses,
Fran

The rain had waxed the night to a high sheen, and Borodin
could not make out demarcations between countryside and town.
The bus drew to a stop before a neon-scarred hulk that the
driver announced to be the Hobart Manor House. Six passengers
rose to get off.

REF. "FLYPAPER" (Z–145–6–239) DOCUMENT 110 AT-
TACHED. OLIVETTI LETTERA 44 PORTABLE TYPE-
WRITER, 1961 MODEL. "E" UNALIGNED. TOP SECRET.

Whitefalls, Thursday June 1

Honestly Fran,

If you don't mean to sound like an old maid then my advice
is stop trying to! You act as though I'm an idiot or something. I
was surprised and that's hardly the word to get your letter this
morning. You seem to forget:

1) I happen to have had one or two dates with men before
and I do know how to take care of myself, thank you.

2) Dad's dinner not being cooked was as much Bobby's fault
as mine. Anyway it hasn't happened again. Next time why don't
you write Bobby and lecture him?

I'm sorry if this sounds angry, but that's a polite word for the
way I feel. I think you're a wonderful person and a wonderful
friend, and in a lot of ways I respect you more than I do anyone
else, but I do think a lot of the time (a lot more than you're
aware) you misjudge people. You ought to be sure of your facts
before you rush ahead with accusations. You might hurt someone's feelings.

Such as mine.

Darcie

Borodin tried to get some idea of Hobart as the headlights
scooped arcs of concrete and store window out of the dark. He
made out a movie theater, its marquee lights dead; a window
of mannequins in janitor's overalls; a bronze man on a matching nag, tethered to the center of a traffic circle.

REF. "FLYPAPER" (Z–145–6–239) DOCUMENT 114 AT-
TACHED. UNDERWOOD PORTABLE ELECTRIC
TYPEWRITER, 1971 MODEL. TOP SECRET.

Excelsior Springs, Sunday June 4

Dearest Darce,

Forgive me. I didn't mean to upset you, but I was worried,

and after your last two letters I'm even more worried. You don't need to act defensively with me, Darce, I am your friend and you can trust me. Above all there is no need to justify yourself to me. On the other hand, as a friend, I feel I owe it to you to warn you when I think you are getting yourself into trouble.

I think your attitude toward other people and toward your responsibilities is becoming casual. Please, Darcie, I implore you, stop now. You could get yourself into serious trouble, especially now while you're still upset (whether you know it or not) over your mother's death. Why don't you stop seeing this person for a while? I think you'll feel a lot better.

All I want, Darcie, above everything else, is your happiness. I pray for you every night. And I know, if you'll just have faith in yourself, and be worthy of yourself, and deserving of your mother and father's love for you, you'll have a wonderful happy life and you'll make some very lucky man a wonderful happy wife.

Do take care of yourself, Darce. Love,

Fran

The drive gave as little idea of terrain as a night flight. Blinder-like banks of earth rose high on either side of the road, and beyond them could have lain pastures, wheat fields, forest, desolation. The tires hummed a steady whine on the seamless asphalt, and the windshield wipers ticked a slow, unsymmetrical beat.

REF. "FLYPAPER" (Z–145–6–239) DOCUMENT 117 ATTACHED. OLIVETTI LETTERA 44 PORTABLE TYPEWRITER, 1961 MODEL. "E" UNALIGNED. TOP SECRET.

Whitefalls, Wednesday June 7

Dear Fran,

I can see there's no point writing you anything more until you cool down a little.

Incidentally, I am in love and having a wonderful time.

When you can control your petty jealousies a little better, I'll tell you about it.

Get well soon.

Sincerely,
Darcie

An occasional blast of wind rocked the bus. They had come two miles, without the road's so much as turning.

REF. "FLYPAPER" (Z–145–6–239) DOCUMENT 119 AT-TACHED. UNDERWOOD PORTABLE ELECTRIC TYPEWRITER, 1971 MODEL. TOP SECRET.

Excelsior Springs, Friday June 9

Dear Darcie,
      That was uncalled for. I think you owe me an apology.

Fran

Borodin counted four cars that they had passed, all coming from the opposite direction.

REF. "FLYPAPER" (Z–145–6–239) DOCUMENT 120 AT-TACHED. OLIVETTI LETTERA 44 PORTABLE TYPE-WRITER, 1961 MODEL. "E" "T" "R" "I" UNALIGNED. TOP SECRET.

Whitefalls, Monday June 11

Fran:
      Am returning dress. Thanks for everything.

D. Sybert

The Pruninghook Arms dated from the turn of the century, when Whitefalls' sulphurous springs had been thought to be health-giving and the town had enjoyed two decades as a fashionable spa. Wars and years had changed all that, and though the hotel still stood, three stories of once-proud gingerbread, its beams had abandoned the pretense of straight lines and right angles and settled into unabashed sags and bends.

Passing close to a pillar, avoiding the overflow of the drain that belched crazily down its side, Borodin saw by the light of the lobby door that the building needed paint. Patches of exposed wood, ten inches square and gray as overcooked beef, had overrun a good 20 per cent of the surface. Presumably, since there were no indications of steps being taken to arrest or contain them, they would spread, and Borodin could foresee a not far-off day when the ceiling above him, the underbelly of a second-story porch, would be cancered beyond salvation.

He felt anger.

He could not in the dark estimate the size of the hotel. He had the impression that wings and additions rambled off deep into the night, that like the dinosaur, the Pruninghook had miscalculated history and overextended itself. Certainly the hotel was understaffed: the visible night help consisted of a solitary soul, a chubby old rustic who limped to the screen door, took two of the suitcases, and left the third for Borodin to carry himself.

"Awful weather," the man commented. His accent seemed stagy, but television dialects had for some years now been taking the edge off Borodin's ear.

The engine of the bus growled away into the rain. Puddles formed at Borodin's feet. He trailed the old man across worn straw rugs and observed, at the desk, that of the rows and rows of boxes, only five were lacking keys.

Borodin filled out his registration form. Carrying two of his bags now—the old man had picked up the lightest and limped briskly to the stairs—he followed to the third story, to the end of a corridor that endlessly readjusted its direction. Along the way the old man switched on lights, and low-watt electric bulbs established small areas of illumination. The shadows that fell between were more ghostly than the dark they replaced. The rain became louder, and not all the lights worked.

The old man tapped a door with a key, and obediently it opened. "You'll be happy here," he said.

Borodin noted an old-fashioned, no-dial telephone on the table between beds; a television set in the heavy style of early

Cold War; enough shelves, tables, and chairs to house in their crannies an entire plague of bugs.

The man waited.

One eye, like a jeweler's, was shut to the size of a pin, and it was this eye that Borodin felt was watching him, even when the other made a broad display of scanning wallpaper. "Bathroom in there."

"Thank you."

"Closet in there."

Borodin sensed that the man wanted a conversation: whether because, like old prospectors, he was mad from solitude, or because he had his reasons, Borodin could not be certain and was not at this hour curious. It had been a long flight, and his body was still on eastern daylight saving time.

"Room service stops at midnight, more or less. After midnight I'm room service. Anything you need?"

The fourth and fifth fingers were missing from the man's left hand.

"Sleep," Borodin said.

"Can't help you there. That's between you and your conscience."

"We're both tired."

"Yup," the old man said. "It's late in the day all right."

Borodin gave him a quarter and with a firm palm to the elbow eased him from the room. He locked his door, tried the handle and found that the lock held. He stood for a moment listening to the clicks of lights going out down the hallway, and then he washed for bed.

*

A gas main had exploded beneath Avenue Q, rupturing a water main, and the District of Columbia police had cordoned off five city blocks. The President's limousine had to make a detour to reach the hotel, and reached it late. The presidential party—Lucky Bill, his wife, and six stocky men whose tuxes all showed noticeably enlarged hearts—made their way from the east ballroom entrance through the already seated guests up to the prefabricated dais. Applause, like the tearing of a garment seam, preceded them along their path.

Party loyalists rose and snowballed the applause into a standing ovation.

"Hello, hello . . . hello," the First Lady said to the right of her, to the left of her. A step behind she heard her husband saying, "Hello, hello . . . hello."

The First Lady wore a dress the nation had never seen on her before, a black silk full-length gown that combined the prevailing chic with a suggestion of mourning. She wore no jewelry at all, not even a wrist watch.

The President wore an ordinary tuxedo, one of six, freshly cleaned and pressed.

The party mounted by six carpeted steps to the head table. It had been arranged in the open layout of the Last Supper, all seats facing forward and three sides unoccupied, save for the microphones that bloomed plentiful as flowers. The two center seats were empty.

The President and his Lady, smiling as the klieg light hit them, suddenly looked very pleased that their dinner companions had saved them places, and they sat—as the beautifully hand-lettered place cards directed—between their very good friends, Vice-President Howard J. Tyson and his wife Maggie.

There came a spattering of flashbulbs from the rear of the banquet hall.

The guards, who had already dined on beefsteak, took seats on wooden chairs near the rear of the dais, at a six-foot remove from the head table, and never once did their frowns stray from the backs of the President and the First Lady.

Maggie Tyson leaned forward, circumventing the President so as to land a kiss on the First Lady's right cheek. "Moni, honey," she cooed, "I love your dress. I've been meaning to talk to you about CBS."

The First Lady removed her napkin from its ring and smoothed it onto her lap. "What about CBS?"

"They want to do a TV thing, just a half hour—"

"I'd rather not, Maggie."

Mild astonishment flashed across Maggie Tyson's face. "Just five minutes of Lexie, some very run-of-the-mill questions and answers."

"I'm sorry, Maggie, I don't think this is the right time."

Maggie Tyson swallowed and studied the program that had been placed beside her plate. The order of events was to be Welcoming Address, by the President's special adviser on national security affairs, Nahum Bismarck; shrimp cocktail; Greetings to our Friends, by Senate Majority Leader Daniel Bulfinch; tournedos Rossini, rice pilaff, and green salad; Remarks, by the year's Nobel laureate in medicine; a Word, from the President himself; chocolate ice cream; and a Valedictory by the new president of Howard University.

It was in the thick of rice pilaff that Maggie Tyson again leaned toward the First Lady. "Now look, Moni, this is not a police state, don't you think the public at least has the right to—"

"The public does not have a right to my daughter."

"The public has a right to be informed. Why, they're sick with worry about that girl, and until they see her on color TV how do they know the news reports aren't faked, how do they know the photos aren't doctored?"

The First Lady stared at Maggie Tyson and wondered at her persistence. "How do we know about anything?"

"Exactly my point, which is why Lexie has got to go on TV."

The President reached an arm into the conversation and snared a breadstick. "Are you two girls arguing again?"

"Just a friendly chat," Maggie Tyson said, "about a little matter."

The First Lady sighed. "Bill, will you please tell Maggie *no* for me?"

The President smiled. "No, Maggie. Now will one of you tell me what's this all about?"

"It's very simple." Maggie gestured with a piece of Ry-Krisp. "The head of the CBS news department, the new man, he's a dear, he has an open slot seven-thirty next Thursday. . . ."

Seeing that her husband had set his smile on automatic, the

First Lady tuned out and thought of Virginia meadows and her daughter's first pony. Salad and remarks drifted by, and the President rose and delivered his word, which was a half-page speech prepared by Nahum Bismarck; and it wasn't till after chocolate ice cream and Valedictory and farewells that an incident brought the First Lady back to here and now.

As she and the President and their Secret Service guard left the hotel through an inconspicuous side entrance marked DE-LIVERIES ONLY, a mob of well-wishers rushed them. The First Lady lost a shoe.

Years later, that shoe turned up for sale in a Manhattan autograph shop.

That night the First Lady returned home holding her husband's hand. Observers noted that, as the First Couple emerged from their obsidian limousine, Lucky Bill paused under the south portico to kiss Moni on the forehead, on the cheek, on the neck. Somewhere in the night a shooting star fell and beyond the steel picket fence a flashbulb went off. The President's right arm clasped his Lady's waist. Her head rested on his shoulder, and its gleaming auburn hung on him like an extraordinary Napoleonic decoration.

Lucky Bill led Moni into the White House.

June 27: Tuesday

Borodin paid less attention now to the sheriff's chattering in his ear. He looked about, thinking.

He had always remembered the squares of small towns as places green and shady, cool in the summer and somehow private, as if by concensus the public left those patches of grass and path to the tall old trees and rain-streaked statues. And so they had done in Whitefalls, except that there was only one statue and the trees were ragged and sun-blistered and the grass had been braised to a bright brown. The store fronts wore more than their share of FOR SALE signs, and the diagonally parked cars were powdered in dust.

The soil was good, Borodin could see that by the weeds leaping up the legs of empty benches; dirt to grow corn in, to grow rich on, crawling with fish bait. Birds had the freedom of the square as though the town fathers had decreed it a sanctuary, and a chirping like a thousand transistor radios gone berserk rained down from the parched leaves. Dust swirled in the uneasy, burning breeze.

At the edge of the square, a few feet from a drinking fountain whose spout trickled sulphur, stood a huge, idle bulldozer.

"What's that for?" Borodin pointed.

"We're putting in a new fountain; gotta keep up with the times." The sheriff flipped the remark out with a little laugh, as though they both knew how silly it was to keep up with such crazy times. But there, nonetheless, stood the bulldozer.

"Doesn't the old fountain work?"

"Sure, it *works*, but the damned thing's an eyesore."

In the shadow of the bulldozer stood a coin-operated newspaper rack. Beneath the plastic and wire mesh of the window, the last copy of that day's Hobart *Times and Sentinel* bannered, POP SINGER SAYS LEXIE DESERVED IT.

On that page were two photographs, one of Jupitra Gorr, the singer, off-the-shoulders strapless and sequin-slinky; beside her a Karsh of Ottawa study of the First Lady and her daughter, Madonna and child-like. A little further on down the same page was another headline, MAGGIE T. REPLIES NOT SO.

Borodin found fifteen cents in his pocket, a Roosevelt dime and a buffalo nickel from the days when newspapers cost two Lincoln pennies, both coins so old it made him reflective to hold them, regretful to spend them on a thing so foolish as the news.

And then it occurred to him, on the edge of that town square, that he was going to die. It came at him without warning, as though he had stepped into a room with no floor. For an instant he was dizzy and falling and there was nothing to grab hold of, and then the feeling passed, and there were trees and the sheriff was ahead of him, a big, tomato-faced man in blue jeans.

The wind was tickling the treetops as winds do and the birds were singing those endless melismas and there was nothing macabre in the fresh air or sunlight. And then he saw the man in a dark suit sitting on a park bench twenty yards away.

The man was feeding a bit of candy bar to a squirrel but there was something willed, unnatural about it, something odd in the way he was not looking at Borodin, as though six seconds earlier he had been staring at him. The man wore a necktie, and no one in Whitefalls wore a necktie; and he was sitting on a park bench in the middle of the morning like an old man with nothing to do but wait for the social security check.

And why shouldn't he be there, Borodin asked himself; *why shouldn't there be agents in a town where someone just tried to kill the President?*

Borodin began walking again, very slowly. He bought the paper; rolled it under his arm; and hastened to catch up with the sheriff, still chattering, who had never realized his listener had fallen behind.

"There's some idea going around that Bill Luckinbill's a good man. Now how the hell, I'd like to know, do ideas like that get started? Why once—you won't believe this—but once Bill Luckinbill let his own dog die. Locked the poor old mutt in a cellar without food or water. You could hear the howling for three days. Long time ago. We were kids. But the kid is father to the man."

Borodin tried to look interested, but chiefly he wondered why the man hated Luckinbill. "Any idea why he did it?"

"Teach the dog a lesson. You know the way Lucky Bill is—always teaching other people lessons. And if the pupil dies, too damned bad."

"You're not too fond of him."

"Any reason why anyone in this town should be? He used Whitefalls for a steppingstone, left us right down in the mud, and now he's in the White House and does he even think of a highway appropriation for his old home town?"

"What kind of mud is Whitefalls in?"

"We're broke."

"And is it Lucky Bill's fault?"

"He could help and he isn't helping. The man's got cheek to come jetting back here with that tacky memorial wreath. Let him do his electioneering somewhere else. He doesn't need Whitefalls, and Whitefalls doesn't need him."

"I see you have a statue to Lucky Bill in the town square."

"That was when we were hoping; thought we'd start seeing some of that federal money. There's a lot more to Lucky Bill than the public knows. He cheated on his high school exams. He got a girl into trouble, I won't say who, but it's common knowledge. He had a job at Abner Seastrom's Mobil Oil station and he lifted fifty dollars from the till. Of course that was all a long time ago, but leopards don't change their spots that I know of. Whitefalls could've told a lot during the last election, but we only told the good part. When it came to the bad we kept our mouths shut. Thought we'd start seeing some of that federal money."

"And aren't you seeing any?"

"Sure, with binoculars you can see to Hobart. Hobart's got a new airport. What was wrong with the old one, I'd like to know?"

"I wouldn't be able to tell you."

"I guess I'm kind of running off at the mouth, aren't I? You want to know about that damned letter. Well, the way I see it, we're both on the same team, working to make Whitefalls a better place to live. So if there's anything I can do to help—anyone I can introduce you to, anyone I can fill you in on—anything I can tell you. . . ." The offer trailed off.

"Matter of fact," Borodin said.

"Shoot." The sheriff's smile hung in suspension.

"Did Hiram Quinn ever mention a girl called Darcie Sybert?"

The reply was cautious. "Nope. Don't think so."

"Do you know her?"

"Works down at the bank, doesn't she? Nice kid. Good kid." A finger snapped in air and sent motes reeling. "Hold it. Her brother Willard was killed in the war. Just a year or so back. And a few months ago her mother died, yeah, her mother got run over. Enough to break your heart. She's a good kid. She tie in with any of this?"

Borodin's reply was measured, testing. "I'm not sure. Quinn intercepted some of her letters. I assume someone monitored her phone too."

"Could be, could be. Now the mail stuff is handled right here in town. You can go down to the post office and talk to Miss Esther Ganaway, sweetest old gal you could hope to find. As for the phone business, that's all handled over in Hobart. Seems we're not big enough in Whitefalls to have our own exchange. Now the man you'd talk to there—oh, I could find out for you. Only . . ." The sheriff smiled. "You said you're just handling mail, aren't you?"

"That's right. Just mail."

*

"It's good to have you with us, Mr. Borodin; and just in time. It's been chaos since Mr. Quinn . . . you know."

"I know," Borodin said sympathetically.

They spoke at the stamp window, voices lowered as though in church. The walls around them hung heavy with international parcel post rates, FBI ten-most-wanted flyers, posters warning that it was a federal offense to assault a postal employee while on duty. The tiers of post boxes, stacked floor to ceiling, stared glassily like the dead eye of a monster fly. A housewife with a baby riding her hip stood at the registry window filling out forms.

"You might as well come on in back, Mr. Borodin." There was humor in the long, memorizing glance of her money-green eyes. She wore her hair in a neat gray bun, and she smelled discreetly of lavender. "We can talk a little easier."

The old woman vanished from the stamp window. An instant later a door marked EMPLOYEES ONLY swung open, and she stood, barely taller than a leprechaun's grandmother, beckoning. Borodin followed the finger.

"Have you kept Mr. Quinn's old intercept lists?" he asked.

Miss Ganaway went to a frail-looking wall safe, and Borodin stood a polite distance away while she fiddled with three dials. She brought him a manila folder of dated, stapled lists.

"Are you married, Mr. Borodin? Not to pry, but I see you're wearing that ring."

Borodin scanned the lists. "I used to be."

"Widowed?"

"Separated."

"Too much of that nowadays."

"I see Darcie Sybert has been on these lists from the beginning."

"Oh yes, indeed, we're always stopping Darcie's mail. Does that girl get letters—writes 'em too!"

"Do you know her?"

"I know her to say hello to. Everyone in town knows Darcie to say hello. She works down at the bank—always smiling and a good word for everybody. Sweet child. Lost her mother a few months ago, and her brother was killed last year. Sad family. The father's in a wheelchair. Still, she's always smiling."

Borodin nodded as though he knew all this.

"Well, you'll be wanting privacy." Miss Ganaway unlocked another door and nudged it open. "Mr. Quinn used to work in here. That's his lamp. Pretty thing, isn't it?"

For furniture, there were crates shoved against the wall, a desk, a stool, and the tiny metal lamp. The room was no larger than a solitary prison cell.

"Pretty," Borodin agreed.

Miss Ganaway handed him a key. "You don't have to lock the door, but Mr. Quinn always did. Sometimes the key sticks, so just jiggle the handle."

She touched the desk and studied her finger for dust.

"We get the incoming mail twice a day, morning and afternoon. It all comes through Hobart now. Mr. Quinn used to pitch right in with the fellows and help sort it, and he'd just put the stuff he wanted to one side, and that way there wasn't too much of a delay."

"I'll do the same."

"That's very kind of you, Mr. Borodin, and we do appreciate it. Folks in Whitefalls are anxious to help their government, but they do get testy if their mail's held up." Miss Ganaway went to the window and let the shade up with a snap. "I'll leave you to your work, Mr. Borodin. If there's anything you need, just holler."

"Thank you."

With a flustered little curtsy she left, closing the door behind her.

The beauty of the infra-red opener was that it left the glue undisturbed on the flap, and all it took to reseal was another lick—no messy, giveaway added mucilage.

Of the 146 envelopes set aside for his consideration, 37 were ads. He ignored these for the moment and studied a note from Harriet Funk to her sister Margaret, wondering (a) what to do about the mortgage and (b) whether to come to Whitefalls for a visit. Though his camera was pre-loaded, he decided not to photograph Harriet's letter.

The ads offered an assortment of magazines, medicines, and

clarinets; he wet a forefinger and found their ink unsmudgeable. He pondered for a moment a *Sports Illustrated* circular addressed to Harry Sybert, then opened a letter addressed, in block printing, to Mrs. Maggie Tyson, care of the White House, Washington, D.C. There was no return address.

Dear Maggie,

Hi, It's me again! If you will allow me to call you Maggie. You are fast becoming my favorite public personality. And I have to confess something. We did not vote for you in the last election, but now I wish there would be a special election to give you a vote of confidence, so that you would know we are 100 per cent behind you.

It is my opinion, and Larry (my husband's) too that there would be a bloodbath if we were to pull precipitously out of Latin America, and you are absolutely right to stand up to those, minorities or not, who preach abortive capitulation. Stick to your guns, Maggie, and stand firm not only to the enemy but to those trouble-makers within who give aid and comfort to the enemy.

If only the quiet ones would raise their voices they would drown out the trouble-makers and let the enemy know we are, have been, and ever will be a united people.

Your friend
Tammy Dufay, remember me? Watson Lane, Whitefalls, S.D.

p.s. Maggie, seriously, if you are ever in this part of the nation *do* stop by for as long as you like—no trouble, honest. Doubtless you could use a rest and that's one thing we've got plenty of!

Borodin photographed the letter, returned it to its envelope, and sealed it. He glanced toward the window.

From across an alley other windows stared back at him, black and blind. Occasional heels click-clacked on pavement and cars moved and braked, unhurried and unseen. The alley was no more than ten yards deep, wide enough for a mail truck; empty. A patch of elm shade fell against the cinderblock wall.

He debated whether to pull the shade, knew that he ought to, decided what the hell, the day was too pretty to blot out. His fingers hesitated at another letter, this one with the return address WHITE HOUSE.

The White House, 1600 Pennsylvania Avenue, Washington, D.C.

Mr. Bart Masters, 4012 Cottonwood Avenue, Whitefalls, S.D.

Your support in our pursuit of peace in the troubled lands of Asia and Latin America means a good deal to me. Although the vast volume of mail that is pouring into my office makes it impossible for me to send you a personal reply, I do want you to know how very pleased I was to hear from you and how very much I appreciate your thoughtful concern for the country.

William J. Luckinbill

The President's signature had been cleverly printed to resemble the scratches of a fountain pen. Borodin photographed the letter and returned it to the envelope.

There remained 123 letters. He did not get out of the post office till after five. The day was already tinged the early pink of evening, and his eyes were weary.

He strolled the town of Whitefalls, nodding to people as though he knew them, for he had the sort of face that at first glance looked familiar. He did not admit to himself that he was strolling with any purpose or to any particular place, but in a while he found himself among the graves.

The cemetery overlooked the town from its hill of oak and elm. Little mausoleums and mini-obelisks rose along a stream and among the plainer, almost deferential gravestones. It was a free-enterprise cemetery, where people had been allowed to put up the monuments they wanted, and the result was the busiest spot in Whitefalls.

Borodin pondered the anarchy of death. His shoes were

deadened of all sound in the thick brown grave grass. It smelled sweet from a fresh mowing. He felt a curious lethargy, a peace steal over him. He had not been in a cemetery since his mother had been buried. The droning of insects lulled him and recalled those boyhood afternoons when time hung suspended like a bee on warm air.

He moved uphill, tracing the stream. A marker made him pause. It was a statue, barely three feet tall, of a woman holding an open book, but since she stood on a pedestal her eyes were on a level with his own. He read the dates and counted the almost fresh daffodils placed on the grave, and he let his eyes drift back to the inscription, THE LORD IS HER SHEPHERD.

She stared not at her book or at Borodin, but into the distance, at the roving weathervane on the County Court House. She had the face of so many of the local women, a look Borodin had recognized even beneath the beehive hair and make-up: stone.

Further upstream he came to another marker, a winged figure holding a stone sword. He had seen this face before also, on soldiers at airports. WHENCE ALL BUT THEY HAD FLED, the inscription declared. He knelt as though laying a wreath, then turned and looked back over his shoulder.

The sight line to the steeple was unobstructed.

Borodin spotted a tall man standing among the tombstones, looking except for the denim blue of his work clothes like a statue himself. His hands and face were the texture of a baseball mitt, he stood almost six and a half feet tall, and he wore a cowboy hat. He was pulling at a rake.

"Hi," Borodin said, and the man leaned on his rake and nodded.

"Help you?"

"Looking for a grave. Where do I find Natalie Sybert, she died a few months back?"

The sky was without wrinkle or movement, and a coolness rose from the stream and out of the tree shade as though an icebox door had been left ajar. Somewhere a car backfired, and a loose axle bumped dirt in an easy-going rhythm.

"You're almost standing on her." The man pointed past a nearby scaled-down Cleopatra's Needle. The rake began moving again and caught up a scrap of scarlet, a ribbon from an old memorial bouquet. The man looked tired, seventy-some. Borodin smiled a thank-you-kindly and walked on.

It was a fine American evening. A robin repeated three notes over and over, as though practicing to get them just right. The smell of living leaf hovered on the air and branches rustled at the touch of breeze. Somewhere down in the town a radio or television set was singing with the soft voice of a woman.

Borodin found the grave in the shade of a boxwood bush. The stone was laid almost flush with the earth, barely rising above acorns and scorched grass; it gave her full name, date of birth, date of death. It said less than a coroner's report.

So: she had existed, she had died. That much of it was real.

He looked at the town, at the view they had given her, and he wondered if the others were real too, if there were Darcies and ministers and old men named Harry Sybert living their lives of diet desperation down there.

It's not my business, he reminded himself. But still he could not help looking.

Stone houses and red brick and white wood frame; tall trees moving to let the winds pass; a silent church steeple. A little beyond he could see the interstate highway that bypassed the town, rushing on to the airport, to the shopping centers and movie theaters that lay hundreds of miles away.

It occurred to him at that moment that he must make a good target standing there on the hill, that anyone with a rifle and a telescopic sight could pick him off from one of the second story windows or the church tower or even from a moving car. It occurred to him too that it didn't make a great deal of difference in the scheme of things whether someone picked him off or not. A money-order thief in Abelard, Kansas, would go uncaught and some mail would go uncatalogued but not much else would be changed and the net change would hardly be for the worse.

He stood still and began counting to ten: *one . . . two . . .*

A lot of men had died in the service of the Agency and gone

on to fame of a sort. Dying in a cause at least had an edge over living without one. And hadn't the Agency sent him here to draw fire?

Far in the distance a television tower rose, beaming quiz shows and soap operas and news reports to keep people indoors, to protect them from sun and breeze and all things living. In the nearer distance branches stirred.

From the church tower, a man with a government badge watched.

Six . . .

To the north ran an arc of farmland, furrowed into corduroy lights and darks. Tractors moved across them, silent and slow, small and red as ladybugs. Borodin saw them plow the far horizon and wondered what the farmers were thinking on this warm, unhurried evening: how did wars and riots and threats to the President mix in their calculations with the price of fertilizer?

He realized he had counted to twelve.

He came down the north side of the hill of graves. Workmen had pressed tar and cracked rock onto a dirt road and given it a veneer of twentieth century, but the tar caught at his heels and came loose with little smacks and the sweet, gummy smell reminded him of long ago, perhaps of a time before he was born.

He passed a road sign: WELCOME TO WHITEFALLS, SOUTH DAKOTA. POPULATION 4000 CHEERFUL PEOPLE, PLUS A FEW GROUCHES. BIRTHPLACE OF LUCKY BILL LUCKINBILL AND CRADLE OF THE NEW AMERICAN REVOLUTION.

The doomed bravado of that hope struck him sadly, like a World War I song or a World War II promise. Yet it was no blinder than dreams he had once permitted himself. He wondered why old, discarded notions, like bravery and enterprise, were floating back into his head. Something to do with the smell of trees, perhaps. He felt he might have walked this very road before, paused at the wood frame gabled house, set foot on the very same porch.

He hesitated; wondered about exceeding his mandate; and then a gaudy piece of jetsam, red white and blue and labeled *initiative,* came bobbing into his brain; and he decided what-the-hell.

The boards echoed hollowly as he walked to the screen door. Through the copper mesh he could see a bead curtain strung across the hall entry, a frosted glass ball clinging to the ceiling light, a deep inviting sofa, a lace doily on the TV. The house smelled of attic and old comforts. He thought he could hear ice tinkling, a breeze fussing with a bamboo harp. Someone was singing along with the radio. He knocked on the door.

*

"I got one son left," the old man said, "and there used to be five people in this house, Mr. Borodin. We were a family. We had our ups and downs, but we were a family. Now I've got one son and he mows lawns. And that's seasonal work, you can't count on it. So I ask you. And now they want us to worry about some assassination that didn't even come off!"

The hairline towered high, jagged and wild; the eyes could have been cracked into the skull with two blows of a pickax, and shock lines radiated from them deep across brow and jowl.

He made a harumphing noise. "I've thought about that shooting, Mr. Borodin; we've all thought about it in Whitefalls. Tell you something. First I said to myself, too bad the President didn't get killed. I'm angry at that man. On account of my boy Willard. Willard got killed last year fighting in Costa Rica."

"I'm sorry you lost a son," Borodin said.

"Lost him, hell. The government grabbed him; Costa Ricans put a bullet in him; and the President wrote a thank-you note.

"That was what ticked me off: the thank-you note. He kills Willard, then he writes a thank-you note. Oh, it was Willard's fault too. Willard didn't have to go. No one has to obey the President. We're just afraid not to. We forget he's an ordinary little man like anyone else, a Whitefalls boy who made good. Only he's got a worse temper. And an army."

Harry Sybert's wheelchair squeaked as he angled for softer light on the half profile.

"And I'll tell you something else. I grew up in a brewery

town, and my father was killed striking against the beer people. Government soldiers shot him. So what the hell am I supposed to care that some President's daughter got bruised by a bullet?"

The chairs appeared to be from a hundred attics and rummage sales. They were oddly placed, more a barricade than an arrangement; and Borodin suspected they were covering holes in the rug. He wondered with some astonishment whether this room had all happened since Natalie died.

"And what does the rest of your family think of the shooting?"

"The rest of my family?" The old man smiled a sour pickle of a smile. "The composition of this household has changed radically over the last year. Bobby, the little one, he finishes junior high this year. You can ask him yourself. He's fifteen. Good marks. Takes an interest in current events, God knows why, they're God-awful nowadays."

Some booted thing somewhere in the hallway kicked baseboard, and a slouchy, blue-jeaned boy passed the doorway: hair long to the collar, mustache and whiskers beginning to sprout. He raised a hand and waved to the old man.

"Hey, Bobby," Harry Sybert called. "There's a man here wants to talk to you."

The boy squinted at the visitor. "I have to go to the dentist."

"This time of day? You just come here and say hello."

"I'm late." The boy aimed another squint at the visitor, then vanished. A screen door gave a sleazy tin slam.

"Kids," the old man muttered.

"Perhaps," Borodin said, "I could ask your daughter some questions."

"Yeah, I'd like to ask her some questions too."

"What time does she get home?"

"Mr. Borodin, you just asked the sixty-four-dollar question. I don't know when the hell she's getting back, and frankly I've just about stopped caring."

"Is she working late this evening?"

"I don't know where the hell she is. She could be shacked up or married by now. She was carrying on some kind of affair I guess you call it. Never met the fellow. But she did try to buy pills. Amos Johnson, down at the drugstore, he couldn't wait to tell the whole town. Darcie tried to buy pills. When a girl tries to buy pills and forgets her Dad's Ovaltine, and stays out till all hours, you know as well as me. She never tells me anything any more. Just packed a bag and kissed me good-by. Nope, she didn't kiss me good-by. Left a note saying my breakfast was in the icebox. Cold Wheatena."

"She just vanished?"

"You might say."

"What day was this?"

"I can tell you exactly when she went. She was acting strange, all worried about the President and his parade."

"The President?"

"It was the very next morning. She went the morning after someone tried to shoot the President. Haven't had a phone call or a postcard or a how-d'you-do from her since."

*

Borodin stood in a vacant lot thinking so hard it amounted to talking to himself.

. . . *I am about to do something very unkosher, very risky and downright suicidal if I value my pension. I am a mail-snoop, mandated to intercept and open anywhere from ten to seven hundred pieces of mail a day, authorized to use my judgment in deciding which pieces to photograph and which to let pass unmolested. I am in no way, repeat in no way, authorized or mandated to mingle with, talk to, peep at, or eavesdrop on people. People are someone else's job, mine's mail* . . .

Borodin toed a clump of crab grass.

. . . *I could be pensionless, I could be jobless, I could be out on my ass if the Agency found out about this, but I have a sneaky feeling I'm about to mingle with, talk to, peep at, and eavesdrop on people* . . .

Borodin took three steps across the vacant lot.

Right from the start Hiram Quinn had focused on Darcie. What had made him so certain?

Borodin had reached a position midway between the Syberts' tumble-down, two-story house and the fresh-painted spire of church that burst like a behemoth tendril from tall, manicured hedges.

. . . *In this town we've had a note threatening the President's life, a near-assassination of the President's daughter, the murder of the mail-snoop who preceded me, and the disappearance of the number one target of his investigation.*

It seemed to Borodin that the matter merited, at the very least, a little inquiry. As he neared the hedge he heard a snipping sound, and when he stepped through a rift in the boxwood he saw a man in clerical collar working over a rosebush with what appeared to be a pair of nail scissors.

"Reverend Oscar Jannings?"

The man peered at Borodin over the rims of his sunglasses. "Yes indeed, what can I do for you, friend?"

"Perhaps you can help me."

*

"Is something the matter?" The First Lady was surprised to find the nurse in the hallway, pacing outside Lexie's door. "Where's Lexie?"

"She's in there, ma'am."

"Why aren't you with her?"

"The television men said my uniform was too bright."

"Television men?" The First Lady gripped the door handle and threw the door open. The room had been lit to a searchlight glare, and it took her eyes a moment to make out the tripod, the cameraman and the sound man, the two men in dark suits, and Maggie Tyson hovering over the girl on the bed.

The sound man glanced up from the tape recorder. "Joe, I told you to watch the damned door," and then a tone of recognition crept into his voice and he rose meekly. "Mrs. Luckinbill. Excuse me."

"Hi, Mom." Lexie's teeth and eyes shone as though they had stored up energy from the sun. "I'm going to be on TV! This is Mr. Evans, and this—"

The First Lady crossed to Maggie Tyson.

"Moni, I want you to meet Mel Elliott." Maggie Tyson was wearing her hostess smile. "He's in charge of documentaries for CBS."

"Get these people out of here."

"Now, Moni, Lexie's loving it."

"I said get them out."

"Moni, be reasonable."

"I'm trying to be."

Maggie Tyson looked at the First Lady, saw something that made her back off. "Mel, can I talk to you for a moment? We've got a snag."

Mel Elliott and Maggie Tyson scurried into the hallway, and the other men and the equipment began scurrying out after them. The First Lady stroked loose curls away from her daughter's forehead.

"I'm sorry, Lexie."

"Don't get angry, Mom. Maggie was just trying to help."

The First Lady began crying softly.

"Mom, don't cry. They didn't bother me, honest." Lexie hugged her mother. "Please don't cry."

*

"Perhaps," Borodin said, "you can help me."

The minister pushed his sunglasses up his nose and smiled as though helping strangers were quite in the line of duty.

"I'm looking for a neighbor of yours. Darcie Sybert."

"Yes indeed. Darcie Sybert lives right over there in that house. Just knock on the door."

"I tried. She's not at home."

A breeze blew, and the whole town smelled sweetly of cut grass.

"Then she's still at the bank. She works at the bank, right down on Main Street. You can walk it."

"Her father hasn't seen her for a week."

The minister frowned. "A week? That's odd. Why I saw

Darcie just last—matter of fact, it *was* a week ago. Has she gone somewhere?"

"I was hoping you might be able to tell me."

"No, afraid not." He was a cheerful fossil with thinning gray hair and veins protruding at the temples. His almost-blue eyes changed color like the sea as they watched Borodin.

"Her father says she hasn't phoned or written."

The minister shook his head. "Poor Darcie, I hope she's not. . . ."

"Hope she's not what?"

"A girl her age . . . so many girls her age. . . . I just hope she's all right."

"You say you saw her a week ago: that would be after the shooting?"

"Yes, we spoke for about two minutes. Why?"

"Darcie Sybert could be in trouble, and you may have been one of the last who saw her before she vanished."

"Vanished, now isn't that a little dramatic? Darcie Sybert is capable of a lot of things, but vanishing is not one of them. Could I ask what your connection with her is?"

"No connection, Reverend. I'd just like to talk to her."

If he had bitten into a blueberry pie and found castor oil the minister could not have looked more dubious. "In that case, when I see her I'll tell her you were asking for her, Mr.—"

"Borodin. I'm staying at the Pruninghook Arms, should be there for a while. I'd be very grateful, Reverend." He nodded a good-by and had gotten as far as the rift in the hedge when the minister called him back.

"Oh, Mr. Borodin—I just happened to think of something. Could you come inside for a minute?"

Borodin made a point of looking at his watch before allowing that he could spare a minute.

The minister held the door, and Borodin followed him along a damp-smelling corridor, past almost-shut doors through which he could half glimpse darknesses of varying opacity, into a study, high and raftered, buttressed with shelves of bound *National Geographics*. The stained glass of the window softened the dregs of evening light to a dull purple. The leather and wicker of the furniture were cracked, and one of the lamps was missing a light bulb and a shade. The cups and saucers balanced on table edges and arms of chairs suggested that a tea party had been in progress for the last week.

"Tea?" the minister offered.

"No thanks."

"My suspicion, my honest suspicion, would be that Darcie just had to get away from it all for a while." The minister blew cinnamon crumbs off a book, forced it into a gap on a shelf. "Darcie has had an exceptionally hard time. I don't know if you know, but she lost her older brother in the Costa Rican campaign, and her mother died this year, and there've been a good many pressures on her. She was tired. Run-down. Needed a rest."

"But you don't have any idea where she might have gone for this rest?"

The minister moved an empty teacup from an empty chair, gestured Borodin to sit. "No, if she's not with her friend in Missouri I have no idea at all. But I do think, wherever she is, she'd appreciate being left alone."

"What makes you think that?"

"While she gets her strength back. 'I will lift mine eyes unto the hills, whence cometh my strength.' I believe Darcie has gone to the hills." The minister looked around his study with dim concern, as though he had just sniffed the burning tobacco of a mislaid pipe.

"She told you she needed her strength back?"

"Not in so many words. But her family life isn't happy and, frankly, I believe she was having romantic problems. Girls her age, you know."

"She talked to you about her romantic problems?"

"We talked about a million things."

"What things?"

"Oh, cabbages and kings. Oil wells, Karl Marx, Tarot. Anything and everything under the sun."

"That much?"

"Yes indeed. Darcie has a very inquiring, eager mind. It's a pity she couldn't have gone on to university." The minister stared at his fingertips, then played piano on his trouser leg.

"What did she have to say about Karl Marx?"

"The usual. She was very unhappy about the turn of events in Latin America and Asia."

"Did she talk much about the brother, the one that died in Costa Rica?"

"I had the feeling that Willard's death was too terrible a loss for Darcie to confront consciously." The minister's eyes were somewhere else, for just a moment. "It aroused feelings of enormous hostility and enormous impotence in her. There was no one she could blame—or rather, there were people she could have blamed, but no way of touching them."

"Who could she have blamed?"

"Oh, the system, the Communists, the Costa Ricans, the Army. . . ."

"The President?" Borodin suggested.

The minister blinked. His eyes had turned the color of tea with too much milk splashed into it. "Obviously, as commander-in-chief of our armed forces, the President was in some way responsible for Willard's death. On the other hand, Darcie admired President Luckinbill—as I think all men of good will must. He's taken some courageous stands. Singlehandedly he's opposing that rider to the gun-control bill. That sort of stand takes tremendous principle, tremendous guts. Of course, you hear stories about him in Whitefalls. . . ."

The minister's voice trailed off as though he had turned to the wrong page of the prayer book and was mentally leafing for the right one.

"What kind of stories?"

"Typical amalgams of small-town gossip and all-too-human envy. It's a difficult thing for Whitefalls to accept—a local boy making good, making that good. On the one hand the town is proud, on the other hand people who knew Bill Luckinbill feel they're just as good and could have done just as well given the same chances. There are even people who go so far as to say Bill Luckinbill was crooked."

"Did Darcie ever say he was crooked?"

"Oh no, not Darcie." The dying sun was playing tag with the stained glass, and the minister's face went an abrupt cherubic pink. He shifted out of the light. "It's only the old-timers, the ones who knew him, who claim they knew him, who talk like that. They all have stories: the day Lucky Bill stole apples from Jay Coots's orchard, the time Lucky Bill pilfered a nickel candy bar from Johnson's drugstore, the time he went skinny-dipping with Hank Watson's girl—gossip four decades old, staler than last week's bread. It's innocent, mostly. As innocent as envy ever is."

"What kind of things did Darcie say about Luckinbill?"

"I don't remember her ever speaking strongly about him one way or the other." The minister added in a flat voice, "Of course she was horrified at Congress's mutilation of gun control."

"Horrified?"

"She's in favor of gun control, naturally, but when it comes to repealing entire articles of the Constitution, she's as outraged as any decent American could be."

"And how did she react to the shooting?"

"She came to me shaking, barely coherent. It was as though the bullet had struck her."

"And then she disappeared?"

The minister looked Borodin over curiously. "You're from the government, I take it?"

"In a way. Federal Security Agency." Borodin showed his ID.

"And you think Darcie had something to do with that shooting."

"At the moment I have no opinion."

"Is she in trouble?"

"Possibly."

"Is there any way I can help?"

"Darcie was under investigation in connection with a threat note sent to the President. Someone attempted to shoot the President. Someone succeeded in shooting the agent who was investigating Darcie. And now Darcie's gone. You tell me if you can help."

"This agent—the man who was shot—what was his name?"

"Hiram Quinn."

The minister cocked his head one way and another, as though catching echoes of something.

"You knew him?"

"Not exactly." The denial fell with a more than rhetorical thump into the silence, and the minister's features bunched into a frown. "Darcie came to me the morning after the shooting. She told me she had to join her lover. She was being taken to him by a woman. That's all she said: a woman knew where he was and she was going to take Darcie to him. I never saw this woman, so I can't describe her. I tried to find out where they were going, but either Darcie didn't know or she wasn't saying. That was odd and very unlike her. But what was odder still, she left something with me for safekeeping. I believe it's a microfilm negative. You have to admit it's very odd she'd have microfilm in her possession."

"Maybe it's not that odd."

"Would it help you—would you care to look at it?"

"I'd care to very much."

*

Borodin took the steps to the hotel two at a time. The funny old room clerk gave him the eye. "Bags all packed, Mr. Borodin."

Three bruised suitcases were stacked by the desk, and on second glance Borodin saw that they were his own.

"Go right on up. Your door's unlocked."

The door was indeed unlocked, and Borodin was out of breath, and the man waiting in his room wore a Humphrey Bogart fedora and pinstripes to match.

"Late," he said, as if this accusation in some way explained his presence and the revolver that he held in one hand, almost casually, aimed at Borodin's heart. He clicked the safety off. "You're to report back to Washington. We're holding a plane." He had the voice of a mustard-gas victim.

Borodin studied the face, as mass-produced and vicious as the gun. "When am I to report back?"

"Ten minutes ago. Your bags are ready."

The closet door was open. Borodin saw that the man had not packed his suits, that his sports jacket and blazer had been reversed.

"Can I take a leak?"

"Afraid not. We're late." The man gestured with the gun as though it were a spatula and Borodin a piece of bacon sticking to the pan.

"You're not going to shoot me in a hotel. Article 117, Agents' Rules of Conduct, Clause 4. There's no silencer on that cap pistol. Besides, we're on the same team, aren't we?"

"I don't know what team you're on, buddy." The man backed into the wall, and his body language gave him away. Borodin smelled bluff.

"Why don't you think about it." Borodin scooped up a pamphlet that the hotel had placed that day on the bedside table, a guide to the month's events in the Greater Wapsinicon River basin area. He opened it to a listing of the movies in Hobart and with a flying flop he landed on the bed.

It was a foolhardy thing for him to have done. He had not considered the full implications of the open closet door. He heard something, a whisper that could have been a voiceless angel or simply a cloth sleeve brushing the door frame, and before he could turn the blackjack caught him, slightly off-center, on the back of the head.

He saw six-pointed stars, and he wondered who had set off the bomb in the barrel of sheriff's badges.

"There's been one development, but it's not exactly mail. Except in a way it might be. Do you remember the Sybert girl?"

They sat at the steel table in the concrete cube. Lumi wore a look of elegant preoccupation, shuffled papers in elaborate permutations, shot dots and dashes of smile at Borodin.

"That's quite all right," she allowed. "You can submit those details in your written report. There's been a development on our side, too; the picture has changed. Thanks to your work, and the work of several others, the picture has changed considerably."

"Thanks to my work?"

"The picture has changed."

"Can you tell me in what way?"

"We can only say that you've worked hard and well, and the Agency feels you deserve a little rest and recuperation." Erikka Lumi's skin had the moist glisten of a ripe, open honeydew. Her tongue made little tracks on her lower lip. "Do you like the Virgin Islands?"

"I like the Virgin Islands, but I like them better after the job's done."

"Your part of the job is done." She leaned forward in her chair. "Is something the matter with your head?"

"I bumped into one of my escorts."

Her eyebrows flinched. "Have you had a doctor look at it?"

"That's all right, the swelling's going down."

She snapped open an ivory-inlaid cigarette box, laying bare beds of parallel king-sized filter tips. "Smoke?"

"No thanks."

She gestured to the bottles sitting on a tray. "Drink?"

"What the hell. Vodka and anything."

"Root beer?"

"Terrific."

"You know, you should be happy."

"I'll be happy when I get over the surprise."

"You were working on a part of the puzzle." She prized the cap off a root-beer bottle. Carbonation hissed. "Other men— agents you know nothing about—have supplied the other pieces."

"I had the feeling my piece was still missing."

"There are several ways of completing a picture." She offered the completed drink. "Let me know if that's too strong."

"No, that's perfect. Health."

"Cheers. And this, by the way, is a little something from the Agency." She placed it on the table: an envelope with a cello- phane window.

He did not bother to pick it up to see how large a check they had given him. "Isn't it a little early for Christmas?"

"In this instance we feel Christmas is just about due. You don't have to be back for three weeks."

"Do I have to go to the Virgin Islands?"

"You can go anywhere you want. We happen to have space on a troop plane to the Islands, and we do have a nice rest and recuperation center there."

"I know it sounds dumb, but I've always wanted to see the Grand Canyon."

"Then go see it by all means. I'm sure we have a transport heading out Colorado way."

"Not on your life. I'm going to rent me a little car." He slipped the pay envelope into his jacket.

"If we can be of any help," Lumi said.

"I only wish I had been of some help."

"You've done a most creditable job."

On his third sip Borodin realized how ridiculously strong his drink was. "What about the written report?"

"No rush. Do it when you get back."

*

INTER-OFFICE MEMORANDUM. LUMI TO JUDD.
COMMENTS ON CONVERSATION, JUNE 28, WITH
AGENT FRANK BORODIN. TOP SECRET.

I must confess, with some confusion and no little chagrin, to administrative misjudgment in having assigned an agent of Frank Borodin's outmoded qualifications to a task as fraught with submerged, subtle, and elusive ambiguities as OPERA-TION FLYPAPER. Not only has the agent demonstrated himself incapable of the simplest sort of mail monitoring, he has also proved reluctant to work within the guidelines which the Agency has set him.

Reports of agents Hadley and Costello indicate, and follow-up investigation has confirmed, that Borodin on at least two occasions compromised the secrecy of his mission by directly approaching and conversing with subjects under mail investigation.

I have recalled and interviewed Borodin. I cannot emphasize strongly enough that I favor all possible haste in the removal of this increasingly unreliable neurotic. The cost of delay could well prove prohibitive.

LUMI

*

Borodin had left the microfilm at a little photography shop on Avenue Q. The print was waiting for him at 2 P.M. It consisted of one typewritten letter.

Saturday, June 17

Dear Fran,

This is one of the hardest letters I've ever had to write in my life. You were right, right about so much, and I should have known but I guess I was too proud. Well they say pride goes before a you-know-what, and I have got what I guess I was asking for.

Hiram has been acting strange for the last few days, very short-tempered, always criticizing me, my clothes, the way I talk and

even my table manners when we were having lunch at the Red
Spot (a new place that opened up downtown.) I swear, Fran,
I was eating a cheeseburger and picked it up in my fingers and
he said when a cheeseburger is that thick you use a knife and
fork!

Well can you believe it, we had an argument right then and
there and I guess I said things and he said things neither of us
really meant, and I said "If that's the way you feel we might as
well call it off," and he said "Fine by me"!! Well I couldn't believe it and I had to go to the ladies' room and have a bawl and
let it all out.

When I came back, Fran, he was drinking with a strange man,
straight bourbons! I said, "Don't let me interrupt," and he said,
"This is my old friend Andy," (or someone) and the man said,
"Don't you believe him, the name is Fred (or something) and
we just met," and I felt so humiliated that Hiram was pretending to run into old friends just to keep me at a distance!
As though two old friends would ever bump into each other in
Whitefalls anyway unless they'd both been born here. So I
guess he thinks I'm really stupid and maybe he's right come
to think of it.

So I decided two could play that game and maybe I shouldn't
have but I kind of flirted with this Andy person—older, very
tan, sort of reminded me of those men in cigarette ads—and I
let him buy me a drink. Just to make Hiram jealous. Well Hiram
walked out!

Well appearances can certainly be deceptive, because the worst
part is that Andy (the guy with the tan) asked me to come
back to his hotel room and Fran, I saw how far I had sunk if
men think I'm that kind of girl, and I thought of Mom and I
just broke into tears. And Andy shrugged and walked out and I
had to pay for the drinks—three dollars and sixty cents plus tip!

Needless to say Hiram did not answer when I telephoned and
he has not phoned me at home and I am feeling just miserable,
down and fed up with life and fed up with men and wondering
why I ever let Hiram touch me or what I saw in him.

Fran, don't leave me now, please write me or maybe I could come out there for a visit. I am going to be nice to Dad who after all cannot help it if he is immobilized.

Please write to me Fran and forgive me for all the terrible things I wrote and did, they were inexcusable. Your friend (I hope),

Darcie

*

Borodin was waiting for her when she emerged from her office. She saw him and blinked. She had put on a dark jacket and pulled her hair back from her face, exposing high cheekbones and soft, almost translucent ears.

"Something else?" she asked.

"Let's have coffee."

"I only have a minute."

They went to the agents' cafeteria and Borodin brought two regular coffees to the table. Except for an old man motionless at a corner table and the counter attendant, they were alone.

"I thought you'd be on your way to the Virgin Islands by now." Dr. Lumi sipped her coffee, and Borodin could see she didn't like it.

"Grand Canyon."

"Well, some place far from this God-awful city. I envy you those two weeks."

"Three. I know you're busy, but there's something bothering me."

Her eyes narrowed. They were a very pale blue, like a reflection of sky in ice water.

"Something happened to a girl out there," Borodin said. "Darcie Sybert."

Dr. Lumi shifted in her chair, showing him a three-quarter profile. "Sybert?"

"She was Hiram Quinn's chief intercept. She was also having an affair with him."

Dr. Lumi stubbed out a cigarette barely half inhaled. "She's nonetheless completely tangential to the case. Much as I admired Hiram Quinn, I'm afraid he was beginning to see code and conspiracy in simple-minded schoolgirl notes. He drank."

"I learned about the drinking."

"Do you habitually exceed your mandate?"

"He was also met by an old friend called Andy or Fred before he was shot."

"You seem to have wandered far from your mail room."

"Is that why I was hit over the head and rewarded with a three-week paid vacation?"

"You've been rewarded because we're pleased with the results of Operation Flypaper."

"What results?"

"You can hardly expect me to divulge that."

"No, I can hardly expect that."

The blue eyes blazed coldly. "Did you pay for the coffee? I meant it to be my treat. Well, next time." Dr. Lumi rose and held out a hand that seemed curiously and perfectly sculpted of white stone.

"You seem in an awful rush not to hear about Darcie Sybert."

"I thought you'd finished."

"My head's a little slow since it got bumped."

"It's looking much better than it did this morning." She slipped back into her chair. "What about this Sybert girl?"

"She vanished. Left a crippled father and a kid brother."

"This is all very sad, but Operation Flypaper is closed."

"Operation Flypaper may be closed, but it's got a hangnail. Hiram Quinn was concerned with her, and I thought we were concerned with Hiram Quinn. If someone snatched the girl it's because she knows something."

"You're working awfully hard to complicate this."

"Apologies. It happens to be my job."

"All right. I'll look into the Sybert girl. Now why don't you go look into the Grand Canyon?"

"It's a deal. I'll send you a postcard."

She rose again, turned, and was gone. Borodin sat and sipped

his coffee to the bottom of the cup, staring at the chair she
had sat in.

*

"What did Hiram Quinn tell you about me?" The Havana
blinked a bloodshot red as the words came spitting through the
ember.

"She can't hear you," Erikka Lumi said.

"Give her another injection."

"The first injection has to wear off."

"We haven't got all year and we've got to know what she
knows and whether she told anyone else."

"There's enough pentathol in her to stun an elephant. Just
leave her alone and come have a drink. She'll come around in
an hour or so."

"Bring her around now." The hunting boots edged nearer
the bed.

"It's too dangerous."

"I'll give her the injection myself, and that's even more
dangerous."

Erikka Lumi's fingers, uncharacteristically, fumbled the syringe. "Her heart can't take this."

"Her heart doesn't have to take much more. All we need is
an answer."

Erikka Lumi pressed the needle tip down into the vein, where
bruises and punctures had made an ugly tattoo the shape of
spilled coffee. The girl did not react.

"She's out," Erikka Lumi stated.

The windburned face knotted like a fist about to strike. "Give
her more."

"If I give her more she'll be fully conscious."

"I want her fully conscious."

"She holds back when she's conscious."

"She won't hold back this time."

Erikka Lumi slipped the second ampoule into the hypodermic
and injected. The girl moaned as though skimming the depth
of a nightmare. The eyelids fluttered and the arm muscle con-

tracted, almost snapping off the needle. "What are you going to do?" Erikka Lumi asked.

"Some old-fashioned remedies."

"I won't have you striking her. Not hard."

"I want a paring knife and some matches and some cuticle scissors."

"What for?"

"You do have cuticle scissors, don't you?"

Erikka Lumi went to the kitchen for the matches and the paring knife. The knife still had parsnip skin on the blade and she had to rewash it by hand. She got the cuticle scissors from the bathroom. They were an old pair, but she rarely used them and they were still sharp.

"You don't have to stay. I'd rather you didn't."

"I don't want you striking her," Erikka Lumi said. "Not hard."

"Does it look as though I'm going to strike her?"

The girl's eyes opened, but Erikka Lumi could not bear to look into them and read their gibbering pleas.

"Go into the other room, Erikka. Make yourself a drink. Make me one. I'll be right out."

Erikka Lumi went into the living room, and when the screams started she turned the television volume as high as it would go. It was not high enough and she had to go walking in the woods to get out of her mind's eye, where it stuck like a glass sliver, the picture of that poor stupid ruin of a child who had once been so soft and white and smooth and lovely.

*

The First Lady reached for the bedside telephone and pushed buttons. Soon a security officer rapped softly on the open door. She recognized the man's mustache and the way he bowed his head slightly.

"Lexie and I will be driving to my father's house in Virginia. We'll need a car and a driver and a blanket and as many men as you think advisable. Her doctor will take his own car. I'd prefer that only one guard ride with us. The rest can go separately. We'll be leaving in half an hour or so."

"Yes, Mrs. Luckinbill."

He vanished, and she pressed more buttons on the phone. The outside line hummed in the receiver, and her fingers composed the Virginia area code and her father's number. Electronic abysses separated the five rings.

The First Lady stared out the window as though for the last time. A 6 P.M. dusk was settling like copper smoke over the fountains and grassy reaches of the south lawn. The Washington Monument had turned a shadowed face to her, and the Lincoln Memorial, half lit and half dark, seemed to be sinking into the leafy haze of the three thousand Japanese cherry trees that Mrs. William Howard Taft had planted around the Tidal Basin.

"Cavanaugh residence."

The First Lady sat straight. "Is that you, Regis?"

"Why, Miss Moni, it's good to hear your voice."

"How's your back?"

"Much better, thank you, Miss Moni."

"I'm so glad. Is my father there?"

"He's in the library, Miss Moni. Just one minute."

She heard the clicks as the call transferred to another extension, and then the familiar voiceless growl of her father clearing his throat.

"Moni?" She could tell he had been smoking again, ignoring doctors' orders. "I was sitting here thinking of you."

"Father, we're coming home."

"You and Bill?"

"No, Lexie and me."

"Why, Moni, that's wonderful. When?"

"Tonight. We'll be leaving in half an hour."

"Then we can all have dinner."

"Sarah's home cooking is just what Lexie and I need." The President himself had tried to hire Sarah for the White House, but the loyal old cook had refused to abandon Colonel Cavanaugh, even when he offered a leave of absence. "Father, ask her to make popovers?"

Her father chuckled. "She'll be glad to. I suppose you'll be bringing guards and people?"

"There'll be a few extra mouths. I'm sorry."

"Don't you worry about it. How long will you and Lexie be staying?"

"I don't know. It may be longish. Would you mind?"

"Not at all, Moni. Not at all."

The bedroom door was open, and for a while the President and his warrant officer stood framed in conspirators' silhouettes against the bright fringe of hall light. Something passed between them, half whispered and half signaled. When the First Lady hung up, the President crossed the room, and the warrant officer closed the door, and the President and his wife were alone.

"Now, Moni," the President said softly.

She turned to him the blank wall of her shoulder.

"What's this about your taking Lexie?"

"Lexie should be in fresh air and sunshine." She watched him move in circles around her, clenching his thumbs white behind his back. Age and suntan darkened his handsome face.

"Lexie is safer here," he said.

The First Lady dropped into a chair. He could see the glistening track of a tear on her left cheek, as though only one eye had wept.

"She'll never get well here. This place is a prison."

He glanced up with great, sad, practiced eyes. "This place is home."

"Virginia is home. I want Lexie in Virginia."

"All right. I'll send a guard with you. How many days will you be gone?"

She huddled against the chair like a prisoner facing a firing squad. "Bill. Listen to me and understand me. Lexie and I are leaving you."

"You're not making sense."

"I'm taking Lexie to my father's for a long, long time. I want to get her away from this place. You can tell the press that she's recuperating and that I'm recuperating too. I won't be with you any more, Bill. And I won't leave Lexie here with you."

"You talk as though I posed some kind of danger to my own daughter."

"You're President. Wherever you go, there'll be bullets and reporters."

He gripped her shoulder. "For God's sake, Moni. I love you."

She dried her eyes with the back of her hand. "And your daughter? Do you love her?"

"What the hell is wrong with you? Of course I love her."

"Then let her go, Bill. And let me go with her."

The First Lady rose from the chair. The President reached a hand but did not stop her. There was concern and there was bafflement in the forward tilt of his head. "I've never seen you this way before."

"You've never looked at me."

He stared at her a moment, then kissed her on the forehead.

Thirty-five minutes later a black government Cadillac carrying an armed driver, a guard, and two passengers pulled away from the south entrance of the White House and turned in the direction of the Virginia hills.

*

"And how do you explain events such as the Whitefalls shooting?"

"My instinct, Walter, is not to explain them at all, but to abhor them. But that would get us nowhere, so I try my damnedest to make sense of these things. And, interestingly enough Walter, there is a pattern."

As his eyes focused on the woman in the TV tube, the President's features clenched into a frown.

"I think our viewing public is ready to hear about that pattern."

Her hair stockpiled like golden armaments upon her head, the wife of the Vice-President of the United States beamed a violet gaze to twenty million TV sets and met the eyes of forty million viewers in home and bars across the nation.

"We are witnessing in our time, Walter, the last act of a ferocious assault upon the very beliefs and foundations that have made America America. I know the word 'conspiracy' has become unfashionable of late, which is a pity, for to my mind there is no better way of describing the systematic undermining of morals, of religion, of marriage and family, which is today in full, unchecked progress."

The President's eye was fixed with effort on the twenty-eight-inch color TV screen recessed beneath the convex mirror on the north wall; in that screen he saw not only the woman who spoke but the gently distorted reflection of the heavy-framed painting behind his head, the Bonnard lilies that his wife had matched with silk shades on the table lamps.

"Not conspiracy in the sense that our courts define the word—though there is that element too. Conspiracy in the literal sense of the word—"

The President, stifling vague yawns, sprawled in a pink chintz chair at one end of the second-story corridor. Generations of those who had lived in the house had used the wide hallway as a sitting room, and it was here, at the western window, that he had met with his wife and daughter—when the schedule allowed—for daily tea that had come at most twice a week. The cream walls, the three-footed mahogany tables, the slip-covered chairs recalled an almost cozy living room, but the gold chandeliers and the heaping bowl of fresh flowers were reminders, like a nagging leitmotif, that the master of this house ruled all wealth and nature.

"Nahum," the President said, "that show's not live, is it?"

"No," his adviser replied. "I believe it's filmed."

"If the organism is strong," Maggie Tyson was saying, "as America was until 1933, it can fight off the attack of these viruses. But if the organism weakens—as America has fatally weakened since Eisenhower led the way to capitulation—it can no longer resist, and the viruses invade the organism in full force, which is what we are witnessing today, and take it over and ultimately use it for their own purposes. Of course, as we know from medicine, the viruses ultimately destroy the very organism they conquer, and they die with it. So theirs is, in a very real sense, a Pyrrhic victory. I pray nightly to God above that this will not be the fate of our Republic."

It was in this same comfortable corner, where one could almost forget the world outside, that the President's family had for three years gathered on Christmas day around the candle-lit tree to hear the President read *A Christmas Carol* by Charles Dickens. Lexie had been a grinning child of sixteen that first Christmas; and now she was eighteen and she was gone, and the President was two and a half years older. The gray at his temples had spread, and he had had two changes of eyeglass prescription, and his ulcer had got a little worse so that, after long nights arguing with his aides, he sometimes passed blood with his morning stools and could read Rorschachs of mortality in his toilet bowl.

"That woman," the President remarked, "would sooner die than use the word *democracy*. Why's that, Nahum?"

"It's a cult thing, nowadays," Nahum Bismarck said. "Read the magazines; read the editorials. Everyone is downgrading democracy."

"Hmmm," the President said tonelessly. "Interesting."

He ached tonight; his entire body could have been a single unhealed wound. The ache was dimmed slightly by the drink in his left hand: a mild bourbon, but his third. His assistant for national security affairs sat in the matching chintz chair beside him, within reach of voice or hand, but he nonetheless felt alone with his gold and flowers.

"It is well known," Maggie Tyson was saying, "but rarely mentioned, that a growing percentage of the heroin reaching this country originates in Communist-controlled lands."

The camera cut to the interviewer, a smallish man with a button-down smile. "It's a Communist plot then?"

The President stared at the whites of the woman's televised incisors. His brow creased. "Nahum, is she trying to torpedo the China alliance?"

His assistant shrugged.

"I frankly think," Maggie confided, "that Communism has

been a red flag distracting us from the true nature of the enemy."

"Are you saying that there are or can be 'good' Communists?"

In an L-shaped studio apartment halfway up a Manhattan high-rise, two young people huddled in the unsteady glow of a secondhand black and white TV with vertical hold problems. It was the only light in the room. The boy watched the screen; the girl watched the boy.

"First of all, Walter, I don't really know the Communists, and I don't think a great many other Americans do either."

"But you do know something of the Russians, don't you?"

"Yes, a little. Of course, many of the political and economic policies of the Soviet Union are morally repugnant to me. But Walter, I am a Christian—unfashionable as that term may be these days—and I never give up hope. I agree with the great philosopher Oswald Spengler that something good can come out of the Soviet Union—not out of Communism, but out of Russia."

The boy played with the contrast button on the set, and the girl played with the top button of her cardigan. "Jordie," she said.

"Shhh," he answered.

Her eyes went morosely in the direction of his, toward the blinking, blipping, side-slipping telecast. "That woman has got to be some kind of Fascist."

"Belinda, cook dinner."

The girl rose from her pillow on the floor, braced herself on the boy's shoulder till the circulation returned to her legs. She took four uneven steps toward the cooking closet. "Rare or medium? It's sirloin."

In the dark—for he would not tolerate room lights when the TV was on—she ran water, clanked pans, set burners to burning and frozen broccoli to thawing. She turned to shout at him, but the sight of the boy gave her pause.

"And what would you call this something that may come out of the U.S.S.R.?"

"I would call it a new awareness, Walter. A sort of ethical socialism."

He was leaning toward the TV as though toward his own mirror-image. His lips formed sounds and his tongue tip brushed his tooth tips, but he spoke with the voice of Maggie Tyson. Or rather, Belinda began to realize dimly, he shaped the words as the television uttered them, but the oddity was that he was synchronous with the machine.

"Jordie?" she whispered. She dropped a pan by accident, but he did not even blink or turn his head so much as a millimeter. She tiptoed toward him and stopped just outside the fringe of TV light. "You're saying her words."

Belinda crouched down on the cushion beside him and pressed a mothering bosom to his shoulder. "Jordie," she whispered, tongue so close she could taste the licks of unbarbered hair that clustered around his ear, "how do you know her words?"

He looked at her, and she cringed at the pity of that fierce wounded gaze.

". . . and don't forget, the Russians are a young people. We see them facing so many, many of the problems, universal human problems, that we Americans face in this country: riots, disorder, greed, disobedience, incitement, anarchy, drugs, kids, desecration of flags and institutions—I could go on forever, but I know you have a commercial coming up."

Old Colonel Cavanaugh sat sunk in a deep chair in the study, watching the weird rainbows of the television set. Regis had made a fire, unnecessary at this time of year but effective in dispelling the chills that plagued the old man's joints. The light of burning pine flickered on walls of leather bindings, and the radiation of the cathode tube flickered in his reading glasses.

He wore the glasses because he had been glancing at the book that lay spread-eagle in his lap, and because he did not like to see people like Maggie Tyson too clearly.

"We've still got a minute, Maggie, and I take it your feelings on the Lexie Luckinbill poster which has been appearing around the country are negative?"

The hairdo of the Vice-President's wife, glossy as a wet albino seal, flickered into focus. "Absolutely. Lexie Luckinbill is one of the sweetest girls I know, and how anyone could advocate harming a hair of her head. . . ."

Cavanaugh's daughter stood at the open window, taking in the soft night air and smelling the rich lawns and fertile fields beyond them. Her eyes scanned a deep blue haze harassed by ghostly bands of starlings. Her father's house stood on a hill, and she could see a good distance over the rolling land. She could see the moon's white blood on the trees, and the moist finger of a river probing a meadow; and a dark rabbit scurrying crazily toward the garden where flowers, colorless now, closed their faces to the toxic night.

Lifting her eyes, she could see a jet plane blinking lights.

Applause from an invisible audience gained behind her with the eerie rapidity of a Geiger counter in heat.

"Why do they let such creatures on television?" the old man murmured.

The First Lady did not turn. "Maggie Tyson is very popular with the public."

"She's making political hay out of Lexie. I don't like it. Lexie looked damned poorly at dinner."

"Yes."

"You look tired yourself, Moni. Can't remember when I've seen you looking so run-down. I hope you haven't got anemia."

"I don't think so."

"It's good to have you here, Moni. You'll get your health back."

"Thank you, Father. We'll talk tomorrow. I have so much to tell you; and to ask you." She came softly to his chair and kissed him on the forehead. He closed his eyes, and when he opened them again she was at the door.

Cavanaugh watched his daughter go. His hand half rose as though to delay her; his lips parted as though to let pass the word that would call her back. But the TV was too loud, and he remained silent in the depths of his chair. He watched her grow bright and then dim as she passed beneath the ceiling lamp. Her hair flared up into a brown torch, and the torch consumed itself in two steps, and he heard her shoes, soft as bare feet, on the stairboards, walking light so as not to disturb his granddaughter's sleep.

The steps faded, he could not tell at what point, and took on the camouflage of the creaks old houses all make at night.

"Maggie, you were saying some interesting things about the Russians. You were saying you'd been to Russia?"

"Yes, my husband and I stayed at the Premier's country dacha last summer."

"And what were your feelings about the Russians—I mean the people, not the system?"

It was almost quiet in the room. The fire was burning down, and the rainbow flicker of the television beat time on the walls like the breath of a living thing.

"Far be it from me to discuss politics—I'll leave that to the men. But I do think we Americans have far more in common with the Russian people than many of us realize."

Hunched in a chair in his penthouse apartment in the Westgate, the once new and still fashionable high-rise on the east bank of the Potomac, Woodrow Judd scowled at his television set and burped softly into his gin.

"We have fought beside the Russians in two world wars; we have both settled this North American continent; we have both had our problems with the selfishness and violence of petty people and petty nations. And Walter, this is my own opinion, but I sincerely believe that many, many Russians are better Americans—and I would rather have them in this country—than all the young hooligans presently shooting dope and rioting in our streets and universities and attempting to dismantle this nation. I would say, send them to Russia—except I know Russia would answer 'nyet'!"

The President heaved his frame, heavy with drink and sadness and ulcer, up from the pink chintz. "I'm sorry, Nahum. I can't watch that woman. You look at the program, will you, and tell me if she says anything?"

The President's adviser, long-faced, nodded. "Yes, Mr. President."

The President took his drink to the bedroom that he had, till this night, shared with his wife. He closed the door on the hallway and stared at the neatly turned-down double bed with its cheerful quilt. He went to the window. Marines in two's patrolled the south lawn. The floodlit Washington Monument pierced the night like a warning sword. Traffic buzzed indistinctly, merging in his ears with the rush of his own blood.

The President stood thinking awhile, then strode to his bathroom and pitched his drink down the toilet. He sat on the edge of the bathtub and lifted the red telephone receiver from its wall cradle. His fingers skimmed buttons and pushed numbers only half-consciously remembered.

It was the direct line, bypassing the White House switchboard.

"Hello?" The woman's voice that answered was as warm as he remembered, and he was lost for a moment in contemplation of it. "Hello?"

"Marion? Is that you?"

He felt a stunned silence; and then came the whisper, "Bill?"

"Can I come over?"

"Tonight?"

"Tonight." He waited and listened to blood accelerating in his veins.

"Some friends came to dinner. They should be leaving around midnight. I'll send the maid and the cook home."

"Twelve-thirty?"

"The coast should be clear by then."

"Thank you, Marion."

The President lowered the receiver to its plastic cradle, sat gazing as though giving it time to ring back and retract.

There was no retraction.

*

The President had the driver take him in an unmarked Secret Service car to Marion Holmes's Georgian brick house in suburban Kenwood. She had left a light burning in the living-room window—their old signal. He told the driver to pull around behind the garage, out of sight of the main road. The driver and the warrant officer got out a deck of cards and the President hurried up the flagstone path.

Marion opened the front door. The honey hair still curved softly around her forehead and her eyes were still that elusive, faraway blue. She took the President's hand, automatically and almost formally.

"You're looking well, Bill."

"You too, Marion."

She closed and locked the door. "I sent the guests and servants home. One of those sudden headaches of mine. Corny but effective."

She pulled and angled blinds and put a record on the stereo, and they sat at opposite ends of the living-room sofa. She asked a rush of questions, managing with the instinctive tact of a hostess to touch on nothing at all. She had heard that the White House curator wanted to restore the chairs in the Red Room: true or false? The chairman of the Ways and Means Committee was off booze by doctor's orders and had taken to pot. Malicious rumor?

"You know it's a malicious rumor," the President chuckled, "because you just made it up. Sometimes I think half the rumors in Washington get started under this roof."

Her nose crinkled in that funny little grin of hers. "Brandy?"

"Terrific."

The President watched her move across the room with the unstudied grace of a debutante. He reflected that if Marion had stayed married and had children, they would by now have been almost as old as Lexie. He wondered if she had regrets, if she ever blamed him. You couldn't tell with Marion: her surfaces were perfect, like the surfaces in the room. It was furnished in uncluttered good taste and it revealed very little about its owner, except that she wasn't afraid of deep blues and wouldn't tolerate vases of anything on the piano and she knew how to frame a Corot. She had inherited the Corot from her grandmother and the money from her father's offshore oil, and her looks came from a John Singer Sargent portrait. The President had known her twelve years, had stopped seeing her two and a half years ago, and couldn't remember what brand cigarette she smoked or how many lumps she took in her coffee. But he could remember the smell of her hair, even in dreams; especially in dreams.

Glasses and bottles tinkled and the phonograph murmured the same intricate Debussy phrase several times, as though dissatisfied with the way it sounded.

She gave him a snifter and took the cushion next to him. They laughed and gossiped about a cabinet member's wife and fell into harmless, easy banter. And then she stopped in the middle of laughing and stared at him.

"Nothing in the papers prepared me for the way you looked coming through that door. You look lousy, Bill. Haven't you been sleeping?"

"I suppose not."

"What do you really want from me?" Marion slid out of her shoes and curled her feet under her on the cushion.

"Really want? I don't know. Or maybe I don't want to know. I'm here, isn't that the important thing?"

"Is it? The mood in this room is not auld lang syne. It's more—me and my true love we'll never meet again."

"She's left me."

"Monica?"

"She took Lexie and she left."

"Does she want a divorce?"

The President moved his snifter in slow circular arcs, as though stirring oatmeal. "I'm not sure."

"Bill—we've been over and done with for almost three years. She can't be using us as an excuse."

"She's not using us as an anything."

Restless strands of Debussy filled the pause.

"Then who is it now, Bill?"

"There was never anyone but you."

"I wish I could say I believed you. I wish I could say it

mattered. But after enough time and enough disappointment things like that stop mattering. Except to women like Monica."

The President took a sip of brandy, said nothing.

"I admire her, Bill. At least she's got guts."

"She left because of Lexie."

"Lexie?"

"She left because she feels Lexie is in danger."

Marion took a deep breath. "You can't deny it, can you?"

"It's more than that though. This country is falling apart, and in some cockeyed way my marriage is falling apart with it."

"Or maybe it's the other way around."

The President's eye was on the Corot. It was one of those moody landscapes and he wondered why Marion liked it. "This country's problems have nothing to do with my problems with Moni."

Marion drew herself up ever so slightly. "Don't they?"

"Don't get paradoxical on me now, Marion."

"There's something dark in you, Bill. Sometimes it frightens me and I think it frightened Monica. You hurt people and you say it's because of the presidency. The presidency's a fact, but it's an excuse too. You've mixed everything up, politics and love and sex. Somewhere in that subconscious of yours you're still a frightened kid from Whitefalls, South Dakota. You think there's cowdung on your birth certificate and you can't believe you've made it to the top and you can't believe you're going to stay on top and you're trying so hard to keep a grip your hands are numb and you've stopped feeling."

"Psychoanalysis is cheap."

"As one who's spent half her life in it, let me tell you it's not cheap, and anyway I'm not psychoanalyzing. I'm telling you you're losing your grip and it's beginning to show. Speaking of which, I'm on my third brandy, how's yours?"

"Okay."

The President made a face, and Marion kissed him lightly on the forehead, like a mother sensing some obscure hurt in her son.

"How am I losing my grip?" he asked.

"For one thing, your wife. She just walked out on you. For

another, the mood of the country. You're in a lion cage and you've forgotten how to crack the whip. The nation's not behind you any more. Look at that Tyson woman: she's on TV every other day, whipping up hysteria. And look at you—calm and fair and reasonable and liberal—even when your daughter gets gunned down by a mob."

"She didn't get gunned down and it wasn't a mob."

"All the same you took it awfully calmly for a father."

"How the hell can I be a father? How can I be anything?"

"I know, I know. The President doesn't have time to be human."

"Don't you start picking on me too, Marion." He set his snifter down on the mahogany coffee table. "Look, maybe I shouldn't have come."

"I'm not picking on you, Bill. And I'm glad you came. It's good seeing you."

He shut his eyes. "God, Marion, everyone's screaming for authority and an iron fist and I just can't give it to them. I must have some sort of pernicious addiction to the personal freedom of others. Maybe I believe in democracy in public and private life. . . . I don't know what the hell I believe."

Marion smiled. "You're in love with her. You're in love with your wife."

"Am I?"

"The way a man gets to love an old pair of slippers or a favorite chair."

"Is that love, Marion?"

"Isn't it?"

He kissed her. She pulled away, her head tipped back, and smiled with self-knowing irony. The President kissed her again, hard and hurting and hungry. Her mouth opened to him and he pushed her down roughly onto the sofa.

Outside the curtained window, a guard lit his tenth cigarette. A car approaching the house dipped its lights.

June 29: Thursday

At twenty-three minutes after seven, after a long day's work and a long hour's drive out from Washington, Erikka Lumi let herself into the house in the woods. She sniffed the gathering darkness, flicked on lights.

Her eyes scanned the four-cushion sofa, the Mies leather-and-chrome chairs, so admirable in their simplicity. She crossed the room, beige carpet muting swift footsteps, and studied the view of the snaking forest, the early stars, and the pines tipped faint gray in the dying light. Dark birds whose name she did not know swept west in funnel-formation, whether pursuing or fleeing she could not say. Night was deepening. Quite gradually the dimness beyond the windows was sliding into blackness, bushes and trees and skies were merging into a single sheer precipice of nothing.

She smiled something foreign.

She went to the front door, eased the bolt soundlessly into place. She could see through the glass the half-bright light of a rising half melon of moon. She got the revolver from the middle desk drawer. She went to the hallway door on tiptoes. Her free hand wrenched the knob. The door was stuck.

Erikka Lumi held the gun in both hands and fired three shots at the doorknob. She yanked the door open.

"Stop where you are!" she cried.

The silence in the hallway was meek and total. She shoved aside a fallen table, stumbled to the guest-room door.

"I'm armed. Come out with your hands up."

She flicked the light switch and stood blinking painfully. A white fetal mound lay inert on the cot. As her eyes adjusted she saw that it was a pillow gnarled in damp sheet.

Erikka Lumi stared at the window, flung open so hard its panes had shattered. She sank into a chair.

After a while she rose, poured herself a drink, and went barefoot into the kitchen. She lifted the phone and dialed a number. When the receiver grunted hello, she said, "It's me."

"Something the matter?"

"They've got Darcie."

"Who's got Darcie?"

"I don't know. They broke in and took her. What shall I do?"

"Jesus Christ. When did it happen?"

"While I was at work."

"Stay there. Don't do anything."

"I'm not hurt," she said. "Not badly."

But the phone was dead.

June 30: Friday

They mounted the slow rise of hill single-file, thirty steps distant from one another, and the mid-afternoon sun projected their flickering, ill-focused shadows onto an uneven screen of three-weeks' mown hay and charred crab grass. They moved high above the creek and seemed to borrow its lack of direction or purpose.

Now and then she stopped to squint back at the patch of sports shirt moving in and out of the brambles, the khaki-sheathed leg tugging itself loose from the briars with quick jerks that sent bushes for ten feet around into convulsions.

She saw that he was not a hunter.

"Hey!" she called out to him.

She waited for him to approach.

"Look, I know you're supposed to be watching me, but that doesn't mean you have to hide in bushes or trail me by twenty paces."

"I'm sorry if I'm annoying you, but those are my orders."

She was not accustomed to voices without humor or self-knowledge, not at all certain of her own attitude toward them.

"I *know* they're your orders, all I'm saying is, since you're stuck with me and we're stuck with each other, well don't you think we might as well be friendly about it?"

The sun was blinding in her eyes, and what faced her had no more depth or detail than a shadow. Yet she believed it was smiling at her.

"Anything you say, Miss Luckinbill."

"Is there anything in that handbook that says you have to call me Miss Luckinbill?"

"No ma'am."

"My name's Lexie." She made her voice very bright and offered her hand, though it had been her experience that the
guardians of democracy were usually shocked at any demonstration of it. "It's really Alexandra, but everyone calls me Lexie, so
I wish you would."

She maneuvered southward, put the sun behind her, and was
able to see the tiny burrs dotting the fresh press of his trousers.
His cheeks were as ruddy as a child's.

"Yes ma'am." He took her hand, briefly and strongly.

"And *por favor* drop the 'ma'am.' What would you think if I
called you 'sir'?"

"You can call me anything you like."

The face that watched her was benign in a neutral way,
through a simple and possibly accidental absence of malig-
nancy.

"I'm going to call you an s.o.b. if you don't stop acting like a
zombie." She fell into the tone that magazines called playful
and vivacious and pert. "What's your name?"

"Charles Beausoleil, Junior."

"So do they call you Charles, or Beau, or Junior? Or do they
call you Soleil, like Louis Quatorze?"

"They call me Chad."

He stared at her like someone who did not know or care who
Louis Quatorze was, who did not know or care that she had
made a pun; like a boy who was too young to have learned to
cover his own curiosity and gentleness and ignorance.

"Chad, come walk beside me."

He walked beside her.

"How old are you?"

"Twenty-five next October."

She wondered whether the Secret Service had demoted her
person and being to a breaking-in ground for colts. She made her
voice very merry. "Isn't that kind of young to be guarding a big
shot like me?"

"I don't think age is a question of years."

They walked.

"Have you told all your friends that you're guarding Lexie Luckinbill's life?"

"I only have two friends and I didn't have a chance to tell them."

When he began trying to hold back and put the statutory distance between them, she held back harder, determined not to give him another glimpse of her back. "Oh, I'm not enough of a big shot to write home about?"

He chewed on something. Striations showed beneath the smooth skin where jawbone connected to skull. "Miss Luckinbill, my job is to guard your life and safety regardless of my opinions."

"You might have to die to save my life, mightn't you, regardless of your opinions?"

The dirt of the path was crisscrossed with shade, deep and scarred where pines shot up alongside, shimmering where tall grass writhed in the passing breeze. The shadows, like a flock of long-winged birds all fleeing some common terror, shot parallel tracks away from the sun, but the path played a curving hide-and-seek among them, like a creature that knew neither danger nor haste.

They walked.

"I do anything," he said, "that's part of my job."

"That would be almost flattering if you weren't such a stick."

He walked with his whole body, shoulders and arms heaving as though beneath an invisible grain sack that kept slipping to one side. His holster from time to time slapped his hip.

"I'm sorry if you find me esthetically repugnant," he said.

"You certainly have a way with the language. Where did you pick up 'esthetically repugnant'—in some cram course in gun school?"

He was silent and she wondered at the hostility that welled up out of her as naturally as her own breath.

"Well, it's a nice sunny day."

He did not deny it.

"You don't like me."

"I don't know you," he said, and this—she realized—was no denial either.

"You've been following me for two days, you ought to know something about me."

He was silent.

"This is ludicrous, I'm not asking you to die for me, I just wish you'd talk to me!"

He pouted, and he looked thick enough to stop a bullet, and the thought that at some cracking of a twig behind them he might throw her into a gully and himself on top made her vaguely uneasy.

"You can talk, can't you?"

His voice was bleached of any emotion. "I don't think it would be a very enlightening conversation."

"Because I'm dumb or because you are?"

"Because there's not very much in common."

"Bullshit, Mr. Beausoleil. We've got a hell of a lot in common."

"If you say so."

"I am not some spoiled rich kid."

"If you say so."

"I say so."

And she turned her back on him and stomped on ahead.

*

"Now you say you traced this girl to the cottage and you broke in and seized her and where have you got her now?"

Borodin told Woodrow Judd the name of the hospital.

"And were the doctors optimistic?"

"She's a bundle of rips and burns and she's been on pentathol and Methedrine for over a week."

"She's an addict?"

"Pentathol and meth are Lumi's way of interrogating."

Woodrow Judd made a face, and Borodin began explaining again how he had been perplexed by the intercepts, suspicious when Lumi recalled him and sent him on vacation; how he had put her off guard and followed her, just on a hunch.

Borodin was tired, beat; he knew he was rambling but he didn't have the energy to rein in his tongue. Woodrow Judd's face betrayed *nada*, but when he finally cut Borodin short his voice was irritable.

"Do you have any explanation for your behavior?"

"I most certainly do, sir."

"I would be curious to hear it."

"Hiram Quinn and Darcie Sybert are my explanations."

Borodin observed his master, his employer-in-chief, and he did not know what he had expected. Certainly not a short, pudgy bureaucrat with sparse gray hair slicked back to cover a silver-dollar-sized bald patch. Certainly not a pinstriped shirt with the monogram showing or manicured fingernails or the faint persistent reek of men's boutique cologne.

He had expected, he realized rather dimly in that day of realizations, someone more like his earliest memories of his father: a strong man moving swift and unafraid through shifting shadows.

The Director moved slightly. His shirt rippled like aspic and his chair let out a mouse squeak. "That's not much of an explanation."

"Do you know about Hiram Quinn and Darcie Sybert?"

"What should I know?" The Director's teeth showed, well-tended for their age, but slightly uneven in color and length. His incisors betrayed the dark stains of the midday wine drinker.

"Darcie Sybert, from what little I can piece together, is the pivotal figure in Operation Flypaper. She may be the only figure in it. A fantastic amount of the mail Hiram Quinn intercepted was letters to and from and concerning this girl."

"Why did Quinn focus so much attention on her?"

"If you want my opinion, Hiram Quinn just picked her out of a hat. The important thing is he opened her letters and he was having an affair with her, and that's warrant enough for Dr. Erikka Lumi to kidnap the girl."

The black marble clock on the gray marble mantelpiece had the basso tick of a grandfather clock, and from time to time it uttered the deep bongs of a church bell. It seemed impossible that so much noise could come out of such a little thing.

The Director's green eyes were carefully noncommittal. His

eyebrows flexed like two caterpillars testing their strength against one another. "In other words you're accusing Dr. Lumi?"

The scalding afternoon sun simmered through lengths of fine lace that hung, incongruous as a bridal veil on a prize-fighter, on the steel-webbed windows. The office was large and long and cool, paneled in ivory wood. A beige rug spread its pale blue-leafed design over the linoleum. Silvery-gold brocade shimmered on four chairs, backed against the farthest wall, where Borodin doubted anyone had ever had the audacity to sit. The bookshelves gleamed with leather bindings that someone's hand had polished to a mahogany sheen. Jonquils bloomed from a turquoise vase set on a sideboard, and there was something restlessly floral in the smell of the room.

"I'm accusing her of kidnaping that girl and acting without the knowledge or authorization of her superiors."

"The same as you?"

"The same as me."

Faint traces of scarlet rose on Woodrow Judd's cheek, like invisible ink warmed over. "Dr. Lumi has only one superior."

"I'm still accusing her."

The Director's eyes turned the color of gravel. "Dr. Erikka Lumi occupies a high and trusted position in this organization. She has occupied it with distinction for eighteen years."

"I'm still accusing her." It came to Borodin with the gradual impact of a headache that his superior-in-chief did not believe him, did not want to believe him. He realized his shirt was rumpled and his shoes were unshined and he felt Woodrow Judd realize it too.

"Perhaps Dr. Lumi should have a chance to answer your accusations."

Borodin nodded. "I'd like to hear those answers."

The Director lifted his decorator-green telephone intercom and dialed three digits. He cradled the receiver between chin and breast, his fingers occupied with pencil and paper, and spoke a mild command.

Three minutes later a uniformed arm swung the office door

open. Dr. Erikka Lumi, barracuda-sleek in an unadorned dark dress, circled lazily into the office.

The Director greeted her. "You know agent Frank Borodin?"

Dr. Erikka Lumi looked mildly surprised at the question. "Of course."

"Please have a seat." The Director gestured.

Dr. Lumi sat in an armchair.

The Director spoke with evident reluctance, relinquishing words only after thoroughly tasting them. "Is the name Darcie Sybert familiar to you?"

"Naturally." Supple and smooth in the highbacked chair, she impressed Borodin with her willful calm, but only because he sensed its utter falsity. He studied it as he would a tarpaulin pulled taut, seeking out hints as to what lay concealed beneath.

"Could you tell us in what connection she is known to you?" the Director asked.

"I believe the question of Darcie Sybert is amply covered in my reports." Dr. Lumi's ice-blue eyes floated in sleepless pockets, and Borodin noticed the hint of a bruised cheekbone, powdered over.

"I'm asking for Frank Borodin's benefit, Doctor; not mine. He claims you have withheld information from me. Please give us the gist of those reports as briefly as possible."

"I see." Dr. Erikka Lumi settled back into the chair in the bored, subtly insecure attitude of a knife-thrower's partner posing for target. "Darcie Sybert is a pivotal figure in Operation Flypaper. Close to thirty per cent of all mail intercepts made by Agent Hiram Quinn were focused on Darcie Sybert, her family, and her immediate circle of friends and acquaintances."

Borodin dug his eyes into her.

"Why," the Director asked, "did Agent Hiram Quinn focus so much attention on this particular girl?"

"It is still not clear to the Agency why Hiram Quinn devoted so much of his investigation to the Sybert girl."

"Was Miss Sybert kidnaped and interned at your cottage in Maryland?"

Dr. Lumi's eyes widened, depthless beneath their trapdoor irises. "No."

"Was Miss Sybert ever in your cottage?"

The doctor's face darkened and angled downward as though to throw an involuntary tic into unrecognizable foreshortening. "Never."

The Director's cheeks puffed, and pent-up air whistled from them. He turned to Borodin, eyes damped to the color of smoldering moss. "Do you have any questions?"

"Why did Dr. Lumi have Darcie Sybert's fingernails pulled?"

Dr. Erikka Lumi straightened in her chair. Something akin to anger flared in her cheeks.

Silence. Tick-tock.

"Do you have any other questions, Mr. Borodin?" the Director asked.

Borodin watched Dr. Lumi's hands grip the armrests. Her knuckles stood out in white relief.

"Thank you, Doctor." The Director rose from his chair. "And apologies."

Dr. Erikka Lumi rose with a rustle and with a good-by nod moved across the beige carpet. The uniformed arm opened the door to her and a gentle, emphatic snap of the latch shut her out.

Borodin and the Director sat and listened to the clock tick. Borodin was careful to meet the man's gaze when from time to time it landed on him.

"You and Dr. Lumi," the Director observed, "appear to disagree."

The overhead fluorescent lights had been extinguished. Above the desk and table lamps with their milky, diffusing bulbs, a vague and unseasonal twilight thickened.

"You joined the Agency in New York City, didn't you, Borodin?"

"Yes."

"And while in New York you handled a breaking, entering, and installation at the residence of the Ukrainian Mission to the United Nations?"

"I was one of two men on that job."

The Director's face drooped as though weary of battling gravity. "You were subsequently sent to Wichita, Kansas?"

"Yes."

"And had a little trouble there?"

"I can explain."

The Director's eyelashes flicked as though staving off sleep. "And subsequently Salt Lake City—trouble; Bangor, Maine—trouble; Butte, Montana—trouble." The Director flipped loose pages in a thick manila folder. "Norman, Oklahoma—misunderstanding; Francine, Nebraska—incompatibility with superiors."

"You've got all the trouble on file. What about some of the achievements? I've had one or two."

The Director's tongue passed along his lower lip and left a visible glistening trail. He gave a fatigued nod. His hand rose to scratch his barbered neck and, falling, lay watch face up on the spotless blotter. "I see you've been with us twenty-two years."

"Almost twenty-three."

"That's a lot of years."

Borodin met his superior's eyes. Neither looked away for a long moment. And then Borodin found himself wondering how the windows could focus Washington so sharply, like high-resolution lenses.

"Let me tell you something, Borodin. You were pulled out of pasture and put on Operation Flypaper as an experiment. We hoped that a man of your 'admittedly outmoded qualifications' might show the type of persistence and doggedness this case required. That's what it says here, Borodin. *Outmoded.*" The Director held up a piece of paper. By the light of the window the reversed Agency letterhead showed through it. "You've been outmoded a long time now. Since that Ukrainian job. You've gone through just about all the pasture land we've got."

They were silent.

"What are we going to do with you, Borodin? Set up a rest home?"

"The Agency is my life," Borodin said dully.

"The Agency is touched to hear it."

"I'm ready to work. Anytime, anywhere." Loneliness filled Borodin and overflowed him.

"Flypaper was your chance to make a comeback. Why did you screw it up?"

"Flypaper doesn't hang together. It's phony."

The Director pressed a button. The office door opened and a very large man stepped in. He was half a head taller than Borodin, and his face had the pummeled look of unfinished clay sculpture. The Director nodded.

"You can have him."

The tall man placed a grip on Borodin that was, for the moment, gentle, and lifted and aimed him toward the door. He did not object when Borodin turned one last time to the man behind the teakwood desk.

"Flypaper is phony, sir. And this agency is going to strangle in it."

The Director sniffed as though something unpleasant had grazed his nostril. "I said take him."

"Where to, Mr. Judd?" the large man asked in a kindly voice.

"The back door."

*

"Ten minutes I had to sit there with Woodrow Judd and that paranoid agent. Do you know, in a senile way, I think Judd's attracted to me? His eyes were on my breasts. Thank God I have good breasts."

"Yes, thank God."

"Not that there was ever any real danger. The way he kept looking at my breasts, I could see he wasn't suspicious."

The light from the window was so strong, the green of the leaves so blinding, that Erikka could see only her listener's black, featureless silhouette, the wisping smoke that rose from time to time in snorts. She paced the perimeter of the living-room rug, wondering whether it was a mercy or not that she could not see the expression on that face.

"It's a shame they have the girl. A shame, Erikka."

Erikka wanted to be kissed. It was a physical craving that ached in her joints and parched her mouth and made her hands tingle. She could barely keep pacing.

"They're bound to check her story. And her story will lead to you. And you will lead. . . ."

"But Judd has questioned me. He believes me."

"Erikka, Erikka, who can say what he believes? I'm afraid all this has raised more questions in his stupid old mind than it has settled."

"I tell you he was looking at my breasts. Fascinated. I know the man. He's a textbook neurotic."

"These are pretty flowers. Did you pick them or buy them? What kind are they? I don't recognize the smell." The silhouette lit a fresh cigar, blew a jet of smoke through the red tip. The room reeked richly of moist brown Havana.

"Would you like cinnamon toast?" Erikka asked.

"Why would I like cinnamon toast?"

"It's no trouble. I can make some in two minutes."

"I've always liked this ash tray. It's volcanic, isn't it?"

Erikka shifted her pacing to a diagonal. "Judd's behavior—and achievement—is a classically perfect realization of the neurotic drive. He's built an organization that is in every respect intellectually and physically superior to the society which it nominally serves and protects. Which is not to say, mind you, that it is morally superior. Really, cinnamon toast would be no trouble."

"Maybe some coffee."

Some women have only to lower their eyes, and men will cross a room to kiss them. Erikka Lumi knew she did not possess this engaging faculty. She did not get kissed unless she placed her lips within kissing range, and even then a fear of seeming forward made her kisses seem stiff and formal. As a result, many lovers thought her either inexperienced or cold.

"Tea goes better with cinnamon toast," Erikka said.

"I think coffee and no toast for me, thanks."

"The toast only takes a minute."

"No, I'm dieting."

The sun had passed its zenith and the forest was a chlorophyl blaze. Above the treetops, visible through the glass wall, the moon was shining, pale and oddly anachronistic. A faint smell of pine crept through the open doors and windows. No need to keep them shut now.

"Why do you want to lose weight? You look just fine."

"The old tum's getting a little soft." The silhouette slapped its belly.

"You should see Woodrow Judd's tummy. I'm not surprised he has coronaries."

"I wonder when he'll have his next." The cigar tip blinked.

Erikka rested her hands on the terra cotta Andean milk jug, drawing peace and cool and steadiness from it. At a window behind her an insect beat its wings, and the screen buzzed sympathetically. "His next is bound to be his last," she said. "What will become of the Agency, do you suppose?"

"By then, hopefully, we'll be living under a different government and no one will give a damn. This is an awfully pretty table. Are the legs hand-carved?"

Look at my legs, Erikka wanted to shout, *not the table's.* She went quickly through open doors into the fully equipped kitchen and began touching appliances.

She spooned coffee into the percolator basket, filled the pot with tapwater, set it on a burner. She lit the flame.

Erikka would have murdered for a kiss. It was lonely and cold standing by the stove waiting for the coffee to perk. Should she go back into the living room; should she wait where she was? All things considered, it was probably wiser to wait, for the mood in the living room had grown thick and dark and kissing did not seem likely there.

She sponged off the formica-topped counter. The first eruptions of coffee were bubbling in the percolator. She raised the flame beneath the pot. There was no wind in the trees outside the window, yet it seemed as if something were shaking the branches.

Mating rabbits, she supposed; or squirrels arguing; or chipmunks. She took some dishes from the machine and slipped them back into their places on the shelf. She changed the position of a potholder that was hanging wrong. She had never realized what a desolate place a kitchen could be. She looked for the cinnamon.

A floorboard creaked behind her, but she dared not hope.

She supposed disagreements were the growing pains of any sort of relationship. *This can only strengthen us,* she told herself.

The bushes rustled again, and suddenly one of those nameless dark birds came screeching out, taking dead aim at the window. Erikka gave a little scream and ducked. She heard a footstep close behind her.

"That bird frightened me," she laughed. "I can't find the cinnamon—you're not disappointed if we don't have toast, are you?"

She turned, and the smile withered on her lips. She shrank back against the open dishwasher, mystified by the two hundred-proof venom in those eyes, not understanding why those strong, blunt fingers were reaching for her throat.

"Darling?" she pleaded. Behind her the dishwasher clanked into action, drowning what little protest she might have been able to utter.

*

"Help you?" a floor nurse challenged.

"I want to see Miss Darcie Sybert." Woodrow Judd's breath came in spasms, and his face was flushed.

"Sybert is in isolation." The edges of the nurse's cap and uniform were starched to the sharpness of knife blades, and a little smile tucked up the corners of her mouth.

"I'm Woodrow Judd and I want to see Miss Sybert."

The eyes sparked. "Of course, Mr. Judd. If you'll come this way."

Around twists and kinks of the corridor Woodrow Judd followed the clacking low heels, wondering that any patient could sleep through the racket of those terrible swift feet.

"She's not contagious or anything," the nurse was saying in an amiable rush of words, "and why she has to be isolated is beyond me. But orders are orders, and in a hospital you obey orders first and ask questions later."

They passed a caravan of steam wagons high-laden with the

detritus of lunch. They passed an orderly who looked to Woodrow Judd for all the world like a junkie, right down to the yolks of his eyes. They passed a room where a patient lay with a hand dangling rigid off the bed and the sheet drawn up over his head.

The nurse made rhythms with her keyring and unlocked a frosted glass door. She allowed Woodrow Judd to go first. A blast of ammonia assaulted his nostrils. He stepped into a darkened room. She flicked on a light, and in the sudden merciless shaft of fluorescence he saw the bed and the thing that lay heaped on it.

"Miss Sybert," he managed to stammer. "Darcie Sybert?"

Great dry cisterns of eyes turned on him. He did not permit himself the luxury of averting his gaze, as though she were a war-atrocity photograph he could close the magazine on.

"My name is Woodrow Judd. I'm here to help you."

He reached out a hand to reassure her, and she sprang back and huddled against the wall for whatever shelter it afforded. Woodrow Judd's hand hovered, unwanted by either of them. Slowly it went to his chin, and a finger grazed stubble with an over-and-over probing movement.

"One thing I promise you, Darcie, I will find out who did this to you and why and if it's any consolation. . . ."

He wondered what they had done to turn her into this mass of bruised bandages; and he remembered what they had done to others, done with his knowledge and consent, and his stomach rode up and for a moment he was in free fall. His eyes smarted and anger pressed like a fist against his heart. "Is there anything you need?"

She stared at him. If only there had been reproach in those eyes he could have borne their judgment, but there was nothing at all, except. . . .

"There must be something you need," he pleaded. "Anything. Ask."

What did he read in that gaze: forgiveness? pity? He felt his left knee go weak.

"Would you like to see your family? You have a family, don't you? Do you have a boy friend? Would you like a television set? Ice cream?"

He braced himself on the metal chair till the room recovered from its unsteadiness.

"God forgive me," he whispered.

He stood a long moment, tried to master the trembling in his chest. When he could no longer bear the softness of those eyes that ought to have hated him, he lurched to the door. The nurse snapped the light off.

"What happened to her?" His voice was halfway between a gag and a whisper.

"You saw what happened to her. It's not at all uncommon nowadays."

"At least you could change the sheets."

"I'm not a nurse's aide."

Through tearing eyes Woodrow Judd memorized the nurse, soldier-stiff and new-money-crisp, and he understood for the first time something about armies. "What's your name?"

"Laurie Caldwell." She drew herself up. "I'm head nurse on this floor."

"All right, Laurie Caldwell. Listen carefully, because I'm saying this only once. I want a doctor to look at Miss Sybert immediately. I want her moved to a private room with sunlight and an open window, not that broom closet you've got her in. I want her sheets changed regularly. I want her to have a nurse around the clock, and I mean a nurse other than you, Miss Caldwell. And if she has not regained some semblance of human shape within twenty-four hours, you will never work again, Miss Caldwell; in fact you will never see the outside of a federal penitentiary. Do I make myself clear?"

The nurse's head gave a dismayed wobble. Woodrow Judd went to the elevator and leaned on the emergency button all the way to the first floor. He walked straight past reception and into the street, never once looking behind him or to the side or even to the front, but threw himself into the idling black limousine and locked the doors and windows as though they alone had the magic to keep gorgons at bay.

Woodrow Judd barked a command at his driver. As Washington, D.C., city in transition, began easing past the bulletproof glass he struggled like the conductor of an amateur symphony to impose some kind of rhythm on his breathing.

The limousine was passing the Folger Library, home of the largest Shakespeare collection in the nation and a detour Woodrow Judd enjoyed. His eye considered the pleasing contrast of stark white marble and lush green lawn and boxwood. Then the thought of Darcie Sybert jabbed and the reds in the panorama washed out and he realized with sickening suddenness that the blood was not reaching his retinas.

He clutched the armstrap; tried to keep a grip on here and now. A steel band was squeezing his stomach in half. He had to shut his eyes to blot out the pain. *Our Father,* he tried to remember, *Who art in heaven.* . . .

When he could see and breathe again, the limousine was passing the National Archives, and the flag at the top of the pole was blue and white and red in all the right places.

I mustn't do that to myself again, he promised. He wondered what kind of fool he was, looked at his wrist watch, and told the driver to step on it. He had been unconscious twenty-two minutes.

*

Alone in his office, willing his heart to beat like a normal, obedient heart, Woodrow Judd took off his jacket and loosened his polka-dot bow tie. He drew the curtains, unlocked the lower left-hand drawer of his desk, set a small bottle with typewritten label on the blotter. He made a face, as though he could already taste the medicine.

It was quarter past four, and except for the ticking of the clock, his office was silent. It had been designed that way.

He tilted the cut-glass decanter, aiming the flow at a paper cup. He measured a teaspoon of medicine, not one drop more or less, into the water. He stirred till the black stain—it looked to him like the excrement of a witch's toad—had evened into an over-all gray. He emptied the cup in two swift, hateful gulps;

crushed it; hid it in the wastebasket under a piece of the morning's newspaper.

He pressed the intercom button. "I want to talk to Dr. Erikka Lumi."

The intercom buzzed somewhere on a distant line, and a staticky voice told him Dr. Lumi had left work for the day. She had seemed in a rush and had given no explanation.

"Where the hell is she?"

The voice said Dr. Lumi had not phoned in; the office had been unable to reach her; there was no answer at her country house. He felt as though a fetus in his stomach were gnawing his heart.

"I want that woman found and I want her here. Put a trace on her immediately."

July 1: Saturday

The bark was cracked, yet clung. Fruit heavy branches spread between earth and low clouds. The rows of trees twisted like city streets, and the afternoon flowed slowly through them, losing direction. The First Lady stood in a shadow. She had not gone to town shopping with her father. She was in the dark of the orchard, gazing toward the stable. The buzz of a faraway airplane meshed with the buzz of a hornet.

A girl stood near the stable door, in shadow also, tips of her hair flowing into the light. She held an apple in her hand. She was watching the branches of a tree. She was motionless as a snapshot. The First Lady could not see the girl's face but she could see the stripes of her blouse which the shadow made ripple like reception lines on a television tube.

The First Lady tried to signal her presence with a wave. From her solitude she smiled at the girl. In the heat, time condensed in droplets. Silence settled on the trees like insecticide.

The First Lady did not know why a girl standing by a stable door, watching a tree, filled her with peace; but she wished she could be that tree, impermeable to the drone of airplanes.

*

"Erikka Lumi was found dead in her country house," Woodrow Judd said. "Several other things were found in her country house. I believe I've done you an injustice."

"We all make mistakes," Borodin said.

Woodrow Judd darted him a quick, sour glance as though not in the habit of having his apologies returned like bad checks. "You feel Operation Flypaper is a phony. Why?"

"The whole approach is half-assed. It's like going after a flea with a cannonball." Borodin's face was dark with bruises and anger. He had spent the night on a Greyhound bus with a paper bag of root beer and a paper bag of vodka, and the federal men had taken him off the bus in Richmond, Virginia, a city of broad, leafy avenues. "Operation Flypaper doesn't make sense unless you're trying to burn up money and personnel and aren't particular about the result. It's a boondoggle. Someone wants to send men into that town and open mail and tap phones till the whole thing turns into an industry."

Woodrow Judd toyed with his intercom. He wore a chastened look.

"Look at those intercepts yourself. They're dumb. There's no code, there's no cipher, there's nothing in those letters, there's no connection with the President or the shooting."

Woodrow Judd had difficulty, now, meeting the eyes of the man who stared straight into his, so he swiveled his chair. It creaked.

"The reason Lumi sent me to Whitefalls wasn't that I was any good, it was that I'm outmoded. You said so yourself."

"Yes, that was the reason."

"And when I started to get something done, when I came up with a real lead, I was knocked on the head and recalled, if you call that recalling. And when I kept going on my own, I found that poor kid half dead in Erikka Lumi's country house."

Woodrow Judd tapped a pencil on his blotter. "Look, Borodin, there *was* a letter threatening the President's life, and it *did* come from Whitefalls, and his daughter *was* shot. That much is real. You can't deny it."

"I'm not denying any of it. Hiram Quinn was sent out to Whitefalls for routine mail monitoring. But he let this thing escalate, and if I were you I'd check out who okay'd his expenses and who gave this operation the green light every damned step of the way. I'd read Hiram Quinn's reports myself and I'd read the report on that damned threatening letter and as a matter of fact I wouldn't be satisfied with reports."

Woodrow Judd raised half an eyebrow.

"I'd go through that whole damned file of intercepts myself.

I'd get hold of that threatening letter and have it right between my fingers just to make sure the damned thing exists. I'd sift every particle of Operation Flypaper and find out for once and all if there's any reality to it. And if there isn't, I'd make a few changes in my organization."

Woodrow Judd made a movement to rise from his chair, then sank back into it as though pushed.

"Something the matter?" Borodin asked.

Woodrow Judd's voice was barely audible. "Will you help me?"

July 2: Sunday

The sun, unable to cling to the apex of noon, slid down the sloping sky, brushed a promontory of cloud, and sent a single, aborted smoke signal drifting into the ionosphere.

One hand shading her eyes, the girl watched the wisping cumulus change shape a moment, and then—with a backward glance at him that her pursuer by now recognized—she began walking again, her stride suddenly purposeful. When she came to the felled tree that someone must have thought an adequate bridge across the creek, she turned off the path and took the bank along the water, the margin of sandy soil vague and insubstantial between the swell of water and the dark press of vines and brush.

He kept pace and kept his distance.

The silence of the woods was a riotous thing, a sped-up tape of bird twitter, a gamelan of creatures that knew how to cause xylophones in trees and percussion in the rattle of dry leaves. And in the peaceful commotion she moved unheard, indistinguishable. One instant her tan blouse melted into the vines and tendrils, in an instant it reappeared; her hair mimicked a sunstruck patch of leaf, and he was certain she had vanished.

He moved faster to close the gap, but he could no more gain on her than he could on his own shadow, a wavering harbinger thrown out ten feet before him, slipping across tree trunk and shrub with an ease his heavy legs could only envy.

She paused at a turning in the brook and leaned on a rock. Then, abruptly, she ran on. When he came to the rock he saw by the footprints that she had taken off her sandals. His own shoes sank soggily into the sand, and tiny grains weighted his foot, but he did not stop to unlace them.

By now the vines and brush outflanked her, pressed in on the margin, drove her ankle-deep into the chilly flow. Her bare foot reached out for a moss-grown stone. A frog leaped up from nowhere, grazing her calf with some cold, fleeting slime, and he heard her cry as though metal had cut her. Two arms, each hand ludicrously shod in leather and thongs, went out like an acrobat's on a rope, and she sank with swift gracelessness into an explosion of rust-colored spume.

He cut directly into the water, aimed for the center of the whimpering little maelstrom.

She battled the brook like a baby in a bassinet; the waves that drenched her were her own doing, and though there was not nearly the depth to sink in, she was making a noble effort at drowning. He reached for her.

"Damn." She was out of breath. "I did that accidentally on purpose and it turned out to be for real."

"I noticed." He caught her by the arms, showing her no more politeness than he would a drowning person. The waves abated, and he lifted her up out of the flow. She clung wetly to him.

"Sorry about that." Her smile was tinged with embarrassment. "I wanted to apologize and I felt kind of silly trying to apologize at twenty paces, so I decided to let you rescue me."

"There's nothing to apologize for."

Her feet dangled uselessly and he moved her toward the bank.

"Oh yes there is." She gave her head a shake, cleared her shoulders of water-tipped hair, sprinkled him. "I've been a god-damned bitch."

He shrugged.

"I'm a foolish, silly empty-head, I know it, and I go around hurting people's feelings all over the place, and half the time I never even mean to. You've got your work cut out for you without me getting all neurotic to boot."

"You can be as neurotic as you want." He set her down.

"Why Mr. Beausoleil, do I detect you calling me neurotic?"

"I'm saying as far as I'm concerned you can be whatever you want."

"Oh. Thanks. For a minute I thought you were taking a minor

sort of interest. I mean, criticizing a person is taking an interest, isn't it? My mother criticizes me all the time, and she says she loves me. And God knows, all those kids with posters and bricks and bombs, they certainly take an interest. They say I'm the number one best-selling poster in the nation—you know. *Next time aim better*, that one?"

"No one's going to shoot you, Miss Luckinbill."

She was pale and frail and putting on a front, and he felt an obscure sorrow for her.

"Sure about that?" She shivered as a breeze fanned her damp blouse, and her arms were coming up gooseflesh. He slipped out of his shirt and helped her wrap it around her shoulders.

"Miss Luckinbill, I'm sorry."

She looked at him.

"I mean about those posters and that shooting. You shouldn't have to go through that."

She smiled. "Oh, it's all part of the political process. Anyway, why in God's name should *you* say you're sorry?"

She moved up the bank, and he saw her eying his holster. They fell into step, and without bothering to weigh the protocol he took the lead and held the branches out of her way. She grinned up at him.

"Look, Chad, could you do me a tremendous favor? Frankly the whole thing was sort of—well, I'm tired and I'd like to think about other things, okay?"

"Sure, Miss Luckinbill." He nodded. She caught his hand.

"And goddammitall, will you please call me Lexie?"

July 3: Monday

"Wait a minute," Woodrow Judd barked. "What was that last one?"

Borodin twirled the dial back. *Dearest Aunt Jennifer . . .* The looping, hand-scrawled letters filled the glowing screen of the microfilm viewer.

"No. Must have been the one before."

Dear Sirs, the letter on the screen ran, *Enclosed please find prepayment for single accommodation the nights of May 6 and 7 in the name of Warner Gillespie.* The letter was signed *with many thanks, Minerva Tate,* and the explanation *secretary to Mr. Gillespie* followed Miss Tate's precisely penned signature.

Woodrow Judd was making one of his annoyed faces, as though a mosquito were buzzing near his ear.

"A letter to the Pruninghook Arms," Borodin said, seeing nothing remarkable in it. "We must have seen a hundred of those."

"It's not the Pruninghook Arms that interests me. It's the letterhead."

Borodin considered the logo of a bespectacled beaver. "Gillespie Ogilvie Thorpe?"

"I've seen that letterhead."

"It's a public-relations outfit."

"I've seen that letterhead recently. In this office."

The marble clock ticked on the mantel. The Director's chair squeaked. Sunlight played in the filigree of the curtains.

Borodin's eyes were dry and scratchy and ached. He and the Director had looked at almost four thousand intercepts, all of them of idiotic inconsequentiality, and they were not even halfway through the file.

"Someone wrote me on Gillespie, Ogilvie, Thorpe letterhead. Someone wrote me personally." Woodrow Judd fussed with his bow tie and stared at the skyline. "A crank. Some kind of request."

Woodrow Judd strode to the desk and jabbed a finger at the intercom dial. "Approximately seven to ten days ago I received a communication on the letterhead of Gillespie, Ogilvie, Thorpe. Bring it to me."

Borodin sat wondering why Minerva Tate drew a hollow circle instead of a simple dot over her *i*. The office door opened and an assistant laid a manila folder on Woodrow Judd's desk. Woodrow Judd opened the folder and scanned a letter and an accompanying report.

Dear Mr. Judd, I must have five (5) minutes of your time to discuss a matter of supreme importance to the Republic. I can be in Washington upon four (4) hours' notice. . . .

*

Chad's step slowed as they approached the white-pillared portico.

"Come on." Lexie tugged at his jacket sleeve.

"No." Chad dug his foot into the gravel drive.

"I'll report you," Lexie teased.

"My job is to guard you out here."

"How do you know I'm not in danger in there?"

"Now please, Miss Luckinbill—"

"I thought it was going to be Lexie."

"Please, Lexie."

Having yielded, he could not meet her eyes, and this gave her a sense of imminent victory. For a long moment they stood silent, rigidly apart as though magnetic fields separated them.

It was a perfect summer day. A thin caravan of clouds stretched across the boundless blue dome of sky; a breeze rippled magnolia leaves, and the air smelled sweetly of cut grass. A man could be seen stooping in the garden to pluck a weed.

"You're frightened of my mother and grandfather."

His reaction was as swift and indignant as if she had slapped him. "I'm not frightened of anyone. I respect their privacy, that's all."

"What's more important—their privacy or my safety? How do you know I won't pop a handful of pills in there? Or slit my wrists?"

He seized her wrists in sudden anger. "Miss Luckinbill, if you do anything to harm yourself, I'll—"

"You'll what?"

He released her. "I'll be very unhappy."

That he could say as much and mean it shamed her, and her coyness rang shrill and false in her ears. "You know something, Chad? You're a dope, but I kind of respect you. All right, we'll do it your way. I am formally inviting you to a late luncheon in the house. The favor of a reply is requested."

He gave a little bow of the head. "And I am formally thanking you and declining."

"Okay. Will you walk me to the door?"

Chad considered a moment. "Yes, I'll walk you to the door."

The door was opened by Sarah, old and black, immense and loyal.

"Well, Miss Lexie," she said.

Later Lexie was to tell Chad how she hated to be called that: *It sounds so—well, so black, and it makes me sound so white; do you know Sarah still calls Mom Miss Moni? You'd think we were back in the days of Scarlett O'Hara and Harriet Beecher Stowe.*

Miss Moni, Sarah told them, had gotten tired of waiting lunch for Miss Lexie. The old servant cast a meaningful eye at Chad.

"Sarah, this is Chad," Lexie said. "He's guarding me."

Sarah scrutinized. "You take care of that girl. Come on, you're letting the flies in." And she gave them both a firm push toward the dining room.

Lexie saw Chad's confusion at finding himself in the house, and she took his arm. "No turning back now," she whispered. "And stop blushing."

"I'm not blushing."

"Yes you are. Right there." She tickled at his shirt collar, and he was dismally aware that the laundry had turned it and sewed it back crooked.

"I'm sunburned, and Sarah can see us."

Lexie threw a glance behind them and saw a frowning Sarah quickly pretend to be absorbed in the phantom dust on a picture frame. She rose on tiptoe and sneak-attacked a kiss onto Chad's cheek. He jerked away as though a bee had stung him.

For an instant she was certain he was going to strike her, and she almost wished he would.

And then he broke into a huge, uncontrollable grin.

"You are a pinko anarchist agitator, and I should lock you up."

"Wish you would."

They turned a corner and were out of Sarah's sightline. "No one can see us now." She hooked her fingers into the lapels of his off-the-rack seersucker.

"Hold on, radical." Chad placed two strong hands on her shoulders and eased her back to earth. "*They* can see us."

He gestured toward the Swiss Guard of portraits flanking the hallway. Lexie's ancestors seemed to be frowning in their massive frames.

"Who cares about a bunch of old Cavanaughs?"

"Cavanaughs and Hancocks and Adamses." He strode forward to read from the gold dog-tags embedded in the frames. "You've got half the signers of the Declaration of Independence watching you."

She caught up with him, but again he dodged her, like the steady old tortoise keeping a hairsbreadth ahead of Achilles. "Kiss me, you bastard."

"Ah ah." He pretended to be studying the likeness of Aseph Larchmont Livingston, 1734–1805. "I didn't know you were related to the Livingstons."

"I'm a living descendant of the whole Who's Who of the thirteen colonies." She succeeded in winding an arm around his.

"You know, you look a little like old Aseph."

"He was a drunk and a lecher, and he fathered eighteen illegitimate children. Furthermore he was a drug addict."

"At least he'd qualify for Welfare. Poor, culturally deprived Aseph."

"What about poor, culturally deprived Lexie?"

"And what are you deprived of, little girl?" Chad puffed out his cheeks and tried to mimic the concern of an Earl Warren.

"Guess."

Before he could guess or even yield to the faint innuendo of her arm, the First Lady stood before them.

"Good afternoon, Lexie."

There were suggestions of shadow beneath Monica's eyes, and the make-up had not quite vanquished them. She looked a good forty of her forty-five years, and she seemed to know it. Lexie could not tell how long she had been watching.

"Mom, this is Chad Beausoleil."

"How do you do, Mr. Beausoleil."

"Chad's guarding me, and I thought—"

Lexie had prepared the explanation last night, lying awake in bed, but her mother was shaking Chad's hand before she could get two words out.

"Won't you come in and meet my father?"

Monica took Chad's arm in a bluntly proprietary manner that Lexie would never have dared. Without a backward glance they were gone, and Lexie was left staring at her mute reflection in an ancestor's glassed-over portrait. *Come on Lexie,* she told herself: *you're not going to run to your dolls or your Mozart this time. You're a big girl now.* She squared her shoulders and marched into the dining room.

At the far, far end of the table her grandfather was slicing his ham into half-inch squares. The task seemed to require more of his attention than the introductions.

"Father, this is Lexie's guard, Chad—"

"Beausoleil," Lexie put in before her mother could toss out the name in her perfect junior-year-abroad French.

"As in *beautiful sun?*" Colonel Cavanaugh inquired dryly.

"No relation," Chad smiled.

"No relation, what a shame," Monica said.

Lexie could not tell whether they were being cruel or dumb or whether they were just, as usual, thinking about far more world-shaking matters than the feelings of other people. They had succeeded in flattening the poor, well-intentioned wise-crack, and she saw that they had succeeded in flattening poor Chad as well. His face had blotched the color and pattern of an open pomegranate.

"No relation?" Lexie sang in her most crystalline coloratura, and she broke into an appreciative laugh that made Lakmé's "Bell Song" sound like a cracked drain pipe. For a moment everyone was quiet. Colonel Cavanaugh sliced ham, and when he had done with the ham he began slicing china with bone-jangling squeaks. Lexie undid her napkin with a flap and sat down; and her mother and Chad simply stood. Lexie could almost hear the sun moving across the window, flattening the Virginia hills into a jigsaw-puzzle picture. And she could almost hear her mother thinking, circuits clicking faster than a computer.

Lexie knew that Monica Cavanaugh Luckinbill was sizing up Chad Beausoleil. She was checking out his jacket; the sleeves were cut short, the neck bunched at the nape, and the lapels were not the width one saw at Washington receptions. She was checking out his posture; he stood a trifle stiff and military; he did not attempt the easy slouch of the State Department charmer. She was checking out his manner and finding it hope-lessly lacking in guile, and she was checking out his accent and probably thinking that Maine was a place you had a summer house in, but no one was born there.

"It's Chad's job to rescue me," Lexie airily told her grand-father, "in case anyone ties me down to a railroad track."

Colonel Cavanaugh glanced at Lexie, the only progeny of his only progeny, his sole posterity and the occasional butt of his wisecracks at fate and genetics. He did not smile.

"Are you enjoying the country, Mr. Beausoleil?" Monica asked; and Lexie writhed at the assumption that the country was the province of the rich.

"Yes, ma'am."

The *ma'am* sounded square and dumb. *He's not like that,* Lexie wanted to shout at her mother: *he's not one of those ignorant rednecks you're always screaming about.* But she bit her tongue and sipped her iced water and wondered whether her mother was going to ask Chad to sit: or did she expect him to stand at attention during lunch?

"Country air's good for the lungs," the old man stated.

"I'll say," Lexie said. "My lung feels terrific." She noticed Chad's toe digging into the carpet. She pushed back the chair next to her. "Chad, aren't you tired standing?"

What happened next was like a ricochet shot in billiards. Chad threw a glance of utter confusion toward Monica; Monica shot Lexie an eyeful of the sternest reproach, a throwback to the time her eight-year-old daughter had shattered a Sèvres figurine at a wedding reception; and Lexie, all innocence, smiled at Chad and patted the seat cushion.

"No one drinks consommé standing up," Lexie said in her most convincing twitter. On cue, Regis set two more cups on the table.

The four of them sat sipping and chewing in a civilized, silent parody of a family meal.

"Mother, may Chad borrow your marc?" Lexie asked so suddenly that Monica scarcely had time to lower her fork.

"Does Mr. Beausoleil ride?" Monica asked in a tone that would brook no yes.

"Of course Chad rides. He was a finalist in the high jump at training academy." Lexie's eyes met Chad's, daring him to contradict her.

"Bless Me is too old to jump," Monica said.

"We're not jumping, we're just riding."

"But Lexie, you can't go on a horse."

"We're not galloping, Mom. I haven't been on a horse in aeons, and Chad's got to guard me or they'll court-martial him. Won't they, Chad?"

Chad smiled neutrally at the others.

"Thanks, Mom." Lexie kissed her mother before she could get

the fork back to her lips to hide the twitch of irritation. Now Lexie beamed a smile toward the far end of the table.

"Grandpa, could Chad borrow your saddle and boots?"

*

"It was thirteen weeks ago this Friday," Jordie said. He was wearing his very best dark suit. "Mr. Gillespie sent out a memo."

"To whom?" Woodrow Judd asked.

"To all the employees." Jordie paid very little attention to the shifting views of the city. His eyes held on Woodrow Judd, only occasionally and somewhat warily shifting to the agent. He spoke rapidly. From time to time his voice, like a balloon on a string, would threaten to rise.

"Mr. Gillespie sends out memos every Friday. He says the company is a democracy and he believes in getting the opinion of the whole corporate family."

"And what was the memo?" Woodrow Judd asked.

They were riding in a limousine: Jordie and the Director on the back seat, and Borodin on a jump seat, half turned so that they formed an almost conversational grouping. Bullet- and soundproof glass separated them from the driver.

"It was a kind of consumer-research campaign. Usually he asks about beer or cigarettes or washing machines. Once in a while he asks about a politician: how could the governor improve his image with factory workers, that type of crap. This time he asked the employees to describe an event or sequence of events that would make them feel the most sympathy for the President of the United States; and an event that would make them feel the least. My idea was to do it all with one event."

"And what made you think this memo should be the concern of the Agency?"

"Not the memo. My reply."

"What was your reply?"

"I wrote nine single-spaced pages. Worked the whole thing out. I outlined the speeches. I said it should be the President's home town. I said it had to be the graveyard where his parents were buried."

The call had come at the offices of Gillespie, Ogilivie, Thorpe. Jordie had been not at all surprised when a voice, refusing to identify itself, told him to go outside to a pay phone and to dial a certain number. Naturally he had recognized the District of Columbia area code and he knew, since no extension was mentioned, that he had been given Woodrow Judd's direct line.

"What precisely did you say in this reply of yours?"

"I said if anyone wanted to create maximum sympathy for the President of the United States, he should shoot the President's daughter. I also said Luckinbill would be incapable of reacting forcefully and this would turn the sympathy against him."

"You wrote this in a reply to Warner Gillespie's memo thirteen weeks ago?"

Jordie had followed directions exactly: told no one where he was going, mumbled something about his ulcer. He had taken a taxi home to pick up his Xeroxes of the scenario, and he had caught the next shuttle plane to Washington.

"I wrote the whole thing almost three months before Lexie Luckinbill was shot. Boy was I mad when that happened."

"So were a lot of people."

"I asked Mr. Gillespie about it. He pretended he'd never heard of me, never seen my nine-page scenario. He wouldn't give me the time of day. That's when I wrote you."

The limousine was following Massachusetts Avenue westward from Union Station, holding to the slow lanes and demonstrating remarkable courtesy to tourists and pedestrians picking their way through traffic.

"Do you have a copy of your reply to Mr. Gillespie's memo?"

"I sure do. I Xeroxed up a whole batch on the company machine."

"I wouldn't Xerox too many of those, Jordie. Could I see one?"

"With pleasure." Jordie extracted a Xeroxed scenario from his attaché case. The initials on the case were not his, since he had got it from a thrift shop. The gilt had almost worn off, but he felt that Woodrow Judd detected the discrepancy. He slid his hand over the initials and drummed a tattoo on the leather.

Woodrow Judd turned pages. "This is quite detailed."

"They added a few things, like the high school band and the Latin on the wreath."

"I see you've got a few speeches in here too. 'If the organism is strong, as America was till 1933—'"

"That's part of the theoretical basis."

"And what does theory have to do with shooting the President's daughter?"

"No major political change," Jordie explained, "can be of lasting or major effect unless it has a solid theoretical basis."

"Who's talking about major political change?"

"Major political change happens to be an interest of mine."

"And is it an interest of Mr. Gillespie's?"

"I don't know Mr. Gillespie personally. I suspect he's an opportunist of the rankest stripe. He'd probably espouse major political change if it served his immediate gain."

It was a typical summer day for Washington. Temperatures hovered in the nineties, the sky was cloudless, and the songbirds were almost broiled in the trees. The limousine was air-conditioned and the interior was as cool as a day in May. Its polarized windows subdued the glare of the alabaster city and at the same time cut the noise down.

Woodrow Judd kept turning pages. "I see your scenario doesn't stop with the shooting of the President's daughter."

"Oh no. There's no point mobilizing sympathy for the President if the sympathy isn't exploited. Power festers when not used. The effect of the shooting is to catalyze the American population into a mob. The mob is one of the most powerful and yet one of the most misunderstood of all political instruments."

Woodrow Judd raised a fist to his mouth and coughed softly.

"It could be compared to a critical mass of uranium. Just as there's no defusing uranium once it passes a certain quantity, there's no stopping a mob once it passes a critical point. In this instance, the critical point can be estimated at one tenth of the nation. A tenth of the nation can swing the country."

"Swing it to what?"

"Swing it to whatever the leader wants."

"And what leader is that?"

At the New York Avenue traffic circle, the limousine slowed to let a group of Ghanaian tourists, in sparkling native dress, cross the street.

"No mob is leaderless," Jordie stated. "It's a contradiction in terms. Just as democracy is a contradiction in terms."

"Tell me, Jordie: how far in this scenario would you say Mr. Gillespie—or whoever is using it—has gone?"

"I'd say we're still at the initial stage. Stage two doesn't come till after the death of the President's daughter."

"Ah yes." Woodrow Judd found a page to stare at. "I see you have several speeches in stage two."

"Leader speeches. I indicated only the leader speeches. For reasons of space."

"And I see there's a long speech in stage three."

"It needs work. It should be short and punchy."

" 'Fellow Americans,' " Woodrow Judd read, " 'I do not think one man, no matter how exalted. . . .' "

"That's the final leader speech. That's where the leader announces to the people that—well, in essence he announces that he's the leader."

"No one knows he's the leader till then?"

"Some of the elect may know it, but the people as a whole aren't aware. It's best for tactical reasons that they be kept unaware."

"I take it then that this scenario is almost a handbook telling the leader how to become leader?"

"Right." A lock of black Irish hair fell over Jordie's unfurrowed brow. "Shoot the President's daughter. For starters."

Woodrow Judd continued reading aloud. " '. . . free from the economic and political contradictions of democracy. . . .' "

"That part's a little technical. In essence he's telling the people that he's bringing them political structure and economic security. In other words, the authoritarian state. The authoritarian state is an organic necessity in the destiny of Western culture."

"I see, I see. The leader is a messiah."

The limousine poked along Embassy Row, which was no row at all but a zigzagging maze of little streets north of Massachusetts Avenue and west of Connecticut. Transition was evident in the burnt-out store fronts that had once been expensive boutiques displaying finery from all parts of the world; but most of the embassies still stood and with them stood the three-story brick town houses, trim and tensed behind their ivied fences. Slate had begun cracking from some of the mansard roofs and, lately, the owners had stopped retiling.

"Yes, the leader concept is very close to the messiah concept."

"Jordie, let me be sure I have this straight. Your employer asked your advice, and several hundred other people's, on how to manipulate sympathy for the President."

Jordie nodded.

"You replied with this scenario."

Jordie nodded.

"This scenario not only describes how to manipulate sympathy for the President, but it goes on to suggest how someone could go about seizing the President's power."

"Oh, much more power than that. The presidency as presently constituted is a feeble institution."

Woodrow Judd allowed as much with a nod. "Why did you answer Gillespie's question with *this?*" The pages of the scenario crackled. "Sympathy for the President is one thing; ousting him is another."

The limousine had found its way back onto Massachusetts Avenue and continued north past the Naval Observatory. At the Wisconsin intersection it turned south again onto M Street, past a white marble fountain commemorating World War I dead but not at the moment functioning.

"Dialectically there's no contradiction, as my scenario shows. Destroy the President's daughter and create sympathy. The sympathy destroys pluralism and creates a mob. The mob destroys the President and creates the Leader."

Cars were moving slowly on Pennsylvania, the city's main artery and favored parade route. The broad boulevard, which two centuries ago had been a deep morass covered over by alder bushes, was now a Sargasso of stalled traffic. Dusty autos lolled in the shade of poplars planted by Thomas Jefferson, whose dream of making the avenue an Appian Way now seemed as remote as the United States Capitol.

"I'm still confused, Jordie. You did a good deal more than just answer Gillespie's question."

"Once I got started it was hard to stop. One thing dovetailed into another."

Woodrow Judd eyed the apple-cheeked boy amiably, as though they shared a secret. "And maybe you were bucking for promotion?"

Jordie's became the smile of an angel caught out.

"Has Gillespie approached you for any more work on this or any other scenario?"

"No, he hasn't. And if he does. . . ." Jordie's smile became cruel.

The Director put a hand on Jordie's shoulder, and Jordie felt himself sinking into a vast peace that far surpassed rational understanding.

"Jordie, you could help us a great deal."

"I'd like to," Jordie murmured.

"If Gillespie or anyone asks you for any further work along these lines, I want you to play along with him. And keep us informed. Tell us what he wants and show us what you give him. We may even have some special material for you to pass on. Of course, you don't need to let anyone know you're working for us."

Jordie's tone was serious, almost devout. "I wouldn't compromise security."

"Security's important, Jordie. I'm glad you realize it. For a start, you could give me all your Xeroxes of that scenario. And if you've left any copies in New York, I'd be obliged if you could destroy them."

Once past the White House, the limousine was able to pick up speed. A breeze ruffled the trees along the mall, and, in the distance the Capitol seemed as bright and scrubbed as a child's fresh-bought toy.

"Yes, sir," Jordie promised. "I'll destroy them."

*

Lunch was long over. Smiling, talking easily now, Lexie and Chad walked side by side beneath the towering blue afternoon. He told jokes about training academy and jokes about the Secret Service, and her laughter rippled like a clarinet arpeggio, on key and exactly on cue.

The groom looked up at Lexie's and Chad's approach. Lexie had dressed Chad in her grandfather's riding boots and cotton jodhpurs. The old man had given permission, grudgingly, for the boots, though not for the jodhpurs; but Lexie didn't see how he would ever find out.

"Your grandpa's jodhpurs sure look nice on your friend," the groom remarked. He was an elderly black, so servile that Lexie could not completely trust him.

"This is Chad Beausoleil, Joe," she said crisply. "I'm teaching him how to ride."

"Miss Lexie's a good teacher," the groom smiled, his mouth half empty of teeth. "She done taught a lot of young fellers to ride."

Lexie had not wanted Chad to know about the other horseback lessons. Rather than let him see her angry, she turned her back and, needing a destination, walked to the clearing where the horses were nuzzling the grass. She could hear Chad and the old groom trading civilities, and when she looked back and saw them shaking hands she was irritated.

She did not lay a hand on the horses or even talk to them. She caught their eyes, and they stopped grazing and came along with her quietly.

Lexie's horse was a docile six-year-old dun gelding fifteen

hands high. His name was Bittersweet, and her grandfather had given him to her when he was a colt. Chad's mount was a five-year-old white mare with a chestnut race down her face. Her name was Bless Me. She was sixteen hands high and given to almost Dionysian seizures of wildness. Since the last of these had been over fourteen months ago and since she had never killed or harmed a rider, Lexie saw no need to frighten Chad with the fact.

Besides, she wanted to see what Bless Me thought of him.

The groom saddled and bridled the horses.

"Mount her from the near side," Lexie told Chad. When he shot her a look of confusion she said, "The left side. Near side is the left side."

Chad mounted, surprisingly graceful for a novice.

"Why can't people say *left* for left," he smiled, "instead of *near* and *port?*"

"*Left* sounds too plain, and horseback riding is very fancy." She gave *fancy* a broad *a*, and the clarinet laugh rippled again.

At first Chad rode like the beginner he was. He sat low in the saddle, held the reins too tight, gripped the horse with his knees. But gradually, with almost no prodding from Lexie, he corrected his mistakes. She suspected he was afraid of Bless Me, but had no way of knowing, for it would have been against his code to betray fear of any sort.

Lexie did not spare whip or spur in keeping Bittersweet docile, but when Chad began imitating she snapped at him to ease up. For more than an hour they walked the woods and trotted the trails and cantered the fields. Slowly Chad learned how to control the horse and, slowly, the horse came to trust him. Bless Me did not trust riders easily, and Lexie could not help thinking this was high recommendation.

They came to a fallen birch trunk blocking the path. Chad's mare took it in a single, not-quite-graceful leap.

"Hurrah!" Lexie laughed.

Chad caught his breath. "I thought she was going to throw me."

"She'd never throw you. You're not the sort."

Lexie hung back when the trail narrowed, letting him ride a length ahead, observing him, liking him. Chad Beausoleil's awkward power had shielded her these last days, and it had begun fascinating her. His was an awkwardness that afflicted both body and tongue: in gait and speech he seemed always stumbling, always catching himself up. And yet, on horseback and silent, he kept his footing; he became one with the animal, like the man half of a centaur.

Lexie's heart syncopated at the sight of his strong, almost too-heavy body borrowing the rhythm of the horse, his face tanned, his pale eyes glinting, his hair short and gold in the sun. At moments he seemed almost beautiful to her, and she marveled at him.

They came to a small lake in a pine wood, deserted and clear as tap water. They let the horses drink, and they stripped to the bathing suits they had worn beneath their riding clothes. They swam, and afterward they lay down on a beach towel Lexie had liberated from her mother's bathroom, eight square feet of striped fleece, an American flag without stars.

"Chad? What do you want? In life, I mean?"

"The impossible."

"Like what?"

"I'd like to see the world a better place."

"But what do you want for yourself?"

"Nothing."

"That sounds like a political promise. And Daddy taught me, never believe political promises. Everyone wants something."

"Not everyone wants something for himself."

"I've never met anyone like you, Chad." She tossed a pine cone into the water. "I can't tell whether you're dumb or a genius."

"I'd say we're both pretty dumb."

"Why?"

He sat up and began drying himself. "You're supposed to have four men watching you, and it's my job to keep you where they can protect you. We've lost them, and I've probably lost a job."

"You'll get another job."

"You could be in danger." He put on one arm of his shirt.

"What kind of danger?"

"All kinds."

"Not with you here." She pulled the shirt off his arm.

"Why do you say that?"

"Because I feel safe with you."

"Do you?"

"Very safe. Kiss me, Chad."

He leaned toward her and kissed her with a gentleness that startled her.

And then they snapped together like two ropes yanked into a knot. The breath was crushed from her lungs and her heart hammered at her ribs as though to break an opening and fly out. Her eyes half shut and she stared into his, seeing herself bent and reflected as in the lens of a camera, and silently, with fierce, entreating telepathy, she dared him, begged him, commanded him.

He lay naked across her. His eyes and teeth and fingernails sparked and shot volts through her. His hands took her breasts, shaping them like raw bread. Her legs sought his. Her mouth fell open. They kissed suffocatingly.

She said his name over and over. His lips pressed her name into her shoulder. An infinity of miles above them, the blue-domed day turned on its axis, like a parasol idly twirled.

*

The minutes limped. Neither Borodin nor Woodrow Judd wanted to speak for fear of sounding as dazed as he felt. It was Woodrow Judd who broke the silence with a cough; it was Borodin who spoke. "He could have dreamed that scenario up after Lexie Luckinbill was shot. That's the reasonable explanation."

Evening in Woodrow Judd's office produced the effect of indirect light in a bar. It was impossible to make out faces or details. The Director preferred to do his thinking without lamps.

"Or," Borodin said, "he could have dreamed it up before she was shot. That one's harder to swallow."

"I don't get the feeling he's lying." Woodrow Judd swiveled in his chair. "He's too goddamned earnest."

"All right. He could be a real psycho. He could have written the scenario straight from the news reports and then conveniently forgotten. He could actually believe he conceived the whole mess."

"Strikes you as that sort, does he?"

"The world's full of bush-league bureaucrats wanting to be Adolf Hitler."

"It couldn't just be coincidence, could it? Gillespie, Ogilvie, Thorpe letterhead in the intercepts; Gillespie's secretary making a hotel reservation in Whitefalls. . . ."

"The letterhead is fact," Borodin said. "And it ties in with what the kid says. We've got to dig. Either the tie-in will stay tied, or it will come apart."

Woodrow Judd, nodding, toyed with documents that lay scattered on his blotter. "I've spoken to the lab. There's no record that the threat note was ever submitted for testing."

"But Lumi handed you a report saying—"

"Lumi made an error." Woodrow Judd's face had the sad finality of a death mask.

*

"Well, hello, Darcie Sybert," the intern said, "how are we feeling this evening?"

The solitude was cold, and she had only a sheet to draw around her.

"She never talks," the night nurse said. "Never a word."

Professional gazes converged on the child. She sat in a ball, never moving, and passed the minutes uprooting the little thoughts and memories that kept sprouting like weeds in her head.

"We'll have you up and about and out of here in no time," the doctor promised. He gave a doubtful little nod, and the nurse followed him out of the room.

In the silence that foamed through the door, Darcie could hear the little sounds of heels and scalpels, wheels and whispers. She could hear the interrogators, pressed against the other side of the wall, waiting with their scissors and needles and lit cigarettes and the questions no answer could satisfy. If they had left her alone this long, she knew, it was only to catch her off guard, it was only to prepare something far worse than before.

But she was working on an escape, and if they left her alone just a little bit longer, she would have it perfected. All she had to do was to make herself small, so teeny tiny she hardly existed at all, and then one day. . . . She smiled, imagining how angry the interrogators would be at that.

But one tiny thought assailed her. "Hiram?" she called, so softly no one could have heard. "Hiram?"

*

"Moni, you can't do it to him." Storm-cloud striations darkened Senator Dan Bulfinch's jaw; his eyes blazed sheet lightning and his voice thundered as though to rouse ninety-nine sleeping senators. It was too much noise for the little book-lined study.

"Do what?" the First Lady said.

"Do what you're doing to him, dammitall. The nation's falling apart and Congress is shoving through a repeal of the Bill of Rights and Lucky Bill has enough on his mind without you running out on him too."

The First Lady sat, and she wished Senator Dan would do the same. The thumps of his booted feet, she feared, might topple a set of Gibbon from a high shelf. Her finger traced a letter engraved on her drinking glass: her father's baronial, Gothic C.

"I only did it to save Lexie," she said.

The First Lady sat with a drink, her fourth, in her hand. She was trying to concentrate on a painting. The painting was her father's garden, framed in tall windows, and it was real, but that made no difference to her enjoyment of it. She often made paintings out of things that were there, just as she sometimes made movies out of things that were happening. It was a strategy of perception that added to her pleasure in life. Sometimes it was the only pleasure open to her.

"Moni, Moni. No man can cope with everything at once. Things are falling apart."

"The center's not holding," the First Lady said, remembering the Yeats doggerel that had become a trademark of the conventional despair.

"That's right. None of it's holding. He's got a hundred senators screaming at him—"

"Ninety-nine. You're not screaming at him, Dan. You're screaming at me."

"And the press is screaming at him, and now you're against him. My God, a man's got to have something to hold onto! This country is holding onto that man—barely—and he's holding onto you—and you're running away."

"I'm not running. I've never run. I never will."

Senator Dan had arrived late that afternoon in a dusty Volkswagen. She had been glad to see him, to warm herself again in the health that poured from him like ultra-violet from a sun lamp. But she had found him angry and incoherent, with fists twisting in his pockets, weapons barely concealed; his talk of Lucky Bill had annoyed her for close to an hour, and—wishing he would go—she tried to think of other things.

"Are you still worried about that woman you think he's been seeing? You're not trying to get even, are you, Moni?"

"No, I'm not worried about any woman. I haven't thought about it in days. I haven't had to think about anything. Lexie's been safe, and I've felt wonderful."

For several days now, since coming to Virginia, the First Lady had taken to three or four light drinks before dinner. Far from making her numb or even tipsy, they brought on a gradual delicious indifference which allowed her, in complete dispassion, to ponder the problems that remained for her to solve. Sometimes, having reached a plateau of inner calm and composure, she would hold a glass for half an hour without so much as sipping, and thus prolong the miraculous state—so rare in her experience—of being mistress in her own head. She was beginning to treasure her consciousness.

"May I make a suggestion?" Senator Dan had the crafty look of a banker about to propose an investment. "Leave Lexie here. You come back."

"No."

"He needs you, Moni. Lucky Bill is a very unlucky fellow without you. He's started drinking."

"Again?" The First Lady looked at her half-empty glass, ice cube a thin remnant. The television set behind her, ignored but left running as though in hope that it would wear itself out, silently flashed pictures at the room, like a peddler respectfully offering wares: Costa Rican jungle, shrimp cocktail, baseball players, a naked woman, floral sachet hygiene mist; the stock market averages. . . .

"Moni, whether you appreciate the fact or not, you need him. And I don't mean as a husband; that's between you and him. But you need him just the way this country needs him. He's the last dike protecting some semblance of political sanity and order in this country, and he just might give. A lot of waves are chipping away at him. And if this nation goes, we all go. You, me, Lexie."

"Lexie is safe."

"You're out of touch, Moni. The temper of the times is bad, getting worse."

"I've never felt better. I've never felt stronger. I've never felt so alive. I can smell trees and breathe air."

"Aren't you being selfish?"

"Of course I'm being selfish. And you're being selfish and he's being selfish. And if you two want sacrifice, you're going to have to get it out of someone besides Lexie and me."

"And you'll let the country go under?"

The First Lady was particularly taken with the colors that followed sunset. She shuddered, safe in her chair, at their pastel violence. The dead and nearly buried day did something quite remarkable to the greens of plants and grass. It brought out a contrast between the color of the stalks and the leaves, lent outlines a holographic three-dimensionality, so that she felt—by reaching out her hand—she might touch each leaf, feel the delicacy of the surface and the roughness of the underside. She could even smell the green: moist, earthy, with a faint sweetness of fertilizer.

She sipped and marveled.

"The country won't go under," she said, "simply because Bill Luckinbill is defeated over a bill and it won't go under because Senator Dan Bulfinch loses his majority, and if the people don't want the Bill of Rights, they have a right to rip it up, don't they? It's a free country."

Over the last quarter hour the painting had changed, by quite miraculous degrees and overlaps, into a black and white woodcut, a tangle of wavering fine lines.

"Aren't you sounding a little like Marie Antoinette?"

"You haven't been married to him for nineteen years, Dan. Bill and I met twenty years ago, and that's enough time to get a good look at anyone. Bill is a realist. The Bill of Rights may sink, but he won't. He'll find some way to keep afloat."

"He took an oath to defend the Constitution."

The First Lady had spent her married life mired in the type of syllogism the senator was trying to force on her now. The reasoning seemed logical, it seemed right even, but if you looked closely you saw that terms kept shifting their meaning and premises were as shaky as condemned buildings; and now that she had crawled out, she had no intention of crawling back and letting the beams fall on her head. She did not care much for logic when the conclusion of every argument was *do my bidding*. She had heard so much of it: *Democracy is threatened—so do my bidding. War must end—so do my bidding. Taxes are high; the poor are rebelling; your daughter may die—so do my bidding.* Doing someone else's bidding never accomplished a damned thing but to make them bid you do more.

"Of course he took an oath to defend the Constitution," the First Lady granted. "Everyone does that if he wants to run the country. And didn't he take an oath to love, honor, and cherish the silly girl that married him?"

"You're not silly."

"And I'm not a girl any more."

At 7:28 P.M. she saw the white mare enter the dark woodcut. She thought it twice as white as it had been in the afternoon. It wasn't, of course, though it had been saddled and freshly curry-combed. What had changed was the background. At night there was less sky than at day, and the dark added layers to the shrubs and foliage. Colors had all but vanished, leaving only a spectrum of black and gray and white. Contrasts, if they existed at all, were starker now. Bless Me was no whiter, but she looked it as she grazed among the hedges and the rose-bushes. In winter, when snow lay on the ground, she would be almost invisible.

"I'll fight my fights, Dan. Not his. Not yours. I'll choose the fight and I'll choose the battlefield. My enemy is not your enemy. My enemies are not Bill Luckinbill's enemies."

Bittersweet, the gelding, was a pale flicker at the periphery of Bless Me's nimbus, like a ghost on a television tube, and it took the First Lady a moment to realize that what she had taken for Bless Me's shadow was the other horse.

"And if this nation becomes a tyranny?" Senator Dan asked, as though it would be her fault.

"We're too big to be a good one. Anyway, the Russians manage. The world manages."

His eyes blazed. "You astound me."

"Thank you."

Bless Me neighed, and Bittersweet replied, and it came to the First Lady—though she resisted the realization, as one resists waking from a dream—that what she saw through the windows was more than mere painting or woodcut. She saw two horses, still saddled, without their riders.

The senator was still talking, and at the back of the First Lady's neck sweat began to run like spiders.

"Where's Lexie?" She jumped up from the chair and pushed the senator aside in her rush toward the door. "What's happened to Lexie?"

July 4: Independence Day

During the soundless hours of early morning, when night hung stifling in the Washington sky, the First Lady sat alone in her husband's bedroom, drawing comfort from the hope that he would return, hold her hand or chide her fear, lend her some splinter of his strength. But the walls whispered to her that William Henry Harrison and Zachary Taylor had died here, exactly where she sat, and she rose, wanting no nearness to death, and paced through corridors where no visitor was allowed, over miles of dismal beige carpet, past portrait after portrait of this dead face or that. And the house whispered names—Lincoln, McKinley, Harding, Roosevelt, Kennedy, cadavers all who had lain within its walls; and she could not blot out her history-book memory of Calvin Coolidge, Jr., sixteen years old, his toe blistered playing tennis on the White House lawn, dead of blood poisoning, and his father's pathetic words: *When he went the power and the glory of the presidency went with him. . . .*

And when there was no power, no glory to begin with, what did the departing child take then?

She stared at restored chair legs and familiar guards and servants, at crisp towels blaring her monogram, and she tasted a despair so strong, so chemical, that it seemed a drop of poison had been placed at the back of her tongue. Her womb felt bloated and burning, as though it had been packed with ice; and a terrible labor contracted her brain, and a thought she did not want to admit was struggling into awareness.

What does the child take then?

It was her husband who found her and led her by the hand. "We were worried," he said softly, as though too loud a sound might shatter her. He was sure-footed in the half-light, and she trusted him as she would have a surgeon in an operating theater.

When she saw that there were others in the room she hung back, ashamed for her nightgown and flimsy robe. But her husband drew her deep into the crowd, and the faces fell back like portraits on a crumbling wall.

"Moni, Moni," she heard them keening.

The First Lady sat, tried not to droop, in a cozy gingham chair that had been Lady Bird Johnson's last decorative legacy to the Pink Room. A doctor bent over her and injected something into the vein of her left arm: to relax her, he said. Whispering servants brought and replaced trays of black coffee. Someone offered her a popover.

"If anything had happened to Lexie," the President said, "we'd have heard."

"Something has happened," the First Lady said. "It's my fault."

"It's not your fault," he said, "and nothing has happened."

The doctor withdrew his needle from the First Lady's arm and asked her to press a piece of white cotton over the tiny puncture. The First Lady watched the night wind play games with the fountain on the south lawn and wondered why it had been left on and tried not to think of death.

"Anything from Virginia State Police?" the President asked a telephone. The doctor locked his bag, wished all a good night, and hurried from the room with the step of a man who had promises to keep. "Maryland State Police?"

Maggie Tyson, gray-clad and as freshly pressed as she had been at three o'clock the afternoon before, crouched beside the First Lady. "You just stay calm, Moni. Whoever's to blame for this is going to get barbecued, don't you worry."

The First Lady recoiled slightly.

"Maggie," the President said, "keep out of this."

"I love that child like my own flesh and blood, and if you expect me to keep out of this, you're expecting the sun to stand still!"

"Lexie's disappearance," the President said, "is not for public consumption. It is not for newspapers, it is not for TV talk shows. Do I make myself clear, Maggie?"

"I don't see how you can put politics above that child's safety!" Maggie cried.

"We have police in an eight-state radius working on this, and we'd appreciate your not making their work any harder."

"How are they going to search every haystack and gully? The sooner you tell every man, woman and child in this nation what's going on, the sooner you'll see results! You can keep some of the people in the dark some of the time, but to gamble your own child's life in a last-ditch play for time on a measly Senate vote is—it's beyond me, Bill, beyond me! But then I'm not a politician, just a woman."

"Maggie," the First Lady said, "please let Bill do this his way."

Maggie's mouth hung open.

"Bill?" Senate Majority Leader Dan Bulfinch beckoned the President to the door. Woodrow Judd stood in the hallway. His face was drawn into a net of wrinkles and he held an armload of clothes and looked like a collector for the Salvation Army.

"Mr. President, we found these in a root cellar in Herndon, Virginia, fifty minutes ago. Do you recognize them?"

"The riding jacket could be Lexie's. I don't know about the breeches. The bootmaker would be able to identify the boots." The President turned back the neck of the blouse and stared at the laundry mark. "We can ask downstairs."

The First Lady peered over her husband's shoulder. The clothes were her daughter's.

"I've already asked downstairs," Woodrow Judd said.

The President looked from Woodrow Judd's face to Senator Dan's. They were the faces of ghosts at dawn.

"Mr. President," Woodrow Judd said, "there is a possibility— only an outside possibility, but I feel in all honesty my oath of office obliges me to advise you of the possibility—"

"For God's sake, Woodie, this isn't an arraignment. Now what the hell are you talking about?"

"I'm talking about the possibility that when Lexie was shot

in Whitefalls, it was not an accident; the possibility that her disappearance today was not an accident."

"Of course it wasn't an accident, we know that!"

"But that these events were part of a calculated, concerted conspiracy."

"Jesus, Woodie! All we're asking for is our daughter. We don't need your anarchists and your neo-neo's. Not tonight."

"Mr. President, I am trying to do my duty in advising you of the possibility that a group of highly placed political malefactors—"

"My wife's half-dead. My daughter could be half-dead or worse. What are you doing about it? Sniffing out Maoists?"

"You may have my badge."

"I don't want your goddamned badge!" The President turned his back and stalked down the corridor. Woodrow Judd turned to the First Lady.

"Forgive him," she said.

"I just feel he should know," Woodrow Judd said.

"Know what?"

They were alone in the corridor. Woodrow Judd drew a deep breath.

"Yesterday a document came into my possession purporting to be a projective scenario for revolution. This scenario involved your daughter. My first reaction was that it must have been written after Whitefalls by a political fantasist. Nonetheless, I feel the President should glance at it."

The First Lady took Woodrow Judd's scenario in its blue paper binder. "All right, Mr. Judd, I'll glance at it."

"No, Mrs. Luckinbill. The President—not you."

"Mr. Judd, if this touches on my daughter in any way, I want to read it."

"There's no sense alarming yourself."

"Isn't there?"

The First Lady took the blue binder to bed with her. Though the contractions in her brain became so painful she thought her skull would burst, she read all nine single-spaced pages.

She could not grasp how anyone could hate her daughter so

much. She could not grasp how anyone could find it right or imperative or expedient to crush the life out of an innocent child. She could not grasp this politics of death and she wanted to deny its very possibility. She would have preferred sleep or insanity to what she read in those pages and she could easily have let the binder slip from her fingers to the floor.

But she forced herself to read it again and again, and dimly—with the flickering clarity of a distant flare sent up in a storm—she began to understand.

*

At 4 A.M., when there still had been no word of Lexie, the President bade his advisers and friends and Maggie Tyson an uneasy good night. He found his wife still awake in the king-sized bed and asked if she wanted a sleeping pill.

"Could there be anything in what Judd says?" she answered.

"Don't think about it, hon, please."

The First Lady began crying.

"Moni, I've had a long day and I have a longer day tomorrow, and I've got to get a night's sleep. Now if you're going to be all worked up I'm going to have to sleep in my own room."

The First Lady blew her nose. "I'll be all right."

"Good night, hon." The President kissed her and went to his room. He stripped to his shorts and threw his clothes onto a wooden chair with the insignia of Northwestern University stenciled on its back. The bed had been freshly turned down, and he propped the pillows so that he could watch the television. Cowboys and Indians committed mutual genocide before his heavy eyes.

He was recalled to consciousness by a familiar ice pick of a voice. "Unquestionably, Tom; absolutely no question about it. The news media in this country are completely controlled."

He was jolted into full awakedness by the unthinkable thought that Maggie Tyson had gotten into the room with him. But his wits came to him and he saw she was safely under the glass of the TV screen, trim and smiling in her gray jacket and Irish lace collar, looking the way one hundred million

American women would have given their franchise to look at that hour.

"Controlled by who, Maggie?"

The President recognized the eastern seaboard drawl of the CBS 7 A.M. anchorman, a specialist in sneers who could have read the phone book aloud and made it sound like a tissue of lies. The camera cut to two eyebrows, skeptical in their arch, drew back to catch a mouth chewing on a yawn, swiveled rightward again to Maggie.

"Controlled by the self-styled opinion makers and kingmakers who sit like spiders at the nerve centers of this nation," Maggie clarified. "I think we all know who they are and what they are, Tom. When the price of beef goes up, when the price of gold goes up, when taxes and crime go up, we all know it's because these men have decreed it shall be so. This nation calls itself a democracy, but in fact it's an elitist dictatorship, and more and more Americans are waking up to the fact and becoming increasingly sickened by the deceptions practiced behind our democratic façade—a façade, by the way, severely in need of updating."

The anchorman's eyebrows had become paralyzed in the neighborhood of his hairline. "Now, Maggie, would you say, for example, that this television station, that this program are controlled?"

The President remembered that 7 A.M. talk shows were live. He muttered "Jesus Christ," and it was a prayer, not a curse. He knew what was coming, and he waited, braced.

"Absolutely. This program and this station are controlled."

The anchorman sat forward in his chair. "Then how do you explain that you and I can sit here and discuss the question of control without these spiders, as you call them, cutting us off the air?"

Maggie controlled her eyelashes perfectly. "Spiders are clever, Tom. I'd have thought you of all people would know that."

"What it seems to come down to is, we've got to take your word for it."

"No need to take my word for it when the facts are staring

you in the face. Let me give you an example, Tom, of what seems to me the most blatant, arrogant example of news manipulation since Jack Kennedy handed this nation's blood and treasure to the forces of militaristic internationalism."

The camera dollied in for the classic tight shot of Maggie staring umpteen hundred thousand televiewers straight in the tube.

"At this very moment," Maggie pronounced, "the nation is faced with what could develop into the most serious crisis of the decade, but have you heard a peep about it on any news show or read a line in any paper? Of course not, because the bosses have unilaterally decreed certain events unfit for public consumption. Now when the President of the United States of America cannot even appeal for help to his own people, when he must kowtow to the powers behind the scenes, I'd say that's pretty ruthless news control, wouldn't you, Tom?"

The anchorman's reflexes seemed to be dragging. "Excuse me, Maggie, but are you referring to any particular event?"

"Damned right I'm referring to a particular event. How many people in this country, at this moment, know that Lexie Luckinbill has been kidnaped by political extremists and that her father is powerless to bring his case to the people? How many folks know that Monica Luckinbill is prostrate, under a doctor's care at this very moment, because she doesn't know if her little girl is alive or dead or worse? How many people know the fear and the grief in the hearts of our nation's leaders? Do you realize, Tom, that if that girl is harmed, why, this country could split right open? And I kid you not. Right down the center, split in two."

The anchorman could not disguise a twinge of interest. "You're saying Lexie Luckinbill has been the victim of a political kidnaping?"

"I'm saying that this nation and every one of us is the victim of that kidnaping, Tom. It happened yesterday evening. Her clothes were found at three in the morning by state troopers in a root cellar in Herndon, Virginia. Her mother's just sick. It's a dreadful business, Tom, just dreadful, and my heart is steeped in woe and compassion for that poor girl and her poor mom and dad, and if this country still has any sort of guts or heart, every man, woman, and child of voting age will telegraph or phone his congressman and senator and make it clear they want laws with teeth in them so that this type of tragedy need never again be repeated. Tie those lines up, folks—tie them up!"

The President turned up the sound so that he could hear Maggie while he shaved.

*

Senator Dan, working over the holiday, frowned at his engagement pad. "Say, Linda—who the hell is Marion Holmes?"

Mrs. Parsons poked her head in from the other room. "She's your lunch date."

"I can see she's my lunch date, but who the hell is she?"

"For a senator you have a very short memory. Did you or did you not ask me to check into the President's love life?"

Senator Dan scratched his head.

"Marion Holmes is it. He's been seeing her again. At least three times in the last two months."

Senator Dan whistled softly.

"I assumed you had something you wanted to talk over with her, and she said this Rainbow Inn is so far out it's really out and there's not a chance of anyone's seeing you there on a Fourth of July, probably not even a waiter."

"You phoned her?"

"Of course I phoned her. What's a girl Friday for?"

"You're outrageous, you know that? I ought to fire you."

"If you haven't got the nerve, cancel. But you may be missing out on something. She said she's been following your work."

"Been following my work, has she?"

"And what's more, she says she likes it."

*

"I've been following you in the papers," Marion Holmes said. "You stick to losing battles. I admire that."

"Perhaps we both stick to losing battles," Senator Dan said.

It was a quiet, dimly lit place with only a half-dozen tables occupied. The bartender was dusting bottles with what appeared to be a feather boa on a stilt, and a few out-of-towners in search of B-girls were nursing drinks at the bar, and a pianist who had once studied at Juilliard was fingering some one-handed hand-me-downs at fifty a week plus tips. The waiter brought Dan's drink, and Marion Holmes pilfered the olive out of it.

"Your losing battle," she said, "is the Constitution of the United States and mine is the President, is that what you mean?"

"Is that what I said?" He tried to pinpoint what it was about her he found beautiful. It wasn't the eked-out youth of a still-beautiful woman, but something quite different. Her forties became her, and he had a feeling her fifties would too.

"You've come to lecture me, Senator, and I need another martini, and if you're a diplomat and a gentleman you'll keep up with me. I had two of these while I was waiting for you. I'm on my third and I'm beginning to feel good and about halfway through my fourth I'm going to feel great and I won't give a damn if the Senate Majority Leader or the Pope himself lectures me about scarlet women."

"I didn't come to lecture."

"Then did you come to stare? To see Marion Holmes with your own eyes? No relation to the Chief Justice, by the way, though I do admire him. You admire him too, Senator."

Senator Dan signaled the waiter that the lady needed a refill. "Yes, I do very much."

"Then you are what we call in my little black book a good guy. That means you're about to hit me, and don't bother denying it, but you're not going to hit too hard." She chewed a roasted peanut, which seemed to be the extent of her interest in solid nourishment. "Booze and age and wasted hope have just about got me down and you're going to deliver the knockout punch. You don't want to hurt me, though. You just wish I was dead."

"You're not going to make this easy for me, are you."

"And why should I? What do I owe you, or him, or her?"

"She's never hurt you, has she?"

Marion Holmes's gaze went out through a shadeless dead land where nothing stirred but ash and phantoms. "Yes, Senator, she's hurt me, and don't ask me to weep for a poor little rich girl sitting in the White House wondering where Prince Charming has gone at two in the morning. I suppose what really kills me is he still loves her and she can't even keep him. If he'd ever loved me like that, believe me, I'd have had him five years ago, White House and all."

"I think he does love you."

"I don't think so. Bill Luckinbill can look at me and I shake like a tree coming down in a gale, but he doesn't even know the color of my eyes."

"Then why did he go back to you?"

The waiter slid an arm and a martini into the conversation and deftly eased the tab out from under a saucer and penciled in the adjustment.

"Why does an elephant go to a graveyard?" Marion Holmes said. "There's a synapse in that head of his with MARION HOLMES engraved on it and when things get tough and your wife leaves you and the country's falling apart you crave a little familiar comfort. That's my theory. What's yours?"

"That he loves you."

"You're a diplomat and a liar and a gentleman, no contradiction intended. And you're warming up to tell me the President is a no-no, you're not going to have me making a widow out of that woman and an orphan out of that kid." She stopped short. "I'm sorry. I didn't mean to joke about Lexie. The whole thing's just horrible."

"Mrs. Holmes, I'm not going to make a pitch about Monica Luckinbill or Lexie Luckinbill. I am going to ask you to help Bill Luckinbill and to help this country."

Marion Holmes's face slowly went pale against the bar gloom as she shed her smile. "You don't ask small favors, do you."

"Maybe I'm not asking any more than you're willing to give. Bill Luckinbill needs all the support he can get. He doesn't need his wife walking out on him, and he doesn't need his enemies fighting dirty."

"In either case, you're afraid I'm the torpedo that could sink him?" The management had placed a pink candle on the table, and it gathered Marion Holmes into its fringe of unsteady light.

"Sink him or cripple him."

She glanced up. "There've been crippled Presidents before."

"I don't think this country can afford a crippled Bill Luckinbill." He watched her. She sat fanning herself with a toothpick.

"Senator, I'm what you'd call a liberal, if anyone's still using that word, and an old-fashioned idealist and a dope. I happen to like people, I mean I really think they're okay, and things may get a little sticky but they straighten out in the end, and I don't think you need whips and chains and wiretaps to make a country work. I think a little tenderness can go a long way, and I've always wondered why they never tried it in politics. I happen to like the Bill of Rights—don't ask me why. Maybe because it keeps the Gestapo and the KGB out of my bedroom. Maybe because it lets me drink in peace. Maybe because it let me see Bill Luckinbill again. That's all I wanted, Senator, just to see him again and remind myself how much I've missed him so I could live miserably ever after. I got my wish. Now you get yours. What can I do for Bill and the Constitution?"

"Never see the President again."

"I kind of felt that one coming." She bent the toothpick in two. "Do you mean never ever, or never till he's out of office?"

"I try not to ask the impossible."

"Try asking some day, Senator. It might just get you somewhere." Marion Holmes downed her drink as though it were lemonade.

"I'll remember that. And, Mrs. Holmes, for what it's worth, thank you."

"Anytime." She began putting things into her purse. "I guess I'll just pack my bags and take a trip around the Cape of Good Hope."

Senator Dan paid the bill, an astonishing eight drinks. He didn't have the heart to try to find out if it was Marion Holmes's math or the waiter's that was off. At any rate she walked straight.

"Drop you anywhere?" he offered.

She laughed without malice. "That's a great idea. Anywhere suits me just fine."

*

At an emergency televised news conference called for 2 P.M., Washington time, the President assured the press and the TV-viewing public that there was absolutely no need for panic and even less need for hasty legislation, that he and Mrs. Luckinbill were in close touch with all internal security agencies of the federal government and with state and local law-enforcement personnel and that they were satisfied that everything humanly possible was being done by these dedicated public servants to locate their daughter.

There was no indication, the President emphasized, of kidnaping, foul play, or violence of any sort; indeed one of the most hopeful signs was that no demands for ransom had been received by the White House. The President thanked the public for their sympathy and help, deeply appreciated by Mrs. Luckinbill and himself, and begged them not to telephone or telegraph unless they had concrete information as to his daughter's whereabouts. Mrs. Luckinbill, he added, was in good health.

Though presidential aides had made clear that the President would answer no questions, the reporter from the Washington *Post* pushed close enough to a live mike to be heard shouting in her familiar moonshine baritone, "Mr. President, what do you think of Mrs. Tyson's breaking this story on a TV talk show? Do you feel it helps or hinders efforts to recover your daughter?"

"Mrs. Tyson," the President answered, before aides could signal to kill the sound, "should be muzzled."

Midday and evening editions splashed the remark coast-to-coast. Afternoon and evening TV news roundups aired it in rerun. It got equal space with Lexie's disappearance and threatened to become an even bigger story. A Gallup poll of Farley, Nebraska, indicated that the President's popularity suffered a precipitous 22 per cent decline while Mrs. Tyson's swelled almost 41 per cent as a result of what the Chief Executive later stated had been a slip of the tongue under tremendous psychological pressure.

If the public could not forgive lack of gallantry, Maggie Tyson showed herself a passed mistress of the turned cheek. Interviewed on the Luana Patterson Happy Hour, live at four from the Hotel Taft in Baltimore, Maggie stated that "The President has got a heck of a lot on his mind and I think we should all show him some understanding. Let's just pray we get Lexie back, and some laws with teeth in them, and I'll be proud to wear that muzzle."

*

At 4:12 P.M., daylight saving time, a young man and woman in blue jeans presented themselves at the south entrance of the White House. The Marine guard admitted them without identification. They went directly to the Red Room, the traditional and sumptuous setting for the First Family's smaller tea parties. It was in this room, in April 1863, that President Lincoln had joked with spirits at a seance, and it was here, too, that President Hayes and his wife Lucy had invited cabinet members and congressmen to Sunday morning services.

Gilt-edged portraits of Wilson and McKinley stared somberly from the red-velvet walls and a butler laid tea service for eight; the First Lady, trying hard to memorize the list of names that had been typed for her—the regional directors of the Boy and Girl Scouts were invited for 4:30—, bit into a cucumber sandwich and wondered whether anxiety had muddled her tastebuds or whether the White House kitchen was going slack.

And then, thinking she heard a voice, she turned toward the paneled door and saw her daughter. For a moment she kept chewing the sandwich. By the time the shock hit her, Lexie was in her arms, smacking kisses on her face.

"Lexie, Lexie," she sobbed, "where—what in the—" And before the scolding words could come, she was laughing tears and holding the girl at arm's length, searching for scratches and breakage and finding no dents in the child she loved, this child who stood before her beaming and jabbering and alive and grinning and snitching sandwiches from the silver tray.

"Your father," the First Lady said, "the police . . . poor Woodrow Judd. . . ."

"I know," the girl laughed. "Chad and I heard all about it on the radio."

The First Lady glanced at the man her daughter had brought with her into the room. Anger came to her voice in a quick flare. "Mr. Beausoleil, you were entrusted with my daughter's—"

"Mother, Chad and I are married."

"Married?" A cucumber seed caught in the First Lady's throat.

"As of nine o'clock last night. Justice Joshua Porter of White Post performed the ceremony in his front parlor. There were no bridesmaids, no guests, and the press was not informed."

"White Post?" the First Lady stammered.

"That's Clarke County, ma'am," Chad said. "Virginia. Eighty miles from here."

"Justice Porter has white hair and an ulcer and he's a Republican." Lexie nibbled a sandwich around the edges. "And we bribed him to keep the marriage secret for forty-eight hours."

"We wanted to tell you ourselves," Chad said. "Before the newspapers found out."

The First Lady stared at the boy, and the light around him shifted subtly as though switches had been pulled backstage, and —yes—there was something fine about him, something she was sure she had seen from the first, because Lexie had never, ever been wrong in her judgment on any place, person, or thing, and the First Lady opened her arms to the stranger and cried, "Oh, Chad, I'm so happy, I'm so relieved!"

And Chad Beausoleil, with infinite, touching tact embraced his mother-in-law.

"You were terrible to steal her from us like that," she said, words gushing, "but at least you brought her back to us, and I don't suppose an eight-state manhunt is any more trouble or expense than a White House wedding. Oh, Chad, thank you for bringing her back to us!"

To me, she meant, but she said *to us* and she kissed him on both cheeks, and her lips left faint, fleeting blushes.

"Chad didn't steal anyone," Lexie contradicted. "I had to steal him *and* seduce him."

"And you left your grandfather's jodhpurs in that root cellar!" the First Lady chided.

"Where's Dad?" Lexie popped a sandwich into Chad's mouth.

"He's in his office seeing Dan Bulfinch about that—you know, that dreadful bill."

Chad Beausoleil's face twitched as though a fly had grazed it.

"Do you suppose I can get an appointment to see him?" Lexie laughed.

"Yes, darling, I think today you can get an appointment."

*

At 4:28 P.M. Mark Hendricks, senior senator from New Jersey, a man who had served five terms in Congress, four of them as chairman of the Joint Commission on Consumer Protection, who had pushed hospital construction through over the vetoes of two Presidents, whose bills had cleaned the air and banned cigarette ads and limited mutual-fund commissions, walked into Woodrow Judd's apartment and announced, "Woodie, I need your help."

"Well now, Mark," Woodrow Judd said, "what can I do for you?"

"I've thought this over for a week, and I think you can do a great deal. I'm being blackmailed."

Woodrow Judd offered a drink and indicated the chair nearest the sofa—the one he reserved for friendly conversations. Worry showed through Senator Hendricks' suntan.

"It's that damned gun-control bill, that rider thing. I'm opposed to it, Woodie, but someone wants me to change my vote."

"That's politics. I hope you told them no."

"I told them no, and they told me they'd publish—this." Senator Hendricks extracted a cylinder of furled print-out from his briefcase and handed it to Woodrow Judd. The rubber band made a *ping* as Judd snapped it off. He scanned the lines of type, pursing his lips.

"This business was twelve, fourteen years ago."

"Fifteen. And you hushed it up for me, Woodie, and I've supported you ever since, you can't deny I've been right in there slugging every time you needed an appropriation."

"You're a friend of this agency, and this agency's your friend, I want you to know that, Mark." Woodrow Judd cocked an eyebrow and twisted a finger in his ear. "Now how the hell did your blackmailer get hold of this?"

"You tell me. It looks like it came from your files."

"It sure does, but only two people can get to the computer bank where this stuff is stored, and that's me and my assistant." But Woodrow Judd remembered that his assistant had falsified reports during his absence and had been found dead in her Maryland cottage and again the most he could feel was a childish resentment at the change in routine her absence would occasion. "When did this blackmailer approach you?"

"Nine days ago, and I've been stewing ever since. Finally decided to do the logical thing and come to you. I can't vote for that bill, Woodie. I just can't. But I can't sit back and let them rake up this old muck either."

Woodrow Judd raised the lower of his chins up from the polka-dot bow tie that bloomed from his shirt. "I've got enough dirt in my files to bury this whole town. So maybe I should just have a heart-to-heart with this blackmailer of yours."

Senator Hendricks sank back into his chair. "I'd be grateful."

"No trouble, Mark. Who is he?"

"It's someone you might say is kind of high in the government."

Woodrow Judd's hand stroked a shaving cut on his cheekbone, and he smiled narrowly. "I don't care how high he is."

"I don't want to get you into any trouble, Woodie."

"You're not getting anyone into anything. You're being blackmailed and I've got a security leak and we might as well plug two holes with one lump of putty. Now who the hell is he?"

The clock ticked and Senator Mark Hendricks told Woodrow Judd the name of his blackmailer.

*

Two hours after sundown, Maggie Tyson's taxi let her off at the high-rise on the east bank of the Potomac. She paid her fare and a twenty-cent tip and walked scowling into the glass foyer. She did not approve of the building's plastic-doughnut architecture, which had copped four-color centerfolds in the nation's left-of-center weeklies, nor of its inhabitants, who were the skim milk of the city's would-be hostesses, congressmen, and administration hangers-on.

Maggie hurried past the armed guard with a *Hi there* and a shout about being expected in Penthouse-J. The guard waved her through with his revolver and she took herself up in the mirrored self-service elevator with Muzak tinkling out its top.

Woodrow Judd himself opened the door. He was dressed in a Chinese housecoat that did nothing for his paunch but advertise it, and when he offered her a choice of stinger or sidecar his manner was positively mandarin.

"You're looking well, Woodie."

"And you, my dear, are looking delicious."

Who but a superannuated fruit, she wondered, would disinter such stale Cary Grant one-liners. She had heard about the apartment with its portraits of poodles past and present, its life-sized porcelain-poodle doorjambs and its crystal poodle bookends, and now she realized that what she had taken for jokes had been merest reportage. Woodrow Judd took her arm and walked her to a sofa upholstered in what seemed to be white poodle fleece. It commanded a view of a bend in the Potomac that was not unimpressive.

Maggie sat, uneasy that the sofa was so totally, so horribly comfortable. She watched the little man whip up two sidecars. He handed her a frosted glass.

"Okay, Woodie: what's this all about?"

"I've had a talk with Senator Hendricks."

"That pervert."

"He's upset with you."

"I don't see that it's any of your business."

"It's my business to investigate any threat to the life or safety of any member of this government, and moreover—"

Maggie cut him short, leaving the tail end of his statement stuck in his throat like a fishbone.

"Isn't it time you stopped taking the side of known moral degenerates like Hendricks? This nation is in trouble, Woodie, and men like him aren't helping any!"

Woodrow Judd looked mildly stymied, as though he would have liked to put his hands to his ears but didn't wish to appear ill-bred. He spoke softly. "It's a fact that the nation's in trouble, but I tend to lay the blame a bit more on your tactics than on Senator Hendricks'."

It was a moment for magnanimity, and Maggie didn't stint. "All right. I've been wrong, very wrong, many many times. I'm the first to admit it. But Washington was dead wrong in the Delaware campaign, and Lincoln was dead wrong to suspend *habeas corpus*, and what patriot hasn't been wrong somewhere along the line? You can't fight to the death for a thing you love more than life itself and not get your hands dirty! The point is, Woodie, you and I are on the same side, and why should we let our petty tactical differences divide us?"

Woodrow Judd's poodle, the living one, came to his side, and he stroked the animal's head fondly, thoughtfully. "Well, in the first place, I'm not sure we are on the same side."

"Of course we're on the same side, Woodie; don't kid me and don't kid yourself. We both know this country can't last long: it's easier to believe Scheherazade than that budget; the oil is almost used up and the heroin is a little too widespread; a lot too many people own guns and a few too many are beginning to think like you and me. But we both know the lid's going to stay on the pressure cooker just long enough for us to sneak a little something out of the pot, and if we happen to go down in history while we pull it off, well why not?"

"Exactly how do you think we're going to go down in history, Maggie?"

"Come on, Woodie: you authored this country's security policies and you run them at a profit, and that alone guarantees you
a niche in Mount Rushmore. As for me—what with Women's
Lib, which to my mind is typical of the surface solution the
nation keeps smearing on its pimples, why, what Jackie Kennedy
had to marry I stand a good 70–30 chance of getting on my
own."

"You actually think—you think *you* can be President?"

"Frankly I think I've got the political awareness and know-
how to do it. And my hands are not tied by any eighteenth-
century ideological crap."

"Good Lord."

"Oh, come on, Woodie. You're not going to get all gooey and
sentimental over a two-hundred-year-old scrap of parchment!
All men created equal, you believe that hooey?"

"I think the Constitution has got a hell of a lot wrong with
it, but I'd hate to see this country lose it to the likes of you."

"What the hell does the Constitution have to do with this?"

"There's a bill pending in the Senate. I think you know the
rider to that bill by heart. For all I know you wrote it. Let's say
it—it alters the Constitution."

"And about time."

"Senator Hendricks tells me you've been urging him to change
his vote on that bill."

"Cut the bullshit, Woodie. I've been blackmailing him, same
as you've been blackmailing him and ninety-nine other senators
every time your appropriation comes up."

"You've threatened to publish a certain incident from his
past."

"If balling twelve-year-old chicks is his bag, that's his problem,
not mine. Damned right I'm going to publish it. He stabs this
country in the back, this country'll stab him."

"This information—the twelve-year-old—how did you come
by it?"

"For Chrissake Woodie, why don't you come right out and
ask me how I got to your dirt bank?" Maggie's voice had the
vibrato of a bowstring pulled taut. "You've been running this

country your way for God knows how many administrations. All right, now it's someone else's turn. When that bill passes the Senate, and when Lucky Bill goes on TV to veto it, and when he signs bye-bye to the greatest concentration of political power the West has ever seen, Maggie Tyson is stepping into that vacuum. You've got a choice, Woodie. You can come along as part of the Administration—or you can be out on your ass."

"Who gave you my files?"

Maggie's pupils narrowed to pinpricks. "Erikka Lumi. I said she could have your job if she helped us. She bit."

"She would have had my job anyway, sooner or later."

"Later would have been too late."

"I'm surprised she betrayed my trust so easily."

"You're not surprised, Woodie—just hurt. But the one thing Erikka needed you couldn't give her—and I could."

"She never said she needed anything."

"Erikka was living the life of a nun, and she wasn't cut out for the convent. She was so goddamned inept she couldn't even shake a man's hand or invite him up for a cup of coffee. That's what security work does to you, Woodie—makes you terrified of your own natural functions." Maggie beamed a gaze directly into Woodrow Judd's eyes. "So I played matchmaker. We had a man available, and we had to keep tabs on her anyway. He kept her happy and he kept her in line and he kept her working for us. Of course, when she got sloppy, we had to get rid of her."

Woodrow Judd slumped like a punching bag that had had one too many. Maggie made a concerned face.

"You seem a little stunned, Woodie. Here, have some of my drink." Maggie proffered her unsipped glass. "It's delicious."

Woodrow Judd refused the glass with a quick headshake. "Not stunned, Mrs. Tyson—just unclear."

Maggie curled against a fluffy pillow. "Look, Woodie, I'm not asking you to join the team blindfolded, so if there's anything I can clear up for you, shoot."

"Hiram Quinn and the fake reports," Woodrow Judd itemized. "The threatening note to the President; Darcie Sybert."

Maggie took a deep breath. "Hiram Quinn was on our payroll. The threat note was a phony, slapped together out of some back-issue magazines. We had it mailed from Whitefalls, and Erikka put Quinn on the job with instructions to go real slow. It took a little planning and a little time and a few jet flights out to Whitefalls to set up that shooting. Luckily you were out of commission when we started this thing rolling."

Woodrow Judd made a sour face, as though unconvinced.

"I know it sounds baroque," Maggie shrugged, "and you probably wonder why the hell we needed a fake letter and a fake investigation. We needed them for you, Woodie, and for the rest of the country. I can't go around shooting Lexie Luckinbill personally, can I? Hell, she's the nation's virgin-in-residence. It had to look like a grass-roots conspiracy, right down to that cornball threat note. Believe me, we had some top minds figure this whole thing out."

Maggie shifted the fluffy pillow under her leg, which had begun to go to sleep. "As for Darcie Sybert, Quinn had to open *somebody's* mail. When he ended up in the sack with her, that— I'll admit—surprised us. To make matters worse, Quinn recognized our assassin two days before the shooting. They'd trained together—can you beat that? We had to find out what Quinn had told Darcie and if she told anyone else, ergo the kidnaping, which incidentally was a pushover. Darcie didn't know Quinn was dead; Erikka said she'd take Darcie to him, but it had to be hush-hush. Darcie came along without a whimper. Erikka got her in the back seat of a car and it was just a question of an intravenous shot and an Air Force jet."

Woodrow Judd nodded slowly. "And who," he asked, "is your assassin?"

"Come on, Woodie. A woman's got to have a few secrets."

"I take it he shot Hiram Quinn."

"He had to. Quinn could have spilled one hell of a lot of beans."

"And don't you think I could now?"

Maggie smiled. "You wouldn't be that dumb."

"I might be dumb to try to fight you, but I'd have to be a

mental and moral syphilitic to go along with you. If you think you can seize the power of this nation over the corpse of that girl—"

"With the mood of the country and the powers Congress is going to pass, it'll be a snap."

"And when the President vetoes your precious bill?"

Maggie smiled. "We've got the votes to override him."

Woodrow Judd stiffened. "You're a lunatic, and I'm going to stop you."

"How?"

"I'm going to the President and if necessary to Congress."

"You would be doing this nation a grave and immeasurable disservice."

"I'd be doing my job."

Maggie paused, then dropped to a note of muted grief. "Then I see I'll have to do mine."

Woodrow Judd investigated each of the poodle's ears. "Your job is none of my business, thank God."

Maggie enunciated distinctly. "Hemorrhoids, Woodie."

"Now what's that supposed to mean?"

"It means your aching ass is no aching ass, it's a worn-out heart that's fifty per cent spare parts. It means I know you've got a pacemaker in your fat gut and you'd be dead without it. It means I've got documented proof you're on the waiting list for a transplant!"

Woodrow Judd recoiled against an armrest. "That . . . is ridiculous. That is a lie. You are lying, Mrs. Tyson, and you know it."

Maggie let him have it, all systems go, full throttle, every syllable staccato *sforzando*. "I have a sworn affidavit, Woodie, and it says that run-down ticker of yours belongs on the junk heap and you have no business meddling in the security of this nation! And do you want to know who signed my affidavit, Woodie? The doctor who installed your plastic and chrome re-tread, that's who signed my affidavit! Furthermore I happen to have one hundred Xeroxed copies of that affidavit here in my purse, ready for immediate distribution!"

"I do not need a transplant. . . ." Woodrow Judd's face began striping like boiled zebra. "I've got a good . . . functional . . . heart . . . miraculous for my age . . . they said it was miraculous. . . ."

"And you keep believing it, Woodie. But you spread one word to anyone—I don't care if it's the President or the men's-room attendant at the Y—and the Washington *Post* is going to know the whole stinking truth about you and your heart and the security of this nation, and there will be a hue and cry from the heartland and the patriots will be crying, 'Barbecue Woodrow Judd!' And you know something, Woodie—you may have the dirt on the President and you may have the dirt on the Washington *Post*—but you don't have the dirt on this nation, and if they say barbecue Judd, they'll barbecue him, and the Chinese will be able to see the flames over in Peking! Think it over, Woodie, 'cause Maggie ain't kidding!"

Maggie Tyson plunked down her unsipped drink and streaked out of the apartment, taking care only to slam the door good and hard behind her. The slam hit Woodrow Judd like a kick in the stomach. He slipped sideways, crushing a silk scatter pillow, and fell to the floor. The poodle came whining to him and coated his cheek with anguished licks.

Woodrow Judd's breathing was shallow and rapid, and his pulse attained the fluctuation of a panicked sparrow's wingbeat. The spectrum before his eyes was green, green, with nary a red in sight, and the light was fading and the darkness was moving entire divisions in from the edge of his collapsing vision. He was barely able to pull the telephone to the floor, and—with his last conscious breath—whisper to a shocked and mystified apprentice operator for an ambulance.

July 5: Wednesday

The telephone rang in Warner Gillespie's New York apartment at 3:20 A.M. "Gillespie," it hissed: "Maggie Tyson here."

Warner Gillespie drew himself into a sitting position and flicked on the bedside tensor lamp. He willed himself awake and focused his attention into a needle that penetrated three inches into the telephone receiver.

"The Senate's going to be voting on that bill day after tomorrow, looks like. I want a new ending to your scenario. A bloodcurdler that'll stand this country on its ear and jolt the nation into a *volte-face*."

"What good is a new ending after the bill has passed?"

"There's going to be a backlash that'll make the race riots look like a college debate. That bill is going to put this nation right where we want it, and your new ending is going to keep it there."

"Okay," he cut her short.

Long after he had made his promise and replaced the receiver, Warner Gillespie sat awake in bed, thinking, frowning, wondering if he dared press his luck a second time.

*

The day came, as Jordie Watts had prayed God it would and as Woodrow Judd had foretold it must. It dawned sunny and clear over New York, a condition so rare in that city as to be chimerical. While the pollution indexers and the federal weather watchers in Central Park triple-checked their instruments and wondered what the hell had gone wrong with the smog, Miss Minerva Tate hurried down to Jordie Watts's cubicle with an urgent communiqué from her boss.

"Mr. Gillespie would like to see you."

Three minutes later Jordie stepped into a room that was half glass, with New York east in one window and New York north in the other. A grayed-at-the-temples gentleman rose, smiling, from his glass and chromium desk and said, "No calls, Miss Tate," and then, "It's good of you to see me, Jordie."

Jordie bridled at the usurpation of his first name, and his tone was even colder than he had planned. "What can I do for you, Mr. Gillespie?" For he knew he was in control, and he knew Mr. Gillespie knew it. The man who perceives the Idea of History is always in control.

Mr. Gillespie made a face that was friendly and almost convincing. "Ah—Jordie, m'boy. I was wondering if by any chance you'd be free for lunch?"

*

Two hours later that same summer day, a man and a boy had lunch at Enrico's, a small restaurant catering to advertising and publishing expense accounts and occupying the lower two stories of an exorbitantly taxed and Mafia-protected town house in Manhattan's East Fifties. Despite the Italian and folksy sound of its name, it served only French cuisine, and its owner, Henri, was famous for turning away customers who looked or sounded a notch below his regulars.

The ground story was a bar, and here newcomers had to wait in hope that Henri would allow them upstairs to the dining room, which had wall paintings of Venetian canals in false, not to say incompetent, perspective. The red velvet chairs and benches at Enrico's tables were mostly occupied, from noon till three, by men whose three-piece suits were tailored and vented like jumbo jets and whose conversations turned on cigarette accounts and famous madames' and ex-Presidents' memoirs. Money, if mentioned at all, tended to be rounded off to the nearest hundred thousand, and tips below five dollars were rare.

Enrico's was probably the last place in New York where anyone would have gone for advice on planning the death of the world as we know it and the birth of its successor. And yet, that lunchtime, advice was precisely what a man well on his way to becoming—if all went well—one of the most powerful ideologues in the nation was trying to extract from his young guest.

The man was tall, in his late forties, with a brooding aquiline profile and a manicured forelock that gave him the look of a Roman emperor during the Decline. He had a disproportionately deep speaking voice and the fearsome syntax of a debating-team ringer. He was Warner Gillespie, economist, ambassador, authority on pre-Columbian sculpture and president of the public-relations firm of Gillespie, Ogilvie, Thorpe, the nation's second largest. The boy he had invited to join him was Jordie Watts, copy clerk at the agency.

By all appearances, the lunch was nothing to cause a waiter's ear so much as to prick. The two inquired about each other's health, commented on the weather, affirmed the supremely obvious state of things. They debated whether to risk oysters; they disagreed as to the advisability of *ris de veau financière*. Gillespie told an anecdote at the expense of the wife of the Secretary of the Treasury. It caused Jordie Watts to explode with laughter.

"More wine?" Gillespie offered, filling the lad's tulip-bulb glass for the fourth time.

Jordie Watts nodded and slapped a spoonful of sturgeon roe onto melba toast.

The *hors d'oeuvres variés* that day included a ravishing *moules ravigote*, and it was because of the *moules* that Warner Gillespie had ordered the two bottles of chilled Montrachet St. Albans 1965. He took his third sip of the wine and smiled at the boy. "It's a delight, Jordie, just a delight to have a bright young man like you in the company to bounce ideas off of."

Delight . . . bright . . . The words rang like antiphonal church bells in Jordie Watts's ears, and like a communicant kneeling at the elevation of the Host, he could barely fight back the tears that came flooding to his eyes. "Thank you, sir."

"More wine?"

A waiter swooped like some gigantic condor, depositing silver eggs of iced vichyssoise.

"What would you think to clear our palates?" Warner Gillespie asked the boy. "Some calvados over shaved ice?"

The boy smiled.

Warner Gillespie signaled the waiter with a crinkle of his nose. "With the tournedos we'll have a Mouton Cadet—two Moutons. You might as well open the bottles now."

*

Nagged by his ulcer, Jordie Watts stirred, kicked loose from the twisted bedspread, and tried to remember what he was doing home during office hours. He squinted toward the window to see if it was morning or evening, but the light stung his eyes, and his head, he realized, ached as though an army tank had driven over it.

Staving off walls with outstretched hands, he staggered to his feet and into the bathroom. He found the empty Maalox bottle in the cabinet right behind the empty toothpaste tube.

The President's daughter—he remembered that much. Hadn't she been at lunch with them? Hadn't she worn a white dress, and smiled at him?

His eyes teared and his vision blurred and some instinct in him cried *orange juice!* and he stumbled to the refrigerator and shooed away the cockroaches and fumbled along the shelves of empty cartons. He tilted a jumbo can of Hawaiian punch to his mouth and drained the last inch of dregs from it. He blinked and saw more clearly.

Valium, the instinct cried.

No: they had not talked with her, they had talked about her. What was the phrase Gillespie had used—*hypothetically speaking*. They had spoken hypothetically.

Jordie's ulcer twinged. The Hawaiian punch can clattered to the linoleum, and bottles cascaded from the medicine cabinet into the sink. He found half a Valium in a topless bottle. He gulped it down with a handful of tap water.

He sat on the edge of the bed and began linking bits of memory to one another. *Hypothetically speaking, the girl is more accessible than ever. She could be in her own bathroom and it wouldn't make any difference. Now using that type of availability, how would you go about standing this country on its ear?*

Jordie made two fists. The bastard had tricked him; gotten revisions out of him, goddammit, gotten a wholly new and infinitely more effective resolution to the dialectic of events in the scenario—and never even mentioned giving him a credit!

Jordie slammed a fist into his ear and tried to remember what the hell that new ending was. Gillespie wasn't going to take bows this time, for Jordie Watts held the ace: a scrap of paper with Woodrow Judd's personal telephone number on it.

Ignoring the prods of his ulcer, he snatched up his telephone and dialed. A genderless voice told him Mr. Judd would be inaccessible for a matter of days.

"This is Jordie Watts," Jordie said, "double-u, a, double-t, s, and tell him it's a matter of supreme importance to the Republic."

III: The Bill

We believe that the situation is likely to be better than we indicate, rather than worse, though the latter possibility cannot be ruled out.

HERMAN KAHN, *On Thermonuclear War*

July 6: Thursday

Borodin stared down at Judd, strapped to an army of bleeping oscilloscopes. The Director's features had been tugged to the left as though a child had slopped a wet sponge across a water color. Spittle running out a corner of the mouth drained the face of any dignity that age or wisdom or suffering might have lent it.

"Has he talked yet?" Borodin asked the nurse.

"No."

"Can he hear me?"

"I'd doubt it very much." The girl consulted a clipboard with graphs and medication instructions and scratch paper clamped to it. "What about the message?"

"What message?"

"Jordie Watts. A matter of supreme importance to the Republic."

"Is there a pay phone?"

"In the hall."

The number was listed with New York City information, and Jordie Watts consented to accept a collect call. The connection had the tin ring of long-distance walkie-talkie. Mines seemed to be going off at the central switchboard, reducing entire sentences to gibbering reverberations. Jordie said something about having been drunk, then added, "I have a hunch Gillespie's aim is maximum emotional impact with a strong play on irrational fears. He's probably going all-out for shock. Can you hear me?"

"Clear as a bell. How's he going to do it?"

"I apologize that my recollection of the conversation is inexact, but I believe I suggested that Lexie Luckinbill be killed, this time for real."

Borodin's hand made a fist around the receiver. "When is this going to happen?"

"I got the feeling Gillespie was aiming at immediate implementation."

"Where will she be killed?"

"Again I'm kind of vague—we had a lot of wine—but I believe I suggested using her home, vandalizing the place, smearing offensive slogans on the walls. The slogans would combine four-letter words with political catch-phrases of the far left and right. Are you there?"

"Still here. Who's going to do this?"

"Gillespie said something about having access to her, being able to get into her bathroom if he needed. I'd assume that one or more of her guards are in on the project."

A flash flood of nausea geysered up Borodin's throat and he had to swallow hard. "Thanks, Jordie. Mr. Judd will remember this."

"Any time."

*

There was no hope of extracting Lexie Luckinbill Beausoleil's telephone number from District of Columbia information, and Borodin didn't waste the time trying. The morning paper carried two possibly helpful items: one was a notice that the First Lady would be addressing a gathering of the Marine Conservation League that morning; the occasion was the gift by the Senegalese nation of a crocodile to the National Aquarium. The other item—lending factuality to what otherwise must have seemed a fairy tale—was a human-interest blurb on Lexie Beausoleil, replete with her married address and her husband's weight, height, hobbies, and birthplace.

Borodin took a taxi, giving the address of the four-story converted town house on Nebraska Avenue where—according to the Washington *Post*—America's newest sweethearts occupied the entire second floor.

Police had cordoned off the block, and the taxi could go no farther than the intersection. Both sides of the street were lined with riderless motorcycles and dead searchlights, as though in readiness for a prison break. Gawkers had gathered at the sawhorse barricades, and the police were using riot techniques, herding them into roped-off areas. Squeals rose to levels more threatening than air raid sirens.

Borodin showed his I.D. to a green-eyed cop. The cop waved him on, shouting to the next cop to let him pass, and he got as far as the town-house steps. He was stopped by a kid with close-cropped hair and a most defensive gleam in his steel-rim specs and a very sturdy arm braced like a roadblock against the front doorjamb.

"Is she in there?" Borodin asked.

"Who?"

"Mrs. Beausoleil."

"Never heard of her."

"I've got to talk to her." Borodin showed his I.D. The steel rims looked at him as though he were some kind of reporter, and from a college newspaper at that.

"Sorry," the kid said, and at his signal two plainclothesmen hustled Borodin to the barricade and eased him back into the mob like garbage thrown to sharks.

*

Time was breathing heavily on Borodin's back, and the heat was melting him into a blob of butter. He had considered the possibilities—the police, the other security agencies, the newspapers—and he had even gone so far as to drop a dime into a phone and dial the CIA—but realism had told him that even if they would listen, which was doubtful, even if any of them would believe him, which was incredible, between the double-check and the delay they would manage to alert every political crank in the District of Columbia and manage to provoke the very thing they were trying to prevent—assuming of course they weren't in on it themselves.

He was standing on a grassy corner near a park. He felt very close to beat and he felt that Lexie Luckinbill might be so close to dead it would be more to the point to alert a priest.

The only bright spot he could see was an oriole singing in the tree above him, and he wondered how the hell the bird managed.

He raised an arm and hailed a cruising cab and told the driver to take him to Constitution and Fourteenth.

The taxi left him at the entrance of the Department of Commerce Building, where for some reason the National Aquarium shared the basement with a cafeteria. His I.D. got him in, and he took the staircase in the main lobby and ran down a flight. A group of schoolchildren who had somehow gotten past Security had clustered at the Siamese tiger fish tank, making faces and rapping on the glass. According to a brass plate, the fish turned black when frightened.

Borodin found that the open turtle tank and the African clawed frogs were the flops of the day, with no gawkers at all. The gigantic green moray eels had attracted an old man with easel and paints, who was most likely a security plant, but the big crowd was at the crocodile tank. Through the forest of bodies Borodin caught flashes of Senegalese robes and the unmistakable broad black backs of the Secret Service guards. A poorly functioning public-address system sputtered something about the ecological balance in West Africa, and from what he could hear of the accent and the grammar Borodin didn't think it was the First Lady talking.

He pried his way through the crowd, scattering *excuse me*'s to reporters and Marine Conservationists and avoiding the men with black suits and gruesome scowls. He finally caught sight of the First Lady, backed against a tank of *crocodylus acutus* and wedged between a man who seemed to be wearing a Liberian flag and another who resembled photographs of the President's adviser on national security affairs.

The woman at the mike wore a purple two-toned feathered hat, and Borodin wondered just how strict a conservationist she was until he got close enough to see that the feathers were cellophane. One of the First Lady's guard had turned his head to blow his nose, and the First Lady was whispering to or being whispered to by an eager young man who had crossed the semicircle of empty floor separating dignitaries from spectators.

Borodin reached the front rank of audience, and before the Secret Service man could spot him or push him back he said, "Mrs. Luckinbill?"

The First Lady looked up and saw a smudged hulk of a human being moving toward her out of the crowd.

"It's about your daughter."

The Secret Service man tried to pocket his handkerchief and at the same time and in the same motion block Borodin. The First Lady put out a hand.

"You've got to warn her," Borodin said.

Nahum Bismarck came forward like shot from a harquebus. "Who are you and what the hell are you doing here?"

"I'm an agent of the Federal Security Agency. I have information—"

The First Lady recognized the note in the voice: despair. It lent him a certain credibility. She tried to see the eyes, but he was a shadow against the back-lit crowd. "What about my daughter?"

"Mrs. Luckinbill! Don't listen to him!" Nahum Bismarck thrust the First Lady behind him, shielding her as though the stranger held a weapon. Borodin fished out his wallet and flung it open. Nahum Bismarck recoiled from the badge as he would have from a degenerate exhibiting himself. He motioned, and two black suits moved in to take Borodin by the arms.

The ecological speech trailed off in static and black-suited men herded the crowd back from the crocodile tank. The Senegalese ambassador stood smiling and seemed to be waiting for a translation.

"Please, Mrs. Luckinbill." Borodin spoke quickly but gently, as he would to a child or an animal. "There's a group that wants to harm your daughter."

She did not budge or blink. "What kind of harm? What group?"

"We don't know, but we have their scenario."

"Scenario? Blue scenario?"

"Your daughter's murder has been scheduled for immediate implementation."

"But she's guarded."

"The guard may have been infiltrated."

"Dear God."

Borodin felt the prod of a revolver in his kidney. Handcuffs flashed.

"Don't touch him," the First Lady said softly. The guards froze. "Have you got a dime?" she asked.

The Secret Service men made confused sounds. The lady in the purple hat said she had two dimes. The First Lady thanked her for one of them. The Secret Service men went with her to the pay phone and waited outside the booth.

The First Lady lifted the telephone receiver and dialed a number. When a voice answered she said, "Are you all right, Lexie?"

"Just fine, Mother."

"What are you doing?"

"Nothing special. Chad's watching the midday news roundup and I'm making a turbot and spinach soufflé for lunch."

"Are the security men there?"

"There are two gentlemen sitting in a black car in front of the building and their names are Fred and Ted, and when they go off duty at five P.M. there'll be two other gentlemen in a black car and their names are Floyd and Mike."

"What about the roof?"

"What *about* the roof?"

"Is it guarded?"

"Mother, what's wrong with you?"

"I only want to be sure you're safe."

"I've got round-the-clock protection. I'm married to a Secret Service man, remember?"

"Could I speak with Chad?"

"Aren't you overdoing the mother-of-the-bride jitters?"

"Just to say hello."

"Okay."

The First Lady heard muffled voices and then the cheerful tones of her son-in-law. "Hi, Mrs. Luckinbill. How's it going?"

"All right, Chad. I was worried about you and Lexie."

"No need to worry about us, ma'am. We're as snug as two bugs in a rug."

"That roof bothers me. I thought someone could slip in."

"The roof's guarded, ma'am, and so's the back door and so's the front door. There are six men watching this house and a squad of cops down the street."

"You sound in good spirits, Chad."

"Married life's agreeing with me, ma'am, and Lexie's one heck of a cook."

"I'm glad she's feeding you. You'll watch out for her, won't you?"

"No one but me's going to touch a hair of her head, ma'am."

"Thank you Chad, that makes me feel much better."

"Hold on. Lexie wants to say something."

Lexie came back onto the line. "Hey, Mom, if you're so worried, why don't you come over for dessert? You can help us choose paint. There's a flat apricot I'd love to use for the dining-room trim, but I need some expert guidance."

The First Lady felt something tear inside of her; Lexie had not asked her advice in a long, long time. "Oh, darling, I'm with some people."

"The more the merrier."

"Thank you, Lexie. That's very sweet of you." The First Lady hung up the phone and turned to the others. "I want to go to my daughter."

Nahum Bismarck made incredulous noises at the back of his throat. "You can't leave the Senegalese ambassador!"

"We haven't got anything to say to one another."

"But you could be jeopardizing the mutual protection treaty!"

"You can finish the ceremonies, Nahum. You're a good deal more important to this government than I am."

"But your guard."

"I'm going to see my daughter and my guard can come with me and this man's coming with me." The First Lady indicated Borodin.

Nahum Bismarck's face was angina-red. "Mrs. Luckinbill, you can't!"

But she could go, and she did go. Avoiding the eye of the Senegalese ambassador, Nahum Bismarck borrowed a dime from the lady in the purple hat and telephoned the wife of the Vice-President. Very rapidly he explained what had happened.

"Shit," Maggie Tyson said. "Okay, Nahum. I'll see what I can do."

Maggie Tyson made another, whispered phone call, and an operative on Nebraska Avenue received instructions to implement the final phase, termination with maximum prejudice, ten-minute countdown, no margin, repeat no margin for error.

*

"Senator Ambler," the clerk called, his voice amplified to an effortless shout.

The senior senator from Connecticut sat straight in his chair. In his neatly tailored dark suit, with his graying, razor-cut hair, he looked more a model for a men's magazine than the autocrat of the Senate Aeronautical and Space Sciences Committee.

Senator Dan Bulfinch watched Ambler milk the moment and quietly detested him. Two weeks ago, in the cloakroom, Ambler had declared himself in full hearing of thirty other senators to be opposed to the bill. A week later, when Senator Dan cornered him at a Uruguayan embassy reception, he had seemed a little less opposed, referring to the measure as "constitutionally questionable." Since then he had returned none of Senator Dan's calls.

Ambler's glance, as it circled the floor and met Senator Dan's, was terse, dour, ironic. The senator voted in favor of the bill. The press gallery buzzed as he took his seat again.

Senator Dan totaled the check marks he had been making on a sheet of personal letterhead. After three votes, the Administration had a one-vote lead.

"Senator Appleworth," the clerk called.

As always during a vote of any controversy, the press and the visitors' galleries were full. What was odd about today was that the Senate floor was full too, as rare a condition as ice floes in the Panama Canal. Senator Dan could see only one empty seat, that of the junior senator from West Virginia: an administration vote, but a perennial absentee. Senator Dan said a mental curse and prayer.

His glance went to Howard J. Tyson, slouched in the chair of the President of the Senate, downright bored as he doodled on foolscap and tried to make it look like note taking. The Vice-President's only hope of getting into the game was a tie, in which case he would cast the deciding vote. At the moment he had the psychotically envious stare of a second-string tackle sitting on the bench during the season's biggest game.

*

"Honey," Lexie pouted, "we had a dozen eggs this morning and now there are none. How do you expect me to make a soufflé without eggs?"

"Don't look at me," Chad said. "I didn't touch them."

"Well, somebody touched them, and it wasn't me."

"Tell you what. It'll take me five minutes to run down to the store."

"Sure you don't mind?"

"How could I mind? It's either that or starve."

Chad kissed Lexie at the apartment door and hurried down the stairs. She waved and blew kisses till he was out of sight, then turned and closed the door. She heard a sound in the kitchen and was surprised to see Andy, one of the afternoon guards, crouching at a cabinet. He was a stocky, taciturn man, and he had the sort of windburned face that Lexie trusted.

"Why, Andy, I didn't even hear you come in."

"Felt a little hungry," he apologized. Chad and Lexie let the Secret Service men snack in the kitchen—it seemed a friendly thing to do. Andy was cradling an armload of ketchup and imported Dijon mustard and Hershey's chocolate syrup, and Lexie couldn't help but think he was preparing an odd sort of snack.

"Chad will be back in five minutes and we're having a soufflé. Wouldn't you like some?"

"No thanks, Mrs. Beausoleil. I'll take these into the pantry and be out of your way."

"I'm worried about your nutrition."

"Don't you worry about me."

"Are you married, Andy?"

"No, ma'am."

"You ought to be."

"Yes, ma'am."

Andy Drumwright, veteran of three Asian and four Latin American campaigns, holder of eighteen decorations for valor in battle, stood for a long moment in the pantry, the command echoing down the corridors of his mind like a mote falling through space. He consulted his wrist watch and saw that there was very little time. They had told him there would be no second chance.

He began in the dining room. He stepped on a Regency chair and, dipping two fingers in ketchup, began at the top of the wall in ten-inch capitals, spelling out the political and pathological obscenities that his superiors, in a last-minute switch, had decided would best achieve the impact required of the terminal phase.

This third, and final, assignment differed from the others. The two Whitefalls shootings had been out-of-doors affairs. His anonymity, and that of his superiors, had been assured by rifle and telescopic sight, by country road and cover of night. The termination of Lexie Beausoleil had to be accomplished indoors, under a heavy guard, and the premises had to be vandalized. The three requirements dictated the timing, the means, and the risks.

Andy began with the vandalizing because it made the least noise. As his superiors had instructed, he spelled *white* without an *h* and *bitch* without a *t*. By the time he reached the hallway he had run out of ketchup and had to go to mustard, which turned out to be scarcely legible against the cinnamon wallpaper, so he finished the job in chocolate. The word PIG was especially jolting on the twelve-foot Victorian mirror at the end of the living room, smeared in two-foot fecal rage that seemed to run across the viewer's own face.

He knew, of course, that he was risking his life, but he had risked his life for his country before and was an old hand at it.

"What in the world?" Lexie poked her head out of the kitchen. Her first thought was that Andy was playing a very elaborate and very juvenile practical joke, and she was furious. Her second thought was that he was having an epileptic fit, and she felt pity for him.

"Andy Drumwright!" She seized him by the shoulder and whirled him around. "You put that down before you break anything!"

He was holding a bust of Lexie's grandfather. He gazed at her with eyes of dark compassion and swung it down mercifully and swiftly into her left temple. Her cry stopped as if a needle had been yanked off a phonograph record. Her arms went up as though to embrace him or cling to him or fend him off and her knees buckled and she slipped to the parquet floor and knelt swaying. He struck her again at the base of the skull, where her soft hair grew dark. It was a hard, precise blow that he had learned in counterinsurgency school, and it felled her.

He saw by his watch that he had seven minutes and twenty seconds left, and he hurried into the kitchen for the electric carving knife.

*

At 12:21 P.M. Clifford Q. Zarkudian, junior senator from Wyoming and a member of the President's own party, stirred in his seat in the Senate and cast a vote for the bill, bringing the tally to fifty in favor, forty-nine opposed.

The voting, on the whole, had stuck to party lines. There had been seven cross-overs, no abstentions, and only one absentee.

The clerk announced that the bill had passed, and the galleries broke into the roar of a zoo at feeding time.

*

The First Lady's limousine with its silent passengers made its way through streets of abandoned, desecrated cars and aimless, wandering junkies and National Guardsmen who stood watch over brimming trash baskets lest an arsonist ignite them.

Not an eye, military or pedestrian, was raised at the seal-black automobile or its fleet of escorts. Government people were forever going somewhere in this city, and the inhabitants were used to having their way blocked by saw horses and bayonets and expensive cars, and very little that any government did nowadays could rouse their attention.

Borodin sat on the jump seat staring through the glass partition and the Polaroid windshield at the red and orange glow on the southern horizon where it seemed the sun had set in the wrong place at the wrong time. There was a suggestion—muted beneath the churning air conditioning—of the distant, lazy roar of a riot.

The First Lady twisted her fingers, her eyes searching the monument-speckled horizon.

It took nine minutes to reach Lexie and Chad Beausoleil's house. The police, recognizing the car, moved the barricades and beat back flurries of autograph hunters. Two very friendly plainclothesmen escorted the First Lady up the town-house steps and opened the front door for her.

Borodin, unescorted and unhelped, hurried up the steps behind her.

The First Lady buzzed her daughter's buzzer and knocked at the door. Borodin tried the door handle. It turned.

"Mrs. Luckinbill," a guard warned.

But the First Lady, ignoring the caution of the guard's drawn gun, was already in the apartment, and her eye had already traveled the cinnamon wallpaper and the living room with its twelve-foot windows and its twelve-foot Victorian mirror.

"Lexie!" the First Lady screamed.

Borodin fired and the guard behind him fired at almost the same moment, and the surprised face of Andy Drumwright shattered in a shower of mirrored shards.

*

"Howard J. Tyson, this morning you and I went down in history, and this afternoon you stand around whining."

Maggie Tyson had just made some amazing confidences to her husband, explaining in precisely what way they had gone down in history, and all he could say was, "I feel bad, Maggie. I feel rotten."

It was chilly in the Georgetown living room. Howard J.'s conscience was singing *Dies Irae*, and Maggie's was needing a drink. Howard J. paced and Maggie wrestled the cap off a fifth of Jack Daniel's.

"I'm not blaming you, Maggie. But the girl. The girl."

Maggie wheeled about. "What about that damned virgin? Quit acting like a kid with a bellyache." She glowered into the sinking water level of her glass; caught a surreal glimpse of Howard J. through the bottom, stretched out of shape like a jelly-fish in a current. "For God's sake, Howie, we're celebrating!"

"I'm sorry. I just can't celebrate."

Maggie dug her heel into the carpet.

"Listen to me, Howard J. Tyson: the closest you ever thought of getting to the White House was a lifetime sentence to an Albany public-works committee; and if it hadn't been for me and my know-how and my ideas and my cash you would never have even seen the inside of the Washington Greyhound terminal men's room!"

"You can be very cruel, Maggie."

"Will you get your mind out of Sunday school? Of course I can be cruel! And you thank your lucky tea leaves! Because the day I stop being cruel is the day you can forget 1600 Pennsylvania Avenue!"

Howard J. spoke with the quiet dignity of a Boy Scout. "I'm not sure being President is worth it."

"Worth it? Howie, baby, the one thing in this country that they have not managed to devaluate is the presidency of the United States of America, and if you don't think that's worth starting a war for, you don't know the value of nothing!"

"Maggie, sometimes I wonder if you know the difference between right and left and wrong. You act as though lying and stealing and killing were all just part of the political process."

"Howie, you leave the political process to me."

"At least you could show some conscience about the damned thing!"

"Like Lucky Bill Luckinbill? Go on television and *cry* because I dropped thirty thousand tons of TNT on some jungle village? *Apologize* when my police clean up a ghetto? If that's conscience, who needs it? The American people have had it up to here!" Maggie made a throat-slitting motion at the level where, if she'd had one, her halo would have been. "Lucky Bill's conscience has sewn him into a sack!"

"But at least he *has* a conscience!"

"Watch TV, baby—watch Lucky Bill's conscience in action, watch him veto the bill this country is screaming for! Watch his polls drop to zero! Watch him get impeached for willful criminal negligence! Watch him get the boot! And watch Maggie move into that vacuum!"

Howard J. watched Maggie.

"When Lucky Bill Luckinbill vetoes that bill—when Lucky Bill blocks the will of the people and of their elected representatives—when he has the blind audacity to put himself above the law and above the people—Maggie is going to hop on that little screen, onto every talk show and every newscast and every panel she can pry her way into—and Maggie is going to say: *Fellow Americans—I do not think one man, no matter how exalted the office he holds, has the right to thwart the manifest will of the people. Is it not, after all, in defense of the free will of peoples the world over that we have poured our blood and treasure into war after war after agonizing war? Is not the free will of the people the very thing we mean when we say liberty and justice for all?* And a howl is going to go up from this nation, and that howl is going to say *barbecue him!* and guess who they'll be running on the next slate—Tyson and Tyson!"

Howard J. kept watching his wife. "Who's going to be President, Maggie—Tyson or Tyson?"

Maggie frowned, swiftly covered with a smile. She refilled his glass, poured herself into his lap. "Momma's doing all this for her baby."

"You're a very selfish woman, Maggie. I don't blame you; you are what you are. I agree that this country needs a strong executive branch, but I'm not certain you and your jigsaw should be let anywhere near it."

Maggie stared at Howard J., understanding what he was saying, why he was saying it, and pitying him as savagely as she had ever pitied anyone.

"Baby," she said, "get drunk."

*

"Stop looking so gloomy, you two. I'm a little bruised and that's all."

The First Lady couldn't help thinking how like a child Lexie seemed, sitting up in bed, how like a little girl recovering from a tonsillectomy and delighted with all the ice cream the hospital is feeding her. And how old Chad looked, how creased and unsteady.

"I'm not gloomy," the First Lady said, "just a little tired."

"Well, stop worrying about me. I'm fine. I could walk out of here right now but for some reason they have to observe me. I guess because I got hit on the head. But I really feel great and I'm going to catch up on my reading."

The books were stockpiled on the bedside table, and the flowers had been moved to the chest of drawers. "Do you need anything?" Chad asked.

"A week's rest, they say." Lexie reached to take her husband's hand. "Chad, it could have happened to anyone. Andy was disturbed and it was just my bum luck he was assigned to guard me. I got a scare and that's all. Poor Andy's dead. Anyway let's not think about that."

"Of course we won't think about it," the First Lady said. But in fact she had been thinking of nothing else. "I was thinking about your honeymoon. You never had one. How would you and Chad like to take a long, long trip?"

"We'll talk about it, okay?" Lexie smiled and kissed her mother. "I think it's time for my shot."

The First Lady had not even heard the nurse come in.

"Good evening, Mrs. Luckinbill."

"Good evening."

Chad stepped back from the bed, and the woman swabbed alcohol on Lexie's shoulder. The First Lady winced as the needle went in. Lexie leaned back against the pillow and closed her eyes.

"What are you giving her?" the First Lady asked.

"Just something to help her sleep. Good night, Mrs. Luckinbill."

The First Lady watched Lexie's breathing become deep and regular. Chad tiptoed to the door and closed it, and the First Lady sat in the chair and opened a volume of T. S. Eliot's complete poems.

She and her son-in-law did not talk, and after a while she closed the book and stared at her daughter.

The First Lady did not know it was 10 P.M. and she did not know how long it was since she had entered the sick room. Her back was toward the window and the city and the riots, and she faced the dark bed with its inert burden and the hovering shadow of the young man. She was shaking despite the arms she hugged about her thin body. The fear and the nausea, and the strength they had lent her, had vanished, and all that was left was the hopeless certainty that this would happen again and again so long as her daughter lived.

Lexie was in no danger, the doctors had said. They were speaking medically, of course. For the First Lady every unguarded window was cause for doubt.

"Moni, Moni," her husband comforted, and a hand was on her shoulder, probing the thinness of her dress.

"Why do they want to kill her?" she asked.

"Don't. Don't ask. Don't think."

"Is it because they can't raise themselves out of the muck and so they've got to pull everyone else into it?"

"Don't."

"Is that their freedom, is that their equality?"

"Don't."

"Freedom to kill, equality to be animals or corpses? No one can be good or honest or kind or beautiful, we've all got to be dogs or get shot? That's what this country is skidding into, and it's dragging the whole world with it! Sometimes I hate America, I hate what it's done to you and me and I hate what it's done to Lexie! Oh my God, Lexie, Lexie. . . ."

"Don't, don't." The President's strong arms held her, confined her. Chad, white and astonished, stooped to pick up the book she had spilled. "You're safe, Moni. She's safe."

The First Lady gazed at her daughter, sedated and sleeping and bruised and half smiling. "Is she safe? Will she ever be safe?"

The President held the door for his wife, nodding to Chad as they left him behind. They passed four armed guards in the corridor. There was another guard in the elevator and he pressed the floor button for them.

"Of course she's safe," the President said. "The security's tighter here than at the White House."

The First Lady squeezed his hand. There were armed guards in the lobby and their faces were grim. The First Lady stopped at the newsstand to look at the headlines. Her husband caught her elbow and pulled her along.

The reporters were waiting outside the hospital, and the flashbulbs excoriated their eyes.

"Bill," she asked in the limousine, "why do the papers say Lexie is on the critical list?"

"Because she is, technically."

"But the doctors say there was no brain damage. She seems well, and cheerful. The news stories are so alarmist. As though she might die. The papers are wrong, aren't they, Bill?"

"Of course they're wrong. Hospitals and papers thrive on alarm."

"We've been getting telegrams. Some people actually think she's dead."

The First Lady saw the profile smile.

"Between hospitals and newspapers," the President said, "I don't suppose the truth stands much of a chance."

"But why can't we just tell them the truth? Why make things worse?"

"You're a great gal, do you know that?"

He patted her hand, and she turned to watch the city glide past the bulletproof glass.

*

"You're looking better, Darcie," the nurse said. "Enjoy your dinner?"

She knew better than to hope. Hope was a provocation, a signal to those who waited, pressed against the other side of the wall. Here, in the little white cube with the electric bed that sat up and lay down as nurses pressed switches, here she was safe.

"I'm going to take your pulse, Darcie. I'll be touching your wrist. You don't mind if I touch your wrist, do you?"

No terror; no hope. White, clean, safe.

She wanted nothing more.

"Did you look out your window today? See how nice the weather was?"

She would not rebel, dream, think, move a limb, make an effort. She would blink—once for yes, twice for no—when the night nurse asked if she wanted pineapple juice, milk, ginger ale. She would live and time would go by her and she would be very, very safe, forever and ever, amen.

"That sheet's loose. Let's tuck you in. There now. Good night, Darcie. Pleasant dreams."

No dreams, she prayed; *no dreams*. She heard a voice after the door had closed, and it seemed to be saying the name of someone she could no longer remember, a name like *Hiram*.

But she had never known a Hiram.

Senator Dan was in the bathtub when the buzzer rang. He slipped into a robe and dripped water across the hallway and cursed the dry cleaner for delivering at 6:30 in the evening. But it wasn't the dry cleaner at the door; it was Marion Holmes. She looked nervous and she looked sober. She asked if she could come in, and Senator Dan knotted the sash of his robe.

"I wasn't quite straight with you, Senator. If telling a little less than the whole truth and nothing but is a lie, then you might say I lied."

He closed the door and locked it. Marion Holmes was standing on the little terrace, staring at the city cradled in mothering smog.

"This Andy What's-it," she said. "Drumwright. The CIA guy with all the silver stars and distinguished service crosses. The one they shot in Lexie Beausoleil's apartment."

"The alleged CIA operative," Senator Dan corrected. "What about him?"

"Whatever he was—has anyone managed to explain how the hell he was assigned to Lexie's security guard?"

"I'm sure there's an explanation."

"I can see you're as pessimistic as I am, Senator. Drumwright deserved better than bullets. He was a nice, soft-spoken guy. Looked as though he'd be kind to children."

"You knew him?"

"Of course his political opinions were a little old-fashioned." Her glance flicked over Senator Dan and he wished he were dressed. "He believed in the Bible and in the government. The stricter the better. He didn't think much of the times we live in. He may have been right."

"How did you know Drumwright?"

"I knew him to say hello to and let in the back door and offer a cup of coffee to." She leaned on the little steel ballustrade—the one Senator Dan had been meaning to get tightened—and gazed down at the evening traffic trying to wend through double-parked cars. "He didn't drink liquor. He didn't smoke. He was very clean. Personally, I mean. He smelled of soap."

"How the hell did you get mixed up with him?"

"Bill Luckinbill has been in my house five times in the last three months. We weren't alone any of those five times. Oh, I don't mean the Secret Service came inside. But Andy Drumwright showed up. Pre-arranged. Bill asked if they could use my place. I guess what he meant was an old mistress is the perfect smoke screen. I didn't ask questions. He said Andy had something to do with counterinsurgents in Bolivia. Well, I'm not very keen on Bolivia, so I just left the coffee on the stove and didn't even bother to eavesdrop. But it was the same Andy. I recognize the photograph in the papers."

"Are you certain?"

"Senator, I haven't touched a drop, that's how certain I am."

"It doesn't make sense. Why would Lucky Bill sneak off to meet a man like Drumwright?"

"Maybe he didn't want to meet Drumwright in the White House."

"Did you overhear anything of their conversations?"

"I was soused, Senator. Bill Luckinbill does that to me. He's very attentive. Keeps the brandy snifter full." She turned away from the street. Her eye played along the building façade as though seeking snipers in windows. She moved back into the living room. "Two nights ago I stumbled into the kitchen and it seemed to me Bill said they'd have to make do with Nebraska."

"Nebraska? What the hell could he have meant?"

"I was very drunk, Senator. Maybe I'm misquoting. But Lexie lives on Nebraska Avenue, doesn't she?"

She picked up her purse from the sofa where she had dropped it. "They were both military. Bill treated Drumwright like a damned good soldier, which apparently he was. Drumwright treated Bill like a commander-in-chief. Bill was briefing him for some kind of mission. That's just an ex-drunk's opinion, take it or leave it. You know where to reach me, Senator."

"Yes. Thank you, Mrs. Holmes." He opened the door for her. She was in a hurry and didn't look back.

*

Maggie Tyson sat in her favorite rocker, waiting for the color TV to warm up. She had reached one of those plateaus in the life of a human being, a plateau so near the pinnacle that a couple of ounces of bourbon, a couple of ounces of self-congratulation, seem not only permissible but warranted.

Maggie rocked and sipped and smiled and waited for the seal of the President of the United States to come into focus; waited for the President to sign *adiós* to the greatest single concentration of political power in the history of civilization.

She glanced at Howard J., nestled on the sofa with a copy of Nixon's memoirs (why was he reading *those?*) and she gave him a tipsy little wave. He smiled back at her.

For the first time in God only knew how long, in the twelve years since she had taken aim and begun that long march to the White House, Maggie could draw a breath. Hell, she felt happy. Her wildest dream had come true, and it was about to be flashed coast-to-coast on all three networks.

Maggie sipped.

The TV voice announced that the Xerox Comedy Hour, usually presented at this time, would not be seen this week. Maggie braced her rocker in forward position as the presidential seal filled the thirty-eight-inch screen.

*

The bill, fresh from the Government Printing Office, and the virgin dip pen and the big inkstand were set out on the lectern.

The floor was splashed with arc-light and crisscrossed with cables. A technician adjusted the big backdrop of the presidential seal, and cameramen, lighting men, network men, advisers, and assistants all shouted at once. The First Lady, from the edge of the studio, watched her husband move through the mob, smooth and flat, as though he had only the two surfaces of a knife to him. She saw Nahum Bismarck urging last-minute changes in the speech, and Mimi Moffett with a clipboard full of messages, and a dozen other desperate men and women trying to converge on the shifting point that was Lucky Bill Luckinbill.

The First Lady was not converging. She was sitting absolutely erect on a folding chair. She was reading the ever-changing message of the electric clock above the door. She sat in a way she knew was stiff and hoped was dignified, quite unsure of anything in the universe except the single point of uncertainty that her consciousness had shrunk to. She knew that in forty-five seconds the red light would blink on and her husband would begin the speech justifying his veto to the nation.

And she wondered if any of it mattered.

The President was striding alone to the lectern and a woman with an eyebrow pencil was running alongside trying to do something to his hairline. The red light flashed and the First Lady watched the monitor, where the colors were subdued to pastels and the President was small and you had the feeling that you could always change to a different program.

The First Lady's eyes met those of her husband's image.

"Fellow Americans," the image said.

*

President Bill Luckinbill gazed straight at the television camera. His eyes focused not on the lens, but on the teleprompter screen just below it, where a slowly unwinding ribbon of typescript unspooled his prepared speech.

"America's leadership must be guided by the lights of learning and reason, or else—" He read in a voice that slightly trembled, and one hundred five million televiewers hung on the emotions registered in the seismographic squint of his eye and pupil. "Or else those who confuse rhetoric with reality and the plausible with the possible will gain the popular ascendancy with their seemingly swift and simple solutions."

The First Lady wondered if the speech seemed as slow to the nation as it did to her. He could draw a quarter hour out like taffy and she felt a terrible foreboding that the present would never end, that time had stuck in this moment.

"The bill before me, which bears the approval of the Congress, is to my mind just such a solution: swift, simple, and misguided. I, of all men and all fathers at this moment, cannot deny that ours is a nation in torment. I cannot deny that there is, perhaps, a cancer eating at the vital organs of the Republic. But I do question that the only cure is to cut the heart out of the patient."

It was not a tragic speech, the First Lady realized. His gestures gave him away. He had won something.

"This bill is a cardiectomy. By in effect suspending the heart of our Constitution, it cuts the heart out of us as a nation, as a power, and as a people. With this type of remedy for the ills civil and politic that afflict us, we risk death as a democracy. And for that reason I am, as you all know, unalterably opposed to this measure, and I can only hope and pray that our Supreme Court will move with all deliberate speed to strike it down."

The President's gaze dropped from the teleprompter to the sheets of yellow foolscap, scrawled and rescrawled over, which lay on the lectern before him, out of sight of the television eye. He paused and swallowed; and one hundred and five million televiewers leaned forward in their seats.

"However, I am but one man in a nation of two hundred and twenty million." The President read from the lectern, his tone softer and wearier. "We are, by the will and grace of God, a government of the people, by the people, for the people. The people, through their elected representatives in the two houses of Congress, by their many letters and telegrams, by public demonstration and through the press and media, have made their will abundantly clear.

"Fellow Americans: I do not think one man, no matter how exalted the office he holds, has the right to thwart the manifest will of the people. Is it not, after all, in defense of the free will of peoples the world over that we have poured our blood and treasure. . . ."

*

Maggie Tyson, cozied in her rocker with a bourbon in one hand, stopped laughing and blinked at the TV and checked the feedback of her ears. As comprehension dawned on her she let out a rasping cry.

Howard J. was staring at the TV, now and then lifting his glass and taking the teeniest of sips.

"Howard—it's my speech!"

It had to be some kind of joke or nightmare. But the words kept coming out of that wishy-washy liberal face—her words— and they went on far too long to be coincidence or a malfunctioning tube, and there was nothing joking about them, and though what was happening was a nightmare, when she pinched herself it hurt, hurt plenty.

"It was, I believe," the television said in the President's voice and likeness, "the Greek poet and tragedian Aeschylus who wrote, *Even in our sleep, pain which cannot forget falls drop by drop upon the heart, until in our despair, against our own will, comes wisdom through the awful grace of God.*

"My friends, my fellow Americans: it is because the people *are* the people that America will meet the challenges facing her and we will build a better, a whole America at home; and that better American will lead the forces of liberty and justice in building a new world. It is because the people have spoken, it is because I am but a servant of the people, that I sign into law the bill which the people have placed before me."

The camera eye dipped down and the nation watched the President touch the pen to the inkstand and scratch his signature across the last page of the measure.

Lucky Bill Luckinbill looked the nation in the eye.

"Thank you."

*

Maggie squinted at the smile on the TV screen, and for the first time in her adult life she knew the ice pick of fear in her adrenal glands. She moved quickly to the bar and poured herself a tumbler of the swiftest courage she could find.

"I've got to talk to him."

"Talk to who?" Howard J. asked.

"That bastard Luckinbill. I've got to talk to him right now."

July 10: Monday

The First Lady huddled in a pew of the cathedral. She was cold despite the press of twenty-four hundred invited bodies, trembling despite the hard grip of her husband's hand around her own. She could scarcely hold the missal or read the responses in a steady voice.

The cardinal, a wavering, faceless pillar of white, stepped down from the altar. He made a blessing motion of the hand over the flower-decked coffin. "Maggie Burns Tyson," he said in a breaking voice, "the day of your baptism you put on Christ. In the day of His coming and resurrection may He clothe you with His glory."

A terrible, stone emptiness filled the First Lady, and she could not hear the cardinal's prayer. She could only hear her husband saying, *Fellow Americans: I do not think one man, no matter how exalted the office he holds, has the right to thwart the manifest will of the people.*

She glanced at him, neatly profiled against the mid-afternoon glow of the Good Samaritan window. His lips were still, yet she heard the words.

. . . no matter how exalted the office . . .

It had been one of those freak accidents. Maggie Tyson, returning from a talk with the President at the White House, had stepped out of a taxicab. To save the expense of going around the block, she had gotten out on the west side of the street and was crossing to the town house she and Howard J. Tyson had rented for twelve years, when the car hit her. The driver, Melvin Brandt—a former government employee and army veteran with two distinguished service crosses, three silver stars, and a medal for humane action—had not seen the red light.

The photograph of Maggie Tyson on a canvas stretcher clasping the hands of the Vice-President had made page one across the nation. She had died in the ambulance, on the way to the hospital.

The First Lady wanted to weep for Maggie, but through some malfunction of memory, some wrong adjustment of knobs and channels, she stood in the house of God and could only hear her husband's address to the nation. Music soared about her. The choir was singing. Her husband was singing.

. . . to thwart the manifest will of the people . . .

The thirty-two-foot base pipes of the organ shook the walls by their roots. The First Lady's hand fell to her side and the missal fell to the little velvet prayer cushion. Her husband stooped gracefully, still singing, to retrieve it for her, and as his hand touched hers the voices and echoes enclosing them begged God's mercy.

*

As soon as she could manage, the First Lady slipped up to her bedroom and found the blue binder exactly as she had left it, in the only place it would fit, beneath the directory in the phone table that Pat Nixon had given to the White House.

The words were on page nine, exactly as he had said them: *Fellow Americans: I do not think one man. . . .* The First Lady was so stunned, so baffled, so frightened as searchlight after searchlight flicked on in her head, that as she came down the stairs she did not at first notice Howard J. Tyson in the corridor twisting a moist handkerchief.

"Moni, I've got to talk to you." His limbs had the odd unjoined look of a marionette with its strings cut. His black suit was wrinkled and there was a stain on his black tie.

The First Lady supposed it was about his wife. "I'm so sorry, Howie. So terribly sorry."

"It's not about Maggie." He mopped his forehead. "Oh, it is about Maggie, but it's about much more. Things we never suspected. Terrible things. About Bill."

"About Bill?" The First Lady glanced to see whether the guards could overhear.

"He used her, Moni: oh, Moni, he used Maggie!"

"Not here," the First Lady said. She took Howard J. Tyson's hand and led him out into the rose garden that the Johnsons had christened for Jacqueline Kennedy.

"He used her ignorance," Howard J. Tyson said, "and he used her ambition, her blind, contemptible avarice for power."

Somewhere, in some dark cistern of his heart or head, a stopper was pulled inside the Vice-President, and the tears that had been bottled there through the years of campaigning and juggling and lying came choking down the rusted pipes, spitting and spilling out like gutter water whose pressure can no longer be contained by dead leaves alone.

"Maggie gave this to me in the ambulance." Howard J. Tyson held in his hand what looked to the First Lady very like a small plastic box, something a child might store pebbles in. "It's a cassette of her last conversation with the President."

Howard J. Tyson pushed a button, and the First Lady listened to the tape and recognized the voices and thought how odd that Maggie was alive again, in the garden, talking. Her curiosity changed gradually to amazement and then to nausea and she realized that every word was hitting her like a karate chop in the neck and that rage and terror were clogging her throat and that her hands, rigid, were ripping fistfuls of roses from their stalks.

"Howie," the First Lady said, "give me that thing."

July 11: Tuesday

Cathedral bells across the nation's capital tolled 2 A.M. In his blue-walled Oval Office, the President of the United States put the final penciled touches to his address to the joint sessions, and wondered with small but growing unease where the hell his wife had wandered off to.

In Woodrow Judd's hospital room, the First Lady and Howard J. Tyson and Frank Borodin sat with the detritus of snacks and coffees stacked on the white table. They listened with faces of grim neutrality as a tape turned on the blue plastic cassette player. They waited for Woodrow Judd's reaction.

"Luckinbill, you scum," the tape spat, "what the hell are you trying to prove?"

"Easy there, big girl," came the President's voice.

"Don't you big girl me. I've put up with about all I'm taking. Did I squawk when you asked me to front this thing? Did I squawk when you kept tinkering with the scenario like some playwright at an out of town tryout?"

"You came up with an extremely clever scenario, Maggie— I'm not denying it. But I maintained then and I maintain now that there was no need to go after Lexie that way. I told you the girl was not to be harmed; you attempted to disobey me."

"All right, maybe I goofed a little. So where the hell do you get the balls to go on TV and sign my bill and deliver my speech?"

"And where do you get the authority to override my command and unleash a zombie on my daughter with instructions to kill?"

"The scenario needed a resolution."

"Not that way. You're an able woman, Maggie, but you're too

easily carried away. I don't think you're ready yet to wield real authority."

"I've got news for you, Luckinbill. If you try to screw me in any way, shape or form, the shit's going to fly. I've got the goods on you and don't you forget it."

"And I've got the goods on you, Maggie. So why don't you just pour yourself a drink and calm down?"

"I conceived and commissioned and fronted this whole stinking operation for you, I carried the ball and put it across the goal line, and now you grab it from me."

"I'm not grabbing anything from you, Maggie. You'll have the presidency in five and a half years."

"You promised next election."

"I had a change of heart. Every President's got a right to a change of heart. You'll be riper in five years. The presidency will be stronger. You'll have real power then if you'll just hold off."

"So you're going to run next year? Yes or no."

"The country needs me."

"Three months ago you said the country needed Maggie Tyson. You said only Maggie Tyson could bring this nation together. You said the U.S.A. needed a strong, fresh executive and you weren't the man for the job. You said if I helped we'd restructure this nation and you'd give me the White House. That's what you said, Luckinbill, and I've got it all down on tape!"

"And I've got everything you ever promised down on tape, and where does that get either of us? You did a great job, Maggie, and I couldn't have swung it without you, and in five years you'll get your turn."

"If you can double-cross me now you can double-cross me in five years."

"Don't be naïve. We're allies."

"Who are you running for Vice-President? Howie again?"

"I'm open to a deal. You might help the ticket."

"Help it, hell, I'd *make* the ticket! They'd be voting for me and you know it. There isn't a tramp out there in voteland who wouldn't give her left tit to be Maggie Tyson!"

"I'm open to a deal. I don't want you or need you as an enemy."

"Maybe that's a chance you're going to have to take."

"No, Maggie. From here on in I don't take chances."

"What about me? How do I know in five years you won't have abolished elections?"

"That's the most politically intriguing thing you've said in a long time."

"Gimme that drink."

The tape turned silently. Senator Dan pushed a button. "Man, that's a politician. He had his cronies tag his own rider onto his own gun-control bill, and he screamed Hitlerism, McCarthyism, death of democracy. He used a scenario dreamed up by a New York public-relations outfit to fan the flames, and he plotted with an old CIA marksman to shoot his own daughter. He had Maggie Tyson figurehead the conspiracy so none of the conspirators even knew he was in on it. And when the time came, he changed horses and dumped Maggie and signed that bill into law so he could sweep into a second term with police powers that Franklin D. Roosevelt and Lyndon Johnson and Richard Nixon only dreamed about."

Howard J. Tyson whistled softly.

"But shooting his own daughter," the First Lady said. "How could any man. . . ."

"There's a precedent," Woodrow Judd said. He was sitting up against his doctors' orders, and he was pale. "Agamemnon sacrificed Iphigenia to get wind for his sails."

"Lexie would have been dead," the First Lady said. "Maggie Tyson was willing to kill my daughter and Bill almost let her do it. I won't forgive them that. Ever."

"He used her," Howard J. Tyson said. "It wasn't Maggie's fault."

"And now Bill's got everything he ever wanted." The First Lady's voice made a fist.

"If we could prove any of this," Senator Dan said, "there'd be a fighting chance of impeachment."

"We've got the tape," Woodrow Judd said. "We've got Maggie's statements to me, and we've got the Watts kid that dreamed the scenario up, and we might be able to break Gillespie down—if we can get to him before one of Luckinbill's veterans does."

"And we've got Marion Holmes," Senator Dan said. "She witnessed the meetings between the President and the assassin."

Woodrow Judd grunted. "If Luckinbill's men don't get her too."

"Don't kid yourselves," Howard J. Tyson said. "If you expect to get witnesses into the Senate alive, with the powers Lucky Bill has now, you're lunatics. He's got preventive detention, he's got search and seizure, he's got eminent domain over the life and property of every man, woman, and child in the Republic. And don't think he won't use them."

"He isn't quite home free," the First Lady said. "He's still got that address to the joint session. That address is very important to him. He's writing it himself."

"That's icing," Howard J. Tyson said. "He's got his cake."

"He's still putting out fake bulletins about Lexie," the First Lady said. "As far as the nation knows she's on the brink of death, and Bill's going to keep her there till the country swallows his about-face."

"Then there's a chance," Borodin said. "If Mrs. Luckinbill is willing."

The First Lady's eyes met Borodin's, and she saw in his something of herself: the freedom of nothing left to cherish or believe in or hope for.

*

They sat in the back seat of a moving black limousine. "I've found something," the First Lady stated. "Something you said."

"What have you found?" the President humored.

She quoted. " 'Fellow Americans: I do not think one man, no matter how exalted the office he holds, has the right to thwart the manifest will of the people.' "

"My speech," he observed, curious that she should remember it but grateful she had found a distraction.

"Not your speech, Bill." She held in her lap a blue binder. "Their speech."

He glanced toward the blue binder. "What's that you've got there, Moni?"

"The scenario. Their scenario. Your scenario."

"Whose *what?*"

"Step one: introduce legislation. Step two: shoot the President's daughter. Step three: stampede the legislation through Congress. Your scenario for the new America. Of course you didn't manage to kill her so you've had to add a postscript and keep her on the critical list just a few hours more."

The President glanced at the glass that separated them from the shaved necks of the guard and the warrant officer and the driver. Black cars and black motorcycles preceded and accompanied and trailed the limousine. Spectators lining the streets stood with hats in their hands. Air conditioning buzzed.

"That scenario was never committed to print."

The First Lady handed him the blue binder. He opened it.

"It was never written down."

"She's my daughter too," the First Lady said.

He sighed and took her hand and when she withdrew it he did not try to take it again. His eyes seemed for a moment to beseech hers, but the glimmer of entreaty could have been a trick of light on German-made contact lenses. His voice was sober, the voice he would soon use to address the Congress and the nation.

"A politician has to make some tough decisions, Moni. He's alone in the dark night of his soul. He has to weigh costs. Sometimes the greatest thing costs most dearly. Lexie was never in real danger, believe me."

She stared at him: saw him, it seemed, for the first time. "Bill," she said quietly, "shut up."

The First Lady rapped on the glass partition and signaled to the driver that she was getting out. The limousine pulled to the curb and came smoothly to a stop.

"Moni, for God's sake—what are you doing?"

"I'm not going to ride in this car with you, Bill. You see, I love my daughter. I even loved you."

He fought to keep her from opening the door. She thrust his hand aside and stepped out of the car.

"Good-by, Bill."

His eyes met hers through bulletproof glass. He tried to measure her intent. For one single moment incredulity paralyzed him. It was simply not possible that the barefoot son of Wilma Boborovsky and Eustace Luckinbill could have come this far if God and History intended to slam the gates in his face. Surely there had to be more point to all he had labored and sacrificed for than a shaggy dog's laugh.

The traffic waited for the red light. The First Lady started across the street, the blue binder under her arm.

"Driver," the President said into the intercom.

"Sir?"

No: he would not tell the Secret Service to bring her back; he would not tell the driver to run her down. He must be sensible. The woman could not harm him. A blue binder could not hurt him. It proved nothing. If she spoke out, told her mad tale, people would think she had lost her mind. The nation would grieve with him.

He watched her hail a taxicab and set off in the opposite direction. A Secret Service car, lagging, U-turned after her. Running to her father, he supposed.

The light changed and he picked up the intercom again.

"Never mind Mrs. Luckinbill. We'll go to the Capitol without her."

*

Now, at least and at last, she was certain. There was very little time, but there was no doubt as to what had happened or as to what she must do. The taxi took her to the hospital. For the moment she was free of her security guard, free of the President, and there was no one to question or contradict her. She moved quickly and she moved ferociously. She made her demand and she made it unconditionally and she crushed all refusal. She left nurses and doctors and guards confused and tangled in argument behind her. She smashed procedure and protocol and snatched what she had come for, the thing that would destroy Bill Luckin-bill, and she swept out of the hospital with sirens and uniforms in confused pursuit.

*

The President of the United States delivered his address—a thing of quiet, understated, and deeply moving dignity—to the joint session of Congress. Silence acclaimed him. He yielded the podium to Vice-President Howard J. Tyson and returned to his seat in the certainty—which he fought to keep from showing at the corners of his mouth—that he had won.

And then, in the thick of that silence, he heard a voice asking to be recognized. He raised his eyes and saw his wife standing in the center aisle.

The chamber buzzed. The President leaned quickly toward the Vice-President, cupping his hand over the still-live micro-phone. "Howie," he whispered, "don't recognize her. Don't even acknowledge her. Have the guards get her out of here."

But the Vice-President, inexplicably, hesitated.

"Moni's been under a terrible strain," the President confided in a deft and rapid hiss. "She was hospitalized this morning. I don't know what the hell she's doing here."

"Hospitalized for what?" The Vice-President sounded con-cerned, and the First Lady was ten steps nearer. Senators and congressmen twisted around in their seats, and the buzz broke into chatter.

"She's hallucinating—fantasizing. Complete paranoid break-down. It's been coming for a long time. For God's sake don't let her get to the podium. She's liable to say anything."

The Vice-President was no longer whispering. "Bill, have you ever heard of the separation of powers? In this chamber, I'm president. Now get the hell back to your seat and stay there."

The President's hand fell from the mike and he sank, suddenly dizzy, into his chair.

"Mrs. Luckinbill," the Vice-President enunciated.

The First Lady's eyes met the President's, coldly, and then she stood before the Congress and the television cameras of the nation, small yet oddly tall in black. As she spoke she glanced at her notes, making no pretense of hiding the little cards.

"Vice-President Tyson, Mr. Speaker, Reverend Clergy, ladies and gentlemen of the Congress, fellow citizens: Two day ago a bill was passed into law. You have been told that dissident forces within the nation conspired and attempted to kill my daughter. You have been told that my daughter is near death at this very moment, and for that reason you have not questioned the President's change of heart in signing that bill. You support the President now and would have the country follow him wherever he asks.

"You have been lied to. There is no emergency but the one provoked by the President himself. There is no conspiracy threatening this nation but the conspiracy led by the President himself. My daughter is here with me. She is unharmed."

A stir like the first hesitant gust of a spring storm passed through the chamber. And then silence, opaquer than before, fell. The President grasped the arms of his chair.

Lexie Luckinbill wore a blue dress. She wore the white face of shock and the red eyes of loss. She came down the aisle on the arm of her husband, whose face—like a soldier's—said nothing. They walked at a mourner's pace through murmuring congressmen and senators, casting bafflement like light rays with each step. They mounted the dais and took their places beside the First Lady; and in a long, sad, questioning glance the girl met the eyes of her father.

"I want to tell you what happened to my daughter and how and why it happened. The President of the United States was willing to trade her life for the passage of a bill."

The First Lady, in a voice that never faltered, explained the plot.

*

"That's Monica Luckinbill," Borodin said in the tone one takes to a child. "You remember who Monica Luckinbill is, don't you, Darcie?"

The afternoon had turned hot, but only its brightness pene-

trated the sealed hospital room, turning the white walls to blaz-
ing Arctic snow.

"Watch her, Darcie. Listen. Some day you'll tell your children
you heard her."

The brilliance held emptiness and silence in spinning solution.
An air conditioner purred, and the eight-inch Japanese television
made the little noises televisions make. In the bounced sunlight
its screen was almost blank, erased but for the persistence of
phantoms. The sounds of machines could scarcely register in
that silence tinged with smells of alcohol and disinfectant.

"Can you understand what she's saying? Try to understand.
You were part of this, Darcie. You helped."

She sat motionless on the center of the bed, huddled into a
tiny sphere, the tendons of her fingers taut as though at any moment she might need to lash out and repel whatever it might be,
in the blinding quiet, that threatened to come too near.

He glanced at the girl on the bed, saw she shared none of his
excitement. He turned down the volume on the television and
spoke softly. "You're going home, Darcie. I'm taking you home
tomorrow. To Whitefalls. Do you remember Whitefalls?"

Darcie Sybert's brow furrowed. On the little screen the President's wife kept talking, and a nation listened.

"Do you want to go home, Darcie?"

Darcie Sybert's face went through a terrible contraction. She
seemed to smile.

"Yes," she whispered.

*

She was nearing the end, and her voice was tired.

"I won't ask by what right of man or God he tried to take her
life. He wouldn't understand the question and I wouldn't understand the answer. It was politics, I understand that much. Wars
must be waged to end war, and freedom must be jailed to protect
freedom, and lives must be spent to preserve life. And if we can
kill a peon in a foreign rice paddy to defend this nation's vital interests, then we can kill our own children to defend those interests; and their deaths will catalyze public opinion, and we won't

need civil war to get our legislation passed: we can panic the people into accepting, begging for the new Republic.

"And so, overnight, we have a new government, and we are a different people.

"If I had lost my daughter, I would have paid more dearly than I ever dreamed possible for my cowardice of twenty years. And this country is paying, and will pay in blood, for its cowardice unless the cowardice stops here, stops now. We are being offered handcuffs in the name of self-preservation, and we are putting them on. We are told not to question. We are told to be patient.

"But patience is the trust that betrays. Patience is the silence that lies. Patience is the inaction that kills. The people of this nation have been patient, and their Presidents and their governments are turning this continent and this world into a graveyard.

"Presidents talk of the political process and the power of the people as though they were the same thing. As long as we believe that, we are doomed to patience. The political process is corrupt, and the power of the people is being polluted and poisoned. It takes power to be good or wicked, to be honest or dishonest, to love or live or hate or die, and that is the true power of the people, and that is the power the politicians take from us when they say politics must be left to those who understand it and the rest of us must be patient.

"We have been patient too long."

The President stared at the figures on the dais: a young man in a sports jacket with leather patches on the elbows; a girl in white on the brink of tears; a woman in black spitting rage and beauty.

He could not recognize them.

And then he heard a sound more frightening than the boom of a neutron bomb. He heard two lonely hands, somewhere out there, clapping. And then two more, then four more, eight more, and then it seemed a quarter of the Congress. His eyes swept the chamber.

Some of the damned fools were on their feet.

O: